RECKLESS PASSIONS

A DANIELLE NOVEL

DONNY HUNT

This is a work of fiction. Names, characters, places, and incidents are products of the author's imagination or are used fictitiously and are not to be construed as real. Any resemblance to actual events, locations, organizations, or persons, living or dead, is entirely coincidental.

World Castle Publishing, LLC
Pensacola, Florida
Copyright © Donny Hunt 2022
Hardback ISBN: 9798842032150
Paperback ISBN: 9781958336533
eBook ISBN: 9781958336540
First Edition World Castle Publishing, LLC, August 8, 2022
http://www.worldcastlepublishing.com
Licensing Notes
Cover: Karen Fuller
Editor: Maxine Bringenberg

Reckless Passions

Long ago I was brazen
Never let go, never backed down
Gave as good as I got
A queen with no crown
You were always by my side
Too dumb to run for cover
Crazy kids against a ruthless world
We had nothing but each other

With Reckless Passions we chased our dreams
It wasn't as easy as it seemed
Reckless Passions led our way to glory
We wrote our own story
Did it in our own fashion
With Reckless Passions

Beck then we didn't know, we couldn't feel
The noose tightening or the devil at our heels
We were running headfirst
Straight into infamy
Never pulled our punches, never shrugged our destiny

With Reckless Passions we had everything we wanted
Everything we could imagine
Reckless Passions helped up make our dreams
While we were tearing at the seams
I guess that's what happens
When you chase Reckless Passions

All these years later we've scattered to the winds
We made our own lives but I still remember us when

We had Reckless Passions
Our fire burned so bright till we were nothing but ashes
Reckless Passions

God, we stood show proud, knocking them all down
Seeking our satisfaction
With Reckless Passions

CHAPTER ONE

The screen flickered to life, and instantly there were the standard B roll shots of Los Angeles: sun-drenched beaches and streets lined with palm trees, luxury cars rolling down Rodeo Drive as fancy women loaded down with bags stepped quickly down the sidewalks. Here was the Hollywood sign, and there was Mann's Theater. The voiceover starts:

"It's not easy putting your life back together after a tragedy, especially when you're trying to raise two boys on your own. We left Wisconsin for California, hoping for a fresh start. Adjusting to life in the City of Angels is quite a challenge for a family of badgers like us."

The stock footage is replaced by a woman. She's middle-aged but trying hard to hide it. Her hair is professionally coiffed, and the bleach job is top-notch, as is the make-up, even if it is a little too heavy. The woman has lost weight, but you can still see the husky frame she'll never be able to hide. She's had work done; a nose job and a face lift. It looks unnatural on her. She's wearing a costume necklace and dangling earrings that would fool the common person and a blue dress with a plunging neckline to show off the boob job she's clearly proud of. She grins into the camera.

"But we're sure as heck gonna give it our best shot." She winks at the camera just before it tilts upward to a clear blue sky, where the title card appears in classy cursive letters. *Life With Nicole.*

***

The screen froze at the push of a button. Franklin Ridgeway, LPC, looked across his desk with professionally kind brown eyes. He softly set the remote down and made a steeple with his fingers. "Now tell me, what is the very first thing that comes to your mind when you see this?" His voice was soft and buttery, the better to put his client at ease.

Danielle Regan was anything but at ease, no matter how hard she tried to hide it. She gave it away with how she pumped her legs up and down and how she drummed her fingers on the arm of the faux leather chair. Although she tried to keep a poker face, Danielle could feel the hate seeping through her body.

Her mind screamed a hundred things she should say, things she needed to say, things the counselor and the courts wanted her to say. She knew them, but she couldn't say them. Ridgeway asked her for the first thing that came to her mind, and she told him in the most Danielle way anything had ever been said.

"I didn't hit the bitch hard enough."

"Danielle," Ridgeway said in that disappointed way that had become common when anyone said her name.

"I know," Danielle said, tearing her eyes away from the TV screen with difficulty. "I know what you're going to say, so don't. I know what you want, but I just can't do it."

Ridgeway gathered himself. "Danielle, you understand that part of your plea agreement is that you successfully complete this counseling. I will not report successful completion until you convince me you're serious about your healing."

Danielle stared across the desk at the man, one of the most unremarkable people she'd ever seen, with receding gray hair and a wiry frame. She thought about her answer, but instead of speaking, she shot up out of her chair and lunged for the remote. Ridgeway was unprepared and couldn't stop her. Danielle quickly found the rewind button and rolled the image back until the smiling, winking Nicole Moore appeared on the screen, and then she paused it.

Tossing the remote haphazardly back on the desk, Danielle stood and pivoted the TV toward Ridgeway. "Look at her. Do you know how much money it cost for her to look like that? The plastic surgery, the dye job, the clothes? She's got her own TV show. She's got two bestsellers. Lifetime is developing a movie about her 'struggle.' She's not taking anger management classes. She's not on probation. Nobody is treating her like a fucking leper. She came out of this smelling like a rose."

"She was the victim,"

"Bullshit," Danielle snarled. "She knew damn well what she was doing. She goaded me. There were fifty people in that room who saw it. There was video evidence. Yet here I sit, and there she is. The only goddamn thing she's done in her whole life has been to capitalize on the screw-ups of others. She's worthless, but everybody loves her."

"This isn't about her, Danielle. We've talked about this. Yes, she goaded you. Yes, she initiated the incident, but it was your actions, your inability to control your temper, that started the riot that got others hurt. You're a smart woman. Why can't you see this?"

"A smart woman," she repeated as she turned and wandered to the back of the room. Ridgeway's tiny office had a built-in bookshelf on the back wall stuffed to the gills with family photos and various keepsakes. Danielle snatched a baseball off a plastic holder and turned it around in her hands, looking at it but not reading the scribbled signatures. "I am a smart woman." Danielle turned back toward Ridgeway. "I'm smart enough to understand what's going on in my own head. If that hag hadn't come into my life, I wouldn't be here. I'd be on a stage somewhere, doing the one thing I'm good at."

Ridgeway started to respond but stopped and instead held up his hands, thumbs touching. Danielle understood and lobbed the baseball to him. He caught it perfectly in his right hand before switching it to his left. "Somewhere along the line, someone would have set you off. That's the root of what we're trying to get at here. You have to dig deeper. You have to quit avoiding the things that take you to the dark places."

"I live in the dark places," Danielle answered coolly. "The dark places are the only places where the world feels right. Some people just aren't made for rainbows and lollipops and unicorns."

"It doesn't have to be about rainbows and lollipops."

Danielle chuckled and meandered back to her chair. "I am who I am, and I never shied away from that. Yeah, I had a rough childhood, but I've never sat around and...." She thrust a finger at Nicole's image, still frozen on the TV screen. "Sat down in front of TV cameras and cried about it. 'Oh, poor, pitiful me. My mommy didn't love me, and my daddy died. Boo hoo, feel sorry for me.' I took it, and I dealt with it because I'm stronger than that." Again, she pointed at the TV. "I've been dumped for another woman, almost raped by my fiancé, and accused of making sex tapes. I've been called a bad role model because I had the gall to maintain my virginity into my late twenties. I've been called selfish, spoiled, and arrogant. Not once have I ever played the pity game. But this woman, this trailer trash whore, gets lauded as a hero. Her husband kills the love of my life, and *she's the victim?* She blames me for it? She ambushes me on the biggest night I've had in seven years, slaps me, and insults the man that her piece of shit husband killed, and *I'm the bad guy?* Nobody says a word about all the youth groups I spoke to over the years. The millions we gave to charity, the Make-A-Wish kids we helped out, and the local jobs we created through a business funded and sustained by my talent. Nobody says a word about any of that. I'm just the lunatic who beat up sweet Nicole."

"No one is a good guy or a bad guy here. I'm not asking you to play a victim or look for pity. What I'm asking you to do is look inside yourself and understand what's going on. You have to understand that all those things you mention created the dark places within you. You have to understand and accept that before you can learn to leave those dark places. You have to take responsibility."

"You think I don't know?"

"I know that you know," Ridgeway answered. "There is a big difference between knowing something and dealing with it. You substitute one for the other. In some ways, you're too smart, too aware, for your own good. It makes you stubborn.

You use that self-awareness as a buffer to keep you from dealing with those emotions. So you internalize until you explode. What happened with Mrs. Moore has happened before." Ridgeway leaned forward and locked eyes with Danielle. "And if you don't learn how to handle things, it will happen again."

Danielle smiled and slid back into her chair. "Oh yeah," she said, sounding too proud in her own ears. "Like the time I didn't speak to my bandmates for six weeks because I was pissed about a bad break-up. Or, how about the time I tried to spear a heckler with my guitar from onstage?" She laughed at the memory. "You should have seen that fat bastard's face when that guitar came flying toward him. Shut his fat ass up. I'll tell you that."

Ridgeway let out a frustrated sigh. "Those types of things are what we're trying to eliminate. You have to before something worse happens. You barely avoided going to prison. What happens if the next time you snap, you hurt someone worse? What if it's your husband or your child?"

"No worries there, Doc," Danielle said flippantly. "No men knocking on my door, and the baby factory got FUBARed in the wreck, not that I ever wanted to have a kid anyway. Last thing the world needs is the spawn of Dorothy Regan passing her genes around the pool."

"Things change."

"I'm not holding my breath on that." Danielle leaned forward and rested her elbows on her knees. "Thing is, in the wild, no one blames a lion for being a lion. It does what it does. I'm a lion. If you prod me, I will eat you. That dumb bitch prodded me, and as far as I'm concerned, she got what she deserved. If you don't want to get eaten, don't poke the lion."

Ridgeway sighed again. Danielle wondered if he'd ever run up against someone like her in all his years of service. She was willing to bet he hadn't. "Our time is almost up." The defeat was thick in his voice. "But Danielle, please, let go of this pride you're carrying around. I know it's an effective shield, but you're not doing yourself any favors. Sooner or later, the bill is going to come due."

Danielle let out a maudlin laugh as she collapsed back into her seat. "Doc, I've been paying the bill since I was eight years old."

***

Danielle let the top down on her blue Camaro and cruised the streets of Austin, enjoying the gorgeous mid-April weather. The skies were dotted with fluffy clouds, and a gentle breeze kept things cool and comfortable. She watched the people on the street as she drove by. Shorts and tank tops were emerging, and there was nary a jacket to be seen. Clearly, everyone else loved the spring weather as much as she did.

The weather was one of the few things Danielle had left to enjoy. Just more than a year earlier, Danielle had viciously attacked Nicole Moore at an autograph session before what was supposed to have been her grand comeback. She had returned to Austin after a six-year exile following the death of her fiancé Kyle in a car crash that had been orchestrated by Moore's husband. She had finally returned, ready to reclaim her spot as one of the top guitarists in the world when Moore had caught up to her. The resulting fight had been dubbed The Scrum at The Drum and had caused a media maelstrom.

Danielle finished her cruise around town and headed home, which was now a lush downtown loft apartment with a stunning view of the capitol and the UT Tower. She parked in the secured access parking garage and rode the elevator up to the seventh floor, thankful that none of the other tenants were there to share the ride. One thing she did enjoy about the place, everyone kept to themselves.

As the elevator rose smoothly, Danielle thought back on yet another failure with the counselor. He had told her that she was a smart woman. So why wasn't she smart enough to just say what he wanted to hear and move on? Why must she remain so defiant?

Those were good questions for which Danielle had no answers. Her pride and her defiance had cost her almost everything. In the wake of the fight, her record label had disavowed her and canceled the last album of her contract, even though they were raking in money hand over fist off her last album, thanks to the scandal. Her best friend Shannon, who starred on the album with her, had seen her own career shoot into the stratosphere. She was on tour now, a tour that they were supposed to be on together. She was a media darling, bravely coming back from a fractured wrist suffered when she'd tried to pull a crazed Danielle off Nicole. It was a dream come true for Shannon, who dazzled in the spotlight in a way Danielle never had.

Danielle's longtime manager Steve had also cut ties with her, no longer willing to weather the storms that Danielle generated. She blamed Steve for the lapse in security that had allowed Moore to infiltrate what was supposed to be an invitation only event with a camera crew. Later it turned out that one of the Erwin Center staff had taken a bribe from a TV producer to slip them inside. The entire thing had been a setup, and Danielle had fallen for it. Still, the damage was done, and Steve didn't need her anymore. He had Shannon now. Danielle was simply a headache he was better off without.

Moore landed her reality show and another bestselling book on top of getting a healthy settlement in a civil lawsuit. Several others who had been injured in the melee had sued as well, and when Danielle's lawyers assured her that she would lose every suit, she settled. Everybody got paid. Everybody benefitted.

Everybody except Danielle.

She was cursed. That simple fact Danielle had understood for a long time. What she didn't know was why. Was it payback for her parent's hedonistic lifestyle? Was it just her personality, something in her genetic makeup that invited scandal and tragedy? Or, perhaps like the bluesmen she had grown up emulating, she had made a secret deal with the devil, a crossroads bargain that explained her sudden rise to fame as well as the dramatic turns of fate.

That idea made the most sense, except for one problem.

Danielle didn't believe in the devil. The only devils she knew of were the ones that everyone carried around with them. Some people controlled theirs while others did not. Danielle was in a constant state of war with hers and losing more often than she won.

In the days immediately after the fight, there had been opportunities. Numerous promoters reached out to her about a fighting career, all trying to strike while the iron was hot. A professional wrestling organization had offered her an obscene amount of money to join their circuit. They promised her that she could be the hero. VH1 offered her a spot on *Celebrity Rehab* even though she wasn't an addict. She needed counseling, they argued. Why not get paid for it?

Danielle had turned them all down. Celebrity had never been her aspiration. She wanted greatness, and once upon a time, she had touched it, even held it. Steve had told her in better days that she had started a revolution, and he was right. Now there were any number of women strapping on guitars and making music, some of them damn good; not as good as she was, but good nonetheless.

The elevator whirred to a stop, and the door slid open soundlessly. She quickly stepped across the hall and into the apartment, which felt more like a museum than a residence. Danielle had reclaimed many of the trophies of her previous life from Steve and now proudly displayed them next to other items, such as the frosty white Stratocaster Eric Clapton had given to her. After the fight and while she waited for the legal system to proceed, Danielle had escaped to England, where she spent several weeks studying at the feet of the masters. Given that she had never pushed to expand her career overseas, Danielle passed with little fanfare. She returned armed with even more tools in her arsenal and a renewed drive to succeed.

There was also a mammoth stereo system and a wall full of CDs, as Danielle had proceeded to fill her time by trying to build the ultimate music collection.

She made her way to the kitchen counter and tossed her

keys down next to her old-fashioned answering machine. A blinking red light told her there was a message waiting. Curious, Danielle hit play, and immediately Shannon's singsong voice crackled out of the old speakers.

"Dani, we rolled into Vancouver last night just as the sun was setting over the ocean. It was so beautiful; I wish you had been here to see it. The organizers really rolled out the red carpet for us. I'm now an honorary Mountie. Can you believe that? Then again, I always did get my man or woman! I met some guy from the local hockey team who wanted me to tell you that you should always keep your feet in a fight. He said you can do more damage that way. He gave me a jersey that I'm going to send to you—it has your name on it and some kind of a whale on the front. You know that if you would just come out here and join us, I would get you on the stage. I don't care what Steve says. He's not here. You deserve to be out here with me. We should be doing this together. You're so quick to fight others; I don't know why you won't fight for yourself. Anyway, it'll be showtime soon, and then it's on to the next. I've gotta go slip into my face for the show. I'm thinking of you every minute, and I love you. Please love yourself for me. You can take that in more ways than one if you get my drift! See you soon."

Danielle laughed aloud and erased the message. Shannon was unlike anyone Danielle had ever known: supremely confident, sensual, and flirtatious. She had also become Danielle's best friend and most ardent supporter, never passing up a chance to defend her to anyone who would listen. Danielle suspected that Steve was intentionally keeping them apart, though that could have been the paranoia talking.

Shannon also desperately wanted more from Danielle than friendship and regularly tested the waters to see if Danielle's attitudes toward sex and relationships had changed. They hadn't, but it didn't stop her from trying.

At least Shannon cared. There weren't too many people left in Danielle's life she could say that about. There was Randy and Terri, the couple who had twice taken her in, though age and bad health were beginning to take its toll on them. There was Ryan Gregson, the longtime Austin DJ who continued to carry her banner and play her music. He did what he could, but Ryan worked at a tiny station that routinely came in at the bottom of the ratings.

Beyond that and a periodic exchange of texts with a former baseball player, that was it. Everyone else had gone on without her.

Danielle grabbed a water bottle out of the fridge, kicked off her boots, plucked the TV remote, a spiral notebook, and a pen off the glass and chrome coffee table, and plopped into an oversized recliner. Soon a much younger Danielle pranced across the giant flat screen.

From the start of her career, Steve had made a point of filming as many live performances as he could. Now he had transferred the footage to Danielle, and she had been curating it. She had plenty of ideas of what to do with the footage, but she doubted she would find any takers. Still, the project gave her something to focus on.

Danielle leaned back, closed her eyes, and let her mind wander. She saw herself on the stage, young and cocky, with her band behind her. The crowd screamed for more, and all she wanted to do was give it to them. She gripped her red and white Stratocaster tight and lit into another song as the cheers from the crowd rose to greet her.

Sitting alone in her living room, Danielle could still feel it: the heat from the lights on her face, the sweat covering her body, the music in her ears, and the smell of perspiration, with a faint undertone of weed wafting through the air. The only time she ever felt alive was with a guitar around her neck. Now even that avenue was largely closed off to her.

Largely, but not quite. Danielle snapped out of her daydream. She had things to do, and the clock was ticking. She made a light lunch and then jumped in the shower. Once out of the shower, Danielle began to put on a new face. She used makeup to dull her sharp cheekbones, full lips, and tanned skin. She slipped on a wig of long scarlet hair with big loose curls, dressed in a rustic broomstick skirt with a white top, and accentuated it all with jangly bracelets and round rimmed glasses.

When she was certain no casual observer would see Danielle Regan, she grabbed a guitar case and headed out. Her destination was a worn-out roadhouse in the hills west of Austin called The Palos Verdes Sudshouse. She had been playing weekly Monday night gigs at Palos Verdes for three months, going by the name of Dixie Anderson, where she entertained the drunks with an eclectic mix of stripped down country and classic rock standards.

This wasn't her only steady gig, either. On Thursdays, she played a Goth princess who went by the name Fairy, playing metal with the house band at a SoCo club called The Rusty Nail. As Fairy, Danielle didn't play, she only sang, and she quickly mastered the art of the primal scream. Turned out that her anger came in quite handy on those nights.

Fridays found Danielle masquerading as Roberta Paige at the Eternal Knight. She rocked through a catalog of eighties hair metal essentials as pretentious yuppie posers rubbed elbows with disenchanted Gen Xers over craft brews.

On her off nights, Danielle wasn't above crashing open mic nights when the mood struck. She had an open invitation to sit in with the house band at Antone's, Austin's premiere blues club, where the club owner would discreetly sneak her in, always in the back, in the dark, and uncredited.

The gigs didn't pay that well, and the crowds ranged from sparse and uninterested to mildly amused, but it allowed Danielle to keep her skills sharp and to lightly touch the life she used to lead. Plus, playing the wild variety of clubs forced her to challenge herself.

The Palos Verdes Sudshouse was a longstanding Austin area club. Originally a blacks only blues club in the forties, the place had undergone numerous name changes and had hosted everything from the Cosmic Cowboy scene of the seventies to metal, grunge, and swing, and was now an old-fashioned honky tonk with sawdust on the floors and outlaw country on the jukebox.

The stage was elevated slightly from the dance floor and surrounded by chicken wire like a coop. It gave Danielle twinges of claustrophobia, but it also served to keep drunken hands to themselves as the night wore on. She took the stage promptly at seven and started, as she always did, with some George Strait, her own little homage to Kyle. From there, she kept a steady stream of danceable songs flowing, usually nineties country. As the evening wore on and the crowd drank more, she'd begin to slip in some rock tunes like "Wild Horses" or "Hey Hey What Can I Do," usually to warm applause.

As she wrapped up a bored rendition of "Independence Day," a drunk old timer with a long beard and a Lone Star in each hand wandered to the side of the stage. "Hey," he slurred up at her. "Hey, play Pancho And Lefty."

Danielle smiled as sweetly as she could. "I'm sorry. I don't know that one."

Undeterred, the man continued. "Well then, play some Willie or Waylon. Give me some real country, not this new-fangled pussy music."

Danielle sensed that the man wasn't going to give up easily. She knelt down in front of him, thankful for the chicken wire barrier. "That's not what I do. You want to come on Saturday nights. That's when the Wagon Wheels play. They're more what you're looking for than me."

The man swayed as he struggled to focus his gaze on her. "You ain't gonna play no Willie or Waylon?"

"No, sir. Maybe some more George?"

The man's eyes got big. "George Jones? Hell yeah!" He thrust both bottles of Lone Star in the air. "That's what I'm talkin' 'bout. That's some country. No Show Jones!" He toasted to no one in particular.

Danielle shook her head. "I meant Strait. I can play some more George Strait if that would work for you."

The man whirled around, his joy instantly turning to

anger. He took a hearty mouthful of beer out of one bottle and proceeded to spray it all over Danielle. "Fuck you then, bitch. You ain't country. You ain't shit."

Danielle wiped the man's spit and beer from her face, her fingers tightening around the neck of the guitar as she imagined the drunk's throat in her hands. "You're right," she said, her words dripping with menace. "I'm not country. But you know what?" The drunk continued to wobble, but his eyes managed to meet hers. She crooked one finger at him. "Come closer, and I'll tell you a secret."

The man somehow managed a crooked smile and leaned into the chicken wire. Danielle leaned closer like she was going to whisper some deep, dark secret in his ear. When the man had his face pressed up against the wire, she pulled back and gathered her feet beneath her. "The secret is, I fucking hate this redneck shit." She jumped up and lashed out with her right foot, slamming it into the wire and the man's left cheekbone. The impact sent him falling back onto the dance floor, where he took out at least three couples and dropped both beers.

Danielle whipped around behind the mic. "If anyone else has a problem with my song selection, you can kiss my ass." She pushed the mic over, and when it hit the floor, it sent feedback squelching through the bar's crappy PA system. Still gripping the acoustic in her left hand, Danielle stormed off the stage, smashing the guitar on a support pillar and letting the pieces fall where they may. Without breaking stride, she snapped up her guitar case and barreled out the back door into the warm, sweet night.

"Hey," a voice called over her shoulder as she made it to the Camaro. "I ain't payin' you for tonight."

She twirled, holding both arms out to her sides. "Oh no! Whatever will I do?"

That wasn't the response the manager was expecting, and it stole his thunder. "And don't come back here again," he said meekly. "You're fired."

Danielle dropped her arms and gave the manager a one

fingered salute. "Best news I've had all week."

He slammed the door and stormed back inside. Danielle threw her case in the back seat, peeled off her top and the skirt, and tossed the clothes aside. Wearing nothing but boots, cut off shorts, and a tank top, Danielle hopped in the car and sped off.

Dixie Anderson was officially dead.

CHAPTER TWO

Fanatics was a popular sports bar that was known for being loud, busy, and dark, just the kind of place Danielle wanted. She stormed in and made her way directly to the bar, where she hopped on a stool at the end, as far away from any other patrons as she could get.

The bartender ambled over to her. "What can I get ya?"

Danielle looked up at him through tired eyes. "Cheeseburger and Coke, please."

"You got it," he said, and ambled back off. She wouldn't be drinking, which meant little to no tip, which meant he had better things to do with his night. Besides, there were busty coeds giggling up a storm at the other end that seemed to need his attention more.

Danielle buried her face in her hands. With luck, the incident at the bar would just go away. If the cops got called, they would quickly find that Dixie Anderson didn't exist and that her address was a Kinko's on Research, and her phone number belonged to a strip club on Riverside. Would they let it go at that? If they dug too deep, they were sure to piece together her real identity. All it would take was one person getting the tag of her car. It was stupid driving her own car to the shows, but then again, she never planned on assaulting anyone.

She suddenly became aware of a presence, a weight beside her. An entire restaurant and some asshole had decided to sit next to her. Danielle turned her head slightly as Steve Redus, her former manager, settled onto the barstool next to hers.

"Danielle," he said softly, his voice just as even and cool as it ever was.

Danielle gave him a quick visual once over. When they had first met, Steve had been a hulking man, his body bulging with muscles. Now time and stress had taken their toll. He was still fit, but the muscle tone was gone, and it made him look sickly.

"Big boss man," she said. "Surprised to see you here."

Steve took a fifty-dollar bill out of his wallet, caught the bartender's attention, and threw it on the bar. "The lady will take her dinner over there." He indicated a table in the corner with a jerk of his head. The bartender acknowledged with a nod. To Danielle, Steve said, "Come have a seat and let's talk."

He didn't wait for an answer, jumping off the stool and moving away. Danielle let out a long, slow breath and followed, suddenly feeling like that little girl back in Chaparral when her mother was angry with her, a frequent occurrence.

Steve pulled out a chair for Danielle, then took a seat opposite her. Danielle paused before sitting. "Always the gentleman." To which Steve responded only with a steel cold gaze. She finally sat. "To what do I owe this honor?"

"Your best friend asked me to come. She keeps insisting that we need to bring you on the tour. That we're your salvation. I couldn't get her to drop it any other way, so I told her I would come check on you."

"And, of course, you picked tonight of all nights. Just my luck."

"I've been here for a week."

"Ah," Danielle said. That didn't make her feel even a tiny bit better. "So, you've been watching for a while. What's the verdict? Gonna give me a chance?"

Steve's gaze softened ever so slightly. "I came down here hoping to see one thing and expecting to see another. You gave me exactly what I expected."

Danielle wanted to plead and beg for him to give her a chance. To promise that what had happened would never happen again. That Shannon was right, they were her only chance. Yet, at the moment, she needed to be humble. Danielle couldn't find it in her. Instead, she felt herself go cold all over. "You know how it is in those clubs. Things get rough. You gotta be able to take care of yourself. He was just a sloppy drunk looking for trouble."

Steve kept his steely eyes on her and grunted in response.

"Have you already told Shannon?"

Steve grunted again and pulled his phone out of his jacket pocket, and slid it across the table. Danielle pulled it the rest of the way. It was a text to Shannon, and he held nothing back in his report. Danielle closed the phone and tossed it back to him.

Steve just shook his head. "Danielle." He rested his forearms on the table. "I'm going to give you some good advice, and I beg that you take it." Danielle met his eyes with her own hard stare. "Let it go. It's over. You keep holding on to this dream of coming back, but it's not going to happen." He leaned in closer. "In this business, very few people get to go out on top. Most of them fade away. Once the industry has moved on, you just don't come back. Do yourself a favor and do what you should have done when you left all those years ago — find a new life. Leave this one behind while you still have a little bit of a legacy to protect."

Danielle collapsed back in her seat. "You think this is about a legacy? This is my life. This is who I am. It took me six years to learn that."

"And you were six years too late. No one wants you anymore, Danielle. We're out there on the road right now, and no one asks where you are. The fans don't chant your name or call for your songs. It's Shannon they want."

"That's bullshit," Danielle snarled, snapping forward. "I produced that album. I wrote it. I taught her how to be a rock star."

Steve stayed strong and still. "But she's the one who sold it."

Danielle turned her face away, unable to counter that argument. She spent a long minute staring into the shadows. Finally, she forced herself to look back across the table. "I still have great music left in me. My skills are sharp."

"I'm sure they are. You've always done your best work when you were upset, so I'm sure you'll go home tonight and write three great songs about this conversation." He paused to draw Danielle's eyes to him. "And I couldn't sell them to save my life. You're poison now. No one will touch you."

Danielle drummed her fingers on the table as she glared at him. "When did you lose your balls?" Steve was finally taken aback. He fumbled for a response and found none. "You used to be my biggest ally. You fought for me, with me. We never backed down, never took no for an answer. Now you just roll over at the slightest inconvenience."

"I'm tired of fighting, Danielle. We're at the point in time where the fights are supposed to be over."

Danielle glowered at him. "Not for me."

"All right," Steve relented. "Let's just say I agree to take you on again. Are you willing to do the things you would have to do?" Danielle started to respond, but he silenced her with a raise of his hand. "I'm talking about working with top producers. Electronic music, programmed beats. Less focus on your guitar work and more on your vocals. Frequent collaboration with other artists, younger artists, embrace hip hop."

Danielle turned up her nose. "Hip hop? EDM?" She felt dirty even saying the words.

"It's what sells. Rock is dead, Danielle. What you and Shannon pulled off last year was a Hail Mary for the ages, but Shannon sees the writing on the wall. The arrangements on tour focus more on beats. She's already growing, changing. Can you do that? Can you change with the times?"

Danielle's silence told them both everything that needed to be known.

Steve stood and straightened his jacket. "Please give some serious thought to what we've talked about. I'm still your friend, and I will still help you when I can." He took a sharp step forward, then stopped and rested a hand on her shoulder. "I am sorry. I was really hoping that you had your act together. Bringing you back into the fold would be to invite disaster, and I'm tired of clearing up your wreckage."

Danielle looked up at him, and suddenly he seemed larger

than life. Feeling the cold yet familiar sting of defeat, she tried to summon a little bit of attitude. "Well, thanks for nothing, I suppose. But I'm not giving up."

"I didn't think you would." He started to leave, sighed, and turned back around. Danielle shifted in her seat as Steve pulled a card out of his wallet and held it out for her. She paused before taking it. "You remember Ashley Brooks? She had that band I was going to hook you up with? Things didn't work out so good for her, either. She's up in Dallas working on a demo, and she'd love to work with you. She's obsessed with you."

"I kind of got that impression myself," Danielle said as she twirled the card in her fingers.

"That's her manager's number. You can give them a call if you want."

He walked away, leaving Danielle alone in the deepening shadows of the restaurant. She surveyed the joint with tired eyes. She was envious of the young women who ruled the bar on this night and the way they flawlessly held the attention of every guy in the place. There was a time she could have outshone them all. Now no one paid her any mind. Sickened, Danielle snuck out, not even waiting for her food to arrive.

***

Back at her apartment, Danielle stripped the last traces of Dixie Anderson away with a hot shower. She slipped into a nightshirt and collapsed on her bed. Steve's final words continued to echo in her head, taunting her. She snatched her phone off the bedside table, but who would she call? It was late, Randy and Terri were already in bed, and Shannon was the last person she wanted to talk to at the moment. She thumbed through her contacts and came to the one name, the one person who might still be up. Without giving herself time to second guess, she fired off a quick text and waited. It took less than a minute for her phone to ring.

Seized by sudden doubt, Danielle let it ring several times before she finally answered. On the other end, Brett Walls's husky voice came on the line. "What's up, Night Owl? Haven't heard from you in a while."

Years earlier, when both were young up-and-comers, Brett and Danielle had spent a promising afternoon together, but circumstances had taken their lives in separate directions. They had briefly reconnected the prior year, just hours before her infamous fight with Nicole Moore. It had been just long enough for them to exchange numbers, and now Brett checked in periodically, never judging and never pressing, simply making sure Danielle was okay. Tonight, she definitely wasn't.

"Is it too late? I can let you go."

"Nah, I was just unwinding a little bit. The Orioles and Mariners are playing on ESPN. Figured I'd catch a few innings. What's up?"

"I...I don't know. Just had a majestically awful day and needed someone to talk to."

"Well, I'm here. I got a Coors in my hand, feet propped up, and baseball on the TV. Lay it on me."

Danielle proceeded to relay the day's events to Brett in detail, and he let her ramble, occasionally giving her a verbal cue to let her know he was still listening. When she had recapped everything, she sat back and waited.

Brett took a long pull on his beer before he spoke. "First of all, I don't believe you're washed up, that you can't come back. It's happened several times. Heart did it. Aerosmith did it, and they were in way worse shape than you. So don't let that get to you. You can't lose hope."

"But if no one will listen to me if no one will give me a chance...." Danielle let the sentence go. She was pacing the cold, hardwood floors of her apartment, the lights of the capitol dome and the UT Tower shining bright in the near distance.

"Then you make them. Have you ever heard of YouTube?"

"Yes, I've heard of YouTube. I'm aware of that social media bullshit. Don't tell me that's your big idea."

"Don't dismiss this so out of hand," Brett said. "Just hear me out. You get some equipment, start a channel, and you start playing. You post a video or two a day. Different things. Maybe you do some alternate versions of old songs, tell some stories, give some lessons, even play some new stuff. Mix it up, keep it fresh. Let the people see another side of you. Let them in."

Danielle scoffed. "I've spent most of my life keeping them out."

"It's a different world now, Danielle. People not only want a more intimate relationship with their stars, they expect it. So you put yourself out there and try to gain an audience. Be patient. If you get enough views, you can monetize. Once you're big enough to monetize, the labels will come calling."

"Yeah, well. I wouldn't know the first thing about all of that. That's way out of my area of expertise."

She heard something that she thought might be Brett's recliner returning to its normal position. "I can help you. I know some guys, and I can get the equipment. Why don't you come up and hang at the ranch for a little while? I can make one of the spare rooms into a studio and get you started. I know a little bit about this stuff, you know."

"Right," Danielle said, recalling an earlier conversation. "You're a sports anchor for the local news, right?"

"Not just a sports anchor," he answered with faked offense. "Amarillo's number one sports anchor. Plus, I help out the social media guys from time to time." After a brief silence, he spoke again. "I would really like to help you, Danielle. I think we can do this. I promise, no funny stuff if you come up. I'll be a perfect gentleman."

Danielle felt herself crashing. "I don't know," she said, fighting off a yawn. "I'm not good at stuff like that."

"It won't be live. We make sure we get good takes. Come on. Give it a chance."

She couldn't fight the yawn anymore and let it overtake her. "I'll think about it. It's getting late, and I'm tired. I'll give you a call in a couple of days."

"Should I go ahead and start lining up some equipment?"

"Not yet. Give me a couple of days. Good night, Brett."

She hung up before he could answer. Danielle shuffled to

bed, put the phone on silent, and climbed in. Brett's idea was intriguing, but she couldn't help but think about Sean Moore. Would opening herself up to the public be a good idea? She was still debating it when sleep finally overtook her.

CHAPTER THREE

The next morning Danielle woke up to find a voicemail from Terri Holder waiting for her. Still only half awake, Danielle pulled up the message, expecting it to be something trivial. Instead, Terri came on, sounding panicked. "Dani, this is Terri. Could you come over, please? Sooner the better? There's some… something I need to ask you. Please let me know as soon as you get up."

Danielle's heart sank, and she felt cold all over. Terri and her husband Randy were her surrogate parents, the only people in the world who were always there for her no matter what. She couldn't stomach the thought of something happening to them. She hurriedly dressed in tattered jeans and a sweatshirt. Dixie Anderson's boots were still scattered where they lay on the bedroom floor, so Danielle pulled them on. She tried her best to brush her teeth with shaky hands before giving up. Did her best to curtail her bedhead before deciding to throw on a ballcap with a Keep Austin Weird patch on it. Then she was ready to leave.

As she waited for the elevator to come up, she called the house but got Terri's voice mail instead. Her message was simple and direct. "I'm on my way. Sit tight."

After what seemed like an eternity, the elevator doors dinged and hissed open. Danielle started to dart in but stopped short when she saw Scott, the building doorman, standing on the other side. He was a large man with squared shoulders and a thick jaw, just the type to quickly discourage interlopers. He held a mustard-colored envelope in his hands. "Ah, Ms. Regan." His voice boomed in the tiny elevator. "I was just coming up to see you." He waved the envelope. "This was taped to the front doors this morning. You're the only Danielle in the building, so I assume it's for you."

"Really?"

Immediately Danielle's warning bells were sounding. The thought of the Moores stalking her danced in her mind. Was this Nicole's work, angling for another showdown? Or had she gotten on some other weirdo's radar? She took the letter cautiously and flipped it over. All it said was her first name, but it was how it was written that shook her. The D was almost perfect, a big swooping cursive D, but then the letters got progressively shakier and hard to read, like whoever wrote it only had the strength to write one good letter. Still, as Danielle studied the writing, especially the capital D, she found it oddly familiar.

A bell rang, and it snapped Danielle out of her thoughts. Scott was holding the elevator, a frown of concern on his stone face. "Something to be concerned about, ma'am?"

Danielle forcibly tore her gaze away from the envelope and tried to put on a confident smile. "I'm sure it's nothing. Can I slip this under my door real quick?" Scott assured her that he would hold the elevator. Danielle hustled back down the hall, popped open the door, and tossed the letter on her coffee table before jogging back. "Thanks."

The doors hissed shut. He asked if she needed the garage level, and Danielle confirmed. "Are you sure everything is all right?"

Danielle was chewing her bottom lip as she replayed Terri's message in her head and thought about the strange letter. She had the very definite feeling that things were not all right. A feeling she was all too familiar with. "Might want to keep an extra eye out for anything out of the ordinary." She glanced up at him as he stared down at her like a protective older brother. "I have a history of attracting trouble."

"I'm aware, ma'am," he answered stoically. He bid her adieu at the lobby, and she went the rest of the way alone, the pressure in the back of her mind getting more intense. If she had somehow brought trouble to the Holders, Danielle knew she would never be able to forgive herself.

The beauty of the day before was gone, replaced by a foreboding overcast sky and whipping winds, reminding Danielle that it was still early springtime in Texas, and nothing could be taken for granted. Where the day before she had cruised with the top down, now she prayed that the heater would hurry up and get warm as she tried to navigate downtown traffic.

The Holders lived in a decaying neighborhood northwest of the UT campus, stubbornly hanging on to their home as the rest of the neighborhood was rapidly taken over by students paying what was jokingly considered cheap rent for the other rundown houses in the neighborhood. More than once in recent years, they had rejected offers to sell. Yet all three of them knew that time was running out in the neighborhood. If the neighbors didn't force them out, eventually, their own declining health would.

Danielle fishtailed her Camaro as she gunned up into the driveway, skidding to a stop next to their white van. She skittered out of the car, past the garage with the tiny apartment above that she had twice called home, through the side gate, and up to the backdoor. When she knocked, Danielle wondered if it sounded as frantic as it felt.

Soon Terri appeared at the door. Instead of instantly opening the door, Terri instead took a careful look around before unlocking it. Before she could even get the door closed, Danielle started in. "What the hell is going on?"

Terri turned around as quickly as a pudgy, sixty-three-year-old woman could. "I didn't mean to scare you," she said, but her voice had a tremor in it. "I just...there's been a person hanging around lately...."

"A person?"

Danielle heard the familiar mechanical whirring of Randy Holder's motorized wheelchair approaching from the front of the house. "Aw, she's seeing ghosts," he bellowed. Randy never took anything too seriously. "Probably just some homeless person wandering around. Damn college kids are always throwing half eaten pizzas near the dumpsters. Brings in the mice and the damn bums."

Danielle looked quickly from Randy to Terri. "Is that what this is about? A homeless person?"

"I don't think so," Terri whispered. A chill visibly ran through her, and she started rubbing her arms to fight it off. "This person. This lady. I don't think she's homeless, and I don't think she's here for pizza, either."

"Okay," Danielle said. She moved to their kitchen table and pulled out a chair. "Come sit and tell me about her."

"Not much to tell," Randy said as he pulled up to his spot at the head of the table. "There's this crazy eyed lady that's been hanging around. She is homeless. Her clothes are all ragged and dirty, and she's weird. Sometimes she stares at the house, and Terri is convinced she's stalking us. I think she's got dementia and gets lost in her own head."

"Have y'all called the authorities?"

"Yes," Terri chimed in. "But they never come."

"Cops got better things to do than hassle old vagrants," Randy interrupted.

Danielle took a deep breath and held Terri's hands. She waited until Terri looked her in the eyes, hoping to calm her down. "I got this, okay? When was the last time you saw her?"

"This morning, when I woke up. I came out to get the paper, and she was standing right at the mouth of the driveway. We stared at each other. She didn't say anything, but I felt very threatened."

"She's a toothpick," Randy howled. "I run over her in my little wagon here and snap her in half. I don't know why she scares you." He patted Danielle on the shoulder. "I told her to grab up my shotgun from the closet and let her see it."

"I hate that thing," Terri shot back.

"Get her to stop coming around," Randy snarled.

Danielle knew that whoever it was, she had gotten to both of them more than they were letting one. She had never seen them snap at each other like this. She put a hand on Randy's shoulder. "Let me handle this." She switched her focus back to

Terri. "First of all, don't get the gun." Over her shoulder, she heard Randy start to interject and slammed her left hand on the table to silence him. "In this neighborhood, with strange people roaming around, brandishing a gun is just inviting trouble. Has she ever come up on the property?"

Terri shook her head no.

"I'm going to go buy you a camera, a digital camera. Every time you see her, you take a picture. That way, you'll have a record with a time stamp on it. Let her see you take the picture. Then you call me, and I'll come over. If she ever steps foot on your property or does anything menacing, you call the cops and tell them you have a prowler. They'll come for that."

Terri didn't speak but nodded her head. Danielle swiveled to face Randy. "Don't you dare take that goddamn gun out of the closet. You do, and sure as shit, someone's going to break in to steal it. Keep your doors locked and your lights on at night, and keep a phone by your hand at all times."

"Oh, come on," Randy said, but she saw the fear in his eyes he was trying to hide. "You know, if I wasn't stuck in this stupid fuckin' chair—"

"I know," Danielle said. "I know you would. But stuck in that chair, you are. So we'll handle this my way. Now...." Danielle stood up and looked from one to the other. "How about I fix y'all some breakfast, and we go on with our day?"

***

Danielle cooked, and they ate together, trying to have a more pleasant conversation, but Randy kept wanting to complain about Obama, and Terri just sat quietly, stuck deep in her own thoughts. Twice Danielle excused herself to the bathroom, only to journey to the largely abandoned front room to peer out of the windows. No crazy eyed ladies appeared. After cleaning up, Danielle reminded them both of the plan and drove back home.

She was safely back in her own apartment before Danielle finally released the tension she had been holding in her neck and shoulders. Terri and Randy had saved her life, but their age and worsening health were taking their toll. Often Danielle felt like she was more a mother to them now than a surrogate daughter. At times it was exhausting.

She kicked off the boots, tossed the hat on a chair, and peeled off the sweatshirt before plopping down on the couch that was more stylish than functional. Steve and his girlfriend Aja had left all their furniture when they left for California, and Danielle had never bothered to replace it. In front of her, the letter Scott had given her rested, waiting for her to open it.

She hesitated, then gingerly reached out and pulled it over. When she picked it up, a business card fluttered to the floor. Holding the letter in one hand, she reached down and picked up the card in the other. It was the card Steve had given her the night before, a simple white card with black lettering. *Mike Campbell, Professional Managerial Consultant.* His business address was in Century City, California. Though the name was the same, Danielle was ninety percent certain it was The Mike Campbell of The Heartbreakers, though, in show business, you never knew.

She stared at the two items in her hands, debating, then flipped away the envelope and darted to retrieve her phone. Moments later, Mike Campbell, Heartbreaker or not, came on the line.

"Mr. Campbell. This is Danielle Regan. My manager gave me your card last night and said your client wanted to play with me?"

"Danielle…. Oh yeah. Yeah, yeah, yeah. Right. You're Ashley's idol. The girl is crazy about you. Yeah. So, listen. We're up in Dallas right now, recording a demo in Deep Ellum. You know where that is?"

"Yes sir, I've been there many times."

"Great," Campbell said, taking no exception to the sarcasm in her voice. "So, she has this song she thinks you'd be great on. And I know you live in Austin, which is just down the road. So if you'd be interested, Ash would be jacked to work with you. We couldn't pay you much—we're on a pretty tight budget."

"I'm not worried about money," Danielle answered. "I'd love to." Then Danielle flashed on Terri and her promise to be there if their stalker returned. "But I'm afraid I can't leave town right now. I've got things I have to attend to."

"Oh, I see," Campbell said with evident disappointment. "Well shoot, Ash is gonna be bummed."

"Well," Danielle said. "I don't know if this would work for you, but I know a guy with a studio. If you could make your way down here, I could get us a couple of hours. He owes me a favor."

"Oh, that would be…. I can't even…. Yes. We can do that. No problem at all."

"Don't you think you should consult your client first?"

"No need," Campbell responded. "If I tell her you're available, she'll come running. When could you have the studio?"

"Let me make a call, but I would say tomorrow afternoon is a safe bet. He's used to artists dropping in unannounced, so he always keeps a studio open for stragglers. Let me know when you get in town, and I'll take you out to dinner."

"That's fabulous. I'll go let her know right now. This is fantastic. Thank you. I'll be in touch. Is this the best number to reach you at?" Danielle assured him it was, and he rang off.

Danielle stared at the phone before putting it down. Whoever this Mike Campbell was, he had yet to learn the art of the poker face. He sounded like a kid. With a sigh, Danielle thought back on her first meeting with Steve. Even then, he had been so polished and together that he inspired confidence in the young artist. She wondered if Ashley Brooks had that same confidence in the overeager Campbell.

Regardless, it wasn't her concern. The prospect of getting back into a recording studio was. It only took her one call, fifteen minutes, and a promised guitar lesson to a young family member to secure three hours of studio time the following afternoon. Finally given something to focus on, Danielle drug out her favorite guitar, a hollow body Stratocaster with a custom purple paint job, and began practicing. She felt good for the first time in a long time.

CHAPTER FOUR

Danielle woke up that morning to a text from Ashley Brooks letting her know that she planned on pulling into town early in the afternoon and asking where they should meet. Danielle shot her the address of a roadside diner a short drive from the studio. Ashley sent her a copy of the song she wanted to work on in response.

The song was called "Club 17," and it was a catchy, upbeat rock song in its rawest form. Danielle listened to it on a loop as she went about her morning routine, letting the song thoroughly seep into her subconscious. By the time she left to make their appointment, Danielle had a firm grasp of the song and several ideas for how to make it better.

The day was not as raw as the previous but still too cool to put the top down as she made her way out of town to the southwest and edged onto an old two-lane highway that wound through the hills outside of Austin. Around a curve, she spotted Raylene's, nothing more than a rotting dive that survived on the repeat business of the locals, who could find the place. It was so far off the map that even the most pretentious Austin foodie didn't bother to look for it.

As she eased off the highway into the gravel parking lot, she spotted two old farm trucks, a flat bed, and a dusty white Mustang that was sorely out of place. She pulled in next to it and noticed a guitar buckled into the passenger seat, which wasn't an uncommon site in these parts.

Ashley Brooks was out of the car before Danielle even put hers in park. She wore black jeans, ankle high black boots, and a sheer gray blouse under a black leather motorcycle jacket.

Her hair was jet black with the kind of natural, loose curls that many women paid three figures to get in the salon. She greeted Danielle with a toothy grin as she got out of the car. "Hey, long time no see."

"I guess so," Danielle said, offering her a handshake that the younger girl eagerly took. She was a good head shorter than Danielle and much more lithe.

"I was so excited when Mike told me you called," Ashley said as they turned to enter the restaurant. "I told him to put everything on hold. I would come down immediately." She talked fast and had just the slightest hint of a Midwestern accent. "I'm really thankful you agreed to do this."

Ashley got to the door first and held it open. Danielle stepped inside, surveyed the surroundings, and took a table by the window where she could watch the cars. Ashley slid in opposite her.

"So, did you listen to the song? What did you think?" Before Danielle could answer, Ashley started up again. "It's about this place I used to hang out when I was in high school. This old abandoned strip mall. Some dude misjudged which way the town was going to grow, you know?" Danielle nodded. "We'd all go out there and drink and fuck and whatever else. Some people did hard drugs, but I never got into that. It was fun, and since we were out away from everything, the cops didn't bug us much. We called it Club 17 since most of us were seventeen. Then some goody two shoes on the city council heard about it and had the place locked up. Typical suits spoiling everybody's fun." She finally paused, and Danielle stared across the table at her. "Sorry," she said, blushing. "I ramble when I get nervous."

"Why are you nervous? We've played together before. We were going to go on tour, remember?"

"Yeah, but that was as your backing band. Now we're here, and Danielle Regan is going to play one of my songs. That's a huge deal. So yeah, I'm kinda nervous."

Danielle chuckled. "I'm not sure that's such a big deal anymore."

Ashley smiled bigger. "It is to me."

Danielle shifted the subject. "Steve mentioned that things hadn't gone so well for you guys either. What's the deal there?"

Ashley grimaced and glanced out the window. "Man...." Danielle waited patiently, and eventually, Ashley managed to look at her. "So, we did get a record deal, and we were all really juiced about it. But it turned out that the label was only interested in our lead singer, not the whole band. They offered to make her a pop princess, and she jumped at it. Left the rest of us holding our dicks, in a manner of speaking."

"Ah, typical sleazy record producer shit," Danielle spat out. She had plenty of experience with those.

"You should know," Ashley said as she popped a fry into her mouth. "It was your guy. Rico Cardenas."

"Ah, shit. Yeah, I know him well. Rat-faced little asshole. I can still remember the glee in his eyes when he tore my contract up right in front of my face. I wanted so bad to jump across that table...."

"Like with the chick in Austin last year?"

Ashley's words hit home, and Danielle realized she had balled both hands up into fists. She released the tension with a slow, hissing breath. "Yeah, I guess so." She felt her cheeks turning red. "So, do you have a new deal now, or are you shopping?"

"Shopping. My sister gave up, went back to St. Louis, and is going after her degree. I don't want to give up yet." She leaned forward, and her easy smile evaporated. "I'm hoping this song we're going to do will get me a deal. Then I can get my sister back in the band, and we can take our shot. This is extremely important to me."

"I'll try not to let you down," Danielle said. "But if you're counting on my name carrying some kind of cache for you, you better think again. Apparently, I'm nothing but poison now."

"I bet we can change that."

Danielle laughed. "You don't lack confidence, do you?"

Ashley relaxed in her seat. "Hey, I'm sitting across from the Queen of Rock, the premiere female guitarist in the world. And

I'm here, not quite on your level yet, but close, and we're joining forces. What happens when you get a queen and a princess, and they're pissed off and out for blood? You get an unstoppable force. That's what we are, an unstoppable force. You'll see. Just wait until we get into the studio."

After a quick lunch, Danielle led Ashley the rest of the way to Iron Star Sound, a nondescript building off the beaten track that promised struggling young artists quality studio access for a minimum price. They were met by John Ryan, the man who owned the studio and often sat in on the sessions. He met Danielle with a hearty hug before turning his attention to Ashley.

"Wow, you two could pass as sisters."

Danielle shrugged him off. "Yeah, well. I'm an only child, and she's a natural blonde, so maybe not."

"Hey," Ashley called as Danielle moved on into the studio. "How did you know I'm a blonde? I never told you that."

Danielle glanced over her shoulder. "Your sister did last year when she was explaining how you learned everything you know by copying me."

"That little shit," Ashley muttered. "That's supposed to be a secret."

In the studio, John introduced the girls to the hired hands he had brought in for the session. Alan Stewart was a well-known local percussionist who had spent time touring behind Willie Nelson and Pat Green, among others. Curtis "Chili" Guinn had earned his stars playing in funk and zydeco bands in New Orleans before relocating to Austin.

With introductions out of the way, Ashley played everyone her song and laid out her plan. She wanted to alternate verses with Danielle and sing the choruses together while swapping lead guitar duties during the song. They spent another half hour working through the arrangement with the others until she felt they had the song under their hands. Finally, they were ready to roll tape.

As everyone got ready to play for real, Ashley sidled up next to Danielle. "This is so awesome, thank you."

"We haven't done anything yet. Stay focused," Danielle responded. Ashley nodded and moved away, acknowledging her role as the most experienced and accomplished musician in the room. Fearing that she might have intimidated her younger cohort, Danielle called her name. Ashley looked up tentatively, and Danielle grinned at her. "Let's see how good you really are, kid." With that, she launched into the song, twisting Ashley's original opening riff around. The seasoned studio professionals fell right in step. Ashley bit her lip, grinned, and started playing as well, quickly concocting a complimentary riff. They ripped through the song of teenage excess and debauchery at breakneck speed, Danielle doing her best to throw Ashley for a loop. Each time she was pleasantly surprised when the young guitar slinger handled the curveballs she threw.

Danielle felt alive as they traded guitar licks and stood at a shared microphone to sing the chorus. This was her true essence; the one time and place Danielle could just be herself and let the outside world go. Sadly, it was over all too soon.

The two of them sat side by side in the control room, listening to the playback and fiddling with the mix. When it was all done, they had a very solid rock anthem in their pocket. Ashley was beside herself as they strolled back out to their cars. "I can't wait to play this for the guys. Man, they are going to be floored. This is so good."

Danielle agreed, but there was something else burning at the back of her mind, something she wouldn't dare say to Ashley. She was flying high, living in the moment, a skill Danielle had never mastered. There was no need to drag her down.

As they said their goodbyes and Ashley drove away, desperate to make it back to Dallas and share her new song, Danielle sat and stewed. Yes, they had recorded a truly great rock anthem.

But what was the point when the music world no longer valued such things?

CHAPTER FIVE

Later that night, Danielle sat in her oversized recliner, the only lights in the apartment coming from the massive stereo system behind her, as she let the music of her idols wash over her. For once, her brain wasn't working overtime. She was focused solely on the notes, letting them whirl her away.

The beauty of the moment was ruined by a phone call. At first, Danielle let it go, not even bothering to see who was calling. When they called a second time, she sighed and reached for the phone. Snatching the remote off the table with her other hand, she muted the music before answering the phone.

Brett's voice instantly came on the line. "Hey, Danielle, I've got some good news for you."

"Oh yeah," she answered, hoping that he could sense her disinterest. He didn't.

"I'm going to be in town this weekend. I figured we could get together. I'd really like to take you to a game while I'm down there."

The thought of having a visitor made her perk up a little, but she didn't want Brett to know. "I'm not into baseball, you know that."

"Maybe that's just because you don't understand the game. But you'll have me, a certified Ph.D. of Baseballology, to guide you through it."

"Well, I could give it a try. When will you be in town?"

"I'm coming in Friday night. The weekend anchor needs some hours, kid on the way, and I've been wanting to take some time off, so he's going to take my shifts on Friday. I told my bosses I'd do a quick interview with a local kid that's playing down here.

It's a working vacation, but it'll only take me a half hour or so to do that. I'll grab him Sunday before I leave town. What do you say? Dinner Friday night, then a game on Saturday?"

"Yeah, sounds good," Danielle said. "No, wait. Friday's no good. I can go to the game with you on Saturday, though."

"Oh, what's the deal with Friday?"

Danielle chewed on her lip as she debated if she should tell him about her Friday night gig as Roberta Paige. She decided against it. "I just have a prior engagement, is all. Fridays are all booked up."

"Oh, really? Hot date?" He tried to sound like he was teasing, but Danielle heard the edge of worry in his voice.

"Oh yeah. You know how I'm beating guys off with a stick." She chuckled. "It's just something I've got to do. Prior engagement, that's all. But I'm good for Saturday."

"All right," Brett said, suddenly sounding chipper. "I'll see you then."

Brett hung up, and Danielle smiled down at the phone. At least somebody was still interested in her.

***

Thursday evening, Danielle stood in front of her bathroom mirror, transforming herself into Fairy, the screaming Goth queen of Austin's metal scene. She had applied heavy white makeup to all exposed skin, applied heavy black makeup to her eyes, lips and nails, and put on a shoulder length block wig with heavy long bangs. She topped off the look with a torn midriff shirt and black leather miniskirt, torn pantyhose, and black motorcycle boots. The boots not only fit the part but were also useful if the crowd got a little too handsy.

She was applying the last touches to her makeup when the phone rang. Danielle took a quick glance and saw it was Terri. Instantly her blood ran cold, and she snatched up the phone. "What is it?"

"It's that woman," Terri stammered on the other end. "I just saw her standing at the foot of our driveway, looking up at the house."

"Did you call the cops?"

"Yes, but they said it could take a couple of hours to get someone over and to call back if she did something threatening."

As Danielle stood in front of the mirror, she literally saw the anger contort her face into something else, and combined with the Goth makeup, she looked like a monster. "I'll be right there," she snarled into the phone.

As the last light of day held on for dear life in the Western sky, Danielle weaved her way through traffic. In times like this, she often thought of the guy in high school who had not only taught her to drive but taught her how to race. Those skills she'd needed to use more often than she ever would have thought.

Once she got into Randy and Terri's neighborhood, she slowed down, keeping her eyes peeled for the strange woman. Fearing, or maybe hoping, that the woman was still at their house, Danielle parked a street over and walked the rest of the way. Darkness had fully fallen, and with her dark getup, she imagined herself to be near invisible.

As Danielle reached the corner, she was able to see the stalker in question. She had her back to Danielle and was stooped and frail, her gray hair a long, matted mess, and as she paced, Danielle noticed that she shuffled more than walked. There was nothing imposing about the woman, but then again, Terri was older and had lost her bravado years ago. Danielle had plenty in reserve.

Quickly but as quietly as possible, she moved to the street, her eyes still locked on the invader. She crossed the street, hoping the streetlight at her back would add to the illusion she was creating. Once she was in position, Danielle started strutting towards the woman and let out a wolf whistle to get her attention.

"Hey, Grandma," she called out, trying to sound as intimidating as possible. The stranger's head whipped around, and she saw shock and fear in the woman's pale green eyes, which flashed against the contrast of her yellowed skin. "What ya doin' out here?" She pulled a butterfly knife out of the waistband on the skirt. The knife had started as a prop during her shows, but she'd actually needed to flash it for defense on a couple of occasions. The Rusty Nail wasn't exactly in a good part of town. Now she flashed it for show, and the weird woman immediately stumbled backwards and pulled her tattered overcoat closer around her shoulders. Danielle broke out into a toothy smile, though she wasn't sure the woman could see it. "You hidin' something under that coat, honey?" Danielle called out. She was trying to affect a New York accent, but it was coming out more like Valley Girl. No one had ever accused her of being an actress. "Why don't you show me what ya got?"

Danielle, knife held out from her body and high so the light would catch it, quickened her pace. Amazingly, the woman, despite her frail appearance, moved quickly, beating a quick retreat. Danielle pursued her to the end of the block and then let it go as the weirdo was swallowed up in the shadows of the side street.

Danielle stowed the knife, feeling cockier than she had any right to. All she'd done was scare some vagrant woman, but she still felt like a protector. Working her way back up the street, she stopped in front of the Holder's house and gave a big wave. She saw the curtains flutter and knew that Terri had been watching. With her good deed done, Danielle hurried back to the car. Though punctuality wasn't required at The Rusty Nail, she was still a professional, and she had a show to do.

***

The phone woke Danielle up on Friday morning. She fumbled for the phone on her nightstand, praying it wasn't Terri reporting another homeless woman sighting. What she got was worse. "Ms. Regan? Franklin Ridgeway. I was wondering if you might come in today for a special session. I've cleared a spot at eleven."

Danielle groaned loudly. "Oh, geez, Doc. I wish I could. I'm afraid today isn't good for me."

"Oh, I see. Well, I guess I can simply report to the judge that you've been unwilling to take the proposed steps in an attempt to speed your process. I'm sure he won't look poorly upon that."

"You son of a—"

"I'm sorry. What was that?"

Danielle grunted again. "I said I guess I'll see you at eleven." Ridgeway agreeably rang off as Danielle tossed her phone onto her nightstand. "Smarmy little bastard," she muttered. A quick glance at the alarm clock told her it was just past nine. She had time, but with an appointment hanging over her head, Danielle got up, knowing that going back to sleep was now impossible.

Back in town and with some time to kill, Danielle decided to pay a visit to Randy and Terri and see if their stalker had returned. She pulled into their driveway and parked on the far side of their conversion van, then let herself in the back gate and strolled up to the back door, only to find it locked. Through wispy curtains, she saw Terri's portly figure moving in the kitchen and knocked on the door.

Terri opened the door moments later, her graying blonde hair like a bird's nest on top of her head. "Good morning," Danielle smiled, but Terri met it with a grimace. "Rough night last night? Did Randy give you the ole two incher again?"

Over Terri's shoulder, Randy rolled into the room on his portable wheelchair. "Hey! Three and a half, I'll have you know!"

Danielle swiveled around Terri. "Get some work done, did ya?" She turned to Terri, who was standing over the stove, still looking dour, and Danielle dropped the playful tone. "Seriously, how are you doing?"

"I'm fine," Terri said unconvincingly. "We were about to have breakfast. I was just poaching some eggs." Terri turned and shuffled back to the stove. Danielle kept an eye on her as she sat at their kitchen table next to Randy.

"Don't believe it," he whispered to her. "They're not real eggs. It's that artificial, soybean egg in a carton shit."

"They're healthier than real eggs," Terri moaned. They had virtually the same conversation every morning as Terri forcibly made Randy eat better. He needed to lose weight to save wear and tear on his knees, one of which was artificial.

"I'd still rather have a T bone and some biscuits and

sausage," he called out. "Eggs in a carton. Who eats that?"

Simultaneously, Terri and Danielle answered, "You."

Terri smirked just a tad. "What brings you around today? Seems early for you to be out and about."

"My therapist wants me in for an extra session today," she groused. "He threatened to tell the judge if I didn't come in. Not in so many words, but the point was clear."

"Passive aggressive," Randy said. "That's what it was. A passive aggressive threat."

"I'd like to passive aggressively put my foot up his ass."

Terri waddled over to the table with a skillet full of eggs and shoved some off onto Randy's plate. "That's the kind of attitude that got you in anger management to begin with, dear. Would you like some?" She held up the skillet.

"No, thank you. I'd hate to deprive Randy of the joy of seconds." She gave Randy a little nudge with her elbow.

"Thanks a lot," he answered. "Don't do me no favors, okay?"

Terri shrugged and then shoveled the rest of the eggs onto Randy's plate. "Suit yourself," she said before easing into a chair across from Danielle. Randy glared at them as he forced the first bit of pseudo-egg into his mouth.

"Do you have any idea why he wanted you to come in?"

"No clue," Danielle said. Terri met her gaze head on, and Danielle blinked first. "Okay. There may have been a slight incident at the Palos Verde Monday night, but I don't know how it would have gotten back to him."

"Danielle Elizabeth Regan," Terri spat out. "What have you done now?"

Randy shoved his plate aside and leaned in closer, an impish smile creeping across his bearded face. "Yeah, give me details. Did you kick somebody's ass? Was it an all-out brawl?"

"This guy was being rude," Danielle started. Terri kept staring, and Randy edged even closer, both waiting for the rest of the story. "So I put him in his place." Still, their eyes bored into her. Danielle wasn't getting off easy with them. "With my boot.

Upside his head."

Randy cackled and slapped his knee. "That's my girl. Take shit off no man."

Terri wasn't quite so pleased. "You are going to wind up in prison one of these days if you don't learn to control that temper of yours. How often are you going to go down this road?"

"If people would quit being assholes, I wouldn't have to."

Randy jabbed his fork at Terri. "She's right. Some people deserve a good boot to the face every now and again. Keeps 'em in line."

"You hush up," Terri snapped at him before turning her attention. "Danielle...."

She sensed a lecture coming on and, knowing that was probably what awaited her at Ridgeway's office, decided that two was one too many. She stood to leave. "Listen, I don't want to get into it. I just thought I'd check in and make sure Randy ate his pseudo-eggs." Randy responded with a vulgar gesture. "I didn't come to get scolded. I gotta run."

"Danielle, wait," Terri called, but Danielle was already two steps to the door with no intention of stopping. Terri didn't give up and chased her down into the driveway. "Danielle, wait," Terri insisted.

Danielle stopped and turned. Terri caught up, but instead of saying what she had on her mind, Terri started fidgeting, checking her surroundings.

"What are you doing?"

Terri gave the entire block a good once over. "Nothing," she finally said. "Now listen to me —"

"If you're worried about the weird old lady, I doubt she'll come around again after last night. You're welcome."

Terri bit her lip and did another visual sweep of the neighborhood. "Thank you for that. I appreciate it. But baby, you can't keep lashing out like you do." She placed a wrinkled hand on Danielle's cheek. "I love you like a daughter, and I'd hate to see you behind bars. You've already ruined your career. Don't ruin your life too."

The sentiment was sweet, but Terri's delivery struck a nerve. She pulled away from Terri's hand. "I'll be fine. I know what I'm doing."

Terri let her go, and soon Danielle was speeding away. At one intersection, she thought she might have seen the old lady again, but she was going too fast and needed to get to Ridgeway's office, so Danielle didn't bother to turn around.

***

Ridgeway was in a beige suit, jacket draped on the back of his chair when Danielle walked in. He stood and offered her his hand, but Danielle refused and dropped into the faux leather chair on the other side of the desk. "You got me here. Now what?"

Ridgeway sat back down and thumbed through a notebook on his desk. "I got a call this morning. There was an incident at a bar outside of town. A man was physically assaulted by a tall female singer. You wouldn't know anything about that, would you?"

"Why? Oh, because I'm a tall woman singer. Talk about your racial profiling."

"It's not racial profiling,"

Danielle ignored him. "People get assaulted in bars all the time. Women get assaulted in bars all the time. Who's to say that this guy didn't come on to some girl, and she put the smack on him?"

"It's really unimportant, Danielle," Ridgeway said as he tried to claw control of the conversation away from her. "The police have no interest in pursuing the matter. The man was drunk and apparently known for getting into trouble. However, since the incident involved an angry female musician and I'm currently treating a female singer with anger issues, I was asked to follow up on it. I'd hate to think it was you. I'd hate to think we haven't made any progress at all and that this entire treatment has been a failure."

"Well, rest easy, Doc. It wasn't me. I was at home doing my hair."

Ridgeway stared daggers at her. "I didn't say what night

this happened."

"And I didn't say what night I was washing my hair." Danielle gave him a big, phony smile. "See? Everything works out. You can tell the judge I'm as clean as the driven snow. Can I leave now?"

Ridgeway removed his glasses and pinched the bridge of his nose. "Danielle. I know your feelings on this, but I think that a stay at an in-patient facility—"

"You're not sending me to The Farm. I don't need that. Those places are for gone people. I mean really far-gone people. I am fine."

"You're a time bomb."

Danielle sat up straight and thrust a finger at him. "I am a magnet for douchebags. That might be annoying, but it's not a crime."

"Well, I can agree that you do invite trouble. I think you need more personal interaction. You live this secluded life, and when you go out in public, you can't deal with the stresses. You need intensive therapy. Not just anger management, but grief counseling as well."

"Whatever," Danielle said as she slumped back into her chair. "I'm so tired of everybody ganging up on me. I will work things out in my own way, in my own time. I always do. I just need time, and I need people to get off my back."

"Would you reconsider anti-depressants or—?"

"Nope. You can't medicate this away, and honestly, I think you run the risk of making things worse, not better. I know that those things help lots of people, but that's not for me. I will get on top of this. I promise you. Are we done?"

Ridgeway sighed. "I'm wasting my time with you, aren't I?"

Danielle stood and made for the door. "It's not you. You seem like a nice man. I don't belong here. That judge...." She made a fist at her side when she felt a verbal explosion coming on. "The judge overstepped when he sentenced me to counseling. I would have paid my fine and done a couple of days in jail, just like a regular person who gets in a fight. He wanted to make an example of me because of who I am. All he's done is make the situation worse."

"Be back here Monday for our regular session," Ridgeway called as she started out the door. Danielle walked on without answering.

***

Friday night, and Roberta Paige was in full voice at the Eternal Knight club. Of all of Danielle's aliases, this one was her favorite, as the music of the eighties was nearest to her heart. It helped that the house band was equally enthusiastic.

The Eternal Knight was a relatively new club and, as such, was just beginning to get popular with the locals. A positive write up in *The Austin Chronicle* helped. On this night, Danielle peered out on the crowd just before showtime to see a packed house. She paid particular attention to a long table full of middle-aged men in dress shirts and blue jeans who were actively calling for the band.

She informed the rest of the band that they had a hot crowd, which brought smiles to everyone's faces. They then proceeded to play with a passion they had never touched before. At the front of it all was Danielle. For Roberta, she kept her natural hair, but teased it up big and bold, applied heavy makeup, and topped it off with a denim miniskirt over fishnet stockings and a lacy corset top under a black leather jacket. Maybe it was the pent-up frustration of the week, but Danielle fully let loose, prancing around the stage and engaging the crowd, who ate it up in response.

The band had a guitarist named Bernie who was perfectly good, and on some nights, she left the playing to him. On other nights she wanted to play. With the show nearing its end and the crowd still screaming for more, she turned to Bernie. "Wanna battle?"

Bernie grinned back and muttered, "You bet."

He tossed Danielle the Flying V he had been playing and snatched a black Les Paul resting on a stand just off stage. Danielle slipped into his rig and fiddled with the strings, adjusting the tuning as she stepped to the mic. The regulars recognized what was happening and began chanting, "Battle! Battle!"

"Y'all seem like a fun crowd tonight, so what if we do something a little different for you?" The crowd screamed, with the biggest screams coming from the group of men near the back. "Bernie here, he doesn't think a chick can play guitar." Boos cascaded from the crowd, and Bernie played along, dismissing Danielle with a wave of his hand. "I think he's wrong," Danielle continued, and sure enough, the crowd roared again. "Will you help us decide who's right?" More cheering. "All right. Bernie, let's go!"

As the rhythm section laid down a loose beat, Bernie and Danielle took turns swapping runs on the guitar. They called back famous rock riffs of the past, mixed them together, and added their own touches to mix. Bernie was very good, skilled, and knowledgeable, and he gave Danielle a run for her money. The battle was fun, but Danielle's pride began to flare up as Bernie continued to surprise her. Her better judgment told her to let it go, but Danielle was never one to succumb to better judgment and instead turned up the heat. Holding nothing back, Danielle let the months of torment loose as she strutted around the stage. She pulled out all the stops, playing behind her head, behind her back, on her knees. Bernie refused to relent and instead joined in, and they brought the performance to a close together, finally collapsing in an exhausted heap together at the front of the stage as the crowd jumped to their feet.

"Damn," Bernie huffed. "I didn't know you had that in you."

Danielle tried to play off her own exhaustion as she patted him on the back. "I'm full of surprises, my man. You have no idea."

The band took a bow together before Danielle bounded off the stage, through the back, and ducked into a supply closet that doubled as a makeshift dressing room. She quickly changed out of her sweaty stage clothes, took down the big hair, and wiped away the make-up. She emerged ten minutes later as a regular girl in jeans and a T-shirt, with a ball cap pulled low over her eyes.

For months she had repeated the routine without incident, but on this night, as she elbowed her way through the crowd, someone called her name. Without looking around, Danielle began to hurry her pace, aggressively moving toward the door. She made it to the door, to the welcome relief of a cool evening breeze, but she made it no further before a strange hand took her arm.

"Danielle, hey."

She spun and found herself standing toe-to-toe with Brett Walls. He stood just a tick taller than her, broad shouldered, blue eyed, and in need of a shave. He wore a Western style dress shirt over dark blue jeans.

"Hey, I was calling you. I guess you didn't hear me."

"No, I didn't," Danielle muttered. "It's loud in there." She backed further away from the door, pulling Brett into the parking lot with her. "I'm surprised to see you here."

Brett smiled big and put his hands on his hips. "So, this is what you had going tonight?"

Danielle shrugged. "It's a regular gig and my favorite one of the week. I didn't want to miss it. Sorry."

"No apologies necessary." Brett jerked his head back towards the bar. "I actually hooked up with some of my college pals, and we've been having a night. Why don't you come inside and have a beer with us?"

"Ah, beers with a bunch of horny, drunk middle-aged dudes. I'm sure nothing could go wrong there."

"I wouldn't let anything happen to you. The women most in danger tonight are those guys' wives. You got 'em all wound up."

Danielle backpedaled. "Still, I'm all hot and sweaty, and I didn't sleep well last night, so I'm going to take a raincheck."

"All right, but we're still on for tomorrow, right?"

He had presented an out, and for a fleeting moment,

Danielle thought about taking it. As she stood in front of him, The Eternal Knight's neon sign bathing them in blue and red light, Danielle felt herself pulled back to time. To another bar parking lot in another city a thousand miles and many years away. Brett looked nothing like Kyle, but they were the same type, big and rugged, but with a soft side they didn't try to hide and a soul that shone in their eyes. For a moment, she wanted to let herself drop into his arms and feel his tender strength envelope her. But this wasn't Kyle.

She forced herself to gaze into his eyes, ready to back out of the date, but the words that came out weren't what she planned. "The baseball game? Wouldn't miss it."

"Excellent," Brett said. "Then I guess I'll see you tomorrow." They stood silently, facing each other, Danielle feeling as awkward as Brett looked. He tucked his hands into his jeans pockets. "Need me to walk you to your car?"

Danielle smiled her sweetest smile. "Nah, I got it, Slick. I can take care of myself."

Brett smiled back, and again Danielle had to remind herself it wasn't Kyle standing in front of her. "I know you can." He slapped her lightly on the shoulder but let his hand linger there. "See you tomorrow."

The warmth of Brett's hand on her shoulder made Danielle tingle. She had missed the touch of another more than she would ever admit. She bit her lip to stop herself from grinning like an idiotic schoolgirl, but a smile crept onto her face anyway. "Absolutely."

CHAPTER SIX

Saturday afternoon was a gorgeous day, sunny and warm with just a slight breeze. Danielle dressed for the occasion in denim shorts, a tank top that clung to her like a second skin, and dark sunglasses. She pulled into the parking lot and soon spotted Brett standing beside a huge red and gold Ford truck. She had to park several rows away as the lot was filling up quickly. By the time she got out, Brett was already on his way over.

Though he tried, Brett couldn't quite hide his approval for the way she was dressed.

"Wow, you look great," Brett told her.

"Thanks." She pointed at his bundle. "What's that you got there?"

"Oh yeah, a little gift to get you in the spirit of the day." He tossed the jersey to her, and she caught it. Holding it up, she saw it was a white Texas baseball jersey. On the back was the number twenty-seven and the name Walls.

"This was yours?"

"Yeah. It's been hanging in the closet for years. I figured, what the hell? Don't worry, I washed it so it wouldn't be musty or anything." He licked his lips and fiddled with the bill of his hat. "You don't have to wear it. I just thought you might want to. You know, kind of fit in. But what you're wearing is fine."

Danielle grinned at him and slid her arms into the jersey. "Is it okay if I don't button it up?"

"Yeah, it's great." He gave Danielle a quick once over. "Oh, and here." He handed her the cap, a white one with an orange bill and a block letter T, just like the one he was wearing. "I got you this too. I broke it in for you."

Danielle took the cap and studied it. The colors were still brilliant, and the hat looked new. "Broke it in? Was this yours too?" She wasn't sure about wearing a hand me down cap.

"Oh no, it's new. I just bent the bill for you," Brett said, pointing out the drastically bent bill of the hat. "Some people don't bend it right, or they don't bend it at all, and then it looks goofy. I didn't want you to look…goofy."

Danielle fought off a grin and put the cap on, sliding it down low over her eyes the way he wore his. "So, what's the verdict? Do I look goofy?"

"Definitely not," Brett answered. "I don't think you could be goofy if you tried." He turned and offered her his arm. "Shall we go inside?"

Danielle took the offered arm with both hands. "Let's."

They walked arm-in-arm into the stadium and found their seats. Danielle settled in while Brett disappeared. He returned carrying a tray with four loaded hot dogs, two soft drinks, and a game program. "Lunch is served." He handed one of the hot dogs to her.

"Wow. I haven't had a hot dog in…a really long time."

Brett sat next to Danielle, leaned in, and pointed down to the field. "We're in white, obviously. The orange and black team is Oklahoma State. They're pretty good, but we're better. We're number three in the nation."

"Out of how many teams?" Danielle asked around a mouthful of hot dog.

"About a hundred and fifty or so. So, yeah, we're good. Went all the way to the College World Series finals last year. This year we're going to win it."

Danielle smiled over at him. "You really do love this game, don't you?"

"Well yeah. I owe everything I have to baseball. It's a great game. You'll understand. By the time the day is over, you'll be a baseball junkie too."

"We'll see about that."

The game began, and Brett's enthusiasm just grew. He

patiently explained everything that was going on from their seats along the first baseline. When the Longhorns came to bat, a player hit a home run, and the crowd of seven thousand people exploded. By the time the game hit the middle innings, she had the art of scorekeeping down, and Brett was still eagerly explaining every nuance and strategy that he saw unfolding.

Danielle didn't follow everything that was going on, but she found herself enjoying the experience more than she expected. She was more impressed by the easy way they related. She didn't feel any pressure when Brett was around like she could finally let down her guard and be herself.

In-between innings, two shirtless chubby young men with orange Ts painted on their bellies started up the steps toward the concession stands when one of them stopped, open mouthed, and pointed at Danielle. "Oh my God. You're Danielle Regan," he yelled out. "Gabe, come here. Check it out."

His friend Gabe, who had continued up the steps, raced back and gave Danielle a hard look. "It is! Dude! You're the one that beat that one bitch's ass at The Drum last year."

Danielle tried to sink into her seat and pulled her hat lower over her eyes, but it was too late. She had been made.

"That was so badass," the first guy said. "You were just like whoosh, over the table, take that and that." He was pantomiming punches, his fat giggling with every move. "You want some, bitch?"

She continued to try to disappear, and Brett picked up on it. "All right, guys," he said, edging up in his seat to position himself between Danielle and her new admirers. "That's enough. She's just here to watch a game, just like you guys are. Let her alone."

The one named Gabe maneuvered around Brett into the row of seats behind them. "Would you sign my hat?"

The other one stepped to the side and produced a black Sharpie out of his jeans pocket. "Would you sign my belly? I got a Sharpie!"

Brett stood, arms outstretched, trying to force them to

keep their distance. "Leave her alone. She just wants to watch the game. Be cool, guys."

The ruckus had drawn the attention of others sitting in their area. Danielle could hear her name being whispered back and forth as the muttering grew louder and louder. From off to Danielle's right, a middle-aged woman stood up quickly and marched down the aisle toward her. "You're Danielle Regan?"

She didn't respond and instead tried to sink even lower in her seat, wishing for all the world she could be invisible at the moment.

"I want you to know," the woman said in a shrill voice, undeterred by Danielle's silence. "That my girls used to look up to you. You used to be a role model. Look at you now. A felon. A disgrace. You should be ashamed to even show your face in public."

"Yeah, you're trash," someone yelled out from behind her. Others around started to laugh. The chubby twins were trying to move in on her, with Brett doing his best to keep them at bay. The first chubby guy was still thrusting the Sharpie at her. Suddenly a pleasant day at the ballpark had turned into a nightmare. The woman was still berating her, people were still laughing, but it just sounded like noise in Danielle's ears. She felt like the walls were closing in around her.

From somewhere further back, a large fountain drink came screaming down, narrowly missing Danielle and hitting the back of the person in front of her. The man leapt out of his seat and fixed Danielle with piercing blue eyes. "What the fuck, lady?"

"I didn't do it," she protested. "Somebody back there."

The man wasn't satisfied. "Will you please just sign this guy's autograph so he'll get out of here?"

"Better yet," the harsh lady said. "Why don't you just leave? We don't want you here."

Danielle finally threw her drink down, shot up out of her seat, and snatched the marker out of the fat guy's hand. "You want an autograph? Here." She quickly scrawled *eat another donut fatty* across his stomach in big black letters before capping the marker and tossing it toward the field. She pushed her way past Brett, and when Gabe shoved his hat at her, she yanked it away and sent it sailing into the crowd like a Frisbee. "Go get it, lard ass," she snarled. Then she was in the walkway and racing up the steps. The anger was rolling inside her, her heart pounding in her ears. All she wanted to do was fight them all, to wade into that sea of taunting, laughing people and swing away. She ran simply to avoid it and hated herself as she ran, feeling like a coward for not standing her ground.

She was out of the stadium before Brett finally caught up to her, latching on to her shoulder and spinning her around. "Danielle, wait. Just slow down."

"Get off me," Danielle snarled, huffing and puffing from her run, the anger still fresh but now feeling the crush of tears welling behind her eyes. She pushed them back with an iron will. "This was a mistake. I was so stupid to think I could go out and be normal. It's always something. There's always somebody there to fuck things up for me."

"Danielle, don't let a couple of idiots run you off. You can't lose your shit every time someone recognizes you."

"It wasn't just a couple of idiots, Brett." She spit out his name like it was an insult. "It was the church lady telling me what a horrible role model I was. It was the hick three rows back telling me I was trash. It was all of them laughing at me. I can't take it. I won't be a laughingstock for those jackasses."

"You don't have to," Brett said calmly. "You don't have to be anything for those people. Screw 'em. There are always gonna be assholes in the world who wanna run you down. Are you always gonna let 'em?"

"I guess so." Danielle wheeled around and started for the car, but again Brett tracked her down.

"Fine then. We'll go. Let's do something else. Let's take a ride, something. Don't let a great day end like this."

Danielle thought it over for a minute. "I don't ride with people. I drive."

"Fine then, I'll ride. Let's go. We can pick up my truck

later."

Danielle shrugged but led him to her car. She put down the top and drove, saying nothing for the longest time as she navigated the heavy Saturday afternoon traffic. Brett remained quiet at her side.

She wound her way out of town, and as she negotiated a curvy country road, she beat the steering wheel with her hands. "I don't get it. What am I supposed to do?" She glanced over at Brett, who was studying her in the dying afternoon light. "Am I just supposed to let people ridicule me? That seems to be what everybody wants."

Brett took a deep breath and glanced out the window. "Well…yeah. I guess you should." He looked back at Danielle, who felt her jaw drop from his answer. "It's not the end of the world to have people make fun of you. God knows I've been on the receiving end a ton. You just gotta develop a thick skin and brush it off." Brett took another furtive glance out the window. "What always helped me was to remember that the people in the stands are in the stands for a reason. They can't do what we do. All they can do is criticize. They don't know what it's like to be us, to be on the field — or the stage if you will. They criticize because they can't do anything else."

"I was just trying to watch a game, though," Danielle responded. "I *was* in the stands. I don't know why people can't just let me alone."

"Well," Brett started. Again, he took his time to compile his thoughts. "Honestly, if you had just signed the autographs, the rest of it probably wouldn't have happened. I mean, those guys, they were obnoxious, but they thought you were cool. They weren't making fun of you. They thought you were a hero. Wouldn't have hurt to have just signed the hat and the fat guy and gone on."

"It didn't feel like hero worship to me."

Brett patted her on the thigh the way her grandpa used to do. "That's on you. You're sensitive, and you overreacted. I know lashing out can feel good sometimes, but there's almost always a better way to handle things if you stop to think about it."

Danielle rolled her eyes. "You sound just like my...." She let the thought trail off.

Brett picked up on it. "Your...?"

Their eyes met, and Danielle looked away. "Never mind." She shrugged. "I know I'm being whiny, and I know I overreacted, but there's just always somebody watching me, judging me."

"But yet, when you were away, and no one cared, you missed the attention. You can't have it both ways, Danielle. You gotta take the good with the bad."

"But there's no good anymore. You heard that one lady. Her girls used to idolize me. Now they don't. All the things I did to be a good role model, they were all undone because of that stupid whore and her loser husband. I didn't change, but now everything I did is no good."

Brett nodded along. "True, but this has always been inside you. It's like with that hockey player you dated who claimed he had a sex tape of you. You could have just blown it off, but you decided to make a show of it, humiliate the guy. You know his career never recovered from that? Or what about the fan you threw the guitar at? You could have walked off stage and been done with it, but you had to lash out. That hasn't changed, either. It was only a matter of time before something like that blew up in your face. That's the exact reaction that woman was looking for. Now everybody knows how easily they can push your buttons."

Incredulous, Danielle glared over at her passenger. "If I'm such a horrible person, why are you here with me?"

"I don't think you're a horrible person Danielle. I think you're great. But you're in a bad spot, and I want to help you out. You strike me as someone who could use a friend."

Danielle's eyes again darted to him, but now she was curious. "Is that all?" Her bullshit detector was screaming.

Brett smiled. "Well, if I'm being totally honest, I have always wondered what would have happened if life hadn't taken us in different directions back in '96. I guess, since I'm single and you're single, and we're here...."

Danielle chewed it over for a minute. "Well, at least you're honest about it."

"I'm also honestly starving. Whaddya say we head this jalopy back into town and rustle us up some grub?"

Danielle laughed out loud. "Rustle us up some grub? Buddy, you've spent too much time out on that ranch alone."

"That I have," Brett agreed. "That's how I know when it's time for a vacation." Danielle looked at him quizzically. Brett smiled bigger. "When the cows start looking too inviting, it's time to get off the ranch for a few days."

"Oh Jesus," Danielle laughed. "You're trouble, aren't you?" Brett just shrugged in response.

***

Brett suggested a local pool hall on Sixth that he swore had the best wings in town. They ordered a smorgasbord of appetizers, a pitcher of beer and another of Coke and picked out a table in the front corner by the window. Danielle watched the Saturday night bar hoppers strolling up and down the street, remembering the days long ago when she could pass among them without notice.

Brett finished racking up the balls and handed her a cue stick. "You first."

Danielle licked her lips as she stood and sauntered over to the table, putting on a show for him, feeling like a whore for reveling in his attention but reveling in it just the same. She chalked her stick and bent over the table.

"So, you got me here. What's your deal?" Danielle asked as she looked over a pool table. "What happened with the baseball thing? Why are you really here?"

Brett took a long tug off his beer. "Those are two completely different stories. I'll give you one. Which one do you want?"

Danielle lined up a shot, took it, and watched as the eleven ball dropped in the far corner. "Stripes," she declared. Standing and rechalking her stick, Danielle eyed Brett. "Give me the baseball story."

Brett took another sip and grinned. "Nope, not that one.

Too personal just yet. I'll give you the other one."

Danielle put a hand on her hip. "Then why did you tell me to pick one?"

He grinned at her. "I just wanted to see which one you would pick, and you picked the one I figured you would."

"Tease," Danielle said as she turned her attention back to the table and her next shot. Brett ambled over to a nearby table, where a sampler of cheese sticks and wings sat waiting.

"I'm not teasing," Brett said as he plucked a wing with bright orange sauce off the plate. "I'll tell you in good time. I gotta save something for the second date."

Danielle peered at him over her pool cue, sneered playfully, and took another shot. This time the ten ball caught the lip and bounced away. "Pretty presumptuous that there will be a second date," she teased. "Technically, this isn't even our first date. There was that time when you were still in college."

"That doesn't count. I was still playing back then. Nice try, though." Brett licked his fingers clean before retrieving his own stick. Danielle took a seat as Brett surveyed the pool table for his next shot.

"Fine. So why are you here?"

Brett surveyed the table, then settled on a shot and indicated where he was going by pointing with his stick. "Three in the side," he said. "And you know why I'm here. I told you I was coming down to interview that local kid."

"No news station sends their top anchor to do something like that. Especially for a small market like Amarillo. Come on, what's the real deal?"

"Sure they do," Brett answered as he hunched over the pool table once again. He took his shot and cleanly banked the three into a side pocket. Danielle caught his smug grin at hitting the shot. "I volunteered for the assignment. Any chance to come back down here. Truth is, I get bored up there, so I frequently volunteer for out-of-town assignments. Gets me to such exciting places as Happy and Kress and Gruver. I even made it to your old hometown to cover a playoff basketball game once."

"Oh really?"

"Yep. The Chaps had this point guard, kid was a D-One talent. They just shredded our poor local team that night." He took aim at another shot. "One in the corner."

"So, how is Chaparral these days?"

Brett ignored her until he slammed home his second shot. "Nice. Did you know they have a huge billboard of you at the city limits?"

"No, I didn't. That's...kind of sweet."

Brett quit studying the table and looked over at her. "Back home, we have this artsy thing that we do with horses. All over town, there are sculptures of horses all decorated up. They kind of do the same thing there, only with guitars. All over town, there are these huge guitar statues painted up in different ways. People actually travel there just to see them all. They've really put themselves on the map, thanks to you."

"Well, good for them. Maybe someday I'll go back and see it. Might be a kick." As Brett went back to studying the table, Danielle changed the subject. "So how do you manage being 'Amarillo's Number One Sports Anchor' while also maintaining a ranch? Isn't that a lot of work?"

"Actually, I don't ranch. I tried, but it wasn't for me. A lot of work for very little payoff. So I sold off the herd but kept the ranch and some of the land. The guy who bought it from me lets me have the run of the place, so I can go up on the mesa whenever I want."

Danielle took a sip of Coke as she watched Brett line up another shot. "So, how did you wind up being on TV?"

Brett hit the cue hard, and Danielle watched with envy as the one ball slammed against the rail and rolled all the way back down the table, settling into a corner pocket. Brett lingered over his shot, admiring the ball as it rolled.

"You're a goddamn pool shark," Danielle spat.

Brett tried to suppress a grin and failed. "I know my way around a table. We're not playing for money or anything, so maybe I'm showing off a little bit." He started scanning for his next shot. "But to answer your question, I totally fell into it. Honestly, I didn't have a fallback plan if baseball didn't work out. What I did have was an idea of what to do with my bonus money when I got drafted, and that saved my ass. It gave me some security for when baseball didn't work out. I had a chance to feel my way around until I figured it all out."

Danielle slid to the edge of her seat. "How long did it take you to figure that out?"

Brett, who was hunched over the table, peered up at her. "It took a while." He returned to the task.

"But how long is a while? How long should it take someone to find a Plan B when their dream goes up in smoke? How long is too long?"

With a heavy sigh, Brett dropped his stick and stood up. "Danielle, there's no rule for something like that. It takes as long as it takes. I would guess that some people never find something to fill the gap." Danielle slumped back into her chair, causing Brett to circle the table and come to her. "Don't rush it. Be patient, and it will all come to you."

Danielle tried a smile, but it died on her lips. "Yeah, right."

Brett leaned his stick against the wall and pulled a chair over to her side. Their knees touched as he sat down, and Danielle didn't pull away as Brett reached out for her hand. "They can't take it away from you. Maybe you can't do it at the same level you did, but you can always play. With all the crazy things I've heard of rock stars doing, I can't believe this won't pass."

"That's the thing, though. I can play the clubs under assumed names, and it kind of satisfies me, but I don't want to be relegated to crappy clubs. I want what I had. Maybe things will eventually blow over, but what do I do until then?" Still, Danielle didn't pull her hands away.

Brett shifted in his seat. "Have you thought any more about my offer?"

Danielle shifted to face him, still clasping Brett's fingers in hers. "The YouTube thing? Man, I don't know. Besides, I've tried running away before, and it didn't help."

"I'm not talking about running away. I'm talking about a vacation. Just let it go for a little while and have some fun while the storm blows over. Besides, this way, you can control the narrative. You get to show everybody out there exactly what you want to show them, say exactly what you want to say. No one can interrupt you or manipulate you." He shrugged and stood up. "It was just an idea."

"I know. Maybe. I don't know what to do."

"Even if you don't want to do that, you could still come up. There's all sorts of stuff we could do. I've got a boat; we could go fishing. I've got motorcycles, ATVs, a pool, you name it. We could just hang like we are now. No pressure. I'll be a perfect gentleman."

"You'll be a perfect gentleman," Danielle repeated. "But I would be alone with a man I barely know in his house in the middle of nowhere. You could chop me up into little pieces and bury me somewhere, and no one would ever know."

"Well, that would solve your problem." Brett tried to laugh off his joke, but Danielle was in no mood. "I'm not going to chop you up. I'm a good guy, Danielle, and I really do want to help you. Even if all I can be is a friend, I'm fine with that. Let me be a lifeline."

It sounded good, too good. Danielle realized she was mentally already there, and it sent a wave of fear arching through her. She stood sharply. "We're not friends. We're acquaintances. There's no way that I would ever put myself in a position like that. That you would even ask boggles my mind. Good night."

She stormed off with Brett in hot pursuit. He waited until she reached the door and stepped out into the night before he grabbed her arm and spun Danielle around. "I know that it seemed a little forward, but that wasn't my intent."

"And I'm just supposed to trust you? We've seen each other a couple of times, and I'm just supposed to have faith? Well, guess what? I'm all out of that." She pulled her arm away and stomped off toward her car, Brett still in hot pursuit.

"You gotta trust somebody sometime."

Danielle was three steps from her car, but she stopped and whirled around. "Do I? Well, it so happens that when I've trusted people in the past, it hasn't worked out so well for me, so I'm sorry if the four hours we've spent together isn't quite enough to put me at ease yet."

Out of the corner of her eye, she noticed a young man walking their way, cell phone in his hand like he was taking a picture or a video. She turned away again and saw the young man with the cellphone had increased his pace and was moving toward the driver's side of the car to intercept her. Danielle's heart was in her throat, fearing what the stranger might have in mind.

"Danielle, I'm sorry you've had problems in the past, but I promise you, my motives are pure."

Danielle stood at the back of her car, Brett in front of her and the stranger coming up on her left, and felt trapped. Panic was rising within her as the stranger, a lanky young man with long red hair, approached her. "Danielle Regan, right? Wow. What an honor."

Danielle tore her glance away from Brett. "You got me, kid." He was definitely filming the entire thing with his phone. "Can I help you with something?"

"Um, yeah," he said, stammering more than a little. "Um, I don't know if you know, I know you've been busy lately, but your former bandmate, Jim Silver, he's battling cancer. I'm a friend of the family. When I saw you, I thought you might want to know, and maybe you'd like to send some good wishes his way? He might like that."

Brett was keeping a respectful distance on the other side of the car and had his eyes trained on the red-haired kid. Danielle edged away from the kid. "I'm sorry to hear that, but I'm kind of in the middle of something right now. It's not a good time."

"It'll just take a second. I'm already recording. Just say something; it doesn't have to be really long. I'm sure it would mean a lot to him."

Brett was slowly coming around the rear of the car, eyes

trained on the stranger, his body tensed like he was ready to leap into action at the first sign of a threat.

"I doubt that. Like I said, it's not a good time."

"It'll just take a minute," Red continued, continuing to come closer. Brett was closing from the other side.

"Listen, kid, Jim and I never got along all that well, and the last time we saw each other, it didn't end very nicely. Now, I'm sorry to hear about him, but I really don't have anything to say. Please just go away so I can finish this conversation."

"Oh, come on," the kid continued. "That was years ago. I'm sure that's all forgotten by now. Besides, I mean, he's dying. Surely it would help him rest easy to know you've forgiven whatever it was."

"Me forgive him?" The very thought was like a slap in the face to Danielle. She turned to face the kid fully. He got excited and adjusted his phone, probably thinking she was going to get deeply personal. Behind her, Danielle felt Brett close the gap even more.

"Danielle...." Brett's voice was a warning over her shoulder. Or was it her conscience? Or both? It didn't matter.

"If anyone should be making amends, it should be him, not me. Jim Silver used me. He bullied me, and he manipulated me. He rode my coattails, and once he got what he wanted, he left me high and dry. You want me to tell Jim how I feel? You really wanna know? Fine." She leaned in toward his phone as her face contorted with anger. Brett was calling over her shoulder, but she wasn't listening. If this kid really wanted to know how she felt about Jim Silver, she would tell him. "Remember me, Jim? The person whose talent made you all your money?" She leaned even closer, raised her hand, and stuck an upraised middle finger toward the phone. "Die slow, fucker."

"Ah shit," Brett muttered. She felt his hands on her shoulders, pulling her back. He was there in a heartbeat, placing himself in front of the kid whose face had gone slack with shock, but he still held the phone up. "Why don't you let me have that for a second, okay? Danielle didn't mean that. She's just upset.

She's upset with me; we were having a bit of an argument. I'll just erase that video and give it right back."

The kid snapped out of his daze. "Hell no." He yanked the phone back and shoved it into his pocket. "She knew what she was saying. What a bitch." He leaned around Brett's frame to look at Danielle. "What a terrible person you are. You used to be my idol, but no more. What a terrible thing to say."

"Like I said, she's upset with me. Just give me the phone for a second. I promise I won't break it."

"Fuck you." He stepped back quickly. "This is going on Facebook, YouTube, everywhere. I'm going to show the whole world what a terrible person you are."

He turned and ran. Brett started to follow, but Danielle grabbed his arm.

"Let him go. It's not worth it."

Brett turned with a look of pure panic written across his face. "If that video gets out…."

"Yeah, I know. I shouldn't have said that. I just…I can't help myself." Feeling like the weight of the world was nestling squarely on her shoulders, she looked up at Brett. "I think I want to go home now. Thank you. I'm sorry I fucked things up." She got in the car and slammed the door.

Brett lightly beat on the window. "What about my truck?"

"Call a cab," she yelled as she sped off, leaving Brett standing in the street looking forlorn.

CHAPTER SEVEN

The phone rang off the hook all morning, but Danielle let it ring. She stayed in bed, covers pulled up over her head and shut out the world as long as she could. It was deep into the afternoon before she finally pushed the covers off and reached for her phone to answer the most recent call.

Shannon's nervous voice greeted her. "What did you do? My God, tell me that this is some kind of sick joke or that it was taken out of context or something."

"Hello, Shannon. How are you today?"

"Don't deflect this on me. It's all over the news, social media, it's everywhere. Tell me that you didn't tell a terminal cancer patient to die slow."

Danielle sat up in bed and finished kicking the covers off her body. "You tell me. Does that seem like something I would do?"

"Damn it, Danielle. You can't keep doing stuff like this. I've been working on Steve, trying to get him to let you join me on the tour, or at least add some dates down there so I could sneak you up, but there's no way he will go for it now. I just... why do you keep making things so hard on yourself?"

"I wish I knew," she whispered. "I'm sure there's some deep seeded reason why."

"That's what the therapy is for. To get to the bottom of it. You are still going, aren't you?"

"Of course I am, Mother. It's court ordered. But it's not doing any good. I don't think therapy is for me. I'm too self-aware as it is. He's not going to find some magical key that's going to open up my head like Pandora's Box. I've always known why

I'm the way I am. I just can't change it."

"Can't or won't, Dani?"

"Shouldn't have to," Danielle responded. "I don't know why I should have to change. I was trying to live a better life, and that bitch Nicole Moore started her shit with me. Last night I tried to get that stupid kid to leave me alone, and he just kept pushing. And that drunk at the bar the other night, interrupting my set."

"What drunk? What bar? What the hell, Danielle?"

"It's not important." They sat in silence before Danielle finally asked, "So how bad is it?"

"Very. You said you tried to get him to leave you alone. Nobody is showing that. Hang on." Danielle heard the clicking of keyboard keys, followed shortly by muted talking. "No. I found the video from the original poster, and there's nothing about you asking him to leave you alone. He asks you to say something, and then you go off on this rant. Man, you look like a mean bitch in this video."

"That little son of a...." Danielle didn't finish the sentence. "Brett could confirm that, but I'm sure he's long gone by now."

"Brett? Would that be the hunk of man meat standing behind you? Ms. Regan, have you been out tomcatting?"

"No," Danielle said, feeling a blush crawling across her cheeks. "He's just an old friend who was in town, so we got together and shot some pool. That's it."

"Well, you need to let him sink his cue ball in your pocket because I think what you're suffering from is some Grade A sexual frustration. Unless you need me to take care of that for you. I'll take one for the team."

"I know you would."

"Hey, what's this?" Shannon went away, and Danielle waited patiently for her to come back to the phone. "You didn't just go play pool. Here's a video of you at a baseball game. Ew. And there's Danielle, insulting people and throwing stuff. Jesus, really?"

"Hey, I was just trying to enjoy a quiet afternoon at the

ballpark, and those guys started hassling me."

"Looks to me like they just wanted an autograph."

"They did, but other people started saying stuff. It got out of hand quickly. I just wanted to be left alone. That's what nobody gets. I just want to be left alone."

"You're in the wrong business for that, dear. There's your bo-hunk coming to your defense. You sure you don't want to climb all over that? He certainly seems protective of you."

"He's just a friend, Shannon. A friend who lives a day away and is probably already on the way home by now. Forget about him. Hell, for all I know, he could have been setting all this stuff up in the hopes that I'd come hide out on his ranch. He asked me that last night, right before that kid cornered me on the street. It could all be a setup."

Shannon laughed out loud. "Oh God, please tell me you're being facetious. You can't possibly think that. If you do, you're going crazy."

"That's entirely possible. Listen, I gotta go. I appreciate your concern, but I'll take care of things, okay? Bye."

Danielle quickly hung up and turned off the ringer on her phone. So the red-haired kid had followed through with his warning. And to top it off, someone had shot footage at the ballpark as well. Fabulous. There was no chance that Franklin Ridgeway wouldn't hear about it, and then she'd hear all about it in their Monday session. Feeling even more defeated, Danielle collapsed on the bed and pulled the covers up over her head, thankful that at least no one could reach her here.

***

"You had an interesting weekend." Ridgeway was eyeing her with that sanctimonious stare he saved for her truly down moments.

"You might say that," said Danielle, being intentionally coy. She plopped her feet up on his desk and crossed them at the ankles. "You know, just keeping it easy and lying low."

"Certainly looks like it," Ridgeway said, flipping a paper over on his desk. "Danielle, you know that a part of your plea bargain is a requirement that you complete this treatment. I can't help but feel that you aren't going to be able to do that. Furthermore, I don't think you care. If you're not willing to work on these issues, you're wasting both of our times. Should I just have the judge revoke your probation and send you to jail?"

Danielle moved her feet to the side to give her a clear view of her therapist. "Do what you want. I don't care."

For the first time, Ridgeway clearly displayed his frustration as he slammed his fists on the table. "That's the problem. You don't care. Why do you not care?"

"Beats me, Doc. Maybe it's just because I feel the deck is stacked against me. Maybe it's because I feel like I will be the one who gets in trouble no matter what I do. Maybe I'm just tired of dealing with it. Maybe it's Maybelline. Who knows?"

Ridgeway stood and paced behind his desk. "You're so flippant." He stopped pacing and put both fists down on the desk. "I really do want to help, Danielle. Why won't you let me?"

Danielle dropped her feet to the floor, shot up out of her seat, and mimicked his stance. "Because I think it's all a crock of shit. All of it. I will always defend myself. Walking away isn't my style."

Ridgeway sighed and pushed away from the desk. "One, you don't have to defend yourself. Sometimes the best thing you can do is turn the other cheek. You could have just signed the autographs for the kids at the baseball game. You could have told the kid with the cellphone some standard line. It's easy. 'Jim, I'm sorry to hear about your condition. My hopes and prayers are with you and your family.' It's that simple. The kid walks away, and you don't look like a horrible person on YouTube."

"I would be lying, though. That's not how I feel. You're asking me to pretend to be something I'm not, and I won't do that. Granted, I could have handled the baseball thing differently, but Brett was asking those guys to cool it, and they wouldn't. They caused a scene that started other people talking. I don't like being called trash, and I won't tolerate it."

"So you walk away."

"I did! I left. I didn't want to. I wanted to waltz right into that crowd and fight every last one of those sanctimonious motherfuckers, but I didn't. And I still get cracked for it. And the other guy, where was I going to run? He was standing right by my car."

Ridgeway sat on the edge of his desk as Danielle fumed. "What about this Jim Silver? Let's talk about him. You said he bullied and manipulated you."

"Let's not talk about him, okay? He was my first lesson in the business part of the music business. He treated me like dog shit, used me to score a record deal, cashed his check, and left me right as my career was gaining momentum. It turned out to be a blessing in disguise because I found a better band, but I'm still sore about it."

"Okay, so give me more details. How did he bully you? Let's talk this through and find a healthier way to deal with those emotions."

"Well, until that punk brought him up, I didn't even—" Danielle was cut off by the vibrating of her cellphone in her jeans pocket. "Hang on a sec." She pulled the phone out and checked the number. It was Randy and Terri. With that familiar feeling of dread gripping her heart, Danielle answered the phone.

"Danielle, it's Terri. That woman is outside again." Terri's voice was a high-pitched whine Danielle had never heard from her before. "She's standing across the street staring back at the house."

"Call the cops."

"I'm not sure they'll even come. And if they do, it could be hours before they get here unless she does something threatening. I don't know what we should do."

Danielle thought it over for a minute. "Just sit tight and keep an eye on her. If she does anything menacing, call the cops. I'm on my way." She hung up without waiting for an answer. "Sorry, Doc, gotta go. My friends need me."

Ridgeway seemed genuinely concerned. "I heard you mention the police. Is there something I should do? Should I call someone?"

"Nah, probably not. Just some crazy homeless woman has been stalking my friends. I'm going to go talk to her and tell her to get lost." She saw his response coming and put up her hands. "I promise to do my best not to do anything stupid."

"Danielle...."

She grunted in response. "Fine." She gave him the Holder's address. "But I'll beat them there. From there...." She shrugged. "Maybe you'll finally get me out of your hair."

Once in her car, Danielle raced through the thick morning traffic. She was keenly aware that if she got caught speeding or some other infraction, it would be yet another strike against her, but it didn't matter. Randy and Terri were some of the only people she had left that she could count on, and if this weirdo kept insisting on hanging around, then she would take care of it, whatever the cost.

She navigated the traffic flawlessly, driving fast but carefully, and soon was coming up on the Holder's place. She scanned both sides of the street but didn't immediately see anyone hanging around. She slammed on the brakes and wrenched the car into their driveway, throwing a cloud of white tire smoke behind her. Without even bothering to kill the engine, Danielle hopped out, ready to confront whoever was in the way.

Terri waddled around from the back of the house as Danielle looked over the neighborhood. "Oh, thank God you got here so quick," she said, grabbing Danielle's arm. "I'm not sure where she went, but she was here just a couple of minutes ago."

Danielle kept her eyes moving, sweeping across the area time and again. "Go inside and keep your phone handy. Let me know if you see her." She spun away from Terri, leaned over the door of her car, and popped the trunk.

"What are you doing?" Terri asked.

Danielle emerged from the trunk with a chrome lug nut wrench. "I'm going to check things out."

Danielle started down the driveway as Terri finally turned off the car before retreating into the house. Danielle started north on the narrow street, carefully watching every bush and tree and any other place someone might use to hide. Along the way, she got more than one curious glance from the neighbors. Three blocks down, she decided it was a waste of time and turned back.

The woman in question emerged from a side street to the south as Danielle neared the Holder house. Gripping the wrench tighter, Danielle quickened her pace. Warning bells sounded in her head. The rational part of her brain realized the anger was taking control, but reason was no longer driving her.

The stranger kept moving toward her slowly, shuffling her feet, noticeably bent over at the waist. Her hair was long and unruly, mainly gray, though a few streaks of dark brown were still visible. She was sickly thin, her arms appearing to be nothing but skin and bones, her cheekbones sharp and protruding. As they neared each other, Danielle noticed a yellowish tint to her skin and eyes, which made the green in her irises stand out. As Danielle closed the gap, the woman stopped and tried to straighten up, forcing a weak smile of crooked teeth.

"I don't know who you are," Danielle snarled. "But you need to get out of here and stay gone. You're messing with my friends, and I don't like it."

The woman smiled bigger, and there was something in the smile that triggered Danielle, something familiar she couldn't quite place. She slowed her pace.

"It has been a long time, hasn't it? I don't look much like myself anymore."

Danielle stopped. She was close enough now that she could have easily hit the woman with the wrench. The way the woman spoke sent shivers up Danielle's spine. She looked at the woman again, carefully studying her features, reaching back in her brain for a possible match to the pathetic looking person stooped in front of her. When it finally hit her, Danielle went cold all over, and the wrench dropped from her hands, clattering to the rocky asphalt. Her breath escaped her lungs, and her heart seemed to skip a beat. She barely managed to utter a single word.

"Mom?"

CHAPTER EIGHT

"It's sure has been a long time, hasn't it," Dorothy Regan said in a wavering voice.

Danielle's momentary shock began to fade, and the anger came back stronger than ever before. In an instant, she was back in Chaparral, in her stuffy kitchen on a hot summer day, covered in sweat and dirt and grease, with her mother's boyfriend groping her, her mother coming into the room and screaming. Danielle could still feel the weight and ferocity of her mother's palm slamming into her cheek. The words that came next had been forever burned into Danielle's memory.

"You little tramp! How dare you?! You just can't stand it, can you? You trifling whore! You can't stand for me to be happy!"

That was the last time she had laid eyes on her mother, who had packed up in the middle of the night and moved away with said boyfriend, ostensibly to escape the pull of her whore daughter. Danielle had almost strangled her mother in a fit of rage that day, and now it all came flooding back.

She knelt down and retrieved her wrench as the familiar sound of Randy's motorized wheelchair came from behind. Danielle clutched the wrench tight, imagining for a moment what it would be like to lash out at her mother.

"What are you going to do with that?" Dorothy Regan may have been old and frail, but she showed no fear. In fact, she almost sounded amused. She seemed nothing like the woman Danielle had scared off just days before. Danielle recognized her mother's stance, the same defiant pose she often caught herself striking. "You really gave me a start the other night with that getup you were in. I felt like a fool once I realized that was you."

Danielle stared daggers at her mother while flexing her fingers around the handle of the wrench.

"Go ahead, swing it," Dorothy Regan taunted her daughter. "You would be doing me a favor. But before you do, I need to speak with you."

"Danielle," Terri called from behind, her own name now a warning. "Stay calm, Danielle. She's not worth it. She's baiting you."

"Don't let her goad you, Dani," Randy chimed in as his wheelchair bumped over the uneven sidewalk. "You don't want to do this."

Dorothy looked around Danielle. "Randy. Terri. I would ask how things have been, but I see you're still pathetic. So nice of you to take in my daughter since you couldn't have one of your own. Little Randy and his defective peashooter."

Danielle took a sharp step forward and pulled the wrench back. "Don't talk to my friends like that. You're the one who abandoned your daughter for a pervert."

Something changed in Dorothy's eyes, and she dropped them quickly. "You're right about that. More right than you know." She slowly looked back up. "That's why I need to talk to you. I'm almost out of time, and I need your help to fix what I screwed up."

"I have nothing to say to you. You played your little game, and you got me here. Good for you. Don't come around here again because it won't work a second time."

"This is about something bigger than you and me," Dorothy answered. "And I haven't got the time to fight with you."

Danielle laughed in her mother's face. "For years, I used to imagine what I would say if I ever saw you again. Then I realized the biggest favor you ever did for me was to walk away from me. Of all the things I need, absolution from you is not one of them. And I have no desire to forgive you. As far as I'm concerned, my mother died in 1992. You. You're just an old whack job with a few screws loose. You're no one, and you mean nothing to me.

If you really are dying, I want you to take those words to your grave with you. They can bury you in the same potter's field they tossed Dad into."

Danielle wheeled around, and Terri put her hand to her mouth in shock. "Jesus, Danielle. It's your mother."

"Butt out, Terri," Dorothy snapped.

"Fuck you," Terri answered, the only time Danielle had ever heard a curse word escape her lips. "I'm trying to help you."

Danielle pushed past Terri and shoved the wrench into Randy's lap. "She gives you an excuse, knock the shit out of her,"

"Danielle, don't go," Dorothy said, making it sound like an order. "We have to talk. It's urgent."

Danielle spun around but kept retreating. "Don't try to boss me, lady. You lost that ability eighteen years ago. We're done."

"This isn't about me, Dani."

Danielle finally stopped. "It's always about you. Always has been. Don't let my name come out of your mouth again. Just crawl back into your hole and stay there."

She turned and hustled to the car. She could hear her mother continuing to talk, but nothing penetrated. She got back in the car, revved the engine, and sped away, hoping desperately to outrace the memory of a woman she'd long ago written off as dead.

***

Danielle was a nervous wreck by the time she got home, and nothing helped her calm down. She turned to the guitar but found that her fingers would not obey her commands. She tried fixing lunch, but the thought of food made her sick. She tried a hot bath and a nap, but nothing would drive her mother out of her mind.

With no other ideas, Danielle picked up the phone and fired off a quick text to Shannon. *Hey, what's up? If you've got a minute, I could sure use somebody to talk to.*

Danielle sat on her bed and watched the phone, waiting for the screen to light up with Shannon's response. Only one never came. Looking at the clock, she realized that on the West Coast, it was mid-morning, and she knew that meant media availability, business meetings, event planning. It would probably be late before Shannon would even have time to talk.

Still, it didn't keep Danielle from feeling like she had been abandoned yet again. She sat in bed and steamed and thought and steamed some more, and then a thought popped into her head. A crazy thought, but one that suddenly seemed to be the sanest avenue left to her. She fired off another text, a simple, *Hey,* and waited.

Not even a minute passed before the response came. *Hey. What's up?*

Danielle started to type, then stopped and put the phone down. She had to be sure; did she really want to do this? She closed her eyes and took a long, slow, deep breath, thinking it all through as she exhaled. She could think of no reason not to continue. She picked up the phone.

Does your offer still stand?

Brett answered back almost instantly. *Absolutely. Whenever you want.*

Danielle chewed on her bottom lip, giving herself one last chance to back out, and discovered in short order that she didn't want to. *What about right now? What if I packed up and left today?*

Brett's response was a Pindrop, showing her his exact location. *GPS will lead you straight to me. I'll have your room ready and steaks on the grill when you get here.*

Danielle felt a goofy grin spread across her face that had no business being there. She was about to run off and play house with a man she barely knew in a town she didn't even know the name of. Yet, for the first time in years, she felt absolutely certain she was making the right move. *I'm on my way.*

Years of living on the road had taught Danielle how to travel light and pack quickly, and those skills once again served her well. She threw some clothes and other essentials in a duffle bag, packed up her favorite guitar—a custom purple Stratocaster Thin line that she had restored herself—and an amp and shoved them in the backseat, and she was ready to go. Just before leaving, she spotted her laptop on the kitchen table. With a sigh of frustration, she went to it and started it up, then fired off a quick email to Randy and Terri, Shannon, and Franklin Ridgeway.

Hello all. Given everything that's happened recently, I've decided I need to get away for a little while. It's not permanent, so don't freak out. I just need a change of scenery. A friend has offered to let me crash at his ranch for a while. His name is Brett Walls. He used to be a baseball player for UT, and he lives somewhere in the Panhandle. I'm not sure where. If you never hear from me again, I'm probably buried somewhere on his property. That's a joke, I think. Please don't tell anyone else where I am. I need a place where I can think and sort things out. If you don't hear from me in a month, call the president. Love, Dani

She read over it one more time, felt the email was okay and sent it. That done, she locked up and took off. It was her first road trip in her new car, and she was anxious to see how it did on the open road. Making a quick stop for a burger and fries, Danielle hit the road. According to the GPS, she was eight and half hours and five-hundred miles from her destination.

Once out of the city, she put the accelerator down. The Camaro's heavy engine roared its approval, and she was on her way. The familiar comfort of the road wrapped around her like a warm blanket. The sun was up, the top was down, the wind was in her hair, and for the moment, all her troubles were in the rearview mirror.

For the first time in forever, Danielle Regan was at peace.

Driving faster than she should have along back country roads, Danielle shaved an hour off her expected time. Eventually, she hit I-40, and from there, she quickly approached the city limits of a town called Vega a little before nine in the evening. From there, the GPS on her phone directed her off the interstate and down a two-lane arm-to-market road. Several miles down, she turned off onto a dirt road and through a metal gate, rattling over a cattle guard. Her lights barely pierced the dust and the darkness, and she crept along, terrified that at any moment, some animal would dart out in front of her or she would suddenly plunge off the road. She topped a small rise, and then she saw Brett's house spread out below her.

The house was a sprawling single story with a gray brick exterior, wood shingles, and a well-lit, paved circular driveway out front. She noticed a three-car attached garage as she got closer. Thankfully, she finally bumped off the rutted dirt road onto the smooth pavement of the driveway and pulled to a stop right outside the front door.

Danielle put the top up on the car and trudged to the front door, weary from the drive. She was getting old; all day drives never used to wear her out. She rang the doorbell, and soon Brett was there, wearing a tattered Texas Rangers T-shirt and dusty old Levi's. When he opened the door, she caught the smell of meat on the grill.

"Hey, you got here fast," Brett said as he held the door open for her. Danielle stepped inside, doubt suddenly filling her mind. "I was planning on putting on something a little more appropriate before you got here."

"Why? I'm just a friend visiting, right? Would you change clothes if I was one of your old baseball buddies?"

Brett pulled the door to behind him and wiped his hands on his jeans. "Probably. Depends upon which baseball buddy." He gave her a full-on smile, one that quickly faded. "Didn't you bring any bags?"

"I've got some stuff, not much. I figured you could show me my room, and I'd like to freshen up a little, and then I'll bring it in."

"Sure thing," Brett said. "This way."

He led her through a smaller foyer into a spacious living room with a stone fireplace in one corner. She noticed a stainless-steel grill smoking away on the patio beyond a sliding glass door. The living room was dark: dark wood and dark carpet with a built-in bookshelf stacked full of books and trophies on one wall. He had a black leather sofa, two matching recliners, and a massive flat screen TV mounted over the fireplace.

Through the main room was a short hallway. Brett led her

to the right, and at the end of the hall was her room. "Here you go. Fresh sheets and everything. Bathroom is attached," he said, pointing out a door on the far wall. "My room is at the other end of the hall if you need something. I just threw the steaks on, so it'll be a bit before they're done. You need any help bringing your bags in?"

"No, I got it. I travel light. I'm just going to clean up a bit."

"Got it." Brett started out the door but turned around. "I didn't ask. How do you like your steaks? Bloody, burnt, or somewhere in between?"

"Somewhere in between is fine," she chuckled.

"You got it. If you need anything, just holler." He ducked out of the room.

It was a tiny room, the bed a single with red and black flannel sheets, a simple nightstand and a dresser for furniture, and a long but narrow closet. The bathroom was more of the same, simple and functional but somewhat cold.

Danielle retrieved her bags from the car, then took some time to wash her face, brush her hair, and change into a fresh T-shirt before seeking Brett out. She found him out on the patio and joined him.

"Man, we got a perfect night tonight," he said as Danielle gingerly stepped through the doorway. "Nice and warm, no wind. I figured we'd eat out here." He jerked his head toward a glass patio table with places set for two. At one was a Coors longneck and at the other a Coke.

"Sounds great." Danielle tucked her hands in her jeans pockets. "You've got a nice spread here."

"Thanks. Oh, check this out." Brett closed the grill lid, poked his head inside, and killed the outside lights. "Come here." He took Danielle's arm and led her away from the house. It was so dark she couldn't see where she was going, so she trusted that Brett wasn't going to lead her into a well. He finally stopped. "Look up."

Danielle did and was greeted with a night sky packed full of stars. "Wow," she whispered. "I haven't seen that many stars since…I guess since I was a girl living in Chaparral. Don't see them like that back home."

"Yeah, I know. Too many lights around. I love it." They both kept their gazes to the sky. "You know, if I take you far enough out on the property, you can't even see the house. You can't see anything. It might as well be 1880 out there. Looks the same." They looked at each other at the same time. "I'll tell you. If you can't get your mind straight out here, then you just can't get it straight, period."

"That's what I'm hoping for."

They returned to the patio and then kept going, Brett still leading her by the hand. "And check this out." He led her through the kitchen, which was a mess, through a proper dining room with a table that had collected a fair amount of dust, and to another room. He flipped the lights on and pulled Danielle the rest of the way in.

The walls had been covered with black sheets. There was a stool in the center of the room with a microphone perched in front of it. A long folding table held a bundle of electronics, and a cheap acoustic guitar sat on a stand. Across from the stool, a video camera sat on a tripod. "This is your studio. We can fancy it up more, and I figured you'd have some of your own equipment. If you need anything else, need to make any changes, then go for it. This room is yours to do with as you please."

Danielle strolled through the room, checking it out. She let her fingers graze the strings of the guitar, and it produced a warm, thick sound. She stopped by the camera and turned to him. "Pull in a bed, and you could shoot some porn in here."

"That was the last girl," Brett answered with a smirk and a wink of his eye. "She didn't do beds."

Danielle's eyebrow went up. "Oh, really now?"

Brett looked quickly to the ceiling and back down. "Taking the sex swing down was a bitch. Come on, let's eat." He turned off the lights, leaving her in the dark and unable to look at the ceiling herself.

"Wait." She hustled out of the room after him. "There

wasn't really a sex swing in there, was there?" Brett ignored her
and kept walking. "Tell me you're just playing about that."

He didn't stop until they were back out on the patio. As
she caught up to him, he was plating their steaks. "Hope you're
hungry. These are some big boys."

She took it but kept her eyes on him. "Tell me you're joking
about the swing."

Brett chuckled as he grabbed his own plate and stepped
around her. "You gotta do something to kill the time out here on
the prairie. The winter nights are cold and long."

Brett sat at the patio table, and Danielle took her spot
opposite him. "You're making fun of me."

"I wouldn't do that. But I will yank your chain now and
again. Nothing wrong with it. Keeps you on your toes."

After they ate and the mess was cleaned up, he challenged
her to a game of pool in the game room, and she accepted. He led
her into a basement to his game room, which would have been
the envy of a lot of the clubs she had frequented over the course
of her career—a pool table in the center that looked perfectly
maintained, a small bar, pinball machines on one wall, an air
hockey table, a foosball table, and a massive stereo system with a
rack stuffed full of CDs.

"I'll rack 'em. You wanna pick some music?" Brett asked.
"I figure you're the expert on that."

"Sure." As Danielle checked out the room, an idea popped
into her head. "Hey, we played pool the other day. Mind if we
play something else?" Danielle answered.

"No problem. What did you have in mind?"

Danielle looked over her options. "I play a killer game of
air hockey. Whaddya say, best of seven? I figure I might have a
chance to beat you in that."

"We'll see about that."

She moved on to the stereo and fiddled with the settings
as she figured it out, then perused his music selection, which was
impressive. Among his CDs was her entire catalogue. She let her
fingers dance along the plastic cases, reading the titles as if they

were some exotic language.

"So, I'm a fan," Brett said. Danielle jerked, startled that he was standing behind her, which elicited a chuckle from him. "Sorry, didn't mean to sneak up on you. You just seemed kinda… mesmerized for a second."

"It's okay," she said. "Been a while since I've seen those." Her fingers slid on. "Your musical tastes seem to be squarely rooted in the nineties, my man."

"I make no apologies for that."

Danielle glanced over her shoulder at him. "Nor should you." She plucked a Matchbox 20 CD off the shelf and put it in. "I think this will do us well."

Soon they were hunched over the table as the clinking of plastic and metal and the hum of the game filled the air. They both played with intensity. Danielle saw the competitive fire in him, just as she had the night they had played pool back in Austin, only this time they were playing a game Danielle could beat him at.

"So, you got me up here. Tell me the baseball story."

"Ah, you don't want to hear that, do you?"

Danielle banged the flat plastic disk past Brett and into the goal for a quick lead. She smiled up at him. "Yeah, I do. You told me that if I ever came up, you'd tell me. So tell me."

Brett retrieved the puck and restarted play. "I don't think I said that in so many words."

"It was implied." Danielle smashed another goal past him. "Besides, I'm kicking your ass, so you might want to distract me."

"Good point. So not long after we met at that photo shoot, I got drafted in the first round by the Cincinnati Reds and started working my way up through their farm system."

Danielle tore her attention away from the table. "Farm system?" Brett took advantage and blew the plastic puck past her. "You sorry son of a bitch," Danielle snarled.

"You gotta keep your eyes on the puck," Brett said with a grin. "A farm system is a series of teams with players of different abilities. You gotta work your way up." He must have noticed the confusion on her face. "Let me put it this way. You didn't start off playing Madison Square Garden, right? You started with ratty local clubs, worked your way up to better clubs like Antone's, then went to regional clubs, then small market arenas, and finally big arenas, right? The big arenas are the Major Leagues, and that would be the Reds. I was working my way up."

"Okay, I got it. Madison Square Garden is a dump, by the way," Danielle said as they bandied the puck back and forth.

"Really?"

"No, it's really nice. Continue. What level were you at?"

"I got up to Double A, which would be the equivalent of playing regional clubs in my example. I was moving up pretty fast, had my eyes set on the big time, and then I stalled. Guys who came up after me started to pass me by. I got frustrated and let it affect me. So they traded me. I bounced around a couple of organizations."

The puck slid in on him, and Brett trapped it with his paddle instead of returning it. Danielle watched as a haunted look crept across his face. Brett was staring beyond her, and she knew he was back there, reliving it all again.

"I started to see the writing on the wall, but I didn't want to believe it. My arm was hurting, but I didn't want to say anything because I was afraid they'd cut me, so I pitched through. I thought if I could make it to the end of the year, I could have surgery and be ready to go by the next spring. Which was stupid, but hey, you do what you gotta do. You know?"

He looked down at Danielle for acknowledgement. She met his gaze straight on. "Yeah, I know."

With a nod, he continued. "So it's late in the year, and we're in a tight pennant race. Important game, late innings, and I'm trying to get out of a jam, and this kid comes to the plate. Real arrogant little punk, big money rookie from Venezuela or some shit. This kid had owned me all year. I hadn't gotten him out at all. Skip comes out to pull me, but I begged him to keep me in, to let me face this guy. I think maybe he knew because he agreed. Count goes full—"

"What does that mean," Danielle interrupted, now transfixed on his story.

"Full count? Three balls, two strikes. I throw another ball, and he walks. Another strike, and he's out. My arm's killing me, but I gotta finish this. So I rear back, and I throw my best fastball. I put everything I've got into it. As soon as I let the ball go, I feel my arm pop, and I know I'm done. Sure enough, I blew my rotator cuff. They put me on injured reserve and cut me at the end of the year. I never threw another pitch."

He let the story hang there. Danielle waited until it was obvious that he wasn't going to say anything more. "So? Did you get the guy out or what?"

Slowly a smile spread across his face. "Fuck yeah, I did. Of course, he made it to the majors, so he won in the end, but I got him that night."

Danielle pushed her paddle away, the game now forgotten. "Didn't you even try to come back? Don't you miss it?"

Brett's smile turned sorrowful as he put his paddle down as well. "Nah. I was done. I was tired of crappy bus rides and fleabag motels. Every athlete gets to that point where they've got to admit it's over. It was my time. And yeah, I miss it like crazy. I go to the ballpark every chance I get. I watch the games all the time on TV. If I could, I'd do it all again, but I'm too old now. Thirty-six is old for a baseball player."

"Huh." Danielle chewed on her lip in thought. "You think that anybody could reach that point? A point where they just know they're done? Maybe that's my problem. Maybe I just won't let myself see that it's over."

"That's stupid," Brett shot back. Danielle's jaw dropped, and Brett quickly added to his response. "You're a musician. You don't have to be done. You can keep playing your whole life. Look at the Stones, for God's sake."

"Yeah, well, I bet they never had their career wash up on the rocks like mine has done."

Brett laughed. "You don't know much about the Stones, do you?" Danielle shook her head no. "Trust me. They dealt with worse. There's no reason for you to be thinking of retirement. You're still young."

"I turn thirty-five next month. I'm not that much younger than you."

"But for a musician, you're just hitting your stride. Don't be foolish. Do you still love it?" Danielle wouldn't look him in the eye, which told him enough. "Then just ride out the storm. You may have to be patient and give it a couple of years, but things will straighten out. I can tell you from experience that you don't want to live your life saddled with regret."

"Oh, I already do that." She reached out and slapped at her paddle, which skidded across the table. "You know, I think I'm going to call it a night. Thanks for dinner." She started up the basement stairs when Brett called out to her.

"We don't have to quit."

"I'm not in the mood anymore. See you in the morning."

Danielle jogged up the stairs before Brett could say anything else. A pleasant night had turned, and she was beginning to wonder if she'd made the right choice after all.

CHAPTER NINE

Danielle got ready for bed before she checked her phone and saw repeated missed calls from Shannon. She tucked the phone into a nightstand drawer, climbed into bed, and then turned off the lamp on the nightstand. She laid there in the dark for only a few seconds before she turned the light back on, sat up, and pulled out the phone.

Shannon answered on the third ring. "Hoochie hoochie. Running off and shacking up with a man. A strange man at that. What are you thinking?"

"I figured you'd be proud of me."

"That depends on his hotness factor and how well you know this guy. Those smarmy little comments about being buried and calling the cops scared me to death."

"He's harmless," Danielle assured her. "I'm not out here looking for a boyfriend. I just needed to get away. Things were getting pretty intense back home."

"Why? Did something else happen, or is this just about those videos?"

"My…." Danielle stopped and thought twice about her answer. "Never mind. Doesn't matter. Things were getting out of hand, is all. I was stupid to think I could stay in the eye of the storm and expect things to calm down."

"I'm worried about you, Dani." She could almost feel the weight of Shannon's words. "I wish so much I could be there for you. This damn tour—"

"Don't tell me you're not having fun."

"I'm having fun, just not as much fun as I would be having if you were here. Steve came out for a couple of days to check on things." Shannon dropped her voice like she was telling a dark secret. "He was talking about how you just can't stay out of trouble. He sounded upset, like heartbroken. I think he really misses you."

The mention of her former manager's name was enough to get Danielle's blood boiling. "Well, he's got a funny way of showing it."

"It was a business decision. I know he second guesses it. If you could just keep a low profile for a little while, maybe he would take you back."

Danielle's heart skipped a beat at the suggestion, but the sting of his rejection followed immediately thereafter. "I don't need him anymore. I've already got other managers sniffing around, wanting to represent me. I could have new management with one phone call."

"Then why don't you call one?" Shannon waited patiently, but Danielle could come up with no good reason. "You're scared. Danielle Regan is scared. Who would have thought it?"

"I'm not scared," Danielle said, but the words sounded meek in her ears. "Just let me work through things out here for a bit, and we'll see where things are."

"All right. But I'll keep working on Steve. Maybe I can wear him down one of these days."

"Steve will see through you like that so-called dress you wore the night you drug me to the Hellcat Club."

"Hey, I'll have you know, that dress got me several phone numbers, a couple of which I cashed in on. It did its job, and it did it well. Such a tragedy that it died like it did, but it was easy to rip, and you know how those football players get when they're all hot and bothered."

Danielle giggled. She wasn't sure that Shannon's stories of sexual conquest were completely true, but she told them with enough conviction that Danielle had never thought to challenge one. "You are such a skank," she said.

"Oh, come on. You could stand to loosen up the chastity belt a little bit. I mean, your horse is already out of the barn. Let her run."

"So, what? I should just strut up to Brett some evening, drop my robe, and give him my best come hither stare and get to it?"

"Danielle, your come-hither stare is more like resting bitch face. You try to be seductive, and you'll scare the poor guy off. But if he makes a move, you ought to run with it. You don't have to marry the guy."

"I'll take it into consideration." Danielle forced a yawn, ready to end the conversation. "Anyway, I'm fine. Brett is a gentleman. There's no need to worry. I'll check in again in a few days. It's late, and I want to go to bed now."

"Okay," Shannon answered grudgingly. "Hey, what did you say that guy's name was again? The guy who wants to manage you?"

"I didn't. Have a good night."

She hung up, turned off the ringer, put the phone away, and killed the light. She laid in the dark for the longest time, rerunning their conversation in her head. Despite what Shannon thought, she wasn't scared. She was smart. Smart and careful. She could do that when people weren't pushing her buttons. That's all she really needed, for people to quit pushing her. Then everything would be fine.

She told herself this, but it felt like a lie. What was the answer: more control or less? Danielle thought about it for what seemed like hours until she finally went to sleep.

***

Danielle awoke the next morning to find breakfast on the kitchen table and a note from Brett informing her that he had been called into the station and to make herself at home. She did, roaming around the house. She discovered little. The house had a separate, more formal sitting room, two more bedrooms, and a formal dining room, all of which appeared to be unused. In the garage, she found two ATVs, three motorcycles, and a sparkling blue and silver speedboat.

She returned to the main living room and decided to

snoop around the large bookshelf. He had trophies going back to youth league baseball. Brett's reading interests seemed confined to books about ranching, biographies, and scrapbooking. Further exploration on a lower shelf revealed the fruits of his scrapbooking fetish. He had one for himself, one for all the sporting events he had attended, and one for all of his travels.

She found another dedicated to concerts he had attended. She took it off the shelf and returned to one of his recliners. Page after page of pictures, posters, ticket stubs, and laminated backstage passes. He had seen them all, from Metallica to Willie Nelson and all points in-between. She also found evidence of several of her own shows that he had attended. In many of the earlier pictures, he was accompanied by a cute blonde, but she was noticeably absent from later pictures. After the blonde, there were occasionally other women, but none who showed up more than twice. The very latest entries were of Brett and his buddies, ballcaps turned around, beers in both hands, having a ball.

Danielle wasn't disturbed by the fact that he had attended several of her shows. Maybe she would have been if it had been all her, but there were several acts he had seen multiple times. Instead of appearing stalkerish, he merely came off as a fan who went to see her when the chance presented itself.

She replaced the book and found another, one that seemed completely out of place, as the book had a strip of lace glued to the spine. Danielle pulled it out to find another picture of Brett and the blonde, only this was a wedding picture. They both wore Western outfits, the blonde falling out of her dress. Brett had a biker mustache and long hair, and they both looked beyond happy. Danielle sat cross legged on the floor and thumbed through it. Their story unfolded inside plain as day. Her name was Jill, and the two of them had grown up together. Both were athletes, but she had been in theater and choir as well. They went to prom together, graduated together, got engaged, then married. The last picture in the album was of the two of them in a group at some sort of function. He wore a suit, she wore a silky blue dress, and they each held a glass of champagne. They smiled, but the smiles weren't the same. Instead of hanging on each other, they stood with a noticeable gap between them. It looked forced and uncomfortable. When she flipped the page, Danielle discovered that only half the album had been filled. The rest were just blank pages.

Danielle was overcome with guilt as she carefully placed the scrapbook away back on the shelf. She felt as if she had violated Brett in some deep way. She stood and wandered around the room, then to the patio and stepped out. It was another pleasant day, and just beyond the edge of the patio, she saw a pool she hadn't noticed the night before.

By the time Brett made it home in the late afternoon, Danielle had swum until exhaustion and was lounging on a plastic pool chair, her black one-piece bathing suit clinging to her body, eyes hidden behind dark glasses.

Brett skirted the edge of the pool wearing boots, starched Wranglers, and a shirt and tie. "I see you made yourself at home. Glad to see it."

"Your pool is fantastic. I should get a pool. Did you know that in high school, I worked as a lifeguard?"

Brett sat on a chair to her left. "No, I didn't. I'm sure you're aware, but not much has been written about your life growing up. I know you were the valedictorian of your high school."

"Yeah. Lot of good that did me."

An awkward silence followed. Danielle closed her eyes but was aware of his presence next to her. Then she felt his fingers lightly tracing the line of a jagged scar that ran almost the entire length of her lower leg. "That's a doozy."

Danielle opened her eyes and turned her leg to look at it. She had become so used to the scar that she scarcely noticed it anymore. "Yep. A doctor told me once that a plastic surgeon could take care of that. It wouldn't go away, but it would be a lot less noticeable, like a line of fishing wire on my leg. I said no. I like having the reminder." She turned her head towards Brett. "Does it gross you out?"

"No, not at all. I've got a nasty one on my shoulder from

my shoulder surgery." He started unbuttoning his shirt.

"I don't need to see it," Danielle muttered. "I don't want to start comparing scars like some sort of goofy action movie."

"Fair enough. Well, why don't I go change into my trunks, and I'll join you out here? We could take a couple of laps together."

"Nah." She forced herself into an upright position and pulled off the glasses. "I've been out here too long as it is. I'll be amazed if I didn't burn." Brett's face fell though he tried not to let it show, but she ignored it. "Why do you have three motorcycles?"

"Ah. You were in the garage. Same reason people have multiple cars, I guess."

"I don't have multiple cars," Danielle said. "I know lots of celebrities do. They buy new cars all the time. I never saw the point. You can only drive one at a time."

"That's true. In this case, though, each motorcycle is for something different. I've got a dirt bike, a crotch rocket when I wanna go fast, and a Harley for cruising. Just depends upon what kind of riding I'm in the mood for. Do you wanna ride?"

"I've never been on a motorcycle."

"Wanna learn?"

Danielle felt herself go warm all over at the suggestion. "You bet I do."

"Let me change clothes, and I'll get one out and give you a lesson."

Danielle hustled inside and changed into jeans. Brett then gave her a long-sleeved shirt and pads. Once she changed clothes, she found Brett sitting on a bike that was little more than a motor and two wheels held together with some dusty orange plastic. The motor idled noisily, and when Brett saw her coming, he revved it a couple of times. He tossed her a colorful, full-face helmet. "Put that on and hop on the back. I'll ride you out to a good spot."

Danielle strapped the helmet on and mounted the bike behind him. With a jolt, the bike darted ahead, forcing Danielle to wrap her arms around Brett's waist to keep from falling off the back of the bike. After a few moments of terror, Danielle loosened up and began to enjoy the speed with which they bumped over the hilly terrain. They rode for several minutes until Brett found a natural bowl in the landscape and stopped.

"This is the learning ground right here. This is where I taught—"

Danielle waited for Brett to come back to her, but he was staring off into the horizon. After a few moments went by, she laid a hand on his shoulder. "So, are you going to teach me to ride this thing or not?"

"Oh yeah. Yeah. Sorry about that. Got distracted for a second." He dismounted and patted the seat. "Scooch on up here, and let's do this."

She edged up on the seat as instructed. She was curious as to what had caused Brett's sudden lack of focus but decided not to press. If he wanted to tell that story, then he would in good time. Brett spent several minutes teaching Danielle the basics of the bike, the brake and throttle, and the clutch and gears. For someone used to having her hands doing different tasks simultaneously, it came quickly for her.

Then he had her practice takeoffs, and Danielle learned quickly that understanding the controls and being able to implement that knowledge were radically different things. With each start, the bike either got away from her or she fell over just after takeoff. Each failure frustrated her more, which drove her to push harder.

After another failed run, Brett gripped the handlebars. "You're making this too hard. Relax." He held the bike up, and Danielle again mounted it and positioned her hands. "Take a deep breath, remember what I told you, and relax. You don't have to take off like a bat out of hell. You're not ready for the pro circuit. Slow and easy, smooth, just be calm."

Danielle revved the motor, largely ignoring Brett's instructions. When he let go, she gunned the engine again and almost immediately, the bike went sideways. Brett lunged and grabbed it as Danielle tumbled to the dirt for what felt like the hundredth time.

"You're not listening," he said, holding the bike up. Danielle jumped back on again. "Maybe we should call it a day and try again tomorrow." Danielle shot him a look that put his suggestion to rest quickly. "Maybe not." He checked the sky and let out a long, slow breath. Danielle realized then how frustrated he was becoming with her. Finally, he snapped his fingers. "You're a fan of Stevie Ray, right?"

"Of course," Danielle answered, her voice muffled through the helmet.

"So, you know how most of Stevie's playing is real aggressive and fast, then. But he's got this song, 'Riviera Paradise,' that's real slow and smooth, jazzy almost. A very tranquil song."

"I know 'Riviera Paradise.'"

Brett didn't let Danielle's nasty tone intimidate him. "Think about that song. Let it play in your head. Be calm, and just ease away. Go slow. Take it easy."

Danielle revved the engine, ready to go again, but Brett blocked her.

"You're not relaxing. You're not listening. Slow. I'm not letting you try again until I see you relax. Breathe a little bit. Calm yourself down."

She was upset that Brett was blocking her, but finally, Danielle relented, closed her eyes, breathed deeply, and remembered Stevie's song. She could hear it in her head, note-for-note. It was never one of her favorites, but now she felt the song penetrating her consciousness, and the frustration began to melt away. She opened her eyes to find that Brett had stepped aside. He gave her a subtle nod.

This time Danielle eased away and was able to maintain her balance and ride. She wobbled and weaved, but with nothing to hit but rocks, that wasn't a problem. She tried to turn and almost lost the bike, but put a foot down, maintained balance, and completed the move. As Brett cheered her on, Danielle pushed the bike a little harder, slowly gaining speed as she got more comfortable. She rode in wide circles around Brett for several minutes, finally skidding to a stop.

Brett ran up to her. "There you go. See? You just rode your first motorcycle."

Danielle pulled the helmet off. She felt as if every inch of her was covered in dirt. "That was awesome. I see now why people ride these things."

"It gets in your blood. I think that's enough for today, though. We're losing daylight."

Danielle wouldn't budge. "I think I can get us back to the house. I'll drive, you ride."

Brett chuckled. "I'm sure you could, but we're not going in yet. I want to show you something, and trust me, you're not ready for this ride. Now scoot."

Danielle faked a pout but took her place behind Brett and strapped the helmet back on. Soon they were bumping over rockier terrain and approaching the big mesa. He circled, then began to climb the massive formation. Danielle gripped him tighter as they climbed but kept her eyes open, enjoying the thrill of the moment.

They reached the top of the hill, and Brett did a quick donut, bathing them both in a cloud of dust. He put the kickstand down and killed the engine. Casually throwing one leg over the bike, Brett shifted to face Danielle, slowly unbuckled the helmet, and took it off.

"Check it out."

Danielle stepped off the bike and stood at the top of the mesa as the land spread out below. Far off to her left, she could see the interstate and the cars and trucks zooming along, looking like toy cars in the distance. She spotted Brett's house, but what really struck her was the land, which was dotted with shallow, dry creek beds, rolling hills, white rocks, and red dirt.

"It's really kind of pretty out here. I'd always heard it was flat and dry, like where I grew up."

"Most of the panhandle is, but up here on the Caprock, it's different." Brett came up behind her slowly, put a finger under her chin, and lifted her head slightly. "And check out that sunset."

Danielle trained her eyes on the horizon and sky that was

coming alive in fascinating shades of purple and pink, orange and gold, and a blue so bright it bordered on white. Danielle whistled. "You know, the main thing I remember about that day we spent together was that you said the sunsets up here have colors that don't have names yet. That line always stuck with me. I even tried to write a song around it, though I never did. Now I see what you meant."

"Gorgeous, huh? I love coming up here, especially when we've got some clouds, just to watch the sunset. This is my favorite thing in the world right here. And I'm glad I could share it with you."

Danielle looked over her shoulder to find Brett had pushed in close behind her, but his eyes were glued to the sky, not her. A ripple traveled through her, a crazy urge to kiss him. His lips were right there—it wouldn't take much. Brett suddenly looked over at her, and she looked away, fearful that he had somehow read her mind.

"Well," he said after a moment of awkward silence. "We'd best make our way back to the house before it gets too dark." He started back for the bike, leaving her standing there alone. She hustled back and jumped on as Brett started the bike up. As they made their way back to the ranch, Danielle wasn't sure if she had dodged a bullet or missed a golden opportunity.

CHAPTER TEN

They both cleaned up before enjoying a simple dinner of sandwiches out on the patio. Brett talked at length about Danielle's adventure on the dirt bike and promised that once she got better on it, he would take her out and let her ride one of the street bikes. She had to trim her wild streak, he warned, because crashing on a street bike would be much worse than just falling in the rocks and dirt. She had to get herself in control.

Danielle listened attentively, at last realizing that her balls to the wall attitude wasn't always the most effective approach to the obstacles in her way. She imagined there was a larger lesson to be learned there, but she wasn't in the mood for deep reflection at the moment. After dinner, Brett excused himself and ran back into town for the ten o'clock broadcast.

After absentmindedly wandering through the house for a few minutes, she worked her way to Brett's makeshift studio. Well, he had gone to the trouble. What would it hurt? She fiddled with the camera, running back and forth to the stool and the camera to make sure she had everything set right, then picked up the cheap acoustic Brett had bought for her and fiddled with the tuning. When she was ready, Danielle turned to the camera.

"Hey there," she said to no one, instantly feeling stupid. Nervously she began strumming the opening notes of "Blessed Poison." She chuckled. "'Blessed Poison.' People talk about artists having a signature song. This one is mine. It's not my biggest hit, not by a long shot, but the song that best encapsulates me. I've never played it acoustic before, so this will be interesting." She started to play, then stopped and looked up at the camera. "I used to imagine myself on Unplugged one day. Never thought my stage would be some dude's living room in the middle of nowhere. Funny how things work out sometimes, huh?"

With that, Danielle put her head down, found her fingers, and began to play the song. The original version was slow blues and a song that always contained a hint of menace to it. Now, it became reflective and melancholy. She finished the song with an extended ride out. "Thing about that song, I wrote it about my mom. She was the blessed poison flowing in my veins, but as I gotten older, I've come to realize that it's me. I'm the blessed poison. That's kind of jarring, learning something like that about yourself."

After a moment of extended silence, Danielle smiled up at the camera. "Sorry. Didn't mean to get deep. How about something a little bit more fun? I mentioned that wasn't my biggest hit. So, what was? It was a song called 'When She Passes By,' my only top five hit. This song was all about my feeling like I couldn't hold a man's attention. Every guy I was with, there was always someone else in the shadows, be it an old flame or just the next girl up. So that's where this song came from."

She played this one more update and closer to the original version. As Danielle wrapped up the song, she felt lighter, as if sharing these feelings was reducing the load on her soul. She put the acoustic aside. "Bear with me. I'll be right back."

Danielle quickly retreated to her room and drug her purple Thinline and Fender amp and set them up. "Now, let's have some real fun. What other tricks do I have up my sleeve?" She picked out another song from her past and started playing. It went on and on, Danielle unpacking the stories of the songs and sometimes even taking a moment to offer a musical history lesson or show how she played a particular part.

As she did, Danielle thought about her bizarre circumstances. Once again, she found herself seemingly in the middle of nowhere, yet she no longer felt like a boat adrift at sea. She'd only been at Brett's for two days, and already things seemed to be turning in her favor.

During a break from playing, Danielle heard the strains

of music coming from the living room. She snuck into the hall, where she peeked into the living room. Brett was in one of his recliners, his computer in his lap, banging away on the keys. Beside him, "Riviera Paradise" played softly on a tiny speaker. He gave no indication that he noticed her watching, and she had been so wrapped up in herself that she never even heard him come in.

Danielle retreated to her studio, grabbed her amp, fiddled with the settings, then, as quietly as possible, drug it to the hallway, slid the guitar strap over her head, and began playing along with Stevie Ray's song. She stepped out of the hall and into the living room to find Brett looking up with a huge grin on his face. She stood at the entrance and played, matching Stevie's delicate solo almost exactly.

As the final notes died in the air between them, Danielle smirked at Brett. "You didn't think I knew that song."

"I figured you did." Another song started, but Brett silenced it with a push of a button on his laptop.

Danielle slipped the guitar over her head and leaned it on the door jamb. "I didn't mean to disturb your work. I just...I don't know. I had an urge."

"It's fine. I'm almost done anyway." He pointed at her guitar. "I've been hearing you in there, banging away. How's it going?"

"Okay, I guess. You can watch it and see if anything is useable. But I do feel...unburdened."

Brett quickly sat up, pushing his laptop off to the side. "Let's take a look right now. I'm excited to see what you've got."

As Brett hustled toward the studio, Danielle was overcome by doubt. She jumped up and trotted after him. "It may all be crap, honestly. I wasn't really taking it seriously. I felt kinda dumb talking to a camera with nobody there. So, if it's garbage, just tell me, and I'll start over in the morning."

Brett was staying a step in front of her and having none of it. "Danielle, the point is to be raw and spontaneous. Don't get too deep in your head. From what I've been hearing, it's great."

He hustled into the studio and pulled a memory stick out of the camera, holding it up for her to see. "This is where Danielle Regan's comeback begins. Let's go look."

He made his way back to his recliner and pulled up the disc contents while Danielle stood behind the chair, peering over his shoulder and chewing away at her thumbnail. Finally, the video came on, and she began her performance of "Blessed Poison."

"Oh God," she murmured as she watched the playback. Brett shushed her, completely transfixed on the computer screen. He watched the entire thing in silence, paying no attention to Danielle's nervous pacing behind him.

When it was over, he shut the laptop and twisted, so he could see Danielle behind him. He had a huge, stupid grin on his face. "That was amazing. I can't wait to post this."

"Really? I was just goofing around."

Brett wagged his finger at her. "Exactly. You weren't thinking and overanalyzing. You just let yourself be you and put yourself out there. That's what I've been talking about. In order to change the narrative, you have to start by letting people see the real you. You have to let people see underneath the armor."

Danielle hugged herself and turned away from Brett's grinning mug. "I don't know."

Brett stood and came around the chair, gently peeling Danielle's hands off her arms and replacing them with his own. She forced herself to look him in the eye. "Danielle, trust me. This is why you came up here." He glanced over at the laptop. "That right there is exactly what you need. Just give me more of that, and I'll take care of all the rest."

Danielle glanced at the computer as well and felt her resolve return. She backed out of his arms. "Fine. But not 'Blessed Poison.' You can't use that one."

"What? Why not? That was the best performance."

"That may be, but it was also way too personal. I can't let people see that deep. It's not good." She knew Brett was preparing a counterargument and wanted none of it. "This isn't up for debate. I forbid you from posting that video."

Brett stared at her, perhaps hoping to break her down, but she wasn't budging on this. "Fine. I won't do that one yet. We'll post some other videos and build an audience, and after you see how this works, maybe you'll change your mind."

"No, I won't. In fact, I want you to delete it."

"What? No way." Brett jabbed his finger toward the computer. "That was one of the best performances I've ever seen you give. I'll hold it back, but I can't delete it. That would be a travesty, and honestly, I think you'd come to regret it if I did."

Danielle stood her ground. "Delete it. Right now. I want to watch you do it."

"No."

They stared each other down, neither willing to give an inch. Danielle finally had enough of the game. "Fine then. I'm going home, and you can go screw yourself. I'll contact a lawyer tomorrow and have him draw up papers to force you to give me the drive, and I'll burn it personally."

"Danielle, you wouldn't...." Her fiery gaze told him everything he needed to know. "Fine," he said with a heavy sigh. "Have it your way." He plopped back down, opened the computer, and closed out the video he had been watching. "Are you paying attention?"

Danielle, peering over his shoulder, grunted an acknowledgement. She watched as he opened a list of files, scrolled through, and highlighted the one he was searching for. He held the laptop up so she could get a better look.

"You see the highlighted file? That's 'Blessed Poison.' I was breaking the songs into individual files while I was watching. You're about to watch it go bye-bye." Brett pulled the computer back down onto his lap, paused, and glanced back. "You sure you won't reconsider?"

She answered with a finger across the throat.

Brett gave another deep sigh, then hit delete. "Goddamn," he muttered as the file vanished from the screen. "And just so we don't have any more problems...." She watched as he navigated to the main page, pulled up the trash can, and hit empty. "There. Completely gone. Forever. Happy now?"

Danielle finally relaxed and softened her stance. "Yes. Thank you."

"Well, I was going to go to bed, but I'm kind of wired. Is it all right with you if I edit one of the other songs and put it up?" Brett's voice had a razor edge, and he made no attempt to hide it or apologize for it.

"Yes, it's fine. I'm going to get my guitar."

Danielle returned to the studio and turned everything off, grabbed the acoustic, and shuffled back into the living room, where Brett was working on one of the videos. She began to doodle on the guitar, just letting her fingers work their way around the fretboard, searching for some magical new combination of notes. It went that way for a long time, neither bothering the other at all. It was a strange occurrence for Danielle.

Eventually, Brett put his laptop away and stood loudly. "I need a beer. You want something?"

Danielle refused. He disappeared to the kitchen and came back moments later with a can in his hand. He sat gingerly on the opposite end of the couch from Danielle.

"So. You don't drink or smoke or do drugs or sleep around. Yet you've managed to carve out a reputation as one of Hollywood's bad girls. I'm not sure how you did that."

Danielle gave him her most serious look and said with an absolutely straight face, "I have anger issues. GRRRR."

Brett laughed and took a drink. "I noticed that today. The harder you tried to ride that bike, the madder you got. It winds up being self-defeating after a while. I used to have a problem with that too. I would get upset when things weren't going well, and I'd start overthrowing. I was in college before one of my coaches finally managed to get through to me. Hardest thing I ever had to learn was to relax when things started going south, but it worked."

"Is that where you came up with the Riviera Paradise thing?"

"No. He just gave me some breathing exercises and visualization techniques, stuff like that. But I didn't think that would work with you. I figured you needed to be able to connect with something personal. Music is your connection to things, so I went with it."

"You just came up with that on the fly? Wow. Either I'm easy to read, or you're really good. Either way, it was very effective."

Brett quickly deflected the praise. "I seem to have a knack for finding ways to relate to people. I guess it's because I'm a people person. I don't know."

Danielle slipped off the guitar and put it down on the couch between them. "You love baseball, and you're good at relating to people. Have you ever thought of becoming a coach?"

"No, I haven't. This job at the station just kind of fell into my lap when my playing career ended. It was the first thing to come along, so I just went with it. Never really thought about doing anything else."

Danielle turned so she could fully face him. "Maybe you should consider it. You might be happier."

Brett grinned at her. "Who says I'm not happy? I've got a great spread, good job, money isn't a problem. A fair amount of freedom."

"And you're all alone out here, making scrapbooks in your spare time. You admitted that you miss the game."

Brett grunted and took another drink. "I guess we're alike in that way. We're both pulled into our own little worlds of isolation."

"I didn't...." But Danielle didn't finish because that was exactly what she had done. "It's hard to pull yourself out once you get into it."

"Yeah, it is." His eyes darted over to the bookshelf, and his grin disappeared. "You were snooping around my scrapbooks, huh? You took that whole 'make yourself at home' comment pretty seriously."

Danielle's earlier feelings came flooding back, and she felt terrible for invading his privacy. She stammered, looking for the words to say. "I'm sorry. I didn't know you were sensitive about anything. I did what you told me to."

Brett let her hang before breaking out in laughter. "It's fine. If it was a secret, they'd be in the attic, not out where anyone could find them."

Danielle let out a sigh of relief. "I was kind of surprised that a manly dude like you likes to scrapbook in his spare time."

"My ex was really into it, so she taught me, and we used to work on them together. After she left, I needed something to do, so I kept doing it. I think I'm pretty good at it, honestly. I once thought about doing it as a side job. I would have called it 'Manly Scraps — Scrapbooks For Dudes.' But I didn't think there would be much of a market for it."

"You may be right about that."

Brett chuckled, but there was no humor in the sound. He drained the rest of the can in one drink. "Whelp, I'm off to bed. You can stay up as late as you want, though. I'm a deep sleeper."

He strolled past her on the way to his room. Danielle felt awkward with the evening ending like that. "Are we going to talk about this ex of yours?"

"Maybe sometime, but not tonight." He started away a second time.

"You should think about the coaching thing."

This time Brett turned all the way around. "I'll make you a deal. When I see you on *The Tonight Show* again, I'll go into coaching."

Danielle raised an eyebrow at him. "Do you doubt that I will?"

"No," Brett said softly. "I don't doubt you at all."

***

The next morning, Brett was gone when Danielle woke up. She planned on another day by the pool, but when she stepped outside, she was greeted with a fierce wind and waves of dust sweeping over the landscape. Instead, Danielle ducked back inside and changed into her bum clothes.

With nothing else to do, Danielle grabbed her phone and sent a quick text to her friends, so they knew she had not been murdered and buried in a shallow grave. Then she went back to the guitar and spent the rest of the day plugging away. Along the way, she began to play new songs she had been working on. Once the tap was open, new songs started coming in fast and furious, but these songs were different. Long known for songs of despair or anger, these songs were hopeful. She even worked on one that tread dangerously close to being a love song.

She lost track of time, and when Brett called her, she had no idea that she'd spent the entire day playing. It was already after five when she answered his call.

"Hey, I got stuck up here at the studio all day, so I was thinking, what if you drove into town and we had dinner? There's this great little Italian place downtown I'd like to take you to. Can you meet me there in about half an hour?"

"Sure, roundabout that anyway. I'll get dressed and head that way. Send me the address."

Driving into Amarillo was easy. She just had to navigate the terrible dirt road back to civilization, then head east on I-40. The GPS directed her into downtown, and she soon pulled up to the restaurant, which luckily had just one spot left to park next to the curb out front.

Brett, still dressed in a suit from work, had a high table for two by the window. There was already a basket of bread and a Coke on the table when she climbed up onto the freakishly high chair. "I feel like I'm sitting on a throne, and the rest of these people are my loyal subjects."

"You look very regal to me."

Danielle glanced down at her faded Levis and vintage Fabulous Thunderbirds T-shirt. "Yes, I'm very stately. The only thing missing is my tiara." They both giggled. "What's the deal with this place?"

"I eat here every Friday night. Goes back to when Jill and I were starting to get serious. This became our date night restaurant." He pointed to a table in the corner. "I proposed to her right over there. Did the whole ring in the wine glass thing. She was a sucker for stuff like that. After we got married, when it was the off season, we'd come here every Friday. I just never stopped."

Danielle studied Brett's demeanor for signs of melancholy but saw nothing. He spoke about his former wife like an old high school friend who had long dropped out of touch. She wasn't sure if that should concern her or not. "Tell me about her. What was she like?"

"Nah, you don't get that story yet. I want to know about you. Weren't you engaged once?"

For whatever reason, he was still reluctant to talk about it, so Danielle let it go. "Twice, actually. Obviously never made it to the altar, though. Guess I wasn't meant to be married."

"Didn't you date some big time actor? McConaughey, wasn't it?"

Danielle let out a full-throated laugh. "Good lord, no. It wasn't McConaughey. I've never met him. No, I was engaged to Adam Quisenberry. Similar actor, less talented."

"Wait, wait, wait. How have you lived in Austin all these years, as a celebrity no less, and never met McConaughey? How did you manage that?"

"I've never been much for hanging out with celebrities. Adam tried to steer me into that life: red carpet premieres and after parties and all that bullshit. Most Hollywood people are so phony I couldn't stand to be around them. Made my skin crawl. I don't do well with posers."

"I've met him," Brett said. "We actually had freshman English together. Of course, he was a nobody back then, so I didn't pay any attention. But I've gone to some of the alumni events over the years for football games and stuff, and he's been there. Pretty cool guy. I don't get the sense that he's a poser."

"Still not interested," Danielle answered as she pulled apart a bread knot and dipped it in marinara. "Like I said, I've tasted just enough of that life to want nothing to do with it."

"Is that why you and this Adam guy didn't work out?"

Danielle frowned. "No. Adam and I have this strange connection. We pull each other together, and then we repel each other. We're terrible together, toxic even. Our personalities, our interests, we just clash too much. There was always heat between us, but it burns out of control. Still, I have to admit that when I'm really down and feeling lonely, he's the one I think about. I even called him not so long ago, just to see if he'd come running. I was looking for an ego boost. He told me to get lost, and that hurt. I always felt like he was my fallback plan. If all else failed, Adam would be there. Turns out I was wrong."

Their waitress came back, and they both took time to place an order before Brett reopened the conversation. "So he's your 'One That Got Away'?"

"No. That was Kyle. He was killed in the crash."

"Right. I forgot about that. I remember seeing the footage on the news. Miracle you survived that. God must have really had some big plans for you."

"God." Danielle spit out the word like a piece of rotten fruit. "Don't get me started." She felt the storm clouds gathering over her head and the pull of the hatred on her heart. She pushed the bread basket aside and leaned in close. "Kyle was driving that night. He'd been whining that I never let him drive, and I was trying to loosen up, so I let him. If I had been driving that night, we wouldn't be sitting here right now."

Brett recoiled, appalled. "Don't say that. I know survivor's guilt can be tough, but—"

"It's not survivor's guilt. I would have seen it coming. I would have avoided it. I wasn't paying attention. I was sitting in the passenger seat dreaming of weddings and babies and stupid, girly shit instead of watching my surroundings."

"That still sounds like survivor's guilt. Is that what's wrong? Maybe you should see someone for that. A counselor or something."

Danielle sat back and glanced out the window. Outside, a long stretch Hummer pulled up near the curb, dangerously close to clipping not only Danielle's car but all the others parked on the street. "I already am," she said, frustrated. "You can talk some things through until you're blue in the face, but that doesn't change facts or make things go away. I'm not saying counseling doesn't help people, but it doesn't help me." Outside, the Hummer doors popped open, and a bevy of teenage girls in fancy dresses popped out, followed soon by lanky boys in rented tuxes. She nodded in their direction. "What's the deal with that? Some sort of formal tonight?"

Brett turned to look out the window as well. "Ah, must be prom night for somebody. I remember prom night. Good night." He glanced back across the table at Danielle. "I bet you were gorgeous on your prom night."

Danielle leaned back in her seat, thankful the conversation had moved away from the wreck. "You would lose that bet."

"Oh, come on. Don't give me the ugly duckling story. I won't buy it."

"On my prom night, I wore a messy ponytail, khaki shorts, and a grease-stained T-shirt." Brett's confusion was evident. She choked off a giggle and explained. "My senior year, I worked in a restaurant with two other senior girls. They wanted to go to prom. I wanted money. I worked a double shift so they could go. So you would be wrong. I was far from gorgeous."

"You didn't go to prom?" Behind him, the party in question crashed through the front door in a racket of giggles and clicking high heels. "That's terrible. Prom is one of those rites of passage nights."

"I have never lost a night's sleep over not going to prom. My life turned out pretty cool. I played Madison Square Garden. I've been on Austin City Limits. I think it's turned out all right for me."

"I'd agree with that," Brett said over his glass. "So back to Kyle—was he a good guy?"

"He was everything Adam wasn't and more," Danielle agreed. "But he's gone now, and I don't want to talk about him. Let's just keep it light."

Brett shifted in his seat. "Yeah, I can do that. So," he

said with a huff, clearly looking for a new direction to take the conversation. "You gotta have some cool road stories, though. Weird things that happened or cool people you met. What's it like out there?"

"You first. Let me hear some cool baseball stories. Then maybe I'll entertain you with tales of my exploits on the road."

Brett grinned. "All right. We'll take turns. I struck out Albert Pujols once when he was still in the minors."

Danielle popped another piece of bread into her mouth. "I have no idea who that is, but I'd love to hear all about it."

***

The weekend flew by fast. Brett and Danielle spent their days by the pool or riding motorcycles. At night, they watched baseball as Brett educated her on the finer points of the game, and Danielle gave him guitar lessons. They worked side by side, editing her videos, and Brett taught her how to upload them. He started pitching her on the idea of starting her own website and selling merchandise, but Danielle wasn't ready to cross that bridge just yet. She occasionally felt the pull of attraction, but true to his word, Brett never made a move, and Danielle happily kept him at arm's length.

On Sunday night, Brett suggested that if she stuck around another week, he'd take Friday off, and they would spend the next weekend at the lake. She wasn't interested in fishing, but Brett assured her that his boat was fast, and she wanted to find out how fast. They made the plans official. With each day, Austin and everything she had left behind slipped further into the back of her mind.

On Monday, Danielle lounged by the pool until she got bored, then snuck Brett's "crotch rocket" out of the garage and practiced riding it around his driveway. When she felt she had the bike under her control, she moved on to the street, but the deeply rutted dirt road wasn't a good learning ground, and the bike was too powerful for her to try to ride it into town unaccompanied.

Monday night, they fixed dinner together, the two of them moving seamlessly around his kitchen. They were a great team, often instinctively knowing what the other was going to do before they did it. It seemed to come naturally to them. Throughout dinner, Danielle kept catching him watching her, and it made her slightly suspicious. Still, she said nothing, and they kept the dinner conversation light.

After dinner, she volunteered to help clean up, and he agreed a little too eagerly. As she cleaned the table, Brett excused himself to the bathroom but came back a little too quickly for the break to feel legitimate. "You okay?" she asked, trying to sound innocent.

Brett struggled to suppress a grin. "Sure, doing good. How are you? Need anything?"

"All good."

Here it comes. He's about to screw everything up. They continued the post dinner clean up while Danielle tried to convince herself that the sinking feeling she felt in her stomach was unfounded. She'd been down this road too many times before, and the signs were all obvious.

Once they were finished, Brett sprang his plan. "Hey, why don't you clean up a little bit? I've got a surprise for you."

Danielle ran her hands through her hair. "I'm not big on surprises, especially ones that require me to clean up. What's going on?"

"Nothing," he said, but Brett's grin gave him away. "Just trust me on this. I think you're going to enjoy what I have in mind."

Danielle rolled her eyes. "Brett, listen. I just came out here to lay low and kick back. So if you're thinking—"

Brett let out a laugh to hide his obvious annoyance. Taking her by the shoulders, Brett looked her square in the eye. "Would you relax? I'm not going to try and take you to bed. I've got something fun for us to do. Trust me. Just go get cleaned up and quit overthinking things," Brett chuckled. "Take the stick out of your ass for a minute and just live in the moment. Have you always been such a buzzkill?"

"I am not a buzzkill." She crossed her arms over her

chest and wanted to defend herself against his accusations, but she knew better. Brett's smirk let her know he wasn't buying it anyway. Finally, Danielle sighed. "Fine, I'll do it. But for the record, I do not have a stick up my ass." Danielle tossed the hand towel she'd been using to dry her hands down on the counter.

"That's debatable," Brett said to her back as she stormed off. "Hey, take your time. We've got all night."

Danielle ignored him and stormed into her room. On the bed was a large package. "You idiot," she muttered. She remembered her time engaged to Adam when he insisted on giving her lavish gifts that she didn't want or need. That had been his way of showing affection, and maybe it was the same for Brett. The obvious difference was she was engaged to Adam, and Brett was supposed to be nothing more than a friend. That friendship seemed to be teetering on the edge.

She plopped on the bed and opened the gift to find a bath set wrapped in cellophane and a powder blue robe with Danielle stitched onto one breast. Inside was a handwritten note, the handwriting neat, considering it was a man's handwriting. *Step one: relax and indulge yourself.*

"What are you up to?" She started to stomp out and let Brett know exactly what *her* step one to him was and how he could go about doing it. How dare he take to giving her such gifts? Then his words hit her. *Take the stick out of your ass.* She really was uptight, wasn't she? She could almost hear Franklin Ridgeway in one ear, admonishing her for jumping to conclusions so quickly.

With great effort, she pushed her immediate feelings away and decided to do as requested, gathered the gift, and went to the bathroom to soak and relax. But just to make sure Brett wasn't planning on slipping into said bath with her, she locked the bathroom door behind her. She wondered briefly if he had some sort of spy camera set up in the room, a nanny cam she couldn't see or holes drilled into the walls. For a fleeting moment, she had a waking nightmare in which a video of her bathing was all over the Internet. Danielle privately admonished herself for entertaining such thoughts, keenly aware of how paranoid she had become.

As it turned out, the bath did help as the hot water, and fragrant oils relaxed muscles she didn't know were tense. At first, she listened for any tell-tale rattling of the door knob that might have given away a darker intent to Brett's actions, but none ever came, and eventually, she slipped not into sleep but into a hyper-relaxed state where time no longer seemed to matter.

When the bath was over, Danielle toweled herself off, wrapped herself in the robe, which was one of the warmest and most comfortable things she'd ever felt, and stepped out of the steamy bathroom to find two more packages on her bed. This time the note was on top. *Step 2: doll yourself up.*

She put the note aside and opened the first box to find a girly girl's treasure trove: makeup and hair products, a top dollar curling iron, the works. All things she had functional knowledge of but preferred to avoid. With a grunt, Danielle put that box aside and opened the second box to find a shimmery purple strapless dress with chiffon edges. "Oh, Brett, you silly man." She was not the fancy dress type, and again she got flashes of Adam. And again, after a moment's thought, she realized it couldn't hurt. "Well, let's see if this contraption even fits."

The dress actually fit like a glove and wasn't as completely uncomfortable as it looked. Impressed that Brett hit it so perfectly, Danielle retreated to the bathroom to check it out and was again surprised to see that the dress actually looked good on her. What didn't look good was her wet, stringy hair and tired eyes. She retrieved the other box of goodies and proceeded to do her best to pretty up.

She found the flaw in Brett's plan, though—he had forgotten shoes. Though Danielle had no trouble augmenting any outfit with her sneakers, it didn't seem right. She laughed lightly to herself and started out the door when she saw the final note lying on the ground just inside the room. *Step 3: Meet me on the patio.*

Danielle exited the room and immediately caught the sound of muffled music. Quickly she identified the source was the patio. Walking gingerly in bare feet, she noticed that Brett had closed the blinds on the patio doors. She opened the door and stepped out to find Brett standing waiting. Lights in the shape of Mason jars were strung up over the patio, while Brett's laptop and portable speaker provided the music, which currently was "You're Still the One" by Shania Twain. Brett wore black jeans, a Western shirt with a bolo tie, and a Stetson. "Welcome to your prom, Danielle."

"Oh my God. You didn't." Danielle felt her face turning red and buried it in her hands.

He was in front of her in an instant, gently prying her hands from her face and lifting her chin with one finger. "You've had *Austin City Limits.* Now let me give you this."

Danielle looked up to find him smiling down at her, and for an instant, she almost felt herself melt. She clenched her jaw to remind herself that they were just friends, while over Brett's shoulder, a slender crescent moon beamed down at her in all its pale glory. The longer she stood there staring at him, the more she felt her control slipping away. She had to say something. Finally, Danielle held up her foot and wiggled her toes. "You forgot shoes."

Brett mimicked her movement to reveal that he was also barefoot. "I didn't forget. I can only handle a certain degree of formality, especially in my own home." He held out a hand to her. "May I have the first dance?"

"Sure." With a giggle, Danielle took his hand, and Brett gently pulled her into his arms. They began to sway to the music, instantly falling into rhythm with each other. "It's almost perfect."

"Almost?"

"Yeah," Danielle said. "This song came out in '97. I graduated in '93, so you missed it by four years."

"Man, you're picky," Brett answered. "But for the record, I did no such thing. I simply pulled up slow songs of the 90s playlist and let it play. You can blame Spotify for the inaccuracies. On the other hand, I'm impressed by the memory. But then again, I guess you're a musician, so you'd remember that better than I would."

"That, and people used to tell me I looked like her, which annoyed the shit out of me."

Brett shook his head. "Why? Shania's gorgeous. I would take that as a compliment."

Danielle faked being offended. "Because, dear, I came first. I didn't look like her. *She* looked like *me*."

"Oh, I see," Bret said with a smirk. "Well, to be honest, you were prettier, but she had the better body."

"Ouch," Danielle said. She pulled away and playfully slapped him on the arm. "I had a great body back then."

"I'm not saying you didn't," Brett defended. "But speaking honestly as a friend, hers was better." He paused and gave Danielle a playful wink. "She had a rack that just would not stop. I mean, did you *see* her *Maxim* spread?"

Danielle feigned disgust. "Yes, I saw her *Maxim* spread. And there I was, having to rely on my talent to get people to listen to me."

"Oooh. Kitten's got her claws out."

As the song switched, Danielle stepped back into Brett's arms. "Shut up and dance with me." They danced through two more songs before deciding to take a break. Danielle took a seat as Brett ducked inside. He came back with two large, salt rimmed glasses filled with a light green drink.

"Now, I know you don't drink, but I make a pretty mean margarita, and I want you to try it. There's more out there than just cheap domestic beer."

Danielle took one of the offered glasses. "You wouldn't be trying to get me drunk, would you?"

"Of course not," Brett said, sounding genuinely offended. "Honestly, there's not a whole lot of tequila in these. Jill wasn't much of a drinker either, so I had to learn to make them light on the alcohol. You'd have to drink a whole pitcher to get a little buzz."

"Well then." They clinked glasses, and Danielle took a sip. It was as good as advertised. "That is good. And I have had margaritas before, so I'm not just saying that to appease your ego."

"I will take that as a legitimate compliment then. I didn't figure you for the kind to blow smoke up one's ass anyway."

"Not at all." Danielle took another drink before putting the glass aside. "So come on, tell me about this, Jill. What is the deal there?"

Brett shrugged. "I'm not putting you off. There's really not much to tell." He took a longer drink of his own, leaned forward, and held the glass loosely as he rested his elbows on his knees. "You know how it is. As a baseball player, I was away from home six months out of the year. It's a lonely life, and it's even worse if you're the one stuck at home. At least I got to move around. Jill was stuck here at the ranch. You spend that much time apart, you begin to live your own life, and chances are good that your lives aren't going to be compatible. That's what happened with us."

Danielle scooted closer to him. "Did she cheat on you?"

Brett grimaced and took another drink. "We both, uh, filled the vacancies in our lives in our own ways. I'm not proud of that, and neither was she, but like I said, it's a lonely life, and our marriage was already over. I didn't fight when she told me she was leaving. She didn't ask for much in the divorce. It all went fairly easy. She just wanted out, and I couldn't think of a reason not to let her go."

Danielle sighed. "Cheating is about the worst sin a couple can commit. If you can't be expected to honor a commitment, then how can you be trusted to do anything?"

"I know," Brett said. "It just kind of happens. It didn't happen all at once, you know. First, you feel distance. Like, you're sitting next to each other, but you might as well be in different rooms. Then you run out of things to talk about. You no longer have anything in common. It gets to where spending time together is awkward, like a blind date with a stranger. Then you start looking for something to fill the places where that person used to live. I can't speak for Jill, but I didn't start cheating until the end when it was becoming clear that it was over. I'm not saying I'm proud of it."

Danielle's mind tripped back to the picture she had seen of them together at the party and realized it was photographic evidence of exactly what Brett was talking about. Yet, her moral compass was unwavering. "Still, once a cheater, always a cheater." She felt herself being both relieved and disappointed at the same time. In one moment, any chance of them getting together flitted away on the April breeze.

Brett put his drink down and shot up out of his seat. "What was I supposed to do?" He walked toward the house before turning abruptly back. "How can you judge? What's your longest relationship? We were married for six years, dated on and off since high school, grew up together. Can you say that? You don't know what it's like."

Danielle gingerly put her drink on the table. "You're right. I don't. I drive my men off way before we can get to that point."

Brett yanked the hat off his head and ran his free hand over his face and through his hair. "I'm sorry. I didn't mean to blow up at you."

"You know, that's the first time you've shown any emotion at all when you talk about her. I was beginning to wonder if you had ever felt anything at all for her."

"It was years ago. I've had time to work through all of that." Brett strolled back to his seat, blushing just a little. "You know, what really burns me up isn't the divorce. Marriages end, relationships break. It happens. What kills me is failure. I failed as a baseball player, failed as a rancher, and failed as a husband. I'm just tired of failing. Tired of screwing up all the time."

Danielle held his hand, her fingers lacing around his. "That's a sentiment I can relate to."

"So here we sit, a couple of thirty something screw ups reliving a twenty-year-old school dance. We're a couple of winners, huh?"

"I guess so." They held hands in silence for a few moments more before Danielle stood. "Well, I guess that's that. Thank you, though. It was fun while it lasted — probably more than the real thing, to be honest."

Brett stood as she passed by. "You're welcome. Glad you enjoyed it. Sorry, I ruined it."

Danielle stopped and turned back. "You didn't ruin it." When she was close enough, Danielle leaned up on her toes and gave Brett a soft kiss on the lips. "And I don't think you're a screw up."

Brett smiled as he lightly ran one finger along her jawline. Before she knew it, he was drawing her in, and she went willingly, their lips meeting in a passionate kiss. They wrapped their arms around each other and pulled each other tighter as if they wanted to see how tight they could squeeze before someone broke.

Danielle finally managed to pull her lips away from his as "Eternal Flame" by The Bangles began to play. Danielle's mind raced. All she wanted at that moment was more, but he was an admitted cheater, and cheaters couldn't be trusted. She looked straight into his eyes. "This is wrong," she whispered. Brett started to protest, but Danielle cut him off. "This came out in '89." They were silent for a moment, and then they broke out in laughter. With the moment passed, and Danielle's flame doused, she quickly stepped back from him. "Goodnight, Slugger."

"Oh, don't call me that," Brett said with a grin. Danielle looked at him with confusion. "Sluggers are hitters, and I was a pitcher. My job was to get sluggers out. Sluggers were my arch nemesis."

"What should I call you then?"

"You could call me a Hurler or a Tosser or a Flamethrower."

Danielle debated it for only a few seconds. "No, those all suck. Sorry, but you're a slugger now. Don't stay up too late, *Slugger*."

She retreated quickly, the taste of his kiss still on her lips. The kiss had been good, too good, and Danielle wanted too badly to go in for another round. She stopped as a stray thought entered her head. She knew the thought was wrong and should remain unspoken, but she couldn't help herself. Danielle turned and rushed back to the patio door. "And just to be clear," she said, intimately aware of the nasty tone in her voice. "All of this is very nice, but don't think for a minute that I need you, or any guy, to come and rescue me. I'm doing fine on my own."

Danielle rushed back to her room, not even sure why she had felt the need to say that to him. She had been the one who initiated the kiss, and he had never said anything about rescuing her. Yet Danielle felt an old familiar fear crawling up her spine again, regardless. She unzipped her dress and was ready to let it fall to the ground when Brett pushed open her bedroom door. With a yelp, she squeezed her arms to her sides to hold the dress in place.

"I'm not sure what that was all about, but I don't think I'm rescuing you. That's not what I'm trying to do. If I overstepped my bounds, I'm sorry, but you kissed me back, so it's not all on me."

"Oh, really?" Danielle let the dress fall, standing in front of him in nothing but her slip. "So is this the point in the story where the big, burly man comes in and throws the damsel on the bed and proceeds to show her what it means to be a woman? Is that what we're doing?"

"What? No." Brett even took a step back. "No, not at all. I just wanted you to know that…I just wanted to defend myself. I'm not even sure why you're mad at me." That was a good question, for which Danielle didn't have an appropriate answer. He gave her a chance to provide one anyway, and when she failed, he went on. "Well, good night." Brett backed the rest of the way out of her room and pulled the door closed with force.

Danielle plopped down on the corner of the bed. "Why are you doing this?" Down the hall, she heard Brett's bedroom door slam shut. "Quit being a bitch," she muttered to herself.

With a growl, Danielle marched herself out of the room and to Brett's bedroom. He had already peeled his shirt off. He wasn't some muscle packed harlequin cover boy by any means, but then again, neither was Kyle. He made no attempt to cover himself up.

"So, question. Would you settle for the story where the

damsel gently leads the big burly man to bed, and together they try to figure out if love still has a place in their lives?"

"Uh, yeah," Brett said, completely caught off guard. "Yeah, I could definitely handle that."

Danielle stood there like a deer in the headlights, both of them half undressed, a big, comfy bed between them. Danielle's head began to swim. She remembered all the tender, passionate nights with Kyle. The love and the intimacy long missing in her life. It was right there for the taking.

"I'm not saying that's what this is," said Danielle, suddenly backtracking. "I'm just asking. More of a hypothetical, really." She shook her head. "Just ignore me and carry on. Good night."

"Hey, wait," Brett called out. Danielle stopped. "Are you always this awkward around men?"

In a flash, she thought back to her first attempts at flirting, her on and off again relationship with Adam, and how she had kept Kyle at bay even when she desperately wanted him. Then she thought of Shannon and her countless advances, most of which Danielle only clumsily swatted away. She couldn't help but smile at the thought. "No. I'm this way with women too."

Brett looked thoroughly confused as Danielle finished backing out of the room. Just before she pulled his door shut, she heard Brett whisper, "Good night, Danielle."

She hurried back down the hall and ditched the silky slip for her trusty old nightshirt. She gathered the dress up off the floor and held the flimsy fabric delicately in her fingers, rubbing the fabric between her fingers. "Silly. Just silly." She started to wad the thing up in a ball and toss it on the floor but stopped and instead gently hung it in the closet with one last, longing look before closing the door.

The entire time she waited, expecting Brett to blow into her room, ready to see how hypothetical her question really was. She climbed into bed, still waiting, maybe even hoping. After all this time, the thought of a man other than Kyle in her bed no longer seemed sacrilegious. Brett never came, and eventually, she gave up waiting, turned out the lights, and went to sleep, feeling disappointed and relieved all at once.

CHAPTER ELEVEN

A trickle of sunlight peeked around the curtains and landed on Danielle's face, which was just enough to rouse her. As her eyes fluttered open, Danielle's senses kicked into high gear. First, there was the tiny tickle of chest hair rubbing on her nose. Then there was her hand resting gently on his chest, and her fingers lightly making figure eights on the skin. She was naked, covered with a thin sheet, a heavy, callused hand running up and down her upper arm.

With a satisfied purr, Danielle craned her neck and peered up at his face. "Good morning."

Kyle's blue eyes glittered back at her. "I would like to think so. Pretty good night too."

"I'll say." She stretched out her 6'1" frame, feeling every muscle pulling to its absolute limit. She released the tension. "Could be a better morning."

"I like what you're thinking. Got plenty of time before the party tonight."

The party? It took her a moment to figure out what Kyle was talking about. "The release party. Right. Almost forgot."

Kyle laughed, and Danielle's head raised and lowered with Kyle's chest. "How could you forget? The album has been all we've talked about and thought about for months." He rubbed her arm more strenuously. "I can't wait to see what people think about it."

"It gets to be old hat after a while," she answered. "But then again, this is your first album release. So I guess it's different." She chuckled and looked up into his eyes. "How about that? I took your virginity too."

"That you did," Kyle said. "It was almost as much fun as when I took yours."

Danielle rose up on one elbow. "Almost? Almost? You think creating a masterpiece is *almost* as good as simple old sex? I think I'm insulted."

Kyle just shook his head and laughed some more. "Honey, with you, it is far from simple old sex, and the payoff is more immediate. I can't believe it's a debate. I guess I haven't done my job well enough. Might have to rectify that."

Under the sheets, Danielle felt exactly how he planned to rectify the situation. She rolled over until she was almost lying directly on top of him. "I'm not sure you're up to the task, Cowboy."

Kyle snapped her over on her back with a move so fast it stole Danielle's breath away. He pinned her arms to the bed and hovered over her. She could smell the morning on his breath. As much as her desire began to flicker to life, another thought entered her head.

"Just a few more hours, and it'll all be done. After tonight, we won't just be playing house anymore. Sure you don't want to back out while you've still got time?"

"Danielle," Kyle muttered, slumping down on the bed beside her. "Why do you do that? We're having a great, sensuous moment here, and you start talking about the future. Why can't you just enjoy this?"

"I am enjoying this. I'll just enjoy it more after tonight. Or after next week when we finally walk down that aisle. We'll have the rest of our lives to live in the moment after that. No interruptions."

This time Kyle was the one who rose. "What do you mean by that?"

Danielle pushed herself up as well and ran the fingers of her left hand through his fine hair. "I'm going to tell Steve tonight that I'm done. No more tours, no more albums. I've spent ten years of my life doing this. It's time for a new adventure."

"No more music? Certainly not. I don't think you can live

without music. It's the air you breathe."

"Sure, I can," Danielle asked. "Music was just my outlet. I have you now. You're my outlet. You're my salvation."

"Danielle, I don't think —"

She silenced him by placing a single finger on his lips. "Shhh. Do you hear that? I think someone is at the door."

Kyle pushed her hand away. "So what if they are. You don't have to answer. I still need to straighten your priorities back out, Missy." He leaned in to kiss her, but Danielle turned her head away. Kyle didn't miss a beat, she offered her neck, and he took it.

"Quit," Danielle moaned. She wriggled out from under his grasp. "Somebody's at the door. I need to get it."

"Danielle." Kyle fell face down on the mattress as she desperately searched for her shirt, any shirt. "Let it go, baby. Don't worry about it."

Danielle finally located one of Kyle's shirts on the floor next to the bed and slid it over her head. "I'll just be a second. I gotta see who's down there. It might be important." She swung her long, perfect legs off the side of the bed.

Just before her feet hit the floor, she clearly heard Kyle whisper, "You're never gonna learn, are you?"

Danielle's feet landed on the carpet, and she turned to look over her shoulder, a big smile on her face. A smile that quickly faded. Kyle was gone, the bed was empty. She looked down to see she was still wearing her favorite nightshirt. The air in the room suddenly seemed to weigh a hundred pounds.

Then she heard it again, the insistent knocking on the front door. "What the hell?" She pushed up out of bed and made it to the door. Just ahead of her, Brett was turning into the living room, moving fast. "Hey, Brett," she called, but he didn't stop. Danielle trailed behind and was just entering the foyer when Brett reached the door, peeked through the peephole, and opened up.

Brilliant morning light filled the room. Danielle caught the silhouette of a hulking male figure in the door and ducked back. She had no desire for one of Brett's buddies to catch her in her pajamas.

"I'm here to speak with Danielle Regan," the man said, his voice booming.

"May I ask why?"

"It's a personal matter, sir. I know that's her car in your driveway. May I please speak with her?"

"Just give me one second." Brett didn't close the door, but he did back up until he reached the entryway to the living room. "Danielle. The police are here to see you."

"The police?" Modesty quickly forgotten, Danielle pushed past Brett and hustled to the door where the hulking man stood, decked out in the familiar khaki uniform of the Texas Highway Patrol, cowboy hat in hand.

"Miss Regan?"

Danielle stopped several feet away. She felt more than heard Brett sidle up behind her. She ran a nervous hand through her hair. "Yes. Something I can help you with?"

"I'm afraid so," the trooper said. He kept turning the hat in his hand. "I'm Officer Sinclair of the Highway Patrol. I've been sent out here to get you. We need you to return to Austin as soon as possible."

"Listen, if this is because I missed my session with Ridgeway, he knew where I was. I told him I was going out of town, and he never said anything to me about coming back. So I don't think it's fair—"

"I'm not sure what that would be about, ma'am," the trooper said, still turning the cap by the bill. "There is a personal matter that needs your attention. It's about your mother."

"My mother," she laughed. "My mother can go fuck herself. Whatever she's done or gotten herself into, I want no part of it. I made that clear the last time I saw her."

The trooper seemed to get even more nervous. He looked at the floor, searching for the right words to say. Finally, he forced his eyes up to her. "Ma'am, I'm afraid I have some bad news. I'm afraid your mother has died."

"Oh shit," Brett muttered over her shoulder. He took her

arms in his hands. "I'm so sorry."

Danielle slithered out of Brett's grasp, her eyes locked on the fidgety cop. "Thank you for telling me. I'm sure it was difficult for you, but we weren't close, and I really don't care. As far as I'm concerned, she died a long time ago, and I have no desire to deal with any of the details. Just do what you would do for any other unclaimed body. Throw her in a hole and go on."

The trooper sighed heavily. "I was told that might be your reaction when they asked me to come out here. There are more than just funeral arrangements to be made, Ms. Regan. It would be better if you would return to Austin where you could discuss this face to face with a professional."

"A professional? You mean, like a counselor? Well, I already have one of those, so when I go back to Austin, I'll call him up, and we'll talk about it, and I'll explain to him why this doesn't affect me."

"No, ma'am." Sinclair stopped turning his cap. "A professional social worker. I'm sure they could explain it better than I could. It really is important that you return to Austin as soon as possible. This isn't just about your mother." He stopped, a look of worry etched across his weathered face.

"What else could it be about?"

Sinclair went back to turning the hat in his hands. "I'm really not supposed to tell you."

"Well," Danielle was flustered and confused. The entire scene was bizarre in a way she couldn't readily define. "I don't know who told you that, but unless you give me a better reason than you have so far, I'm not going anywhere."

Sinclair seemed to relax a bit. "We need you to return to Austin to discuss what needs to be done about your sister."

Danielle felt her legs go weak, and she fell back into Brett. "My what?!"

CHAPTER TWELVE

Danielle stumbled away from the door, somehow making it back to the living room on legs that didn't want to work before she collapsed on the couch. She heard Brett talking to the highway patrolman, but it sounded distant in her ears, like a TV playing in another room. Danielle's mind was a swirling storm.

Sister. She had a sister.

Then immediately, she rejected the thought. No, Dorothy Regan had a second child, most likely with that sleaze Sean she had run off with. Biology be damned. That didn't mean this mystery girl was her sister.

Brett was suddenly there, kneeling in front of her. "Danielle, are you okay?"

She tried to play it casual. "Yeah, I'm fine. I just...I think I need to go back to bed for a bit. I woke up too quick, and I'm a little disoriented, you know."

Brett lifted her chin. "You need to go home. There are things you need to deal with."

"No, I don't. I'm fine here." She started to stand, intent on returning to her bedroom. "I just need some sleep."

Brett pushed her back down. "Danielle, you have to go back home. I love having you here, and I hate to see you go, but you're needed. You can't tell me this doesn't impact you. I can see it. It's okay." He got up off the floor and sat beside her, holding her close with one arm. "I know this is a shock. You can cry if you need to. I won't judge you."

Danielle pushed him away with whatever strength she had. "I don't need to cry. I cried my last tears over that woman years ago. I don't need anything. I don't need to deal with this.

Let's just go back to bed and pretend it was all a weird dream, all right?" She knew he was going to argue and tried to put on a seductive face. "If you want, you can come to bed with me and help me feel better."

Brett's face contorted with disgust. "Danielle, no. That would be a terrible idea."

She had expected such an answer. "Wow. I had no idea I was that undesirable."

"Don't even start that," he scolded her. "You have to go back. If you want, I'll be happy to go down with you. I could take a few days off and lend some support."

Danielle tried to put on an indignant face, but she knew it was a losing battle. "You're not going to let this go, are you?" Brett shook his head. "All right, fine, I'll go. Let me go get dressed."

"Do you want me to go with you?"

In her heart, she desperately did, but Danielle was used to handling her business alone. "You really don't need to do that. I can handle it."

Brett stared at her for a moment, then jumped up. "Give me ten minutes, and I'll be ready to go. I'm not letting you do this alone. I don't care what you say." He pushed past her to go pack, and Danielle let a tiny smile pass across her face before turning to get dressed.

Fifteen minutes later, they were on the road. She brought nothing but the clothes on her back, having every intention of being back in just a few days. Brett did his best to make the trip tolerable, telling a steady stream of light-hearted anecdotes from his past, along with the occasional dirty joke. Danielle was in no mood to talk, and eventually, he fell silent.

As the miles rolled on, he started up again. "Sure you don't want to talk about it?"

"I've already told you," Danielle answered, eyes still locked on the road ahead.

"It couldn't have all been bad. There had to have been some nice times. Can you think of just one time when you got along? One good day?"

Danielle let her mind drift back, searching not for the terrible moments for once but for the nice ones. Ones that she had tried so hard to bury. "There was this one time Mom tried to make some fancy new dish. My grandparents were gone by this time, and it was just the two of us, and she was working two jobs and was always tired. We lived on pizza and TV dinners, but she wanted to cook. I could see it meant a lot to her, so while she cooked, I did the table up prim and proper, candles and all. She almost cried when she came out of the kitchen and saw it." Danielle felt the cold, salty evidence of tears on her cheeks but left them alone.

"How old were you?"

Danielle did some mental calculations. "Twelve, thirteen, somewhere in that area. Anyway, she put the plates down, and we sat, and we were both so excited." She interrupted her own story. "God, what did she make? I can't remember."

"So you had a nice dinner together?"

"Oh no," Danielle let out a bittersweet chuckle. "It was awful. She took one bite and just lost it. Started bawling and threw her plate. Had a total meltdown. Before she stormed upstairs to her bedroom, she stopped and looked at me and said, "I'm sorry I'm such a shitty mom." That was the only time she ever apologized to me for anything."

"That's not quite what I was expecting, but I guess it's kind of nice."

"That's not the nice part," Danielle said. "I felt bad for her. I couldn't cook, but I knew how to make a grilled cheese, so I made her a grilled cheese and her favorite soup and took it up to her in bed. She hugged me, and we snuggled together on her bed and ate and watched some old movie on TV. It was almost like a real mother-daughter relationship. I hoped it would carry over, but the next day it was like it never happened. One night. One goddamn night I got inside her walls."

"I know that feeling,"

Danielle's head snapped around, and she caught Brett staring at her. She knew what he meant, and the realization was more than she could bear. "I don't want to talk about this anymore." Brett agreed, and they finished the drive down in silence.

Several hours later and weary from the road, as well as the emotional burden she was carrying, Danielle finally pulled into the parking garage and led Brett up to her penthouse.

He whistled as he surveyed Danielle's place. "Wow, look at that view. Man, this place must cost you a fortune."

"My manager was good with money too. In fact, this used to be his place." She paused and took in her surroundings. "I once designed and built this beautiful house by the lake that was supposed to be my home. It had all this room for the family I thought I was going to have. It was everything I ever wanted." She caught Brett watching her. "And it turned into a prison. Now I know better, so there's no need for a big, fancy place."

"I get that," Brett said, turning a full circle. "Still, this is a great apartment." He inspected Danielle's massive stereo system. "Decorated like a high school boy lives here."

"It's just a place to sleep and eat," Danielle shrugged.

"So is a prison," Brett answered

Danielle could only meet his gaze for a moment before she broke it off. "Come here. I do have a guest room, but it's not done up or anything. I'll have to get you some sheets and stuff. Bathroom's down there. My room is there. It's a simple layout; you shouldn't have a hard time finding anything."

Brett followed dutifully behind as Danielle gave him the grand tour. Together they made the bed in the guest room. After that, they ordered a pizza and ate quickly before Danielle excused herself for the night.

"You really don't have to go with me tomorrow. I can handle this myself."

Brett, still working on his last piece of pizza, was having none of it. "You shouldn't do this without some support. I'm with you every step of the way."

Danielle looked back, barely able to keep her eyes open. "You'll probably live to regret that."

***

The Health and Human Services Building was located in an abandoned elementary school, and the entire place felt scuzzy, from the broken playground equipment outside to the floors that looked like they hadn't seen a mop since 1987. Danielle walked into the lobby and saw into the faces of the defeated and hopeless, joyless moms and an occasional dad, their eyes all dead and flat, while kids ran wild around them, snot seeming to ooze out of every nose.

She recognized that same look in the eyes of the receptionist, who sat behind bulletproof glass and looked at Danielle like just another burden she'd have to carry. Behind her, Danielle noticed that several workers glanced over, each bearing the same dead-eyed stare.

They were rudely told to sit down and wait. Danielle just wanted to be done with the entire thing. She kept glancing at the door and feeling that familiar urge to run. Beside her, Brett took it all in.

"Damn, man, look at this. These people are all so broken. I've never seen so much misery at someplace that wasn't a funeral. It breaks my heart."

"It's a tough world," Danielle answered, though she was impressed to see Brett's empathy. He had a good heart. But then again, she knew that already.

"Have you always been so cold?"

"Every moment of my life has been a struggle, so yeah, I'm a little hard." She turned away, but her words echoed in her ears. She scanned the room full of broken people and joyful, unknowing kids and took a deep breath. "It's not that I'm not empathetic. I'm just a realist. Not everybody makes it. You start trying to save the world, and you're just going to drown in the waves."

Brett's response was cut off when a slender, middle aged black woman poked her head out of a side door. "Danielle?"

Eager to drop the conversation, Danielle shot out of her seat and quickly made her way to the door, followed by Brett.

The woman held the door open until they were inside. "Good morning," she said, though her voice was as emotionless as everything else. As the metal door clicked shut, she held out her hand. "I'm Rachel Luster. Thank you for coming. Right this way, please." Luster led them down a darkened corridor into an expansive room jam packed with metal desks that may have been left over from the building's school days. Her desk was in a corner with an aging PC on top and papers covering everything. "I'm not sure how much you've been told about all of this."

"Just that my mom died and that she left behind someone you suspect to be her daughter. That's all I got."

Luster clasped her hands in front of her. "First of all, I am very sorry for your loss. I understand how much it can hurt to lose a parent. However, I must warn you that the details of what happened are not very pleasant."

Danielle remained just as hard and unemotional as everyone else. "I'm sure they're not, but frankly, I don't care. The officer was insistent that I come down. I really want nothing to do with any of this." She paused as an idea came to her. "This kid that you've got are you even sure she's Dorothy Regan's kid?"

Luster cracked a sad smile, reached into a desk drawer, pulled out a Ziploc bag full of papers, and tossed them down in front of Danielle. "We have no reason to believe she's not. The girl had this on her when the first responders got to her. Everything seems to match up."

Danielle stared at the package as if it were some sort of venomous snake waiting to strike. Slowly, she moved the bag with one finger, turning it so she could read the top document inside. It was a birth certificate from the state of Utah. "August 21, 1995. Talitha Grace McLain. So she is Sean's kid." Danielle turned to Brett. "He's the winner that molested me in front of my mom, and I got blamed for it. And what the fuck kind of name is Talitha?"

"It's a biblical name," Luster answered for her. "It's the name of a girl Jesus resurrected in Mark."

Danielle scoffed. "Of course, it would be some weird ass

biblical name. That woman, I swear." To Brett, she said, "You know those fake Christians we talked about once? Meet my mom."

"I think there's more to it than that," Brett said. "A girl resurrected. A second daughter." He looked over at Danielle. "A second chance."

Danielle rolled her eyes and turned her attention back to Luster. "So, where is her dad? Why don't you get his worthless ass down here?"

Luster started to answer, stopped, sighed, dug around on her desk for a paper, and finally peered up at her. "The father, Sean McLain, is...unavailable."

"Unavailable," she scoffed. "He ran off and left them. Exactly what I'd expect that piece of trash to do."

"No. We know exactly where he is." Luster left it at that. Danielle peered across the desk with anticipation. Finally, Luster glanced both ways and leaned forward. "He is incarcerated in the Idaho State Penitentiary." Danielle continued staring, waiting for the rest of the story. "He has been convicted on a number of sexually based offenses, many involving minors."

"There it is." Danielle turned to Brett. "The man my mother abandoned me for: a child molester. And they had a little girl together. Isn't that sweet? What are the odds that this girl hasn't been abused?"

Luster's posture gave the answer away even before she spoke. "None. Talitha has been very forthcoming with investigators. Her story...." A shiver ran through Luster's body. "Her tale is a strange and depressing story." Luster's mood suddenly brightened. "However, the girl is quite remarkable." She pushed a stack of papers aside and leaned forward, resting her elbows on the desk. "She has a will and a spirit that I find quite admirable. She has an incredibly strong faith, and frankly, she is mature beyond her years."

"That happens when you grow up with monsters. You have no choice but to grow up fast," Danielle answered. "This is all fascinating, but I don't see what it has to do with me. Surely

Sean has family somewhere."

"One of the documents in that baggie is a notarized will from your mother naming you as her guardian. It's rough, but our lawyers assure me that it meets the necessary requirements. You are her legal guardian." She saw Danielle's next question coming. "We did a preliminary investigation in anticipation that there could be a legal issue. Sean didn't have any immediate family, and the family he does have demonstrated no desire to be involved."

Danielle certainly understood that. Why would anyone want to be saddled with the love child of a pervert and a lunatic? "And what if I refuse? What then?"

"Danielle," Brett interjected. "Don't be so quick to dismiss this. Your sister needs your help. You heard what Ms. Luster said. She's had a hard go already. She needs somebody to stand up for her."

Danielle whipped her head around. "Don't call her my sister. I don't have a sister. I didn't even have a mother."

Luster jumped in. "If you choose, you can waive your rights as a guardian. In which case, she will be put into foster care until she becomes an adult. At that point, she gets turned loose."

"Don't let that happen, Danielle," Brett warned. "I've heard all sorts of horror stories about foster care. So many kids get put in really bad places. They get abused, neglected."

"We do our best to assure that doesn't happen," Luster said. "But I must admit that even under the best of circumstances, foster care is something we prefer to avoid if at all possible. As her closest relative and appointed guardian, we strongly suggest that you take custody."

Danielle took a moment to glare at Brett before she leaned in toward Luster. "You wanna help that girl? Take her out in a field somewhere and put a bullet in her head."

"Danielle!"

She turned to Brett. "This girl has been used and abused, and I know what it's like to grow up with Dorothy Regan as a mother and having her crazy running through your veins. She has zero chance of living a normal life. She's going to be a bigger basket case than I am."

Luster collapsed back in her seat with a heavy sigh. "Euthanasia is not an option. I take it that I should have the papers drawn up for you to resign as guardian?"

Brett cut in before she could answer. "No. Don't. Danielle, at least meet her. Ms. Luster here said she has an incredible spirit. Maybe if you meet her, talk to her, you'll feel different. This could be a great thing for both of you."

"I would feel better if you would at least take the time to talk to her," Luster agreed. "I have a good idea of what your relationship with your mother was, and I understand your reluctance, but don't punish the child for the sins of the parent."

"Exactly," Brett said. "Listen to her."

"Why do you care so much?" Danielle snarled.

"Because you saw those people out there. How broken they all were. You have a chance to help someone, to give someone a better life. I think you have to take that opportunity."

Danielle glanced from Brett, a look of pathetic pleading on his face, to Luster, who suddenly had the tiniest glimmer of hope in her otherwise dead eyes. "If I meet this girl and I don't like what I see, for whatever reason, then I walk, and I don't want grief from either one of you."

"Just go in there with an open mind," Brett said. "Give her an honest chance. Don't go in there with your mind already made up."

Danielle glared at Brett, then turned to Luster. "So, where is she?"

Luster led them out of the room, through an outer door, into a long, narrow room with a simple table and two chairs planted in front of a large window that looked in on another room. The girl sat at a table with her back to the window. All Danielle could see was a mane of straight blonde hair. The room was decorated with cartoon animals on the walls, and a Crayola bookshelf jammed full of books in one corner, with toys scattered around the floor. The girl was hunched over a book.

"We'll observe from here. This is one of the rooms we use for supervised visitation. The door is locked from the inside, so when you need out, just signal and I will meet you at the door. All I ask is that you be patient and have an open mind."

"Yeah, I get it," Danielle sighed. "Let's just get this over with."

Luster and Brett exchanged worried looks with no effort to hide them from Danielle. Then Luster opened the door, and Danielle stepped through.

The first thing that hit her was the cold, antiseptic feeling of the room. The girl turned her head quickly, her hair flowing around her like a dancing golden cloud. Danielle got her first look at the girl's face, and it froze her in her tracks. She very well could have been staring at a fifteen-year-old version of herself.

Cosmetically there wasn't much similarity. Her eyes were bright blue, her hair blonde, her complexion fair, but a deeper look showed that they had the same high, sharp cheekbones, short rounded nose, and full lips. As the girl recognized who Danielle was, a huge smile spread across her face, one that seemed to make her glow. In all her life, Danielle had never seen such a welcoming smile as hers. She wore a green shirt that proclaimed Property of Baylor Bears in bright yellow letters, the shirt swallowing the girl, her arms like tiny twigs jutting out from the side.

"You're finally here." Her voice lilted, full of childlike joy.

Danielle edged her way around the table and sat opposite the girl. Doubts continued to swirl in her mind, and she quickly checked to fix the location of the door. "I'm here," she finally said in a throaty whisper. "So you're...." She couldn't bring herself to say the words.

"Your sister," the younger girl added eagerly. "Or, I guess half-sister, if you want to be accurate. My name is Talitha. I've waited a long time to meet you." She closed her book and held out her hand for a shake.

Danielle looked at the outstretched hand but refused to shake it. Talitha dropped her hand, the first sign of disappointment creeping onto her pretty face. "Mother said you probably wouldn't like me. I had hoped she was wrong."

Danielle sat at the very edge of her seat with her hands folded in her lap. "I don't know you. I didn't even know you existed until yesterday."

"She tried. She tried to reach out to you. She said she saw you once, but she wasn't able to talk to you." She left Danielle a gap to respond, which she did not take. "If it's any consolation, Mother felt terrible about the way she treated you. She felt very guilty about abandoning you. She used to talk about you often. Especially late at night when things were quiet, and she could think. It's just a shame that she wasn't able to tell you."

"Uh huh. So were you there when Mom...?"

"Died? Yes. I tended to her the best I could, but she needed a doctor." Talitha's voice started to crack.

"That's just so typical," Danielle spat. "To expect a little girl to take care of her instead of going to the hospital like a normal person."

"I didn't mind taking care of her," Talitha responded. "It was my responsibility as her daughter to care for her. She knew she was dying, and though she never said, I believe she welcomed it. Her spirit was in great pain. I tried, but I couldn't help."

"You couldn't have helped. You're just a kid. What could you have possibly done?" A mental image formed in Danielle's mind, and it added to her disgust to think of this poor kid forced to play nursemaid to a terminally ill woman.

"It was my duty and honor to help her."

Danielle started to push the topic but instead let it go. "So...what...?" She let out a nervous chuckle. "I don't even know what to say to you."

"The other people who came to see me wanted to know my story." The twinkle in Talitha's eyes faded at the comment. "Do you want to know?"

"No, I don't. I got the gist of it from the social worker, and that's all I need to know." Danielle noticed the relief in Talitha's eyes. "Besides, no use in opening old scars."

"Thank you," Talitha whispered. "I get tired of telling it.

Sometimes I think people want me to tell it so...." Talitha couldn't bring herself to finish the sentence, but Danielle saw where she was heading.

"So they can get off on it? People are weird that way. Living through others so they can live out their own peculiar kind of kink." Talitha nodded knowingly. "It's usually harmless. Until some weirdo gets it in his head that it's not just a fantasy." The room disappeared, and suddenly Danielle was back in her old Camaro screaming down the Capital of Texas highway, Kyle at the wheel talking foolishness about weddings and kids and families. She could almost feel the wind in her hair. "And then they decide that they have to make the fantasy reality," she whispered softly.

"Did it happen to you too?"

Danielle snapped out of her daze. She was back in the room, her sister sitting across from her. "Ah, not like what happened to you, but somebody became obsessed with me and the man I loved died because of it. So I get where you're coming from." Danielle flashed quickly to that last day back in Chaparral when Sean, her mother's boyfriend and Talitha's father, had tried to assault her in the kitchen. For a moment, she thought about relaying the story but passed. She couldn't see where that bit of information would do the girl any good.

"Mother told me that you're a musician," Talitha said, switching gears at just the right time. "I remember once when I was little, and we saw your face on a billboard somewhere. I thought you were the most beautiful person, and Mother told me you were my sister. That was in Boise, I think. Or was it Salt Lake? We moved around a lot."

"Well, I definitely played both of those cities more than once."

"Is it fun? I bet it's fun, traveling all across the country and playing music like the minstrels of old."

"Minstrels?" Danielle laughed. "Never considered myself a minstrel. A troubadour, maybe, but never a minstrel. Where did you hear that?"

"One of the women in our camp was very knowledgeable about medieval times. She used to teach us. I haven't gone to a regular school in a long time, but the women in the camps made sure we were educated. After we left the camps, Mother would take me to the library and leave me there all day to read. Some days she would make me read about certain things, and some days I got to pick what I wanted." Talitha picked up the book and held it in front of her. "This is my favorite. Have you read Harry Potter?"

"No, I haven't. I'm not much of a reader." Talitha's reference to a camp sent shivers running up Danielle's back. What kind of life had this kid lived? Suddenly, all the worst things she had envisioned seemed to be entirely inadequate.

"I can see by your reaction that you didn't know about the camps. They didn't tell you much, did they?"

"I didn't ask," Danielle said, her blood running like an icy river through her veins. "I don't want to know."

"You look at me differently now," Talitha said, dropping her eyes to the table.

"No. I—"

"I'm okay," Talitha answered sweetly. "We have no control over the things that others do to us, only how we react. I choose forgiveness. Mother promised me that things would get better one day once she got me to you."

Danielle shot up out of her seat, sending the flimsy chair rolling along the ground. "I am not the one who makes things better. I'm not some kind of savior. Hell, I can't even take care of myself most of the time." Talitha was cringing, and it stirred something inside of her. Danielle took a deep breath and kneeled in front of Talita. "Look, kid, your mom sold you a pipe dream. I'm sorry, but I'm not the mother type or even the sister type, and I can't be what you want me to be. I just can't. I don't know how, and I don't want to be. I'm sorry for...everything. That you were born into this fucked up bloodline. That you've endured what you have, that your mom saddled you with caring for her dying ass. I'm sorry she built your hopes up. I'm sorry."

She stomped to the door and banged on it until Luster finally popped it open. She did not look back because she knew she couldn't. One more look into that innocent face would have made it impossible for Danielle to leave, and that was all she wanted to do.

CHAPTER THIRTEEN

Danielle darted out of the room, stepped across the hall, and slammed her right forearm into the opposite wall. The aged drywall cracked and sagged at the impact. Danielle whirled and buried her face in her hands. "Oh, Jesus. That kid…. Oh my God."

Brett was at her side in an instant, putting a reassuring hand on her shoulder. "What's wrong? It seemed like things were going fine. What is it?"

With great effort, Danielle pulled her hands away from her face. "My mom convinced that kid that I was going to fix everything. That I was going to make things better. How am I supposed to do that? If she kept tabs on me all these years, how did she not know what a mess I am?"

Luster stepped forward. "Compared to the life that little girl has led, your problems are nothing." The woman's voice carried an edge that Danielle was not used to hearing. "How can you make things better? For starters, you can put a roof over her head. You can give her three square meals a day and put her in some decent clothes. You can enroll her in school. At the least, you can assure her that some strange man isn't going to come to her bed at night." She waited for Danielle to look at her. Her face was stone cold now, but her eyes burned with passion. "It's not hard to give that girl a better life than what she's had. She's fifteen, and the only person in the world that has ever cared for her is gone. But with the last little bit of energy she had, Dorothy Regan tried to bring her to you because you're the only family she's got. You owe it to that girl to do this."

Danielle felt the fire ignite within her. She stepped right up to Luster and glared down at her. "I owe that girl nothing," she hissed. She slid past Luster to the one-way window and stared down at Talitha, who had gone back to reading her book. "I'm not equipped for that."

"But you can," Brett pleaded. "If you could escape your own upbringing and become what you are today, then you can help her. All you need to do is be there for her. It's not like having to raise a baby or anything." Danielle shook her head fiercely, but Brett wouldn't let go. "I'll help you. We'll do it together."

"Oh really," Danielle snapped, her words dripping with venom. "You're just going to move in, and we're going to play Mommy and Daddy, is that it? You must be joking."

"Not like that. But...we'll bring her back to the ranch with us. We can do all the things we've talked about doing. She won't be a bother. Plus, it'll give y'all a chance to connect without just being thrown together alone." Danielle's façade must have faltered just a little because Brett pushed. "Come on, Danielle. I don't want this to be one of those moments you look back on and regret in several years. This is a chance to help someone who really needs you. And you may need her."

"I don't *need* anyone," she said to Brett, pausing to drive home the point.

"Nevertheless, I think Mr. Walls has a point," Luster added as the double team continued. "She is a remarkable young woman. You'll see if you give her a chance."

Danielle turned a slow circle as she ran her fingers through her hair. "I'll screw her up. I'm telling you now."

Luster stepped forward, blocking Danielle from pacing anymore. "If she isn't already screwed up from all she's been through, then I highly doubt you can do anything to make it worse."

Danielle's eyes darted from Luster's to Brett's and finally to the window, and the frail girl hunched over her book. "This is a bad idea," she muttered. She glanced over her shoulder at Brett. "I'm telling you, it's a bad idea."

"I'll be with you every step of the way," he assured her. "Take a chance."

With a groan, Danielle marched back to the door, took a deep breath, and went back inside. Talitha glanced up at her quickly, started to smile, but stopped herself. Danielle settled softly on the seat across from her and gently pulled the book away.

"Listen. I'm gonna be honest with you, kid." Talitha's shimmering blue eyes met hers and held fast. She had no problem looking someone in the eye. "I'm not a great person. I've got a bad temper, I'm impulsive and selfish, and I'm not even remotely used to having to take care of someone else. Your mom didn't set a great example for me to follow. I will have no clue as to what I'm doing, and I'm probably going to be a nightmare, but if you really want to stay with me, I'll give it a shot,"

Talitha's face lit up, and her eyes crackled with energy. "Do you mean it?"

Danielle instantly felt her doubt beginning to claw at her. "I'm not making any promises as to how this will all work out. I let everybody down eventually, so don't have too much faith in me,"

"Oh, thank you. I promise I will be good. You won't have any trouble with me. And I'll do chores. Whatever you need me to do."

Something in her face suddenly changed, and Talitha reached across the table to take Danielle's hand. The second they touched, Danielle felt something she had never felt before. She was used to that instantaneous crackle of chemistry between a man and a woman, but this was different. Was this what new parents were talking about when they spoke of holding their baby for the first time?

Talitha waited patiently for Danielle to cycle through the rush of emotions before speaking again. Softly but assuredly, Talitha looked deep into Danielle's eyes and spoke. "I do have faith in you. Probably more than you have in yourself."

Danielle was locked in on those blue eyes and felt herself falling. Until the beast inside her woke up. She snatched her hand back. "I'm not looking for a housemaid," she snapped, knowing that the comment didn't even make sense. "We'll have to get you into a normal school and whatever the hell that entails. And my job comes first. I want you to be clear on that. My music is all I have, so it's very important to me. You're going to have to be okay with that."

"Yes, ma'am," Talitha chirped. "I understand. I will stay out of your way. I can be very self-sufficient."

Danielle stared across at the girl, her fear almost nauseating as she thought about the challenge Talitha was going to present to her. Still, Danielle couldn't deny that something else was brewing somewhere deep in her soul. Was it hope? Did she even have any of that left? "Well, I guess I'll have Luster go pack up your stuff."

"Thank you," Talitha said again. Nimbly, she shot up from her seat, circled the table, and wrapped her arms around Danielle's neck. "Thank you so much."

Danielle let the girl, who smelled vaguely of dollar store soap, linger before gently pushing her away. "Don't thank me yet. Like I said, I let everybody down sooner or later."

Talitha ended the hug but left one hand lingering on Danielle's shoulder. "You won't let me down. I believe in you."

"That's usually people's first mistake. Come on, let's get your stuff."

Luster let them both out of the room and called a coworker to take Talitha in the back to gather whatever belongings she had while she led Danielle and Brett back to her desk. There she laid out the minutia of things Danielle was expected to keep up with. There was the list of agencies she would need to contact, a court date she would have to make in order to finalize everything, tips on how to be a caregiver. Luster pored over all of it thoroughly, but Danielle couldn't focus on it. Instead, she continued replaying the recent events that had led her to this point. She thought of her mother on that last night, trying to get through to her and failing. Maybe things would have played out differently if she had given her mother a chance to talk. Then again, even with Death riding on her shoulder, Dorothy Regan had let her own pride get the better of her. So, crazy wasn't the only legacy her mother had left.

Finally, it was over. Talitha was led into the room, still wearing the ill fitting clothes, clutching a paper sack in both hands. In a building full of miserable people, she beamed like a star. Brett saw her enter and stood up, and Talitha's smile instantly evaporated. She stepped back quickly, bumping into the worker who had escorted her into the room.

Luster noticed and sprang into action. She took the girl's arm and gently coaxed her forward. "Talitha, this is Mr. Walls. He's a friend of your sister's."

Beside Danielle, Brett muttered, "Oh damn," as he witnessed her reaction. "That poor kid."

A sudden, jarring thought hit Danielle, and she looked into his eyes with barely controlled panic. "You know, if you have any weird feelings or kink or anything, this is the time to let me know."

"Danielle," he rebuked her.

"Well," was all she could say in response. Instead, she turned her attention to Talitha. "It's okay, kid. Brett is here with me. He's a good guy."

Brett stepped around her, knelt in front of Talitha, and held out his hand. "I'm Brett. Nice to meet you."

Talitha shuddered and backed away, yet she kept her eyes trained squarely on Brett. "Hello," she said without offering her hand.

Brett dropped his attempted handshake. "It's cool. Danielle and I we're going to make sure you're taken care of. You can consider me the big brother you never had."

Talitha shuddered again, still staring daggers at him. "I had brothers in the camps...." She let the sentence trail off, but she didn't need to finish the thought.

Brett stood fully upright, a stern look on his face. "Not that kind of brother. I swear to you. Nobody will lay a hand on you with me around,"

"Well, this is going to be fun," Danielle sneered as she edged in front of Brett. "Come on, kid, Let's get out of here."

"Thank you, Ms. Regan," Luster said as she handed her the Ziploc bag of important papers. "I can't tell you how nice and how rare it is to place someone in a good home. If you need anything, please don't hesitate to call me."

Danielle snatched the bag. "Yeah, I got it." She turned to Brett. "Can we please get out of here?" She hurried back through the halls, past the human debris in the lobby, and finally out into the fresh air and daylight. She looked to the sky. "God, I need a shower after that."

Behind her, Talitha let out a long, slow breath as the sun hit her face. She closed her eyes and looked up as well. "Hmm. The sun feels so good," she whispered. "I haven't been outside in days."

Brett nudged up next to Danielle. They both took a moment to watch the girl soak up the sun's rays before he turned to her. "All right, Captain, my Captain. What's our first move?"

Danielle studied Talitha as she basked in the sunlight. "I guess we take her shopping. Get her some clothes that fit."

"By all means. Got to get her out of that God ugly Baylor gear," Brett agreed. "Poor girl has been through enough without being subjected to that."

Danielle rolled her eyes. "You athletes are so weird."

"Hey, it's our culture."

"Just shut up and get in the car," Danielle responded. "And get the kid. Otherwise, she'll stand out here all day. "

"You got it, boss," he said. He turned to see that she was still standing, basking in the sun as the gentle breeze ruffled her golden hair. "Hey, Tal...Tal...Tally. It's time to roll, kid. We're going to take you shopping."

She let her arms drop to her side and began to shuffle forward. "It's Talitha," she said coldly. After a moment, she looked over at him with something that might have approached a grin. "But you can call me Tally if you want."

Brett fell in step beside her. "It's a deal then. So let me give you the lowdown on Danielle here. First thing, she drives like a bat out of hell, but she's good, so don't sweat it. Second, she's had a really hard go of things lately, so she's a little prickly sometimes. Don't take it personally if she gets on you a little bit." Talitha slipped him a glance out of the side of her eye. He instantly caught her drift. "I'm not saying it compares to whatever you've been through, but it's been a challenge. She's not in the best frame of mind right now."

Danielle reached the car first, unlocked it, and started the engine while the others climbed in. Talitha's eyes got wide as she settled into the black leather passenger seat. "Wow. What a nice car."

Danielle smirked. "You like? Check this out." With a push of a button, the top began to retract, letting the brilliant sunshine flood over them. "I think you might like this better."

"Oh yeah," Talitha muttered. "Wow."

Danielle looked over her shoulder at Brett, who was clearly amused at the childlike innocence Talitha displayed. "Watch this." She put the gas down while keeping her other foot on the brake. The back tires spun, throwing thick white smoke into the air. When she let off the brake, the Camaro fishtailed, then shot down the road. It threw Talitha back in her seat, and for a moment, she looked absolutely terrified, but the fear faded as she let out a whoop. Danielle tore through the parking lot and slid into a right turn but soon ran into the typical Austin gridlock. Talitha groaned as Danielle had to slow down.

"Yep," Brett said. "She's definitely your sister."

Danielle worked her way across town to one of the glittering new malls that had gone up in the years she had been on the run. "Ah, you're bringing her here?" Brett complained. "We're in Austin. Let's take her to some cool vintage stores and get her something unique."

Danielle and Talitha exchanged a quick glance. "Right now, let's just get some clothes, and we'll see what her style turns into later. We can get everything we need right here."

"If you insist. But we should take her by the Co-Op later so I can get her some Longhorns gear. You gotta at least give me that."

The mall proved to be another eye-opening experience for Talitha. Danielle noted with sadness how she eyed the other teenage girls that traveled in packs, all decked out in the latest fashions, sipping on iced coffees and speaking in code that only the other members of the group could fully understand. Talitha's initial joy faded, and she tried to disappear anytime they passed a gaggle of girls. Danielle pulled her in close and whispered in her ear. "Don't let these privileged little daddy's girls make you feel bad about yourself. "

"I'll try," she agreed.

The first place Danielle took her was to a spa, where she laid down the money for the works. She and Brett made small talk as Talitha was enveloped in the full luxury experience. The process took forever, but when it was over, Talitha had a stylish new haircut and her nails glittered with fresh teal paint. She wiggled her fingers at Danielle. "What do you think? It was the woman's idea. I couldn't pick a color."

"Do you like it?"

Talitha shrugged, looked down at her nails, and wiggled her fingers some more. "Yes, I do."

"Then they're perfect. Next, let's get you some new clothes."

Danielle steered her into an upscale boutique and helped her find a new outfit, then took her to the fitting rooms. Once she knew the clothes fit, she gathered the hand me down Baylor duds and handed them off to Brett. "Dispose of these, will ya?"

Brett could barely contain his joy. "My pleasure." She watched as he made a production of tossing the old clothes in the nearest trash can, then pretending to dust himself off as if he had been contaminated by touching them. He strutted back towards her. "Now that Baylor crap is in the trash, right where God intended it to be."

Danielle cocked her head to the side. "Isn't Baylor a Christian school?"

"So is Notre Dame, doesn't mean that they don't suck. Besides, Baylor is full of Baptists, and that is all I have to say about that."

"And how are Baptists different from all the others?"

Brett put his arm around her. "I'll explain it to you sometime. For now, just know that Baptists are like the weird branch of the family tree."

"Oh." She looked over at Brett and cracked a smile. "Then my whole family must be Baptist."

Brett's response was cut off by Talitha emerging from the dressing room, now looking every bit as stylish as the girls she had eyed with envy earlier. "Wow. All right. You look like a whole new person. I guess big sis here has better fashion sense than I thought."

Talitha looked down at her outfit curiously. "It's strange. How something as simple as changing clothes can make you feel so different."

"That may be true," Danielle stepped in. "But clothes don't define you." She waved a hand toward the front door that opened up into the mall. "Most of these kids have no idea who they are. Their entire self-image is tied to what somebody else tells them is cool."

Talitha thought it over for a moment, then nodded solemnly. "Got it."

"All right then. That's one outfit down. Now, all we gotta do is get you a crapload more. Come on, more stores to hit."

Danielle paid for the new clothes and then led them back out into the mail. They hit every store in the mall and exited most of them with something. All three were loaded down with bags as they finally left. The brilliant sunshine had faded, and a beautiful Austin sunset was taking shape as they crammed all the bags they could into the Camaro's tiny trunk.

After everyone piled back in, Danielle looked over her shoulder at Talitha. "So, I bet it's been a while since you've had a good meal, hasn't it?"

She answered with a firm "Yes, ma'am," but Danielle could see the hunger in her eyes.

"Any special diet or anything I need to know about?

Allergies or anything?"

She shook her head.

"All right." She turned to Brett. "Your call, Tex-Mex or bar-b-que?" Brett's immediate answer was bar-b-que, and they set off once again, this time for a historic eatery on the outskirts of Austin called Lonnie's. Talitha's eyes got wide as she caught her first glimpse of the massive array of meats cooking in the center of the room.

Brett nudged her in the side. "Kid, if you leave here hungry, then you did something wrong."

That wasn't a problem. Despite her slight frame, Talitha put down a surprising amount of food, eating like it was the first time. It wasn't her massive appetite that had Danielle's attention during dinner, though. Brett kept routinely checking his phone. Danielle had only made so much peace with cell phone culture, and letting it distract from dinner was still a major sin. He finally checked it once too often, and she called him on it.

"What the hell is going on?" She fixed Brett with a look that had crumbled several people over the years who had irritated her in some way. "I swear to God if you take the damn phone out again...."

Brett blushed as he clicked off his phone and slid it back into his pocket. "Sorry," he said, embarrassed but not intimidated in any way. "Just trying to keep up on some things."

"Is it job related?"

"No, not quite. More like a side project I have going, and I'm liking what I'm seeing."

Danielle cocked her head to the side and studied him intently. Again, he didn't break down when faced with one of her withering stares, which might have impressed her had she not been so annoyed. "You're checking on a game, aren't you?"

At her side, Talitha was holding a rib poised just a fraction of an inch from her mouth but had stopped eating to watch the exchange like she was casually observing a tennis match.

Brett hesitated slightly before breaking out a shit eating grin. "You got me. Yeah, I've been checking scores. But hey, cut me some slack. Even if I'm on vacation, I'm still a sports reporter. I need to stay abreast of what's going on."

"You're an anchor for a two-bit sports station in a tiny market in the middle of nowhere," Danielle fired back, but her inflection gave away the fact that she was needling him.

Brett took it in stride. "Two-bit? Man, we've stepped up in the world. When did we get the other bit?"

Danielle smirked, impressed by how he stood his ground when so many others had fallen apart when she had played the bad cop routine. "I'm being generous." She glanced over at Talitha. "If the bottomless pit here ever gets full, we'll head on back to the house."

Talitha answered by finally taking the bite she had paused, chewing a couple of times, and then mumbling, "Almost there." She had bar-b-que sauce smeared all over her face and suddenly looked more like a little girl than a teenager.

"Take your time," Brett said. "You deserve it. Eat as much as you can." He slid his eyes over to Danielle. "Big sis is picking up the check."

She finally did finish, and after she cleaned up, they piled in the car and headed back to Danielle's apartment, where it again took all three of them to carry Talitha's new wardrobe to her room. They dropped the bags just inside the door.

She turned to Talitha. "I only have two bedrooms, and Brett is in the second room. So I'll make up the couch for you tonight, and tomorrow we'll drive back up to the ranch where you can have your own room."

"Nope, nope, nope," Brett interrupted. "You can't put her on the couch. This is her home now. Come on."

"I don't mind," she said, sounding like she was hoping to avoid a fight. "I've slept in much worse places."

Brett looked at her kindly and gently put a hand on her arm, causing Talitha to pull back. "Whoa. Sorry." He pivoted to Danielle. "Sorry," he said again. "But I'm a guest here. This is her home. She should take the bedroom, and I'll take the couch. That's all I'm saying."

Danielle was watching Talitha, who had taken another long step away from Brett, trying to inch closer to her without making it obvious. She let out a heavy sigh. "That's fine. But I don't have any other sheets, and since you slept there last night, they smell like you, and I am not washing sheets at this time of night. I'm too tired."

Brett dismissed her concerns with a wave of his hand. "Oh, that's nothing. It was one night."

Talitha continued to ease toward Danielle. "They will still smell like a man. A strange man." She glanced up at Danielle. "I would rather sleep on the couch."

Brett looked hurt for the first time, though he tried to hide it. "All right. Whatever y'all say. If that's how it's going to be, I'm going to go ahead and turn in. It's been a long day." He didn't wait for an answer and instead shuttled off to the guest bedroom.

Talitha watched him go while chewing on her bottom lip. Once the bedroom door clicked shut behind him, she spoke. "I'm sorry if I hurt his feelings. It's just—"

"Hey, it's okay. I get it. He gets it." Danielle moved over to her black leather couch, a holdover from Steve's ownership that looked a lot nicer than it sat. "He's a strange man, and you have no reason to trust strange men. He'll be fine. He's a big boy." She sat and patted the cushion next to her. Talitha sat gingerly next to her and politely folded her hands in her lap. "He's an all right guy," Danielle confided. "He's had a couple of chances to come on to me and passed, so I think you'll be okay. He genuinely wants to help. But, we move at your pace, and if you don't feel secure around him, then that's fine. It'll take time."

Talitha fixed her gaze on the floor in front of her. "It's just... that's how it starts. A hand on your arm, then an arm around your shoulder. They're always so nice, and then...." She shuddered and swallowed hard. "I lived with it so long and just did the best I could. Tried to take the attention off the other girls. When we ran away, I thought that was behind us, but...." She shrugged, managing to look up at Danielle. Her eyes were wet with tears that wouldn't fall. "Life on the road for two women is hard. Mom was older and worn down, and sick. Sometimes people would offer to help us, but then they wanted something in return."

Danielle started to put her hand on Talitha's but thought better of it and pulled away. "Hey, really. You don't need to paint me a picture." She looked over her shoulder at her own bedroom and the California king bed that was calling her name. "If you would rather," she started, swinging her head back around. "You could sleep in there with me. It's a huge bed."

Talitha rubbed the tears out of her eyes, and when she spoke again she was more firm. "I'm fine with the couch."

"I've got a couple of spare pillows and a blanket in my room. I'll bring them out." She pointed to a closed door located equidistant from the bedroom doors. "That's the bathroom there. I'll get the couch ready while you change clothes."

She stood and trotted towards her room when Talitha called out to her. Danielle stopped and swiveled. Talitha was standing by the couch, still holding the fingers of her right hand in her left. "It wasn't just men. That's why I can't share a bed with you. Mother was the only one I could trust."

"Say no more," Danielle whispered.

When she got to the bedroom, Danielle gently closed the door and sat easily on the edge of her bed before letting out a long, slow breath. It was becoming clear that everything Danielle had imagined Talitha had gone through was actually underselling the truth. The baggage the girl was carrying was much heavier than she expected, and it was going to take a lot of effort to make this work. Though deep down she knew it would, Danielle was hoping that just giving her a safe place to stay and some nice things would make it all better. How was she possibly going to be able to help Talitha sort through all her emotional trauma when she couldn't even face her own?

She heard the bathroom door close, and almost immediately, the shower turned on. Danielle sprang into action, gathering what she could and going to the living room to make up the couch. With the shower still running, she padded quietly across the floor to the guest room and knocked.

"Yeah?"

She entered the dark room slowly, trying to fix his location. She felt for the end of the bed and sat down. She could feel his leg under the sheets pressing up against her. "She wasn't trying to hurt your feelings or anything."

"I know, Danielle. I'm not upset about that." Brett threw the covers off, grunted, and sat up. "When we came down here, I thought we were just coming to help an orphaned kid. All day long, the picture has gotten uglier and uglier. Man, the evil that men will do. It just pisses me off. I didn't think I should try to process it in front of her. Oh yeah, I'm so offended or whatever. She lived it."

Danielle, facing away from him, nodded in agreement. "Not just men," she muttered. "She told me that a few minutes ago."

"Jesus. What kind of camp was this?"

"It was a cult, Brett. One of those places you read about sometimes where a bunch of pervs carves out someplace out in the middle of nowhere to live out their sick fantasies while trying to convince people that they're some sort of fundamentalist Christian organization. Without even reading the file they put together, I can tell you exactly what happened."

"Hang on." Brett switched on the bedside table and sat up against the headboard. Danielle looked over her shoulder to see him shirtless, the sheets bunched up at his waist, and for a fleeting moment, other thoughts entered her head.

She turned away in order to push them aside. "Sean, her dad, had a predilection for young girls. I don't know how much he had embraced it when I knew him, but he made a run at me. That's what ended my relationship with Mom. She chose him over me."

He tried to offer a feeble condolence, but Danielle sloughed it off. "So people like that have a tendency to find one another. They're living up in the mountains in Utah or Idaho or something, somewhere where it's easy to get lost, and he finds some like-minded dudes. They decide to pack up their families and start a commune somewhere—or maybe it has already started, and he just joined up. He tells Mom that everything wrong with the world is because people have lost touch with God, and the modern church is more about singing songs than worship and convinces her that they're going to get back to the true roots of religion. Mom was a sucker for shit like that. Once he gets them out to one of these camps, they're stuck. At some point, Mom figures out what has happened, but it's not easy to get out once you're in. Then Sean gets his ass busted, and the other men take responsibility for them, and it gets harder."

"Sounds like a movie," he said. "That poor kid. I'm amazed she can even function."

Danielle looked back over her shoulder, and this time she was all business. "We don't know that she can."

CHAPTER FOURTEEN

Danielle awoke the next morning to the smell of bacon cooking and coffee brewing and muffled music bleeding into her room. She was confused as she got out of bed, her hair a tousled mess atop her head. After finishing her conversation with Brett the night before, she had collapsed into a deep sleep and awoke in a thick mental fog.

She stepped out of her room and was greeted by the sight of Brett and Talitha preparing a quick breakfast while Willie Nelson's voice materialized out of somewhere unseen. She had to shake her head to make sense of it all. The vision of the young girl scuttling around her kitchen was proof that the prior two days hadn't been some sort of strange fever dream.

Brett noticed her shuffling across the room and called out to her. "Hey, good morning, sleepy head. You look like you just went ten rounds with a rabid mountain lion."

"I'm not a morning person," she mumbled. "What's going on?"

"I couldn't sleep," Talitha said as she whirred around the kitchen. "So I thought I would make breakfast. I hope it's okay. I haven't been able to cook in an actual kitchen in a while."

"I'm sure it's fine," she grumbled as she plopped down at her tiny kitchen table. Ordinarily, she would have passed on the bacon, as it appeared underdone, but given Talitha's obvious nervousness and possible delicate nature, she made the best of it. As she gnawed on a piece, she turned to Brett. "What is this shit you're playing?"

Brett, sitting to her left, plucked his phone off the table next to him and waved it in the air. "Willie Nelson. You should know that."

To Danielle's right, Talitha chirped in. "Brett was telling me that if there was a Mount Rushmore of Texas music, he would be on it. He said that Willie is an essential part of beginning my musical journey. So who would the others be?" Talitha asked, sounding genuinely interested.

"Good question. Willie is on there, and George Strait definitely. Then probably SRV — that's Stevie Ray Vaughn — and the last one is probably —"

"Me." Danielle smirked before turning back to Brett. "I've gotta be on your Mount Rushmore, right?"

Brett looked her dead in the eye and, without hesitation, said, "No." The firmness of his answer took Danielle by surprise. "There was a time when I think you might have been," he continued, either unaware or unconcerned by Danielle's reaction. "But then you just disappeared, and people forgot about you. Can't be on Mount Rushmore if people forget about you."

Danielle suddenly felt sick, and it wasn't from the undercooked bacon. She pushed away from the table violently. "Hurry up and eat. I want to get back on the road as soon as possible." Neither of them tried to stop her as she stomped back to her room.

She got dressed in a hurry, trying not to think too much about the conversation but still seeing Brett's face as he calmly told her she was a nobody. She knew it shouldn't have stung as much as it did, but she was hurt nonetheless.

It took much longer than she wished, but finally, everyone was ready to hit the road for the return trip to Brett's ranch. The ride down the elevator was silent and uncomfortable. Danielle breathed deep and loud, doing her best to keep her seething rage contained. Once the elevator doors opened and they started for the car, Brett ambled up beside her.

"I didn't mean to hurt your feelings about the Mount Rushmore thing."

"You didn't hurt my feelings," she snarled. "I love being told that I'm a nobody. Makes me feel good."

"I wasn't saying you're a nobody. I was just being honest."

"Well, Brett, how about you honestly kiss my ass?" She called to Talitha, who had walked ahead. "Kid, you got shotgun. Brett's going to take the backseat."

"I was going to suggest that anyway," he pouted.

"Good for you."

They stuffed Talitha's new wardrobe, still in shopping bags, in the trunk and piled in the car. With a quick check of his handy dandy phone, Brett also informed her that they would be driving through rain and possible thunderstorms, which put an end to the idea of making the drive with the top down.

"So, where are we going?" Talitha asked as Danielle navigated Austin's mid-morning traffic nightmare, which was actually better than trying to beat the early morning crunch.

"My ranch," Brett chimed in from the backseat. He was stretched across the entire backseat, earbuds inserted into his ears, but no music pumping through them yet. "I got a spread up in the panhandle, about seven hours from here. Great place, plenty of room. I think you'll like it."

"Oh," she said politely, but Danielle noticed her wringing her hands. She reached across the cramped confines of the Camaro and gave Talitha a nudge. "Don't sweat it. It is a nice place, not as far off the beaten path as you might think, and lots of fun things to do. Trust me, he won't do anything to you, especially not with me around."

That seemed to comfort her some. By the time they reached Belton, Brett was snoring in the back. Danielle was aware that Talitha had been watching her for some time, but she finally worked up the courage to speak. "You seemed really upset about the Mount Rushmore thing earlier."

Danielle tried to play it off. "That was stupid. Not sure why I got my feelings hurt about that." She glanced over her shoulder at him, some sort of muted music escaping his earbuds. "I actually respect the fact that he told me the truth. Didn't bat an eye. It's pretty impressive."

"It still hurt you."

"Yeah, it did," Danielle admitted. She stared straight ahead, but her mind was elsewhere. "When I was younger, I told myself that I didn't care about how people viewed me, but that was easy to do when every record I released was hitting the charts. I always kind of thought I had carved out my place in the music world. But over the last couple of years, I've come to see that I didn't, and it does bother me. I guess it's just arrogance and ego, but I thought I was one of the greats, you know?" Talitha just nodded, and Danielle chewed the thought over in her mind. "Had I known that I would have been so easily forgotten, I'm not sure I would have left."

"Brett said you disappeared for a while. I know Mother tried to find you once before but said you were gone. Where did you go? What did you do?"

"That's a long story," Danielle said, tightening her grip on the steering wheel.

"Didn't Brett say this was a seven hour drive?" Danielle confirmed that it was. "Seems like a perfect time for long stories. I'll tell you mine if you tell me yours."

"I've heard plenty enough of yours. But you want mine? What the hell? My therapist says I need to talk about these things anyway. So how far back do you want me to go?"

Talitha squirmed in her seat to get comfy and gave Danielle a warm grin. "Start at the beginning."

"Okay, but I warn you. It's not all a happy story. Gets pretty dark at times." Talitha stared at her with unblinking eyes. "Well, it was dark for me anyway."

Danielle laid the whole story out for her as they drove, holding nothing back. Along the way, she came to a few points in the story where she had to admit that perhaps she hadn't made the best decisions. The picture began to form in Danielle's mind of how others were seeing her, and it all began to make a little more sense for her. They were well past Waco and steaming towards Dallas by the time she reached the end of the tale.

"You've had a fascinating life," Talitha said. "I hope I can live a life as interesting as yours."

"Hope you live a better one," Danielle answered. "Hope that all your stormy seas are behind you. Of course, coming from where you are, I don't suppose what I've gone through seems to be anywhere as bad as it does to me."

Talitha looked out the window at the scenery flying by. "It all depends, I guess. If you hadn't stood up to Mother that day in your kitchen, maybe they would have eventually scooped you up and taken you into the mountains. We might have grown up together, and you might have gone through the same things. You never can tell."

"Never thought about it like that."

"You wouldn't. You were strong enough to resist. I never did." Talitha sank back into her seat with the declaration, growing suddenly silent.

After a few miles of uncomfortable silence, Danielle tapped her on the shoulder. "Don't feel bad that you didn't fight back. You were just a kid."

"So were you," Talitha responded.

"I was hardly a kid. I was sixteen and, all modesty aside here, built like a brick shithouse." She giggled at the term, which Danielle herself never quite understood. She caught Talitha glaring at her and realized the giggle was out of place. "What I mean is, I was an athlete. I worked out constantly. I was all muscle. Honestly, if Sean...your dad...hadn't caught me off guard, I would have pulverized the little runt. But even with all of that, when he started in on me, I froze. I was in shock. You just don't expect that."

Talitha made a noise and looked away, staring out the window silently. Danielle turned her attention back to the road. After several minutes, Talitha spoke again, her eyes still peeled on the passing scenery. "I was eight the first time. It was in the basement of our church."

"I really don't want...."

Talitha looked over at her with a seriousness Danielle had not witnessed before. "I know you don't, and I believe you, but I think you need to hear this." She looked straight ahead and swallowed hard. "Father was late picking me up from a lock in, and I was the last kid there. It was just me and the pastor. They had this big game room type area down there, and I was playing around, not paying attention to anything."

She paused, took a deep breath, and closed her eyes. Danielle felt her skin crawling, the picture already forming in her mind. "I get the point."

She continued unabated. "When he got there, the pastor took him aside, and they whispered about something. I noticed it then, but I didn't think anything about it. Then the pastor calls me over to him and tells me to lay on the couch, and starts telling me that Father needs my help with something. That God has called him to purpose, and only I can help him."

Danielle glanced a sideways glance and caught unchecked tears making their way down her sister's cheek. She was deep in the memory now, and there was no pulling her out of it.

"I don't think he wanted to at first. He resisted, but the pastor kept telling him it was God's will. By the time I realized what was going on, it was too late."

Danielle tightened her hands around the steering wheel. "That's bullshit," she spat. She caught Talitha's surprised look. "If he didn't want to, he wouldn't have. A real man would have kicked that pastor's ass, church or no church."

"Is that your answer to every problem, violence?"

This time Danielle looked hard at the younger girl. "Yeah, I guess so." She let her own mind wander back. "I guess that's wrong, but I'll tell you something. That day in the kitchen, when she picked your dad over me, and I wrapped my hands around her throat, this woman who had treated me so terribly, who had scared me to death. I looked her dead in the eye, and she just crumbled. She wilted right in front of my eyes, and I felt so powerful at that moment. I swore I'd never let someone get the best of me again, and I damn well haven't."

Talitha again made a humming noise as she thought about it. "But look at where that path has led you."

The point hit too close to the mark, and Danielle felt herself get defensive. She couldn't help herself. "And sitting back and taking it did you so well." Talitha's eyes got wide with shock, and she turned away. Danielle looked the other way, instantly regretting her statement but refusing to take it back.

After another elongated silence, Talitha picked up her story as if nothing had happened. "Not long after that, Father packed us up and moved us to the first camp, and everything went downhill." She paused for effect, waiting for Danielle to look over at her. "As I got older, I started volunteering, hoping to save some of the younger kids in camp from the same thing." She shrugged. "Problem was, everybody had their own preference. I aged out of one group's desires and right into another's. But I did try as best I could."

Danielle couldn't hold Talitha's steely gaze and looked away. She continued.

"After Father got arrested, things got a lot worse for both of us. Finally, Mother decided we had to leave, no matter what."

Danielle had braced herself for righteous fury or maybe sorrowful tears, but instead, Talitha just seemed to blow off her previous comment, so Danielle pressed on. "How did y'all get away?"

"It's not some big story," Talitha said with a shrug. "We waited until the leaders decided to switch camps. They piled a bunch of us on this old school bus. On the drive, we pulled over at a truck stop for everyone to use the bathroom. Mother and I walked toward the bathroom, circled around the back of the building, climbed in the back of a flatbed truck, and waited for it to drive away. We didn't know where we would wind up, but we knew it couldn't be worse. Then we started making our way down here, and...I won't say that life on the road was worse, but we both had to do things we weren't proud of. But Mother was sick and knew she had to get me out of there."

"That's just insane. It's 2010, and people are living like this, and nobody cares?"

"They don't advertise it," she said with a smirk. "People have a tendency to not want to look too closely at anything that disturbs them. Can't say I blame them."

"Well, kid. I'll give you credit for surviving it. You're stronger than you know.

"It wasn't strength," Talitha said. Her voice took a cool, confident tone. "It was faith. I had faith that I would be delivered. Faith in Mother, faith in you, even though I had never met you. Faith is what got me through. Faith and God."

Danielle made no attempt to hide her revulsion. "God? God had nothing to do with it," she sneered. "What kind of God would have left you in that situation? Or all the other kids? Why would He tolerate the things men do in His name?" She put up a finger to silence the rebuttal she knew was coming. "Don't give me that, 'God's got a plan' bullshit, either. I used to talk to God. I used to believe. But every time I needed Him, God let me down. Hell, I even begged him to kill me, called him out, and nothing."

"If he had, you wouldn't have been there for me, and where would I be now?"

Again, Talitha looked her in the eye, and Danielle blinked first. "Well...you don't know me that well yet. I ain't no great shakes, kid," she said, exaggerating her West Texas drawl. She meant it to be funny. Talitha didn't laugh.

"Still better than where I was."

Danielle looked away. As she drove, Danielle wondered if this was how it would always be with Talitha. Would the horrors of her childhood always be a tool she could use to one up her big sister? It was annoying and frustrating. With the conversation over, she reached for the stereo controls. "How about some music instead? Makes the drive seem shorter."

The rest of the drive was uneventful, and eventually, Brett woke up to take the pressure off her by entertaining Talitha with his baseball stories. Talitha responded with some cute stories of growing up in the mountains. She'd actually had a normal childhood at one time, and it sounded as if Dorothy Regan had finally discovered her maternal instincts. At least there were no stories that involved getting slapped for playing records.

The entire gang was running on fumes by the time they

pulled into Amarillo. Brett suggested that they stop for an early dinner, but Danielle wanted to get home, so they pressed on, grabbing some pizza and Cokes on the way out of town.

Upon arriving, Brett joyfully took Talitha on a tour of the grounds, leaving Danielle to unpack the bags. She stood in Brett's living room, surrounded by all his dark furniture and manly decorating, and realized that this place already felt more like home to her than her sterile Austin apartment did. She was absolutely sure that was not a good thing.

With Brett still keeping Talitha distracted, Danielle slunk off to the studio. The videos they had been making were doing more good for Danielle than any of Franklin Ridgeway's therapy sessions, but she now had a whole bundle of new feelings she needed to sort through. After a quick setup, she flicked the camera on.

"Hey there. I know it's been a few days since I've posted anything, but there's been some heavy stuff going on. Maybe I'll tell you about it someday. I've gotta figure everything out before I can start telling y'all about it. So let's see." She looked down at her fingers on the fretboard of the acoustic. She sat on the stool, fingers poised, but nothing would come out. "Guess it's not happening tonight." She shut everything down. Brett was still giving Talitha the grand tour, so Danielle quietly snuck off to her room, where she fell asleep the second her head hit the pillow.

CHAPTER FIFTEEN

Danielle woke up the next afternoon and instantly chastised herself for sleeping so late. She threw on an oversized T-shirt and some athletic shorts, brushed her teeth and hair, and padded into the living room to find Talitha buzzing about the kitchen. She was softly singing a song that Danielle recognized but couldn't quite place.

"Hey, what are you doing?"

Talitha jumped. "Oh goodness. You scared me." Her fair cheeks instantly turned bright red. "I was thinking I would bake some cookies. I'm good at baking."

Danielle stretched, trying to get her body to wake up. "Really? That's cool. Where's Brett?"

"He's in the garage fiddling with his boat. He said this weekend he'd take us to the lake. Doesn't that sound like fun?" Talitha's excitement shone through, and it made her glow. Danielle couldn't believe what a difference just a couple of days had made.

"Well, you get back to your baking. I'm going to go chat with the man of the house."

"Okay," she said joyously.

As Danielle started for the garage, Talitha started singing again, and this time Danielle instantly recognized the song. It was "Blessed Poison," only she wasn't singing it right. It was too slow. She had only played it that way once.

"Where did you hear that?"

Talitha jumped again. "What?"

"That song. Where did you hear that song?"

Talitha's face went slack, and it dawned on Danielle that

she probably thought she'd made some sort of terrible error. But Danielle was focused on other things. "Um, Brett played it for me last night. It's one of yours, isn't it?"

"Yeah, it's one of mine," she hissed. "How did he play it for you? On his computer?"

"Um...YouTube?"

"I knew it." She stormed towards the garage and flung the door open. Brett was couched in the boat, the engine cover off. He had a smear of grease across his forehead. "You asshole."

Brett let the crescent wrench he was holding go, and it clambered to the deck of the boat. "What? What are you talking about?"

"You posted that, didn't you? I expressly told you not to. You told me you deleted it. You lying sack of shit."

"I didn't lie." He struggled to his feet.

"Save your bullshit," Danielle snapped. "I can't believe I trusted you. I must be losing my mind." She stormed out of the garage with Brett desperately scrambling out of the boat to catch up.

"Wait, Danielle. Just listen to me." He finally caught up to her in the living room and spun her around by her arm. Behind them, Talitha stood shocked in the kitchen, cradling a mixing bowl in the crook of her arm. "Would you just wait a minute?"

"Why, so you can spin some crock of shit? Why would I believe anything you say to me now?"

Brett sighed and wiped at his sweaty brow. "Why don't you just shut up for half a second and let me tell you what happened? I think you owe me that much."

"I don't owe you anything," she said, knowing that was a lie.

"Come. Sit." Brett took Danielle by the elbow and gently led her to the couch. He retrieved his laptop from the table beside his recliner and brought it to her. "I showed you that I deleted the file. That wasn't a lie. I deleted it from the memory stick." He licked his lips nervously. Danielle was staring holes in the side of his head. "But, I had already saved the files on my hard drive, and I didn't delete that file." Danielle started to protest, but he silenced her with a finger. "Not a lie. Just not the complete truth. Yes, it's splitting hairs but...."

"But what?"

Brett shifted so he could look at Danielle straight on. "You agreed to come up here and do this so I could help you. I'm the one who knows about all of this. I expected you to trust my judgment. That performance is exactly what we, what you, needed. It sucks that you wouldn't trust my judgment."

"It's my song. I should get to decide what gets done with it. I'm the artist. You should do what I tell you to."

Brett shrugged. "Well, it was filmed on my camera, with my guitar, in my house, so I think that entitles me to some say on it." Danielle smirked, and Brett again cut her off. "I don't want to get into some sort of debate on legal ownership of the performance. The point is that this song is exactly what I was going for, and you wouldn't let me use it. So, I honored your wish, and I posted some of the other songs you recorded, and nothing really happened. You weren't getting many views or likes—nobody seemed interested. Then I posted 'Poison,' and everything changed. Views shot through the roof."

"When did you do this?" Danielle said, her anger beginning to dissipate.

"Right before we left for Austin," Brett admitted. "And by the next day, things were happening. Once word got out, once people started sharing this, it blew up."

"That night at the restaurant, you weren't checking scores, were you?"

Brett gave her a lopsided grin. "No, I wasn't. I was checking the stats on the video." He laid a hand on her knee and leaned in close. "Danielle, you touched people with that video. You did, not me. Look."

He backed off and tilted the computer so she could see the screen. "Read some of these comments." Talitha had crept up closer, watching the scene play out. He started reading for her. "'Thank you so much for sharing this. I've always loved this song, but now that I know the story behind the song, it means so much more.'" He scrolled down. "'I know what you're talking about. I grew up in an abusive home and have seen those same things in me, and it terrifies me. I feel so much better knowing I'm not the only one.'" He found another. "'Such a delight to see true musicianship in this time of computer programmed, generic pop garbage. I had forgotten what a wonderful artist you are.'" Brett kept scrolling. "It goes on and on. This is all you. I just did what I did to get you out of your own way."

Danielle gently took the computer from him and read through the comments herself. "Wow," she muttered. "I had no idea."

Again Brett laid his hand on her leg. "If you would just trust me, we can do this. *You* can still do this. Will you trust me?"

Danielle nodded her head while she read through the comments. "Um. Yeah." She finally handed the computer back. "I...I'm sorry. I guess you were right. It's just so weird."

"What's weird?"

Danielle stood and walked away. "Letting people in." She turned and looked at both Brett and Talitha in turn. "Letting people get close to me usually doesn't end well. It usually ends in pain."

Talitha spoke up first. "Isn't pain better than nothing? Isn't having people around better than being alone?"

"Yeah, I don't know about that," she said. "I'm going to go...lay down or something. I need to think."

She beat a quick retreat, but the walls of her room weren't enough to keep out what she had seen. The comments kept reverberating in her mind. She had touched people, lots of people. People were still out there and willing to listen. Somewhere along the line, she wondered if Steve had seen it yet.

***

Days passed, and the three fell into a comfortable routine. Brett hired a friend to come to the house and work with Talitha during the day, trying to gauge her level of education and getting her ready to return to school. They discovered that she was extremely intelligent, but there were serious gaps in her education. She took to the sessions passionately, gobbling up any and all knowledge she could gain.

Danielle spent most of the days in the makeshift studio, learning to make herself vulnerable.

Once she decided to lean into the idea, Danielle quickly upgraded the equipment and decided to start using a mixing console so she could make the arrangements more complex. In the evenings, Brett taught her how to use the editing software so she could post the videos herself.

Tiring of just redoing her old songs, Danielle began to throw out newer songs. One in particular, "Austin Sunsets," struck a chord with the public and soon began to rival "Blessed Poison" for views and likes. "Austin Sunsets" was the closest Danielle had ever come to a true love song, saved only by the searing blues solo in the ride out. Brett told her it reminded him of early seventies Rolling Stones songs with Mick Taylor on lead guitar. Which sent Danielle to the Internet to research Mick Taylor.

Danielle's loneliness shone through in songs such as "Kill the Lights," a mid-tempo rocker where she sang of her desperate attempts to reclaim her lost fame, and "Chase the Highway," a bluesy piece about her life in exile.

They began spending their weekends at the lake, where Brett taught her how to pilot the speedboat, then instantly regretted it. Speed always brought out Danielle's daredevil, and now, between the boat and the motorcycles, she had plenty of opportunities to indulge the beast.

Talitha took to outdoor life. Danielle taught her to swim, and Brett taught her to fish. Spending so much time in the sun, her hair turned near white while she bronzed in the same way Danielle used to do in her younger days. The more time they spent together, the more Danielle began to see herself in the girl.

Two months passed. Danielle resumed her sessions with Ridgeway via video, and he remarked about how the time away seemed to be helping. He assured her that if she could avoid further incidents, he would report the successful completion of his program to the judge. Everything was coming together.

Then Shannon called.

Danielle was sitting in bed, working on a new song, when the phone buzzed on the nightstand. She picked it up hesitantly, suddenly feeling like the air around her had gotten heavy. "Hello."

"Hiya, gorgeous, long time no speak."

Danielle pushed the guitar off her lap and stretched her legs out in front of her. "Well, we've both been pretty busy. How's the tour going?"

"Fabulous. After Canada, we hopped over to Europe for a bit and returned to my old stomping grounds, if you will, and it was fantastic. The crowds were amazing. Steve tells me you never went overseas?"

"Nope, I was strictly a North American artist. Had some chances to go, but you know how I feel about flying. You can't drive to London."

"Well, you're missing out. It was fantastic. I could stay on the road forever, but Steve is starting to harp about recording a new album. He wants me to do it on my own, but I'm not so sure. I think I need you with me."

"No, you don't," Danielle assured her. "You can stand on your own two feet. Besides, I'm blacklisted, remember. If you try to bring me in and the suits will throw a fit. Going to have to fly solo."

"Maybe not," Shannon said with a hint of teasing in her voice. "I've been thinking about that. And by the way, congrats on the YouTube thing. That was a great idea. I've been watching your videos, and they are amazing. Steve watches, too, though he tries not to let me know. It's helping rehabilitate your image. Now I think I can help you with the next step."

Danielle sat up straighter. "What next step?"

Shannon gave her a throaty life that dripped with sex. It was no wonder that Shannon could have anyone she wanted with a snap of her fingers. Almost anyone. "I'm going to get you back on the stage."

"And how are you going to do that?"

"We're heading back your way. There was a show in Colorado Springs that got snowed out earlier in the spring, and we're going to play a make-up show there on Saturday. Steve's arranged to have a camera crew there to film it for a possible DVD release. And I'm going to sneak you into the show."

Danielle's temporary interest caved, and she collapsed back on the bed. "Never happen. Steve won't let me within ten miles of you."

"No. But he's already approved a backstage pass for Taylor Hale, my best friend from high school. He's even put her on the list so she can come up to my room at the hotel. It's all been set up...Taylor."

"You've got to be shitting me."

"I shit you not," Shannon responded. She was quite proud of herself. "So this is what you're going to do. You're going to go get some wild clothes, crazy stuff — stuff that Danielle would never wear — and some makeup and hair dye, and you're going to make yourself unrecognizable. I've told Steve that you're a fashion maven that loves to dress up in crazy costumes, so he'll be expecting it. You'll meet us in Colorado Springs and come up to my room, where you'll stay until showtime. At the show, you'll stand just offstage and wait for my cue, then run out on stage, grab a guitar, and we'll just start playing. It'll be so fast no one will see it coming. By the time Steve or anyone else realizes it, you'll be playing, and security won't dare come on stage during a performance to get you. And it'll be on video."

Danielle breathed out as she thought about it. "A lot of things could go wrong."

"Don't think that way. Thinking that way is how things go wrong. Be confident, have faith. Have faith in me. I've been setting this up for weeks now, ever since I heard about the make-up show. I've been talking about you...Taylor, that is...for weeks. Everybody is expecting you. All you have to do is not be Danielle for about thirty-six hours. You did it for six years. It should be easy."

"That was different. No one was looking for Danielle or expecting her. The second Steve sees me, he's going to know, disguise or not."

"Steve is going to be busy with the filming and everything. I've got a handler who takes care of my needs. She doesn't know you. With any luck, Steve won't even see you, not until it's too late anyway."

Danielle felt the stirring in her soul. The idea of being on stage again as herself, not as some wannabe. When she closed her eyes, she could see the crowd and hear them chanting her name. She hadn't trusted Brett, and he had been right—maybe Shannon was too.

"I can tell by your silence that you're thinking about it. Come on, Dani. We've never gotten to share the stage together like we were supposed to. The world owes us this one—owes you this one. Come on, let's do it."

She flashed on Talitha and Brett. Despite all their time together, Talitha was still reluctant to spend time with Brett without her present. She couldn't leave her. Then again, she was confident Brett wouldn't do anything to her, and maybe the best treatment for Talitha was to throw her in the deep end and make her swim. Nobody had ever treated her with kid gloves, so why should Danielle be any different?

"Come on, Danielle. You know you want to say yes. Just do it."

Danielle's internal struggle continued for only a few more moments. Danielle, the performer, wanted out. Playing house with Brett was fine, and the YouTube videos helped, but she longed to be *Danielle* again. "All right, I'll do it. But I'm going to have to move fast. I'll have to leave early Friday, so I've only got three days."

"I'm on it. I'm going to email some things. I've done some sketches to give you an idea of how to dress and lists of some local stores that have what you'll need."

"Local to where?"

"Austin, of course. Silly. Where else?"

"I haven't been to Austin in weeks, remember? I came up here to Brett's ranch? I sent the email about getting cut up and buried somewhere on the property?"

"Oh yeah. I do remember that." She paused a heartbeat. "So you're still shacking up with the athlete, huh? Have you let him step into your batter's box yet?"

"It's not like that. We're friends. He's helping me figure things out."

Shannon's disapproval was clear. "Oh, come on, Dani. Your vagina must look like a haunted house by now. All full of cobwebs and spiders and stuff. You need to let that boy clean you out. Unless…." Shannon's voice dropped an octave. "You're saving that up for our reunion? I would be more than happy to do the job."

Danielle groaned. "Jesus. Are you ever going to give up on that?"

"Nope," she answered. "I'll break you down sooner or later. No one can resist me when I set my mind to it. The fact that you've held out this long is a tribute to your willpower. But I will convert you."

"You're dreaming. Send me the list so I can start tracking things down. I'll see you Friday. You better be right about all this." If she was going to do this, she would tackle it with the seriousness of a military operation. "Because if you're wrong, it'll destroy whatever chance I have left. I'm putting myself in your hands here."

"It's a short trip from my hands to my arms," Shannon teased.

"Three days," Danielle shot back. "Be ready."

She hung up, wanting no more of Shannon's flirting. For a long while, she had basked in Shannon's attention, even egged it on. Though she had no interest in a same sex relationship, Shannon made her feel desirable and wanted, and the ego boost was helpful. Now she found it irritating. She thought instead of Brett, and the night on the patio when he had thrown the prom for her, the night she almost let him in her bed and wondered if she hadn't made a mistake. If the police hadn't come the next morning and things had continued on their course, she might have let him. Danielle sat back and wondered if she'd blown the opportunity.

She daydreamed, imagining a scenario in which Brett would indeed sweep her off her feet. The type of scenario you'd see in sappy movies. Maybe a twilight picnic on the mesa while the colors of the sunset danced in the sky above them. He would lay her down gently the way Kyle used to do....

The stray thought of Kyle snapped her awake. Why was she even considering such a thing? The only man she would ever love was gone. How could she let anyone else take his place? Besides, she had more important things to worry about. Shannon, annoying or not, had laid out a path for her. She couldn't let anyone distract her now.

Danielle dressed quickly and snapped her car keys up. In the living room, Talitha was laying on the couch, reading a book. Brett was on his computer, prepping for the newscast that night. They both looked up when she walked into the room. Danielle twirled her keys on her finger. "I've gotta run into town and grab a few things. I'll be back later. Don't hold dinner for me. I don't know how long this will take."

Talitha tossed the book aside and jumped up. "I'll come with you."

Danielle put out her hand. "Not this time, kid. I need to do this alone." Talitha's eyes darted to where Brett sat. Danielle knew what she was thinking. "I'm just going to town. You'll be fine." She leaned in close and whispered in Talitha's ear. "He's not going to touch you." She gave Talitha a playful slap on the arm and pulled away. "Don't worry. I'll be back soon." Danielle caught just a glimpse of Talitha frowning at her, looking like a scolded puppy, before she turned away. "See ya in a bit." She hustled out of the house and nearly ran to the car, fearing her sister would follow her out. She didn't, and soon Danielle was on the highway speeding toward Amarillo.

Speeding toward her future.

CHAPTER SIXTEEN

Danielle's obsessive side took over. She neglected the YouTube videos, much to Brett's dismay. She spent all the time she could practicing with the make-up and working with the outfits she bought, coming up with different looks and trying hard to make Danielle Regan disappear.

It had been easy to disappear when she left Austin seven years earlier. No one was looking for her. All it took was a different haircut and a dye job. The ethereal quality of being a celebrity was both a blessing and a curse. Drop off the radar for just a bit too long, and a new crop of fresh faced starlets popped up, and you were forgotten.

This would be different because they would be looking for her. Shannon had even told her that in the early days of the tour, security had been told to double check any unusually tall women. Steve was convinced that Danielle would try something crazy— something like crashing the stage during a concert. Though by now, the edge was sure to be off, Steve would be there, and no one knew her better than Steve. If she didn't do this just right, he would see right through her.

Danielle realized early on that the thrill was driving her as much as the possible payoff. Living the life domestic with Brett was growing old fast. He was a nice guy but hardly exciting, and she could only take so many bike rides and trips to the lake.

Talitha knew something was up. Danielle could see it in her eyes every time Danielle excused herself to her room. Brett probably suspected too. Neither pressed her, which was for the best. When she set her mind on something, Danielle's normal responses to being pushed were considerably unkind.

Thursday was the worst day of all, just hours from leaving. The plan was laid out, and the look was pre-chosen. She had even worked on her voice to try and disguise her West Texas drawl as much as possible. She only needed the clock to hurry the hell up.

They ate dinner before Brett went off to film the ten o'clock newscast, and Danielle quickly excused herself as well. She planned to sleep early so she could wake up and be gone before sunrise. The drive to Colorado Springs was roughly five hours if she drove the speed limit, which wouldn't happen. She planned to be there well before lunch.

She double checked her bags and stowed them in the closet. She would not be taking any of her equipment. There was no way to smuggle it, and it was a dead giveaway. Instead, Shannon promised a guitar would be available. Her combination of anxiety and anticipation was like the return of an old friend, a reminder that she was, in fact, still alive.

Then Danielle had nothing to do but lay awake in the dark and pray for sleep that didn't want to come. Just as she began to feel it tugging at the corners of her mind, the screen on her cell phone lit up the tiny room. Squinty from the sudden brightness, Danielle fumbled around for it. Shannon had texted her.

All set up in Colorado Springs. Hilton West, room 421. We have the entire floor. Security at the elevator and stairwell. When you get here, text Lucas. Identify yourself as my friend Taylor, and he will come to get you and get you past security. Can't wait to see you! Be careful.

She ended the Tweet with Lucas, the Roadie's number. Danielle put it in her phone and went over the plan one more time. On the night of the show, she would stand backstage and slowly work her way to the edge. Shannon assured her that a guitar would be placed just offstage, tuned, hooked up, and available. Toward the end of the show, Shannon would stop to talk to the audience, and that was when Danielle would grab Shannon's guitar and dart onto the stage. Security was always more focused on threats coming from the audience and wouldn't be ready for her. Once she was on stage, it was over. Shannon was convinced that security would not dare follow her onto the stage, especially once the star of the show embraced her. She only needed a few seconds.

She visualized it all in her head, over and over again, and then suddenly, her alarm was going off. Danielle hadn't even realized she'd fallen asleep. Time to move. Being as quiet as possible, she made her way to the bathroom and took care of the basics. She threw on some black tights and a loose T-shirt and threw her hair into a ponytail before killing the bathroom light. In the dark, she snatched her keys and phone from the nightstand and retrieved her bags from the closet. She cracked the bedroom door and found the house dark in the predawn.

Danielle crept into the hall and gently pulled the door closed. She had toyed with the idea of leaving a note for Brett and Talitha but decided against it. She would explain everything when it was over. With a garment bag in one hand and a duffle bag over her shoulder, Danielle tiptoed through the house, thankful she had spent enough time here to memorize the layout.

She was halfway through the living room when the whisper came from the couch. "Where you going, sis?"

Danielle froze, a breath caught in her throat. She let out a jagged breath to calm her nerves. "I got something I gotta go do."

"At five in the morning?"

"Gotta get an early start."

Talitha paused. "You don't have to sneak out. All you have to do is tell me this isn't working out, and I will leave. It's clear you don't want me around."

Talitha's words struck a nerve. She could hear the bitter disappointment in Talitha's voice. She knew the tone well. "This isn't about you," Danielle sneered. "This is about me. Something I have to do. Things will be better once I get back. *I'll* be better once I get back."

"How long will you be gone?"

"Just a couple of days. The time will fly by. I'll be back sometime Sunday, and I'll explain everything, and you'll see."

"And in the meantime, you leave me alone in the house with a man I hardly know, in a house several miles away from anything. You're okay with that?"

Danielle turned. The sky outside was slowly beginning to lighten, and Danielle could make out Talitha's silhouette on the couch. "Brett's not going to hurt you. We've been here for weeks. I can't believe you still don't trust him."

"He hasn't been alone with me for an extended period of time. If I couldn't trust my own father, why would you think I could trust him?"

Danielle's shoulders slumped. "Because not every man is a pervert. That's why. Now I'm wasting time. I've gotta go. I'll be back Sunday. I promise."

She shuffled on to the door, but she could hear Talitha get up off the couch and heard her bare feet padding behind. Danielle made it to the door and opened it up. As she stepped into the cool morning air, she looked over her shoulder to see Talitha standing behind her. She was haggard and disheveled. Her tired eyes caught Danielle's.

"I don't think your promises mean very much."

Danielle stared into those icy blue eyes without flinching, held the gaze, and then shrugged. "If that's what you think. Personally, I think I've done pretty good lately. I'm sorry my life can't completely revolve around you." She didn't wait for a response, whirling and pulling the door shut behind her.

Walking to the car, Danielle felt the treason of her conscience tugging at her, but this was no time to roll over. Talitha was going to have to toughen up someday. There was no time like the present.

Once she was on the highway, Danielle reached across and dug a CD out of the glove box and put it in. The CD was *The Fairie Meets the Fury*, the CD she and Shannon had cut the year before, the one they were supposed to have toured behind together. Since the big fight, Danielle had refused to listen to any of the songs, but now she needed to refamiliarize herself with them.

Early in Danielle's touring career, she had tired of playing the same set night after night, so she and Steve had come up with a new way. Instead of one fixed set list that rarely changed, the set list was different from show to show. Some songs were "fixed" and therefore always played, but their place in the show would change, and there were several "floater" slots where the band would decide on the day of the show which songs to slot in. Everyone got to pick at least one, be it one of theirs or a cover. It helped keep the shows fresh, and Steve had extended the practice to Shannon. Danielle's performance would be one of these "floaters," and Danielle got to pick. She hoped to have her mind made up by the time she reached Colorado Springs.

The music helped push Talitha to the back of her mind, but Danielle soon found that the girl wouldn't stay there. She kept seeing Talitha's disappointed face in her mind, and though she was far too used to being a disappointment, the hurt in Talitha's eyes stung a little more deeply than it should. She regretted her flippant comments, but what should she have said? Danielle's promises didn't mean anything. That was hardly up for debate anymore.

The trip was uneventful, even if the road no longer held the same solace it used to, and she pulled into Colorado Springs just before noon. She fixed the location of the hotel before finding a convenience store with a somewhat clean bathroom to change.

Shannon had concocted an entire backstory for the fictional Taylor Hale, complete with phony childhood memories that Danielle had spent days memorizing. The official story was that Taylor had left Minnesota for Los Angeles after graduation and was now one of Hollywood's premiere costume designers (working under an assumed name) as well as a committed cosplayer.

Thankfully alone in the rest stop bathroom, Danielle transformed herself. She tucked her hair under a bright pink pageboy wig and used glittery makeup to make her eyes and cheeks sparkle. She squeezed into a sequined silver dress and used a push-up bra to make her breasts more prominent. Dark stockings covered the nasty leg scar that would have given her away, and faux platform shoes were there to explain her height.

Danielle had gone to the trouble of hollowing out the shoes and dropping the soles to the bottom so that from the outside, they still looked like platforms. She hustled back to the car and the glory of the air conditioner, where she quickly painted her fingernails a sparkly pink to match her hair and went back over her cover story while she waited on them to dry.

An hour later, she whipped the now dusty and bug crusted Camaro into a guest parking spot and fired off a quick text to the mysterious Lucas. He responded two minutes later, telling her to wait in the lobby near the stairwell. She gathered her bags and went inside, talking to no one. Her head was on a pivot, constantly on the lookout for the one person most likely to recognize her.

Lucas poked his head out of the stairwell a short time later. He was a beefy guy with a face full of stubble and nicotine stained teeth. He whispered her assumed name. Danielle smiled big and said, "Yes, dear," making sure to fully pronounce both words. Lucas rolled his eyes and jerked his head, holding open the stairway door just enough for her to squeeze by him.

"For the record," he said, jabbing a finger at her. "I'm against this little idea Shannon has cooked up. And if you fuck up her show, I will personally fuck you up, got it?"

Danielle was not used to being threatened, at least not physically, and it shocked her. She assessed the man and promptly realized he could easily do exactly what he had promised. "I'm not here to fuck things up," she said in her natural voice.

He grunted and started up the stairs. He didn't even offer to help her with her bags, not that Danielle needed it. Just outside the fourth floor door, he stopped. "My guys are used to seeing hot chicks hanging around, so there's no reason for them to notice you." Danielle gasped at the insult, but he kept on trucking. "But she has a personal assistant named Faye. Look out for her. She's a nice lady, but months of trying to handle Ms. Olausson have made her a little edgy."

Danielle nodded at that. "She can do that to you."

Lucas stared hard at her for a heartbeat, then shrugged.

"421 is ahead on the right. Walk quickly, keep your head down, and don't talk to anybody." Again he jabbed that meaty finger at her. "Don't leave the room for any reason. You go wandering around, and I can't and won't help you."

"You got it, hoss."

Lucas cracked the door and peeked out. "I got two guys at the end of the hallway yapping. I'll distract them. Then you go. No one else in the hall. Two quick, quiet knocks on the door when you get there. Give me thirty seconds, then haul ass."

He stepped out in the hall, and Danielle caught the door before it latched, counted to thirty, and then stepped out. As Lucas had promised, he had the other two security guys turned around. She moved quickly, found room 421, and started to knock when the door opened, and she was suddenly jerked inside.

Danielle dropped her bags as she stumbled, barely catching herself before she fell. She whipped around, ready to bitch at Shannon for the violence of the move, but before she could get a word out, Shannon's arms were around her neck, and she was planting a lingering kiss on Danielle's lips. She broke the kiss but kept her arms around Danielle.

"It's so good to see you again. It feels like forever."

"Tell me about it."

Shannon Henderson, stage name Rikka Olausson, was the walking personification of a dream girl. She stood 5'9" with shimmering blonde hair, frosty blue eyes, and flawless fair skin. She had pouty lips, perfect teeth, perky breasts, and shapely legs. She was a goddess and she knew it, flaunted it, and reveled in it. Standing so close, it was easy to see why so many people, both men and women, fell easily into her bed.

"So," she said playfully. "What do you want to do first?"

Danielle slithered out of her grip. "Not what you want to do." She peeled the pink wig off and tossed it on Shannon's unmade bed, letting her dark hair fall free and shaking it out. Shannon's suite was a mess, with room service trays and liquor bottles scattered everywhere. Clothes littered the floor. Danielle bent over and picked up a tiny, pink laced bra and held it up.

"Miss laundry day?"

Shannon put her hands on her hips. "Now, does it look like that little bitty thing could hold me?" Danielle tossed it, and Shannon caught it and rubbed it on her cheek. "One of the collection."

"You keep girl's underwear?"

"I keep all sorts of things that my conquests leave behind. One of these days, I'll open a museum to a life lived well. I've even got something of yours to put in it."

Danielle spun around. "What do you have of mine?"

Shannon strutted like a peacock. "One of those dowdy nightshirts you wear. I stole it out of your suitcase before you left Cali."

"My Longhorn one. I wondered what happened to that. That was my favorite one."

"Mine too. It's so thin I could almost see through it. You must have had that thing since you were in high school," she said with a giggle.

"Damn near." Danielle stretched, trying to get the knots out of her muscles. "What sounds really good is lunch and then a nap. I feel like I've been up for days."

"Consider it done, my love," Shannon said. She ordered room service while Danielle dug her road clothes out of her bag and prepared to change.

"This sure was a lot of work for twenty minutes," she said as she unzipped the torturous dress.

"Wait, wait." Shannon rushed across the room and stopped Danielle mid-zip. "People pop in and out unannounced, so I need you to stay in costume. Unless you want to crawl in bed and hide under the covers. Nobody ever looks in my bed."

Reluctantly Danielle zipped the dress back up. "Fine, toss me the wig."

Shannon did and watched as she put it back on. "Is it so bad being a girl for a little while?" she asked with disdain. "My sad little tomboy. You act like your skin is going to fall off."

"I don't have a problem being a girl," Danielle said. "But

I feel like I just stepped out of a goddamn comic book. I feel like fucking DiDi the Slutty Clown."

Shannon laughed, but abruptly cut it off. She rushed to the built-in desk, knocked a collection of wine bottles off the corner, sat down, and dug a battered spiral notebook out of a drawer, plucking a purple glitter pen from the rings. "Would you do me a favor and bring my bag over here?" Shannon asked, pointing at a leather handbag that probably cost a week's stay at the Hilton. Danielle brought it, her curiosity raging. Shannon took the bag, pulled out a pair of black framed glasses, and slid them on.

"You wear glasses? I didn't know that."

Shannon peered up at her. "Only on occasion. I haven't put my contacts in yet. I needed to give my eyes a break." She returned her attention. Danielle watched as she scrawled in the book with picture perfect handwriting. When she was done, she looked up at Danielle, then drew a quick sketch. She turned the spiral around so Danielle could see the finished product, an idealized and exaggerated version of her as a clown.

"What is this?"

Shannon licked her lips, showing the first blush of modesty Danielle had ever seen in her. "When I'm not singing or banging every hardbody in a five mile radius. I write stories. This is my story journal. I think I can do something with DiDi the Slutty Clown."

"Well, I'll be damned," Danielle said. "I had no idea."

"Imagine that. I'm not quite as shallow as you thought," Shannon teased. "This is my little secret. I wouldn't have let you see it, but I was afraid I would lose it."

Danielle thumbed through the spiral and found dozens more sketches and pages upon pages of story ideas in various stages of development. "Why do you keep it a secret? I think this is cool. Do you publish any of these?"

Shannon removed her glasses and put them back in the case. "I've put some of them online, anonymously, of course. Maybe one of these days, I'll really sit down and develop some of them. After all, I won't be able to do this forever." She paused, which caused Danielle to look up. "I learned that lesson from you."

A stern knock on the door interrupted the conversation. Danielle felt her eyes go wide. Shannon put her glasses away, suddenly looking more serious than Danielle had ever seen. "You're Taylor," she warned. "*Be* Taylor."

"Why don't I just go hide in the bathroom?"

"You're going to have to face someone sooner or later, or this isn't going to work." Shannon pushed away from the desk as a second knock came. "Coming," she called out. Turning back to Danielle, she said, "If nothing else, act like me because I'm as un-Danielle as they come."

Danielle nodded as Shannon moved to the door. She tried to calm herself by reiterating that most of the people she would run into didn't know her and wouldn't be looking for her. A thought that calmed her until she heard Steve's booming voice from the doorway. "Ready to head to the arena?"

Danielle murmured and scrambled to the bathroom anyway, leaving the door open a crack so she could hear and taking a seat on the toilet.

"The arena," Shannon asked.

"Shannon," Steve said in that slightly disapproving way that Danielle knew so well. He pushed past her and into the room. "We talked about this. We've got the production meeting with the film crew in forty-five minutes. Then you've got the one-on-one sit-down with the reporter from *The Denver Post* and the VIP Meet and Greet after that."

"I thought all of that was tomorrow. You told me I would have an afternoon off to spend with Taylor."

"I said I would try to get you an afternoon off," he sighed. "But it didn't work out. I told you that. The tour is almost over, so you can have all the time you want to spend with your friend. When is she getting here, anyway?"

"She's already here." Danielle heard Shannon moving across the room, and soon she stuck her head in the door. "Tay, hurry up and come here. I want you to meet my manager."

Danielle mouthed "What the fuck" at her, and Shannon promptly sneered back at her. Danielle rolled her eyes, licked her lips, and concentrated on making her voice sound different. "I'm almost done...sweetie pants."

Shannon giggled and ducked back out. "She just got here," she told Steve. "Flying has always messed with her system. She's delicate."

"Uh huh. I need you to get dressed and come on. I'll send Tara for your things. The car is ready to go now."

"Fine," Shannon resigned. "Let me change clothes real quick." Danielle heard some rustling, and then she called out, "Tay, hurry up. I gotta go."

"I'm coming," she answered between gritted teeth. Knowing Shannon wasn't going to let it go, she stood and flushed and went to wash her hands, which let her turn her back on the rest of the room. In the mirror over the sink, she saw Steve standing impatiently in the room. He looked rested and relaxed in a scarlet polo shirt and freshly pressed khakis, his head shaved with sunglasses pushed up on his forehead. He looked her way, and she turned her head, ostensibly to look over her shoulder at him.

"Nice to meet you," she muttered.

"I hope you enjoy your stay, Miss...."

"Hale," Danielle said, turning back to the sink and turning on the water. "Thanks for setting this up." She washed her hands, drawing the process out and praying that Shannon would hurry the hell up and get him out of the room. She was standing by the bed, slithering into a deep purple velvet dress.

"Anything for my star," he answered.

Again she glanced up into the mirror and saw Steve studying her. She remembered Shannon's plea to not be Danielle. She noticed the ridiculous amount of cosmetics Shannon had scattered on the counter. She dried her hands, trying to be dainty about it, plucked a shade of bright pink lipstick off the counter, and pursed her lips. "I'm disappointed by your collection, sweetie," she said to Shannon. "I'm not sure what you expect me to do with this."

"That's just my travel collection," Shannon said, acting mildly insulted. "I didn't want to be carting my entire make-up cabinet around on tour."

Danielle half turned to look straight at Shannon. "Isn't that what your people are for?"

Steve interjected on her behalf. "Travel being what it is, it's important that we bring as little excess baggage as possible. Shannon has someone who takes care of her make-up and clothes for shows and public appearances. Trust me, she's not wanting for looks."

Danielle pouted, looking quickly from Steve back to Shannon. "Um. Still, if I had known my choices would be so limited, I would have come prepared." She turned back to Shannon's cluttered counter, shuffled things around, and grabbed another tube. "Turquoise, dear? Are you so out of touch that you don't realize that turquoise is last season?"

Shannon stammered. "I just...it's been a long tour."

"Like that's an excuse," Danielle snapped. She dropped the lipstick tube with disgust.

"Shannon, we really need to get moving," Steve said. Danielle fought hard to suppress a smirk as Steve looked away from her reflection, moving quickly to Shannon's side. "We're on a short schedule." He took her by the elbow and started guiding her to the door. "Pleasure to meet you, Ms. Hale," he called over his shoulder.

Danielle kept fiddling with the make-up until they were gone. Blissfully alone, she slumped and peeled the wig off. "That was a nightmare," she said to herself. Looking at her reflection, she said, "This isn't going to work."

Several minutes later, room service arrived, and Danielle found herself with two meals to eat. No sooner had room service left then the door suddenly opened. Danielle froze as a tall, skinny blonde rushed into the room. The girl yelped when she saw Danielle sitting on the end of the bed.

"Um, I'm...here to get Ms. Olausson's bag. You must be

her friend."

"Yeah," Danielle said, not trying to hide her drawl. "Saw her for about five minutes before the bald guy whisked her away."

The girl laughed uncomfortably. "Yeah, we're always on the run," she said. Her eyes drifted to the room service cart and quickly away. She dug into Shannon's closet and came out with a garment bag and an overnight case.

"Hey, what's your name?"

"Tara," the girl said, flustered. She again eyed the food in front of Danielle.

Danielle picked up the plate with Shannon's wrap on it and held it out. "Tara, would you like Shannon's wrap? I can't eat all of this by myself."

"Um, yeah, I would, but I got all of this, and I gotta get."

Danielle stood and took the garment bag from her with one hand while pushing the plate of food into Tara's other hand. "I'll help you," she said. "You eat." She plopped on the end of the bed and took a lustful bite. "When's the last time you ate?"

Tara struggled to get the bite down. "I don't remember. We're on such a tight schedule that I just grab when I can. I'm usually too tired to eat."

"She's pushing y'all really hard, huh?"

Tara took another bite and shrugged. "Life on the road," she said. "It has its advantages, but I will be so glad when it's over. I think I'm going to sleep for a week when I get home." She took one more bite and pushed the plate away. Standing, she took the bag back from Danielle. "I gotta get going. Thank you."

"Think nothing of it," Danielle answered.

The girl raced out of the room, and Danielle stood and wondered if life had been so hard for her staff when she was touring. She certainly hoped not.

CHAPTER SEVENTEEN

Danielle fully stripped away her disguise after lunch and felt instantly better to be out of the ridiculous get up. Then she spent an hour cleaning up Shannon's room. She wondered how the room had gotten so bad so quickly, but knowing Shannon, that was probably a question she didn't really want answered. When things were more presentable, she wanted to take a nap but found herself doubting the cleanliness of the sheets and requested a maid to come change them out.

Exhausted and bored, Danielle melted into the bed, looking forward to a restful sleep. She pulled the covers up to her chin and turned her back to the door—just in case another one of Shannon's people came busting in—closed her eyes, and drifted off to sleep.

The kitchen was hot and stuffy. Sweat poured off her as Danielle stood among the outdated appliances. She was young and tan and grimy, in a grease stained tank top and cut off jeans. Something wasn't right, but she couldn't put her finger on it. This place was familiar.

Strange hands wrapped around her shoulders, and Danielle instantly stiffened. Someone nudged her neck, hot breath dancing on the cool sweat, chapped lips grazing her skin. She wiggled in the grip, twisted, and turned. Sean McLain stood in front of her. His dishwater blond hair and pencil thin mustache made him look unassuming, but there was a predatory glare in his eyes. His hands moved down her arms and then to her breasts as he pushed her back against the refrigerator. He pushed in close, stronger than his wiry frame would indicate, pulling at her shirt, lips coming in for hers. She felt panicked, scared. What was she going to do?

Then she remembered who and what she was. Danielle gathered her strength, put her hands flat against his chest, and shoved him off her. "Get the fuck off me!" she growled. The anger, the sweet, sweet anger that had never let her down, gathered in her muscles. She clenched her fists. "Not then, not now."

But Sean didn't cower or back down. His toothy smile just got bigger. "That's fine. I don't need you. I've got someone better." The lights went off, and a spotlight came on. In the center of the room was a large bed, and in the center of the bed was Talitha, stripped to just her underwear. Black clothed men with white priests' collars held down her arms and legs. She squirmed under their grip, calling for help. Sean climbed on the bed, hovering over the girl but watching Danielle.

"Get off her," Danielle snapped.

"What are you going to do way over there?" He looked down at his own daughter and licked his lips. "So sweet." He glared back at Danielle. "Don't pretend you care." Talitha's eyes widened in terror, and she called out Danielle's name in desperation.

She finally forced herself to move, but there were people everywhere, all of them calling for her attention. They waved papers and phones in her face. She could still hear her sister's cries, but she could no longer see through the masses. Then Nicole Moore was there in her big boobed, phony Hollywood best, sneering at her. The sounds of Sean raping Talitha filled the air, but all she could see was Nicole Moore's stupid face. "Why don't you just turn and walk away, Danielle? Isn't that what you're best at?"

Unable to get around her, Danielle whirled around, and Kyle stood in front of her. "Kyle!" She yelled, and ran to his arms. "You've got to help me. I need to help her."

He pushed her away, all the kindness she remembered gone and his face gray. "I've been trying to help her, but you never listen. There is no help now. For you or her."

"No. That's not true. It's not too late. Please help me."

But Kyle just shook his head and turned away. "You wanted to be on your own, and so you are." He moved away quickly, and Danielle chased after him, pleading for him not to go. She reached for his arm, but he was gone, and she stumbled and fell.

"Danielle?" A tiny voice called from behind.

From her hands and knees, Danielle turned. Talitha was on her knees, her clothes torn, her eyes black, and her lip busted. She was white as death. "Where were you? Didn't you hear me calling?"

Sean emerged from the shadows behind her, his hands like claws wrapping around Talitha's arms and drawing blood. Nicole was at his side, and dozens more faceless people appeared from the darkness surrounding her. "She's mine," Sean said. "You had your chance."

"No!"

Danielle shot up in bed. Darkness had fallen, and the only light came from the cheap alarm clock on the nightstand and the few city lights that snuck through the cracks in the blinds. A jagged breath escaped her lungs as the images of her nightmare faded. She spied her cell phone on the nightstand and reached for it with shaky hands. She pulled up Brett's number but couldn't bring herself to dial it. Instead, Danielle threw it down on the bed.

"Jesus," she muttered as she ran her hands through her hair. "God, what have I done?"

The door opened, and Shannon's familiar silhouette stepped in. She turned on the lights, and Danielle flinched away from the light.

"Now that's what I like to see," Shannon said. She pushed the door closed with her foot and climbed into the bed, crawling on hands and knees to the far side of the bed.

"I swear to God, if you touch me, I'll kill you," Danielle whispered, meaning every word of it.

Shannon recoiled. "Are you okay? Did something happen? What's wrong with you?"

Danielle threw the covers off and paced to the window. "Nothing happened. I didn't do anything. That's the problem. I never do anything, do I?"

"What are you talking about?"

Danielle looked back at Shannon, who had genuine worry etched onto her face. At that moment, Danielle wanted to lay it all out for her. She knew Shannon would listen without judgment, but with the concert less than twenty-four hours away, she lost her nerve. Shannon would probably tell her to go home and forget about this silly idea of theirs. She knew it was the right answer, but she had come too far to back out now.

"I guess I'm just nervous about tomorrow night. Seeing Steve today kind of shook me."

"You did so good, though," Shannon said, leaping up off the bed. "He had no clue. That whole schtick with the make-up was so good." She made her way to Danielle and wrapped her up in a tight hug. "It's going to work, babe. Trust me." She broke the hug but laid a cool hand on Danielle's cheek. "You just need to relax and have a little faith."

Danielle put her hand over Shannon's and leaned into the embrace. Her eyes found Shannon's. "Faith is one thing I'm all out of."

"Then let me give it back to you," Shannon said softly. "By tomorrow night, you'll be Danielle Regan again, and the whole world will know your name. Trust me."

***

Danielle couldn't sleep that night. While Shannon sprawled across the bed, dead to the world, Danielle perched by the window and gazed out at the sleepy city. The images of her earlier nightmare kept dancing through her head, but they weren't alone. As the hour of the show drew slowly closer, Nicole Moore started popping into her head. She could see the phony as clear as day standing in front of her, telling her it was all a waste of time. She could never get back what she lost.

As the dawn began to creep over the mountains, Danielle felt a modicum of relief. The day was here, and she knew that meant a hectic rush of activity. She needed the distraction from her racing mind. Now with sleep creeping at the back of her mind, Danielle left the window and took a steaming hot shower. As she stood under the spray, she tried to visualize the show. She saw herself edging closer to the stage, Shannon's guitar strategically placed close. Shannon began to address the audience, all eyes on her. Danielle saw herself confidently stepping forward, plucking the guitar from the stand, and striding out on stage as the spotlight found her. The crowd went wild. Shannon beaming at her as she approached, strapping the guitar around her with a sly smile, her fingers finding the first chord.

But no sound came out. She felt herself tighten up—her fingers wouldn't move, she couldn't sing or speak. The crowd's cheers turned to laughter as she stood frozen and ineffectual. Even Shannon began to laugh, and then Nicole Moore walked onstage. "It'll never happen. You're done."

"Fuck!" Danielle slammed her fist against the shower wall. She closed her eyes and tried to drive the image out of her head. She focused on the water cascading over her. She tried to will the water to seep into her pores and penetrate deep into her soul, to awaken the old Danielle that she was sure still lived there somewhere. The fearless one. The confident one. "Wake up," she whispered. "Please wake up."

She stepped out of the shower and wrapped a cheap hotel towel around her, shivering despite the steaming water she'd been in. Shannon leaned against the bathroom door, naked as the day she was born, watching her. "You all right? Sounded like you fell."

"I'm fine," she said, her voice wavering slightly. She hoped that Shannon hadn't picked it up as she picked up a hairbrush and began to run it through her hair. Shannon moved up behind her, and they both looked at their reflections in the mirror. Danielle saw in her eyes a fear she'd never seen before.

"You cannot freak out," Shannon said. Her voice held a firmness that was out of character. "You're going to draw attention to yourself. You have to be calm." Danielle couldn't answer—she was transfixed by the silent panic etched on her face. Shannon spun her around and gripped her arms. "Where is my fierce, take-no-shit Danielle?"

"I'm here," Danielle whispered, but she could see that Shannon wasn't buying.

Shannon pulled her in and hugged her. "Don't sabotage this, Dani."

"I won't," she whispered. She just didn't believe it.

Shannon had just finished helping Danielle slip into another Taylor Hale disguise when the previously mentioned Faye hustled into the room, pushing a room service cart full of breakfast foods. She was a kindly but harried woman on the other side of fifty, with short blonde hair and worry lines at the corners of her eyes.

"Showtime, my dear. Are we ready for this one?" she asked Shannon, who had just managed to slip into a robe at Danielle's insistence.

Faye's eyes quickly shifted to Danielle, already dressed in a ridiculous emerald dress that threatened to cut off her oxygen, while a push-up bra was a nice touch to throw off Steve, who knew Danielle's modesty well. She topped it off with more wild, glitter make-up and a deep purple wig.

"Oh, hello there," she said as she took in Danielle's strange outfit. "My, aren't you a fetching one? You must be Taylor, right?"

"That's me," Danielle said, holding her arms out at her side. She made no attempt to disguise her accent. She also picked up one from Faye. "That's an interesting accent. Are you from Australia?"

Faye smiled warmly, and it was a pleasant smile. "New Zealand," she answered politely.

"Wow. You're a long way from home."

Faye's eyes quickly slipped to Shannon, who was investigating half a grapefruit and paying no attention to them. "You can say that again." Danielle gave her a knowing grin before the older woman shifted her attention to the star of the show. "Now, Shannon, dear, the big man wants me to remind you that tonight's show is being filmed, so he needs you at 100%."

Shannon stabbed at her grapefruit with a pointed spoon. "Yes, Mommy. Will you please tell Steve to make sure Josh has my guitar ready for tonight? I want it right off stage so I can get at it quickly."

"I will. Now hurry up and eat your breakfast. Lots of things to do today." Before leaving, Faye turned back to Danielle. "Pleased meeting you, dear. If you need anything, my name is Faye. Just ask for me."

Shannon's personal assistant/nanny left, and Danielle sat opposite Shannon. "So what song are we going to sing tonight? I was thinking we might do 'Already Fallen.'"

"We're going to do 'Girl's Night Out.' I've already added it to the set list."

"Wait a second," Danielle said. "I thought we were going to decide that together. I've been debating this for days, and you just decide this and don't even bother to tell me?"

Shannon poured herself a cup of hot tea from a stainless steel carafe on the cart. "I did because that's the song I want to do." She doused her tea with a generous shot of honey and sugar and took a quick sip. Danielle was glaring at her, to no effect. "Dani, that song is special to me because you wrote it specifically for me, and it's the most rocking song I do. Nobody else can play it like you. I took it out of the set list because my current guitarist can't play it right. I really want to play this song." She took another sip. "Besides, we haven't done any of the songs you sang on the album during the tour, so if I had added one, it would have raised suspicions."

She was disappointed, but Danielle had to admit that the decision made sense. "Fine. But I wish I could get a few minutes with your guitar so I could tune it the way I want. And to do that song, I need a good crunchy sound. I need to fiddle with your amp too."

"We can't, Dani. That'll make people suspicious. Josh, my guitar tech, he knows what to do. But I'll ask him if he can make it a little, what did you say, crunchy?"

"Yeah." This felt better, talking about set lists and tunings. Thinking about camera crews and lighting and all of that. Felt like business. The nerves were still bubbling inside her, but she tried hard to keep it hidden.

"I know," Shannon said suddenly. "Once you get out there and we get that first song under our belts, and everybody is cheering, and Steve sees that you're not going to wreck everything, then we can do your song. How about that? Of course, most of them were there when we recorded it. And we rehearsed all the songs on the album." She paused, and Danielle waited for the explanation. Shannon swallowed once. "Steve wanted me to sing your songs on the tour. I did the first night, but I didn't feel right about it. But the band can play them."

"Nice." Danielle pushed away from the cart and ambled back to the window. The town was now alive with morning commuters. Early morning fog was just starting to lift as the sun broke through the clouds.

"Don't be upset."

"I'm not upset with you," Danielle said. "But Steve trying to get you to do my parts, that stings."

Shannon shifted in her seat and fiddled with a napkin in her lap. "It's just business, Dani. Besides, he was hurting too. You were supposed to be with us."

"And I fucked it up. I know." She tore her eyes away from the window. "We better get you dressed. You'll have to go soon."

Shannon tossed the napkin on the cart. "You'll be okay here alone until Faye comes to get you for the show? You're not going to panic and run off or anything?"

"I'm good," Danielle said, trying to project confidence she didn't quite feel yet. "This is what I do."

They got Shannon ready to go, and soon she was off to do the typical whirl of pre-show press and preparations. Danielle picked at the breakfast cart but found that she had no appetite. She paced the room, fiddled with Shannon's things, tried to watch TV, but found nothing to draw her interest. Her mind drifted back to Brett's, and she wondered if Talitha was all right. Danielle moved to the desk and picked up the phone, paused, and put it back down. To call now would just make things harder. It was almost over, and Danielle convinced herself that she'd be a better sister once this was done.

Danielle wasn't aware that she'd fallen asleep until Faye shook her awake later. She was still sitting in the office chair, her head tilted back. She sat up, startled, and immediately felt her neck and shoulders tighten.

"Oh, I'm sorry, dear," Faye said softly. "You didn't look very comfortable."

Danielle rubbed at her stiff neck. "It wasn't." Faye circled Danielle and began massaging her neck and shoulders. Almost instantly, Danielle felt all the tension and nerves melt away. "Oh my God," she muttered. "You're an angel."

"That's what the mister tells me," she said.

Danielle smiled over her shoulder. "Ah, you got a guy waiting for you back home?"

"Sure do. He works construction, and when he comes home at night, he's just all seized up. Poor man is probably nothing but one gigantic knot by now. But after tonight, I get to go home."

"I bet you're ready for that."

"That I am," she said. Faye quit massaging and gave Danielle a pat on the shoulder. "Once I get home, I'm never leaving again. I'm too old for a life on the road. I'm just going to enjoy my family and read."

Danielle peered up at her. "Will that be enough for you?"

"Darling, that's all I need."

Danielle took a moment to freshen up, and then Faye led her down to a black Crown Victoria that idled at the door, waiting for them. Faye rode shotgun while Danielle slid into the back and found herself sitting next to Steve. Out of nervous habit, she sucked her bottom lip for just a second before she caught the gesture and quit. She casually slouched, trying to make herself look shorter.

"Ms. Hale," Steve said with his trademark booming voice.

"Hope you've enjoyed your time here."

"Very much," she said, barely remembering to put on her fake accent. "It's a very interesting life Shannon leads. Very hectic."

"Can't be too different from the movie business," he answered. "Being a make-up artist in Hollywood, I'm sure you've got some wild stories."

As the car moved away from the hotel, darkness overcame them, and Danielle was thankful for the camouflage. "It's not really that interesting. You sit and put fake faces on fake people all day. Most Hollywood types are a bore. Very shallow and self-absorbed. That's why I enjoy this," she said, sweeping her hands over herself. "This allows me to be my true self instead of altering someone else's truth."

Steve chuckled. "That's an interesting way of putting it. So no war stories for the drive?"

Danielle tried to think of the most non-Danielle thing she could do. She turned and let her fingers of her left hand dance across Steve's jawline. "I could think of more pleasant ways to pass the time than swapping stories." She licked her lips slowly. "This is the Mile High City, after all."

Steve pulled away from her. "That's Denver. We're not that high here."

Daniele ran her hands over his chest and found that he was still just as hard as he used to be, even if the years were starting to show on his face. "Close enough. I don't get too hung up on details."

He took her wrist and pushed Danielle's hand away. "My fiancée wouldn't care too much for that. We'd best stick to small talk."

"Oh," she said, putting on a face pout. "That's a shame."

Steve grunted, pulled out his cell phone, and lost himself in it. Danielle looked out the window, trying hard not to break into a laugh. She wondered what he was going to say when all of this was over, and he found out who she was.

Steve remained quiet and distracted for the rest of the

trip, just as Danielle wanted. Once the car pulled safely into the backstage area, Steve jumped out and disappeared. If she had to guess, Danielle would have bet that he was on his way to the sound booth to oversee things from his catbird seat. One of Shannon's beefy security guards led her to the side of the stage, showed her where to stand, where she wouldn't be in the way, and the areas to avoid. She knew it all, but Danielle nodded and went along with the lecture anyway.

The familiarity of the organized chaos brought a small smile to her face, one that the security guy noticed. She rebuked herself for being careless and did her best to disappear. The longer it took to get to showtime, the more antsy she got. She hoped that once the show started, it would go faster.

In front of the stage, the crowd began to buzz as showtime drew ever closer. Danielle wanted to take a peek but didn't dare draw the notice of security again. She felt a tiny charge when Josh, the guitar tech, positioned Shannon's guitar, an Ibanez with a paisley pink and purple paint job. She longed to put her hands on the instrument.

Then the time finally arrived. The house lights dimmed as canned intro music began to play. It was some sort of Celtic sounding instrumental. Lights began to sweep the crowd, which brought the first loud cheers of the night. Shannon's band emerged and hustled their way to the stage. Finally, Shannon herself appeared, looking like a queen in a flowing emerald gown, her blonde hair flowing wild and free under a rhinestone jeweled tiara. She checked Danielle briefly as she passed by but showed no other recognition. The instrumental died out, pyrotechnics went off, and the band lurched into the opening song, Shannon standing at the mic and letting her voice cast a vocal net over the crowd. After the first song, she tore the bottom of her gown away to reveal her long legs encased in silk stockings and a miniskirt that left little to the imagination.

Danielle soon got sucked into the show. Shannon was a far better showman than she had imagined as she pranced and twirled across the stage, engaging and sometimes titillating her audience. Occasionally she sat at the piano and let her underrated musicianship shine through. The band behind her was tight and gave Shannon plenty of room to improvise.

As Shannon had predicted, once the show started, the staff became focused on their duties, and no one paid attention to her. So Danielle casually began to edge toward the wings of the stage. She hadn't needed to memorize the set list—it was written in grease marker on a plexiglass sheet positioned just behind the band. She followed along, her heart beating a little faster as each song got played.

She was almost within arm's length of Shannon's foofy guitar when her bassist caught sight of her and shook his head violently at her. Danielle stopped instantly. The bass player gestured to a security guard, who slammed down a clipboard and stomped over to Danielle, taking her arm roughly and pulling her back. "Don't get any closer than this," he growled. "Or I'll have you sent back to the hotel."

Danielle showed the proper humility and vowed to stay put. Now things were going to be more difficult. The distance to the guitar wasn't that great, but she would need to be faster now. She rubbed her hands. Looking like a nervous habit to the uninitiated, she was actually loosening up her fingers since she couldn't warm up with some playing.

Shannon's band brought the last song to a close, and Shannon, who had retreated to her piano, jumped up and strode to the front of the stage. "Thank you all so much for coming tonight. We've had a blast tonight, Colorado Springs, and we're just getting started."

Danielle looked around, fixing the positions of everyone she could. The security man was watching the crowd, the bassist was getting a drink of water while Shannon riffed. Steve was nowhere to be seen. She took two small, quick steps to give herself a better angle on the guitar. She focused on it. Everything had worked out just as Shannon had thought, and now there was no one between her, the guitar, and the stage. She was ready to make her move when the bassist put his water bottle down and looked up at her. Their eyes locked, and Danielle knew she was on—Shannon was giving her the cue.

"Tonight is such a special night that we're going to play a song from the new album, one we haven't done much on tour. But for you, we're making an exception. And not only that...."

Caught in-between, the rational part of Danielle's brain screamed to abort, to back away. Danielle's pride wouldn't have it. She was too close now. She flashed back to her discussion with Ridgeway, where she had compared herself to a lioness. This was her savannah, her hunting ground, and no one could deny her now. She gave the bass player a wink and started running. He yelled out for security, but nobody was close enough. She snatched the neck of the guitar. The stage lights were just ahead. She could hear Shannon building up. "I've got a special surprise for you tonight. A special guest that I think you will be very interested to hear from."

Then, the unexpected. Instead of just freezing or hanging back, the bassist player moved to intercept her, trying to block her way to the stage. Behind her, staff were screaming, panic raging. She couldn't turn back now. She shifted left, trying to stay out of the bass player's grasp. He lunged for her and caught her shoulder just enough to spin her.

She spun out of the wings onto the stage, into the light. The crowd screamed, and then Shannon yelled out, "No! Wait! Stop!" Danielle was trying to complete her spin and reorient herself when someone hit her in the legs, and she started to fall. She tossed the guitar, putting her hands out to cushion her fall. Three hulking guards were rushing her, the angry males of the pride coming to put the cocky lioness in her place. "Please stop!" Shannon cried out.

Just before Danielle hit the ground, she saw the person who had grabbed her legs and was shocked to see tiny, scrawny Tara, Shannon's make-up artist, with her long arms snaked around both of Danielle's legs, her eyes shut tight. The day before, Danielle had given her a wrap, and she had been paid back like this.

She hit the stage hard, the impact knocking the breath out of her lungs. She craned her neck to see Shannon being carted away by her bandmates, still screaming for everyone to stop. She kept saying, "I asked her to come. It was my idea!"

Danielle tried to wriggle free of Tara's grasp, and then the bass player was standing over her, holding his instrument over her head like a sword. She stopped moving, certain he would smash her in the face if she didn't. The cavalry arrived, and Danielle felt herself yanked up, just like the cops had done to her the year before after the big fight with Nicole Moore. There was no chivalry, no kid gloves for a girl in this scenario, as they manhandled her away from the stage. She struggled, but there was no way she was getting free of their grasp.

They took her to Shannon's dressing room, where a Colorado Springs police officer turned her around and slapped the handcuffs on her wrist. He was talking shit about how they were going to love her fruity ass at the station when Steve's voice rose above the din. "Put her in the dressing room." The cop argued, but Steve was insistent, and finally, he complied and pushed Danielle into the room. He sat her roughly in a folding chair in front of a dressing table.

Danielle looked at herself in the mirror. Her wig had fallen off, and several strands of her natural dark hair had broken free. The ridiculous makeup was smudged and smeared, her eyes were red, and her front teeth-stained purple from the ruined lipstick. She looked exactly how she felt, like a mess.

She sat perfectly still for several minutes while the cop hovered over her, his hand positioned on his nightstick, ready to strike if she made any sudden moves. Outside the dressing room door, havoc slowly faded, and peace seemed to ensue. Steve pushed through the creaky door, sighed, and drug another chair over to her side.

"Dani."

"How's it hanging?" Danielle tried to sound flippant, maybe even a little cocky, but like the rest of the night, her attempt fell flat. "So, what's up?"

"Danielle, damn it. This was stupid."

"Yeah," she agreed. "Not one of my better ideas. I just figured that maybe enough time had passed." She tried to turn, but the cop's hands clamped down on her shoulder. "Back off, Barney Fife," she snarled, and he raised the back of his hand to her.

"Officer," Steve said. "You can go now. We won't be pressing charges."

"I think our D.A. might have something to say about that," the cop pouted. He gripped her shoulders harder. "She put people in danger. I'm taking her in."

Steve didn't get flustered or raise his voice at all. Instead, he locked his steely gaze on the cop and laid it out. "And my attorney will have her free by sunrise, especially once I point out the bruises you're sure to leave on her. I'll have a brutality charge, and a civil suit ready to go before your shift even starts tomorrow."

He didn't like that, but finally, he let go of her shoulders and shuffled out of the room, leaving her handcuffed.

"Thanks, big man,"

Steve nodded and stroked his chin. "Thanks for trying to take the blame, but I know this was all Shannon's idea. She's got a lot of talents, but advanced planning isn't one of them."

"This was supposed to be my tour, too," Danielle whispered. "I just wanted a slice of what was mine. After all this time, I thought I was entitled to it."

Steve's brown eyes seemed as deep as her despair. "You know, if you two had just come to me and made a case, I probably would have let you do it. I would have worked it out. It would have made for a great video. But you have to do things the hard way."

"You wouldn't have let me," Danielle sneered, feeling the slightest bit of fire. "You made it pretty clear how you felt about things, about me. I had to do this the hard way. I had to show you, show everybody, that I was still...me."

"I also pointed you at the Brooks girl. I was trying to edge down a more patient track. But you always have to be so balls to the wall. You still haven't learned that there are better ways to handle things."

"It's not my way," she said. "But I guess I'm the clown," she said as she looked at her idiotic reflection. "Just a fucking clown now." She looked at Steve solemnly. "There's no coming back from this, is there?"

"No, Dani, there's not. You're Axl Rose now, just a crazy, washed-up shell of yourself. The press will never let you live this down."

He stood and made his way to the door, where he summoned a different cop. The cop released her from the handcuffs. Danielle stood and rubbed at her chaffed wrists.

Steve stood more than an arm's length away. "Go home, Danielle. And stay there."

"My stuff is at the hotel."

"I'll have someone drive you. Get your stuff and hit the road. I'll be doing damage control here for hours, and I'm going to have a little sit down with your co-conspirator as well. I want you out of town before she gets back to the hotel."

Danielle walked past him to the door but stopped there. Turning back, she said to him, "Go easy on Shannon. She was just trying to help a friend. Her heart was in the right prison."

"Her head was up her ass," he answered. "And this stupid stunt could have seriously hurt someone. She'll be lucky if this doesn't ruin her career too."

"Maybe," she answered. "Or she'll come out of it smelling like a rose. I'm the only one who winds up in the shit. See ya around, Steve."

A taxi whisked Danielle back to the hotel, where she took enough time to change out of what was left of the costume before she hit the road. It was late at night, and she hadn't slept in what seemed like forever, but she was determined to make it back to Brett's. She drove with the radio off. The only sound to keep her company was the sound of the road as she replayed the evening over and over in her head.

Somewhere in the wilderness between Raton and Clayton, a stray thought crept into Danielle's head as the first of a convoy of big rigs flew by, heading in the opposite direction. *One little turn of the wheel, and it would all be over. You'd never even feel it.*

Never in all the down moments of her life had suicide actually entered Danielle's head. She thought about Kyle, the flash of headlights across his face as the truck bore down on them. It would be fitting. Yet Danielle didn't turn the wheel.

It wasn't because of self-preservation. Danielle Regan's will was gone. She was finally and truly broken.

CHAPTER EIGHTEEN

Halfway through the drive home, the adrenaline wore off, and Danielle began to crash. The rumble strips on the shoulder of the road saved her from putting the Camaro in a ditch on multiple occasions. She managed to pull herself together long enough to limp into the tiny town of Clayton, New Mexico, where she was relieved to find a twenty-four-hour convenience store.

She parked right by the door and stumbled into the building. Behind the counter, a slightly overweight kid with frizzy black hair tore his eyes off his phone long enough to assess her. Danielle managed to give him a half-hearted smirk and made her way to the bathrooms at the back of the building.

She was relieved to find a spacious and recently cleaned restroom. Several splashes of cold water to the face did nothing to wake her up, so Danielle walked to the handicapped stall, locked the door, sat down, rested her head on the toilet paper holder, and went to sleep.

She awoke forty-five minutes later with a horrible crick in her neck. She sat, stretched, and rubbed at her neck as she tried to drive the last tendrils of sleep out of her aching body. She was beginning to feel the effects of the beating she had taken at the show in her shoulders and back, and even her butt, which had taken the force of her landing when Shannon's assistant had taken her down.

Back to the sink for some more water in the face. Danielle was horrified by what she saw in the mirror. Her hair was a tangled mess, and she had black bags under her eyes. She looked like she had been put through a ringer. She did her best to straighten up, using her fingers to work out the tangles in her hair. Eventually, she gave up. Hell, nobody else was going to be in the car anyway.

She finally stepped out of the bathroom, thinking only of snacks, gas, and hitting the road. Only the kid from the counter was standing just outside the bathroom door. He smiled at her with crooked teeth, and he smelled like stale Cheetos. "Been in there for a long time," he said. "I was just coming in to check on you. Thought you might have been ODing or something."

"I'm fine, Sparky." She put her hands on his chest and pushed him back, finding him softer than she expected. "Thanks for the concern, though."

She moved quickly through the store, grabbed a bottle of Coke, a bag of chips, and a big bag of M&M's, and moved to the counter. Sparky was following behind her, and she couldn't blame him for thinking she was some sort of meth head, given her appearance. As she stood at the counter, he made no attempt to move to the register, and eventually, she turned.

"You know, nobody's been in here for like two hours." Sparky gave her his misaligned smile again. "No need to burn your cash on that stuff."

So, it had come to this. She'd gone from fending off Hollywood action stars to having laconic teenage losers trying to extort sex for snacks. "Oh yeah?" She nibbled at her bottom lip and thrust her chest out. Thanks to the stupid push up bra she was still wearing, that was a lot more impressive move than it should have been. "You let me take this stuff for free?"

He shrugged and smiled bigger. "I think we could work something out." He moved in closer, pinning Danielle against the counter. She would have been worried, but she already knew he was a cream puff.

"How about a tank of gas too? Will you throw that in?"

"I bet we could figure something out."

She hummed and bit at her lip again. "What are you thinking about, Sparky? You want me to jump up here on the counter and spread 'em for ya? Or you wanna go in the back?"

A quick glance down showed his hard on growing under his loose fitting khakis. "We could do that," he muttered. "But for the gas, I think you'll need a bit more."

"Oh," she said, drawing it out. She hooked her fingers in his waistband. "Well, big boy. What are we thinking? You want me to drop to my knees right here? Cause you know, I give mean head. Like, porn star quality."

"Oh yeah?"

No hiding his erection now. He pushed closer against her and tried to kiss her, but she turned her head. She easily pushed him back again. This kid was a marshmallow compared to the hard men she had dated in the past.

"Don't confuse things. Whip it out. Let's see what you're packing." He stepped back further, undid his belt, and as soon as his pants dropped, Danielle snatched his balls and squeezed hard, fingernails digging into the skin. He called out in pain and crumbled to his knees. Danielle leaned in close. "Listen to me, you dirty nothing. I'd rather nibble on the end of a shotgun that let you put that puny excuse for a dick anywhere near me. How fucking dare you try to force yourself on me? I ought to call the cops and let them come find you with your wanger hanging out. Now, I am taking this shit for free, not because I can't pay, but because you pissed me off. And you're going to ring up thirty bucks on pump one for me too. And if you don't, I'm going to call the store manager and tell him to watch the security footage."

"Okay, okay," the kid moaned. He tried to take Danielle's hands off, but he didn't have the strength. "I'll do it, I'll do it. Just don't call my boss. Please let me go."

Danielle squeezed harder. "Beg me."

"I beg, I beg. Please, please let me go."

Danielle squeezed even harder. She began to worry that she might be causing permanent damage, but a lesson had to be learned. "You do this to any other girls? I bet you have. I bet you're the kind of guy who needs roofies to get laid, aren't you?"

"No, no. Seriously. I'm a virgin. I never...I just thought...."

"You thought you found a distraught and tired girl in a vulnerable situation, and you'd take advantage? You piece of shit. Guys like you are why girls go gay. You're not a man. You're a fucking snake."

"I fucked up. I'm sorry. I'll never do it again."

Danielle dug her fingernails in more and twisted, eliciting fresh howls from the kid. "No, you won't, because every time you even think about taking advantage of a woman, you're going to flash back on this night and you're gonna do the right thing, right? You're gonna treat the women in your life with respect from now on, right?"

"Yes, ma'am," he blubbered. "Please let me go."

She finally did, violently pulling her hands away and letting her nails drag across his scrotum. Sparky went to the floor and curled up in a fetal position. She pulled out her phone, snapped a picture of him on the floor, then forced his hands away so that she could snap a picture of what amounted to his manhood hanging out of his pants. Then she took a picture of the sign on the wall with the owner's name and number, as well as the corporate number. She waved the phone in his face. "Little insurance policy, Sparky. Thirty bucks, pump one. I wanna get on the road, so pull yourself together."

He struggled to his feet, and Danielle stepped around him and hustled back to the cooler, where she plucked a tall can of Coors out while Sparky finally made his way back to his proper place. Tucking her phone back in her pocket, she slid the can of beer across the counter toward him. "Put it on my tab. Use it as an ice pack or drink it. Doesn't matter to me. But don't forget this night."

"I couldn't if I wanted to," he muttered as he sat gingerly on a stool and placed the can between his legs.

Danielle gathered her snacks, took her keys out of her pocket, and made it to the door. She turned and said, "Be a better person," as she backed out of the door. She moved the Camaro to pump one and found that the kid had rung up the requested amount. As she pumped the gas, she watched him through the window. She knew if he called the cops, she'd be screwed, but he seemed eager just to have her gone. She finished gassing up and sped away.

As she drove, pounding the Coke down and devouring the snacks, she thought back on the experience. She could have handled things better. She knew that. But the truth was, it felt good lording her power over the kid. When she had him by the balls, she had control, and control was something she hadn't felt in a long time. Good Lord, she was messed up beyond recognition, but in moments like this, she felt like her old self again. She knew then exactly how deeply fucked she was.

The rest of the drive flew by, and as she made her way off the interstate and down the lonely farm-to-market road north, the first colors of the morning were lighting the Eastern sky. Bumping over the cattle guard and finally cresting the hill, Brett's ranch spread out in front of her, but it no longer felt like home — rather like the smoldering ruins of another bridge burned.

She whipped the car into the circle drive, noticing that Brett had left his truck out overnight, which wasn't like him. She wondered only briefly what his reasoning might have been. Leaving her bags in the backseat, Danielle walked up the driveway, hoping he hadn't changed his locks while she was gone. Relieved her key still worked, she stepped in, quietly pushing the door closed behind her. The house was still pitch black, but she found her way to the couch without incident and collapsed on it.

Sausage sizzling in a pan and muttered voices were the first sensations to penetrate her slumber. Danielle groaned and sat up. She flashed on the convenience store and hoped that maybe she had dreamed the entire thing, using her left hand to work out the kink that was still in her neck. Standing on shaky legs, Danielle shuffled across the living room and made her way into the kitchen.

Brett was shoveling scrambled eggs onto two plates when Danielle walked in. "Look what the cat dragged in." Sitting on the other side of the bar, Talitha looked over her shoulder, and the disappointment and disgust on her face was palpable. "I would ask what you've been up to, but it's all over the news."

"I figured as much," Danielle said. "It wasn't supposed to go like that." She walked into the kitchen, retrieved a glass from the cupboard, and poured herself some orange juice. The first drink was just to fight the nasty case of cottonmouth she woke up with. "But I'm sure they're not reporting the whole story."

"Video says it all. You tried to crash the concert. One of the stagehands tackled you. Not much more needs to be said." Brett sat and started in on his breakfast.

"Actually," Danielle said, leaning against the bar. "Shannon invited me up. It was her idea for me to wear the crazy costume, so I could hang around backstage, and no one would suspect me. It was in the process of introducing me. I was supposed to run out, but her bass player freaked and tried to stop me, and then her make-up girl fucking tackled me."

"You got tackled by a make-up girl?" Talitha said.

"Better stick with the stagehand story," Brett agreed. "Makes you seem like a little bit more of a threat."

"I wasn't supposed to be a threat." She slammed her glass down, spilling some of the orange juice on the table. "If I had really crashed the concert, don't you think I'd be in jail right now? No way they would have let me go. It was a misunderstanding, pure and simple."

"Well, that's not what the news is saying," Brett said around a bite of sausage. "It's your word against the entire national media. Even if what you say is true, the optics are not in your favor."

"Fuck the optics."

Brett finished scarfing down his breakfast, stood, and gathered his dirty dishes. "More like the optics fucked you." He shifted his attention to Talitha. "Are you ready?"

She took a last bite of egg and handed Brett her plate. "Yes, sir."

Danielle noticed how they both seemed to be moving fast. "So, what's up? Why are y'all in such a hurry?"

Brett had moved deeper into the kitchen and was putting their dishes in the sink. "We gotta get on the road."

"Stop," Talitha said firmly. "I'll tell her."

"Tell me what," Danielle asked.

Talitha stood in front of her and looked Danielle straight in the eyes, coming off as much more confident than she had when Danielle had left just three days earlier. "I'm going back to Austin. Brett is taking me to the bus station. I've already contacted Ms. Luster. She's going to place me with a foster family."

"What? Why? I told you that when I came back, things would be different."

Talitha didn't bat an eye. "There's no room for me in your life. There never was. If it hadn't been for Mr. Walls, you would have left me down there alone. I don't want to be a burden on you, so I won't. I learned how to take care of myself a long time ago. I'll be fine."

"I see," Danielle said. It was what she wanted to hear and what she knew in her heart was best, but yet the words stung more than she wanted to let on. "Well. I told you I'd disappoint you."

"You can't be disappointed in someone you never got to know."

Danielle looked hard at the girl and saw in her the same defiant stance that she used to have. Danielle remembered coming home after spending a few nights at her mentor's house to find that her mother had moved away while she was gone. She hadn't been much older than Talitha was now. She tried to swallow, but the cottonmouth had returned. "I think I'll go to my room now."

She stepped around Talitha and started for the room. Behind her, Brett said, "I'll get the bags," to Talitha. Danielle pushed on to her room and then to the bathroom, where she freshened up the best she could. That woman was in the mirror again, the ghost of someone who used to matter, staring at her with dead eyes. How had she fallen so far? She knew what she had to do.

Danielle stormed out of the room, found her keys on the floor beside the couch, scooped them up, and stomped out into the driveway, where Brett was placing Talitha's bags in the backseat of his truck. "I'll take her."

They both turned.

"I'm her sister. If this is how it has to be, I should at least be the one to take her." She looked square at Talitha. "I think I owe you that much."

Brett violently shook his head and slammed his truck door. "No. I don't think so. You left her here with a strange man, knowing she doesn't trust men. No warning, no explanation. You just left."

"I know what I did," Danielle said. "Did you do anything to her?"

"Of course not."

"Then I was right. You weren't a threat. I trusted you enough for both of us, and I was right to do so. I don't apologize for that."

Brett strode up to her and faced her. "You don't apologize to anybody for anything."

"No, I don't." Danielle was not about to back down, finding some hidden resolve somewhere deep inside. "I don't apologize for leaving because I had to. I had to do that for me. The timing sucked, I know. I handled it like shit. I know that too. I don't expect forgiveness here." She turned away from Brett and toward Talitha. "You're right. I didn't want you and didn't know what to do with you, and I still don't. I'm a complete train wreck, and you're better off without me. I'm not going to try to convince you otherwise. But I would really like to drive you to your bus. At least if I see you off, then that will be more than I ever got, and I'll feel like maybe I did something right."

Talitha looked from Danielle to Brett and back again. "Whatever you want, kiddo," Brett said, though his voice had a tone.

"She can take me," Talitha finally said.

Brett sighed but turned and retrieved her bags from the backseat of his truck and took them to Danielle's car, carefully placing them in the backseat. "There you go," he said as he closed the car door. He approached Talitha and took her hands in his. "You've got my number. Let me know when you get settled, and keep in touch, okay?"

"I will. And thank you for your kindness, Mr. Walls. I did enjoy my time here."

He leaned forward and gave her a delicate kiss on the forehead, then turned and started to say something to Danielle but let it go. Muttering to himself, he went back inside.

Danielle and Talitha stood, eyeing each other before Talitha finally spoke. "My bus leaves in a half hour. We need to go."

"By all means," Danielle said, and they both got in the car. They were both quiet until Danielle got up on the interstate, heading west toward Amarillo. "So," Danielle said. "It seems like you and Brett hit it off. Why don't you just stay with him?"

Talitha was staring intensely out the window and wouldn't tear her eyes away. "He offered, but he has his own life and doesn't need me in the way. Besides...."

She got silent, but Danielle read her line of thought. "He was good for a couple of days when he knew I could come back at any minute. It would be another thing if you lived with him, alone, way out in the country."

"He's a nice man," she said. "As far I know, anyway. If he did something...it wouldn't be the first time a man played the good guy just to lower my defenses."

Danielle wanted to defend Brett. He hadn't done anything to her, and he'd had plenty of chances, but Talitha's experiences were entirely different, and she couldn't say he wouldn't do such things and be 100% certain of it.

After a couple of more miles of silence, Danielle finally spoke again. "I really did plan on trying to make it work with you. I did. But I know why you're doing this, and it's the right decision. I'm in no condition to be taking care of someone else. I guess I proved that this weekend."

Talitha finally tore her eyes off the passing scenery. "I just don't understand. You have money and freedom. Why are you pushing so hard?"

That was a question Danielle had been asking herself a lot. She chewed on it for a minute. "I guess...." She thought it over a little more. "I had this great life, and it was just about to get better. I was happy, really, truly happy, and then all of a sudden, I got ripped out of it. I never had a chance to adjust." She glanced over at Talitha, expecting to see judgment on her face, but instead, finding blue eyes full of understanding. "Most musical acts reach a point where they're not topping the charts anymore. The industry passes them by, but it happens over time, and they can adjust. I never got that. I was on top of the world, and then I woke up, and my fiancé was dead and buried, and my body was broken, and I was lost. So I went away, hoping to find myself, and I finally did, only when I came back, nobody wanted me anymore. I never got to adjust. I never got to say goodbye, you know?" She started to tear up and turned away so Talitha wouldn't see the tears. "I never got to say goodbye to Kyle. He was there, and then he wasn't."

"You need closure," Talitha said. "Have you gone to his gravesite?"

"Yeah. But it was nothing. Some unfamiliar piece of ground and a headstone somebody else bought. The spot next to him is empty. It was reserved for me in case I died. Steve's holding onto it. I don't know if that's sweet or disturbed."

"Steve?"

"My manager. Ex-manager. I never knew Kyle there. I slept through the funeral."

Talitha seemed genuinely interested. They flew past the city limits sign, and the first tendrils of Amarillo business greeted them. The downtown exit was just a few miles ahead. "Where did you know him?"

"When he came to Austin, we mainly stayed at his house. We didn't go out much. But I sold that house when I left town. The new owners renovated it, so it wouldn't be the same. Mainly, when I think of Kyle, I think of when we first met in Nashville. I think those were the best times. I was falling in love and didn't even know it."

Talitha sat quietly, making a gentle humming noise. Finally, she spoke up. "Maybe after you drop me off, you should go to Nashville. Revisit the places you went. Find a way to say goodbye."

That was something Danielle hadn't thought of. She slowed, switching over to the right lane to take the downtown exit to the bus station. "Maybe I will. I mean, what the hell? It's not like I have anything else to do."

She focused on driving as she took the swooping exit that led her north, then worked her way over to the old Greyhound depot, which squatted in the shadow of Amarillo's tallest building. Danielle eased the car up to the curb and put it in park. "Here we are."

Talitha nodded, popped the door, got out, and fetched her bags out of the backseat. She bent over and looked inside one last time. "Best of luck, Danielle. I hope you find something that will bring you some peace."

"Thanks," Danielle muttered. "Good luck with the new family."

"Won't really be family, will it?" Talitha didn't wait for the answer. She shut the door and started to walk away, but stopped and came back. Danielle rolled down the window, and Talitha stuck her head inside. "I don't want you to feel guilty," she said with her sing-song voice. "I know you were doing what you had to do, and it was unfair to you for Mother to force me on you. I have no hard feelings toward you, and I really do hope you find happiness. Everyone deserves happiness."

Danielle felt her stomach drop. "Thanks, kid," she said, barely able to force the words out. Talitha turned and walked away. Danielle watched until she disappeared inside the building. She started to get out, to rush inside and bring her sister back out, but instead, she forced herself to put the car in gear and pull away. If she did go to Nashville to chase Kyle's ghost, Talitha would just be in the way.

Instead, Danielle worked her way through downtown's one way streets, trying to decide between returning to Brett's or taking Talitha's advice and going to Nashville. She wasn't sure she had another long road trip in her. As she sat and idled at a red light, a noisy Greyhound bus rattled by in the opposite direction, heading for the station.

Danielle made a rash decision, which was the only type she ever seemed to make. From the inside lane, she pulled out into the intersection and made a hard right turn. Driving far too fast for the tight streets, Danielle double backed toward the bus station. She caught sight of the bus and turned the wrong way down the one way street, racing the bus. The bus driver's eyes got big as he saw the Camaro racing toward him. She got to the turn in first, skidded into a rough turn, and slammed on her brakes once she was in the bus bay. The expectant riders screamed and flipped the bird at her, but Danielle paid no attention.

Danielle threw the station doors open and quickly located Talitha sitting in a ratty chair, clutching her bags to her chest. "You," she said. "Come here." Confused, Talitha stood and crossed the distance between them. Danielle put a hand on her back and guided her back outside. "You're coming with me."

The bus was idling behind the Camaro, its ass still out in the street. The driver laid on his horn. "Hold your horses," Danielle barked at him. "Get in the car, kid."

Talitha did as instructed, and as soon as she closed the door, Danielle pulled away. Talitha quickly fastened her seatbelt. "What are you doing?"

"I'm taking your advice, and I'm going to Nashville, and you're going with me."

"Um, don't you think you should do that on your own? I'll just be in your way. And besides, Ms. Luster will be expecting me."

"I'll call her from the road," Danielle said. "I need you. I haven't wanted to admit it because I'm proud, and I don't want to need anyone, but I need you. I need you to teach me how to let go. I mean, you should be furious with me. You should hate my guts, but you don't. I've never been able to let go. I hold stupid grudges, and I never ever believed in second chances, and you see where it led me."

Danielle cleared the last of the red lights and sped up,

taking a new ramp that brought her back up to I-40 and pointed them both east. She quickly accelerated to get into the flow of traffic and worked her way into the center lane. "I never believed in second chances," she repeated. "But I'm asking you for one. Give me another chance to be a sister to you. I'll take you with me to Nashville, and I'll make a complete effort to be available to you. I might not always succeed, but I will try. Once I've done what I need to, if you still want to go back to Austin, I'll take you myself, but no sister of mine is going to ride a goddamn Greyhound bus."

She thought she saw Talitha suppress a smile. "I'll go." She reached over and rested a delicate hand on Danielle's thigh. "Second chances are good. Jesus died to give us all a second chance."

Danielle sighed uneasily. "Okay, kid. One thing, don't hit me with the God thing too much. That kind of creeps me out. My feelings about God are...let's just say we're not on real good terms with each other."

Talitha laughed out loud. "You think God has it out for you?" Danielle answered with a look. "That's not how it works, silly. But I'll try not to 'hit you with the God thing' too much," she said. "I may not always succeed." Danielle was happy enough with that, but Talitha wasn't done. "Can I ask you one thing?"

"Sure."

"Why do you never call me by my name? You always call me kid or something like that. Is that a way for you to keep your distance?"

Danielle flexed her hands around the steering wheel as she tried to come up with some way to spin it, but then she decided if this experiment was going to work, she had to be honest. "It's because I hate your name. I think it's stupid, and somebody should have slapped your momma upside the head when she suggested it."

Talitha giggled, which wasn't at all what Danielle expected. "Father gave me that name. Can I tell you something?"

"Go for it," Danielle said.

"I never cared for it much either. Even before everything got twisted. Kids used to make fun of me all the time. Once we moved to the camps, any time somebody called my name, it was usually a bad sign. I've thought about changing it."

"Then let's change it," Danielle eagerly agreed. "I'll pay for it, and it'll be totally legal. Anything you want."

"Anything?"

"Of course. It's your name, after all."

"I had a friend once, a long time ago, and she couldn't pronounce my name right, so she just called me Talia, and I always thought that was a pretty name. I would like to be Talia from now on."

"Talia," Danielle repeated. "That's nice. Nicer than Talitha. Such a weird ass name. You want to keep McLain as your last name? You could take Regan like me."

"But I'm not a Regan," Talitha said. "I wouldn't feel right about that. What was Mother's maiden name?"

"You don't know Mom's maiden name? She never told you?"

"It never really came up," the newly minted Talia said. "If you've forgotten, we were kind of busy being assaulted a lot of the time."

The tone took Danielle by surprise, but when she looked over, Talia was grinning at her. "Were you just using sarcasm on me? I didn't think you had a sarcastic bone in your body."

Talia giggled again as she squirmed in her seat. "Maybe it's the name change bringing it out of me. Or maybe you're just a bad influence."

"Yeah, that's probably true," Danielle agreed. "James. Mom's maiden name was James."

"Talia Grace James," she repeated. "I like it. Kind of rolls off the tongue. A new name for a new start. Thank you."

"No thanks needed." They reached the city limits, and traffic began to lighten, so Danielle put the pedal down. "Well, Talia, let's say you and I have a little adventure."

Talia smiled back at her. "Let's."

The instant she agreed, Danielle felt a weight lift off her. She leaned back in her seat, set the cruise control, and relaxed her grip on the steering wheel. "Well, let's do it right then. Reach beneath your seat."

Talia leaned over, her tiny hands groping under the seat until they grazed on something, and she pulled it out to find a black plastic case. "This?"

"Yep, It's time I start educating you. Open it up." Talia pulled the case into her lap and unzipped it to reveal a collection of CDs. Danielle glanced over. "Pick one, any one. It's not a true road trip unless you've got some road music."

She studied the spines of the cases, carefully reading each one and occasionally taking one out to inspect it further. Finally, she picked one, opening the jewel case and carefully removing the disc. "Here."

Danielle took the CD by the edges and checked the label. "Um. Stevie Ray Vaughan. Nice pick." She slid the CD into the stereo. As the first strains of "Love Struck Baby" began pouring out of the speakers, a thin smile broke across her face. "SRV. You know, Mom knew him. When I was little, and we lived in Austin, my parents would have these wild parties, and all sorts of people would be there. I remember him singing me to sleep once or twice. I really like him. Of course, back then, he was a nobody, just a struggling Austin bluesman."

"Is that how you got started playing music?"

Danielle mulled that over for a minute. "I guess it was, in a way. But the path that led me here was kind of a long and winding one."

"It's a long drive to Nashville," Talia said. "So give it to me. All of it."

CHAPTER NINETEEN

They made it to Little Rock before Danielle ran out of gas. Along the way, Danielle laid out her life story in intricate detail, and as promised, she held nothing back. The stories flowed freely, as did the music as they rolled from one CD to another. Each new CD opened up a new line of discussion as Danielle took her sister beyond the tracks, regaling her with stories of the road. It was amazing when Danielle let herself think about how she had actually gone on to meet or even play with many of the artists who had inspired her.

Danielle found them a Holiday Inn just off the interstate and checked in before grabbing some drive through burgers and calling it a night. After the dinner mess was cleaned up, they took turns showering before hitting the bed.

To Danielle, it felt like she had just closed her eyes when Talia started gently shaking her shoulder. "Get up," she whispered with urgency. "Get up. We're going to miss breakfast."

Danielle struggled to pull herself out of her slumber. "What?" She raised up on one elbow. "What time is it?"

"It's almost nine. They quit serving at ten." Talia was kneeling beside her bed, already fully dressed in jeans and a loose navy blouse, her hair pulled back, which accentuated the roundness of her face. "I'm hungry. Come on."

Danielle groaned and collapsed back on the bed. "You know that there are places that serve breakfast twenty-four hours a day, right?"

"Yes, but here it's free. Mother taught me to never waste a free breakfast."

Danielle groaned louder. "Then go down and get

something. You can bring it up and eat it here."

"Alone?" The tremor in her voice was clear.

Danielle finally forced her eyes open. "Yes, alone. We're in a busy hotel on a Monday morning. Nobody is going to mess with you." Slightly annoyed, she tossed the covers off and swung her legs over the side of the bed. She ran both hands through her tangled hair. "I know you've got good reasons for being timid, but you're fifteen, and adulthood isn't that far off. You're going to have to learn to be self-sufficient. You start with small steps. You'll be fine."

Talia stood and smoothed her jeans, trying to hide her shaking hands. "I will. Do you want something?"

"Orange juice," Danielle said. She watched Talia gingerly make her way to the door, hesitate when she got there, and then finally step out into the hall when Danielle made no effort to stop her. She wanted to drop back into the bed for more sleep but knew it was too late, so she made herself get up instead.

She was squeezing into her own jeans when Talia knocked on the door. Barefoot, Danielle hustled to let her in, and Talia ducked in, balancing two Styrofoam plates, on one hand, a cup in the other hand, and another held in her teeth. She grunted, and Danielle got the meaning and took her cup of orange juice from Talia's teeth. Talia let out a relieved breath. "Didn't spill a drop."

She rushed to her bed, which she had made, and set her plates on the corner. One had a collection of fresh fruit, the other had a thick waffle. Talia set her cup on the nightstand that separated the beds, then held the waffle out to Danielle. "I got this for you."

Danielle grabbed the plate. "Don't suppose you got syrup and butter?"

Talia looked slightly panicked. "I didn't. My hands were full, but I can go get you some if you want."

"It's fine," Danielle said. "Eat your fruit." Danielle plopped on the edge of the bed and began tearing small bits of the waffle, which would have been so much better with syrup and butter. "Have you always been an early riser?"

Talia stabbed a bite sized chunk of pineapple with a plastic fork. "Yes. I don't sleep much." She took her bite and licked the juice off her lips. "Nights were...uneasy."

"Say no more." Danielle put the waffle aside. "I'm more of a nighthawk myself, but I guess you're starting to figure that out. I can get up early like you do. I just prefer not to. When we used to roll into a new town, I always wanted a day to just sleep and recover. I refused to do that whole burning the candle at both ends thing that a lot of bands did. We took things a lot slower."

"Was it fun, though? It seems like it would be a lot of fun."

"At times. Sometimes it was like an actual job and got to be a drag. Looking back, I don't think I fully appreciated it at the time." She moved to the window and pulled back the drapes to let the brilliant morning sunlight into the room. "It seems like I've spent my whole life either racing towards the next thing or running from the last thing. Kyle used to get onto me for not living in the moment more."

"You still do that." Danielle glanced back at Talia. "Isn't that why we're here? You're racing toward something, even if you don't know what. Or are we doing this because you're running from what happened in Colorado?"

Danielle turned all the way around. "Wasn't this your idea? Go to Nashville and find closure?"

"I'm fifteen. What do I know?" Talia poked a piece of watermelon and scarfed it down. "You seem to be the type that needs a quest. Besides, I thought I'd be on a bus to Austin."

Had she gotten played by a teenager? "It's too late now. I'm going, and you're coming with me. Joke's on you. Finish your breakfast so we can hit the road."

Once back in the car and on the highway, Talia dug through the glove box and found the copy of *The Fairie Meets the Fury* that she had been listening to on the way up to Colorado Springs. "I want to listen to this."

"Uh. Have we already gone through all the others?"

"No," Talia defended. "But I want to hear you. I've heard a bunch of your influences, and I've seen your videos on YouTube, but I want more."

"Go ahead," Danielle sighed. "But honestly, if you want to get to know my music, that's not the best place to start. That album is only half me, and I was in a weird place." She caught Talia staring at her. "Okay, I'm always in a weird place. I don't have any of my other CDs in the car."

"You have a phone. You can listen to music on your phone, you know."

"Phone is a shitty way to listen to music. Albums aren't mastered to be pumped through a phone. It just isn't right." Danielle hit the brakes and wrenched the car to the right, darting down an off ramp.

Talia braced against the dashboard, eyes wide with fear. Danielle ignored it as she came down off the interstate too fast, cut off traffic on the access road, and made a hard right turn at the intersection. "What are you doing?"

Danielle smirked at Talia's terrified reaction. She had a lot to learn about riding shotgun with her. "You want to hear my work? You're gonna hear it right. I saw a mall back here. If it's any kind of mall, then it'll have a record store."

"Are you serious? You almost got us killed because you want to go buy CDs?"

"I didn't almost get us killed. I know what I'm doing. I'm an excellent driver." Danielle picked her way through the mid-morning traffic with ease. "I'll have to tell you about the guy who taught me to drive. He used to take me out in the desert and just let me put the hammer down. He had this awesome '79 Z-28 that ran like a bat out of hell. We'd have these races out there in the middle of nowhere. He let me drive because he said I was fearless. If I hadn't fallen in love with music, I could have totally been a race car driver."

"You certainly drive like it."

They wasted an entire afternoon ratting around Little Rock, going from mall to mall and then seeking out used record stores to find the albums the malls didn't have. When it was all said and done, Danielle had managed to piece together her entire discography for Talia, including the ultra-hard to find *Marina Del Rey Soundtrack* that had been, by far, her most disappointing album. With the task complete, Danielle pointed the car back east, only to find herself stuck in rush hour gridlock.

At Danielle's insistence, Talia started at the beginning and began to work her way through the catalog. Eventually, traffic cleared, and they started making time. "Five hours to Nashville, kid. Then we'll find out if all of this was even worth it."

"It's worth it already," Talia whispered as she studied the liner notes to Danielle's first album. She didn't look up and probably thought, or maybe hoped, that Danielle hadn't heard her comment. She let it pass without a comment.

Listening to her own music, really listening to it, was an eye-opening experience for Danielle. The songs were like pieces of her soul, and she knew them intimately, but sharing them with Talia allowed her to experience them in a new way. Maybe it was vanity, but damn, she was good back in the day. She always knew when Talia found a song she liked because she would instantly play the song again while reading along with the lyrics. Danielle wondered if the music bug was biting her too.

Danielle hadn't stepped foot in Nashville since the day she tearfully left Kyle behind, choosing her art over her heart. On her last tour before the world fell apart, she had expressly forbidden Steve from booking a show there. She couldn't stand the thought that Kyle would find her and she'd have to face the consequences of her actions. He eventually came to her in Austin, a move that had left Danielle feeling that she had an eternal upper hand on him.

Still, she flawlessly navigated her way to the same downtown hotel she had stayed in back then. The place had a different name now and had been massively renovated, which took her reason for staying away. She passed on the high dollar suite for a more economical room with twin beds, and they headed upstairs for the night. Danielle tried hard to imagine Kyle riding the elevator, his cowboy hat pushed back on his head or strolling down the hallway with that slightly bowlegged walk he had, but every time she almost had it, he disappeared in the mist.

As they prepared to go to bed later that night, Danielle pulled Talia down to sit beside her on the bed. "I know you're a morning person and all that, but I've spent most of the last week behind the wheel of a car, and I'm wiped out. I'm gonna sleep, and I'm gonna sleep until I'm damn ready to get up. If you get hungry, call room service, get whatever you want. You wanna go downstairs, go for it, but please let me sleep."

"I will," Talia promised.

True to her word, Talia let Danielle sleep, and she slept for twenty hours straight, finally stirring for good just before ten that night. Talia was sitting cross-legged on the end of her bed, watching TV. In the corner, she had piled room service trays.

Danielle sat and stretched, feeling rejuvenated. "How ya' doin', kid?"

Talia jabbed the remote toward the TV. "Mother never let me watch TV, even when we had one."

"That's probably a good thing," Danielle said as she drug herself out of bed. "Give me fifteen minutes, and we'll head out."

"Where are we going to go? It's ten o'clock already."

Danielle paused at the bathroom door. "It's a music town, baby. Things are just starting to get interesting. We'll find some dinner, and then I'll find a club."

"I'm too young to go to a club."

"You let me take care of that. Fifteen minutes."

Once she was ready, Danielle took Talia to a twenty-four-hour diner that Kyle had frequented named Marshall's. Talia ordered a salad while Danielle scarfed down a plate of roast beef and mashed potatoes. "This place," she said between bites, "hasn't changed a bit. It's nice to know that something hasn't." She turned around and pointed toward an occupied table for two by the window. "That was our table. Kyle would actually wait for that specific table to open up."

"Why that one?"

"You see the open sign hanging in the window there? He said he liked the way I looked in the glow of the light. He was a sap like that."

Talia took her hand, and it brought Danielle's attention back to the table. "He sounds like he was a really sweet guy. I've read about guys like that, but I wasn't sure if they really existed."

Danielle sighed. "Yeah, they exist. But they're few and far between, unfortunately." Talia hummed gently and looked down at the table. "Something on your mind?"

Talia shrugged, eventually managing to look up. "Is Brett that kind of guy?"

"Maybe. Why?"

"He really likes you. It hurt him a great deal when you ran off. He tried to hide it, but I could tell. Maybe you should give him a chance."

Danielle chuckled and pushed her plate aside. "Trying to hook me up with a new boyfriend while I'm trying to chase down the ghost of my last one? Kind of weird." Talia dropped her eyes again. "Listen, Brett seems like a good enough guy, but my heart is closed. I've got nothing to give him, and honestly, he could do better."

"If you say so."

They stared across the table at one another before Danielle broke the contest. She threw some money on the table, stood, and held her hand out to Talia. "Come on, let's get you ready."

"Ready for what?"

"You'll see." Danielle led Talia through the restaurant to the bathroom and stood her in front of the mirror. "If I'm going to sneak you into a club, I gotta make you look older."

"You don't need to—"

Danielle placed a finger on her lips. "Shhh. This is what big sisters do. Now hush up."

She took the clip out of Talia's hair and let it fall over her shoulders, using her fingers to puff it up and position it so that her bangs covered half of Talia's face. "That's good. Now, no twenty-one-year-old would dress like this." She untucked Talia's blouse, this one a soft peach color, and tied off the bottom of it, leaving just a hint of skin exposed above her waistline. Then she undid the top two buttons.

"Are you sure about this?" Talia asked as she studied her reflection. Danielle stood beside her and crouched so that they were cheek-to-cheek.

"Absolutely. I've still got some of that stupid makeup in the car. I'll do your face out there, and we'll be good. Where we're going is pretty dark, so people shouldn't be looking too close."

They hustled back out through the restaurant, and Danielle felt vindicated when she noticed some guys checking out Talia on their way by. It was going to work. In the car, Danielle took the make-up case out of the back seat and did a classy touch up on Talia, not going for slutty, just mature. Feeling far too confident, she stashed the case and started the engine.

While Danielle made her way across town, Talia looked at her face in the visor mirror, particularly focused on her now ruby red lips. "Are you sure about this? I've got a bad feeling."

Danielle swatted her playfully on the thigh. "It'll be fine. Just let me do the talking and keep your head down. Anybody looks too close, and we're busted."

The club Danielle found was now called The Buenos Noches Room, but she had known it under another name. Kyle had tracked her down here once. She got lucky and found a parking spot between two oversized pickups not far from the door. Danielle took a moment to finger comb her own hair. "Remember, keep your head down and let me talk. You're about to experience a legitimate Nashville honky tonk."

"All right," Talia said with a quivering voice. She reached for Danielle's hand as they made their way to the door.

The bouncer was the typical kind of redneck tough guy, short and square with broad shoulders and thick thighs, muscles bristling under his Western shirt. He was the kind of guy who got his strength from throwing hay bales, not bench pressing in overpriced gyms. Danielle pulled Talia to her left side as she sidled up to him.

"ID?"

Danielle produced hers out of her back pocket and held it

out to him with two fingers. He studied it for a moment, and if her name made an impact, he didn't show it. He pushed it back. "And her?"

Danielle smiled sweetly. "She's with me."

"Uh huh. ID."

Danielle plopped one arm on his shoulder, rubbing up close to him. "Big sis is trying to show the small town girl a good time. Come on." She ran one finger along his unshaven jawline. "I bet you used to go to clubs when you were slightly underage."

"How slightly?"

Talia was doing her best to keep her distance, peering up at them through strands of hair.

"Just turned nineteen," Danielle said. "We're not drinking, we're just here to listen to some real life Nashville country."

He wagged a meaty finger at her. "No drinking."

Danielle stood back. "Cross my heart, no drinking. Just hanging out." The bouncer paused, then slumped and jerked his head and stepped aside. Danielle smiled wider and squeezed his bicep. "Thank ya, darlin'," she said with her exaggerated accent that she knew well how to use. She turned to Talia. "See? I told you it would be fine."

The Buenos Noches Room was a spacious club with a polished oval dancefloor circling a DJ booth, bars running down both sides, and a stage at the back of the club. It was ensconced with chicken wire, but Danielle figured that was more for show than purpose. She found them a table with a view of the stage, which was occupied by a pudgy dude with a ZZ Top beard who was doing a semi-credible country/blues mashup. An impossibly hot girl in Daisy Dukes and a skin tight tank top came for their order, and Danielle ordered two Cokes.

"I was just going to have water," Talia protested.

"Ah, live a little. You don't drink water at a club. Come on, loosen up." She gestured toward the stage. "This dude is pretty good, don't you think? I like his voice. Nice and gruff."

"I guess," Talia said as she hugged herself. "It just feels wrong." The waitress returned with two glasses of Coke, and

Talia took a careful look at her. As she sauntered on, Talia leaned in. "I don't look like that."

"Neither one of us does. Don't worry about it. I got you past the bouncer, so it worked."

"You told him I was underage."

"Yeah," Danielle said after a sip of watered down Coke. "But there's a huge difference between nineteen and fifteen. He bought nineteen, and I'm happy with that." Talia rested her elbows on the table and chewed at her thumbnail. "Don't sweat it," Danielle assured her. "We'll just stay for a half hour or so and then go back to the hotel."

The band launched into a new song, and instantly couples flocked to the dance floor. "This is a good two-stepping song," Danielle said. "Kyle insisted that I learn how to two-step. You wanna learn?"

"I'm fine."

"Ah." Danielle pushed away from the table and pulled Talia up. "Come on. It's a dance. I'll show you. Just follow my lead."

Danielle led Talia through the dance, occasionally giving her little pointers and encouraging her to loosen up and go with the music. Just as she was starting to get it, the song ended, and the band started playing a slow dancing song instead.

"We'll catch the next one," Danielle said as they shuffled back to the table. "Don't tell me that you didn't have at least a little fun," she said.

Talia cracked a shy smile. "Just a little. But I do want to do it again if we can."

"Of course. You have good rhythm. It comes natural to you. You're kind of built like a dancer. Maybe we should get you in some classes."

"Really?" She seemed struck by the idea.

"Ladies." They were interrupted by a middle-aged cowboy with a deeply weathered and hard face. He wore his hat low over his eyes and held a Coors loosely by the neck. His teeth were stained yellow from nicotine. "That was quite a show y'all put on out there." He turned his eyes toward Talia. "What about you let a man take you round the floor a time or two?"

They both caught the predatory edge in his voice. Talia tried to pull back into herself.

"Thanks for the offer," Danielle said as politely as possible. "But we're having a girls' night out. Just trying to have a little fun, not looking for anything."

The stranger pulled out the seat to Danielle's right with his foot and slithered down into it. "That's all I'm doin' is looking for a little fun. Just one dance with the young one."

Talia tugged at her sleeve. "Let's just go."

"You two aren't muff munchers, are ya?"

Danielle leaned toward him. "So what if we are? Means that we don't have any need for you at our table. So why don't you move on? I'm sure there's some washed out honky tonk queen here you can take home tonight. I'm trying to show my girl a good time, don't make it ugly."

"Or you can take me home, and I can show you what it's like to be with a real man."

"Danielle, please, let's go," Talia begged. "I'm scared. Come on." She stood, trying to yank Danielle to her feet. "Please come on."

She swatted Talia's hands away. "A real man would know better. Now do us both a favor, Billy Bob, and get lost. I owe my sister another dance."

"Sister? Ah. Ain't never been with no sisters before. You almost had me goin' there for a minute."

"You just don't get it, do you, pal? I'm telling you to fuck off. So move along, hillbilly."

"Danielle, don't antagonize him, just come on." Talia wrapped both of her hands around Danielle's arm, but she still couldn't get her to budge. "It's late, and I'm tired. Come on."

The stranger deliberately set his beer down and stood. "I'll take ya home, darlin'."

"The fuck you will," Danielle snapped. She stood quickly and squared up to the stranger. "You even think about laying a finger on her, and I will fuck you up. I've handled my share of drunk cowboys before. Kicking your ass won't be a thing for me."

"You talk a lot of shit," he said with a chuckle. "Let's see if you're really as tough as you talk." With one hand, he shoved her, and despite setting her feet, he was strong enough to push Danielle off balance and into Talia, who stumbled and fell. The sight of her sister on the ground sent a fresh wave of anger surging through her.

"All right, fuckhead," she growled. "That's it." She lunged at him, put both hands on his chest, and shoved hard but barely made him move.

"That all you got?"

His laugh smelled like cheap cigarettes and stale beer, and it pissed Danielle off even more. She clenched her fist hard as she stared daggers at him. He glanced down and saw the fist.

"Go ahead, girlie. First shot's free. But I should warn ya, I got no problem hitting a girl. Especially if she thinks she's a tough girl."

"Stop! Enough!" Talia was on her feet and positioned herself between them. "We're leaving, Danielle. Right now."

A couple of bouncers who were copies of the one at the door stepped through the crowd. "Yep," one of them said. "Time for you girls to go home." He pointed at Talia. "Ain't no way this one's of age. Get your ass outta here."

Begrudgingly, Danielle let Talia lead her away. "Catch ya later, girlie," the stranger called out, openly mocking her. She tensed up, wanting to go back after him, but instead let Talia finish dragging her out the door.

"What were you thinking?" Talia yelled as they got back in the car. "Were you really going to get in a bar fight with that guy? Why wouldn't you just leave like I wanted you to?'

Danielle held the steering wheel in a vice grip, the stranger's stupid face still fresh in her mind. "Because I don't back down. I don't take shit, especially from a piece of trash like that. You can't let guys like that get on top of you. You can't show weakness."

"Weakness? Walking away from a fight isn't weak. It's smart." She shivered. "Please don't ever put me in a position like that again." Talia pulled down the visor and began to frantically wipe the makeup away from her face with the sleeve of her shirt.

Danielle grunted as she pulled out of the parking lot and back onto the street. "Well, isn't this a fine way to end a fun night."

CHAPTER TWENTY

Danielle woke up the next morning to find Talia still asleep. She was curled into a tight ball, barely taking up any space despite having a huge bed all to herself. Danielle got dressed quietly and snuck out, hoping to get back before Talia knew she was gone.

In the lobby, she studied a map of the town, fixing some locations that she didn't remember as well as she thought she would. Once she had her bearings, she made a quick drive across town, bought some six-inch subs from a local deli, a gallon of sweet tea, and paid extra for an old fashioned picnic basket, and raced back to the hotel.

Talia was just stepping out of the bathroom when she got back to the room. Though she tried to hide it, Danielle could see the worry in Talia's eyes. Fear of abandonment was something Talia would probably struggle with her entire life, and Danielle knew she would be a big reason for that.

"Hey, sleepyhead. I'm having an effect on you. Starting to sleep late already."

Talia washed her hands and then splashed some water on her face. "But I didn't fall asleep until after dawn. I couldn't go to sleep, so I sat and watched the sun come up. I wasn't really sleeping that long. Where did you go?"

Danielle smiled big. "Just prepping for the day. Hurry up and get dressed."

"Fine," she muttered. Talia shuffled to her bed and threw her suitcase up on it. "You know, if you're going to do something like that, a note would be nice. It's kind of jarring to wake up, and you're not here."

"I know, kiddo. I'm sorry. I was hoping to get back faster."

She watched Talia carefully pick through her clothes before pulling out some jeans. "Why don't you wear some shorts? It's gonna be hot today."

Talia glanced up and bit her lip. "I'm not comfortable showing that much skin."

Danielle sat down on her own bed, facing her. "Does that come from the camps?" Talia answered with a subtle nod of her head. "You're not in the camps anymore. I remember buying you some."

"Yeah, but...." She shivered. "I don't want to invite attention. I don't want to put myself on display, especially after that guy last night."

"That is your mom talking," Danielle said. She leaned over and lifted Talia's chin with one finger. "First, that guy last night was just a drunk looking for trouble—forget him. Second, wearing shorts and showing a little skin isn't an invitation for anything. You've spent most of your life up in the mountains. You're in the South now, and it gets hot down here. It's survival. Third, you're a pretty young girl who is going to grow into a gorgeous young woman—guys are going to notice you regardless. You could walk around in burlap sacks. It wouldn't matter. Guys are gonna be guys. But I'll teach you how to take care of yourself so that one of these days when some drunk in a bar comes on too strong, you can put him in his place. For now, you got me, and nobody's gonna mess with you and get away it. So come on and get dressed. We've got plans."

Talia did find the courage to put on a pair of faded jeans shorts that hung halfway to her knee and a short sleeved red and white baseball shirt. Danielle tried to make her feel better by switching from a T-shirt to a tank top so that she was showing more skin and, therefore, attracting more attention. Danielle ripped the blanket off her bed, and they were off.

She took them to a city park not far from where Kyle had lived and pulled the Camaro up to the curb. Taking the picnic basket out of the backseat, she encouraged Talia to follow her, and she found a level, grassy spot under an old oak tree. Danielle spread the pilfered blanket out for them to sit on. "I got to the deli and realized I don't know what you like, so I just bought a whole lot of different stuff. I figure that whatever we don't eat, we can leave for the kids in the park."

"Or we could give them to homeless people," Talia said. "They would appreciate it."

"We could do that," Danielle agreed. She started taking sandwiches out of the basket and reading off what they were. Talia went with a simple turkey and Swiss. Danielle took a club and poured some tea into some clear plastic cups.

"Is this place special in some way?"

"Yeah," Danielle said. "This whole thing. Kyle would bring me here for picnics, and he would always get sandwiches from this one particular deli. Unfortunately, that place went out of business, so I had to settle for this place." She pointed across the way to a playground that was at present deserted. "That playground wasn't there. There was a gazebo there, and the playground was over there. An old school playground with a teeter totter and even a wooden merry-go-round. It looked dangerous and fun as hell. Of course, they've changed it all."

Talia was watching her and listening carefully. She swallowed and asked, "How long ago was all of this?"

"Ten years ago. Wow." She studied her sandwich, then tossed it on the blanket. "A lot can change in ten years, huh?" She looked over at Talia. "I was on the run, a big surprise, I know, and I rolled into town, just planning on spending a day or two. Something about this town grabbed me, and it held me here. I got it in my head that I needed to record my next album here, and eventually, Kyle came into my life."

"It was God's plan," Talia said softly. "He brought you here and held you here for a reason. You were supposed to meet Kyle here at that time."

"I knew you were going to say that," Danielle groaned. She had a dozen well-rehearsed arguments for the God's plan idea, but she left them all unspoken. "Whatever it was, those few weeks were some of the best of my life. That's what I'm hoping to find, just a tendril of that feeling, and so far, it's not working."

"I thought we were here so you could find closure."

"That too," Danielle whispered. She scooped her sandwich back up. "Well, let's finish up and move on." Talia finished first, and Danielle caught her staring at the playground. "What's on your mind, kid?"

"Just thinking, that's all."

"Obviously. What are you thinking about?" She followed Talia's gaze to the playground. "Is that bringing up some kind of bad memory for you or something?"

"No. I used to see kids playing at parks like this on playgrounds like that when we'd go into town for supplies or when we moved camps. I always wanted to stop and play, but of course, we weren't allowed." She closed her eyes. "They looked like they were having so much fun. All the laughter and the squealing." Her eyes opened slowly. "And I'd be pressed up against the glass of an old school bus, a sweaty man beside me who claimed to be a Godly man while his hand crept up my skirt." Her face went hard. She began to shake, but this time it wasn't fear but anger.

Danielle took another look at the playground. "Bet I can beat you there."

"What?"

Danielle stood and dusted herself off. "I bet I can beat you over there." Talia still wasn't getting it. "A race. I'll race you to the playground."

Talia was still confused. "Why?"

"Because the first one to the playground gets the best swing. That's the rule of the playground. You may not have gotten to play on one, but I'm an old veteran of the playground. Not the pussy ones like that, with all the plastic set in a rubber base, either. I grew up with metal equipment that scalded you in the summer and hard dirt and rocks. We were fucking tough."

"You want me to play on the playground?" Talia shook her head. "I'm too big. I'm a teenager. That's for little kids."

"Fine, have it your way. I'm going."

She left Talia behind and started the long walk across the park. She heard Talia softly call for her to wait, but she ignored it. Ignored her until she heard urgent footsteps coming up on her quick. Talia was running to catch up. She looked over her shoulder once to see Talia awkwardly running and realized that she probably hadn't done much of that either.

"There ya go. Now catch me." She turned and ran, but not anywhere near full speed. She did indeed beat Talia to the playground and took her choice of swings as her trophy.

Talia, breathing hard, took the swing next to her. "Watch me and do what I do," Danielle said, and she started to swing. Talia watched, then copied her, and soon they were arching high in the air. Talia squealed in delight. They spent over an hour there, climbing up plastic climbing walls and sliding down twisty slides. Talia let herself go, and in her exuberance, she looked so much younger than she really was. It made Danielle want to mourn for what the girl had lost.

Eventually, they packed up, and Talia collapsed into an exhausted heap in the shotgun seat. "That was fun. Thank you."

"There was no merry-go-round," Danielle said. "Brooke and I used to take turns trying to make it go so fast that the other one would go flying off. Lots of skinned knees and elbows playing that game."

"Brooke?"

"A girl I grew up with. I haven't seen her since...." Danielle reached deep into the corners of her mind. "Shit. I guess we were about your age. Her family moved away. I wonder whatever happened to her."

"Do you want to look for her?"

Danielle smirked. "Nah. I think I'm spending too much time chasing my past as it is. Besides, I wouldn't know where to start."

"You could try your phone. That seems to be where everybody else finds what they're looking for. I see people on those things all the time. Even Brett when you left me there. He was on his phone a lot."

"Yeah, people spend their entire lives looking at screens while the world passes them by, and they don't even see. I've made a little bit of peace with the damn thing, but I still try to avoid using it as much as possible." She dug hers out of her pocket and waved it in the air. "These things are more addictive than heroin." She tossed it on the console.

She weaved her way through the cramped residential streets until she found the street Kyle had lived on, turned right, and crept down the street. She didn't remember the exact address; she just knew that she'd recognize the house. She crept that way for several blocks, earning herself plenty of hard stares from the residents who were outside, most of them black and understandably wary.

She eventually did find the house, but like everything else, it had changed for the worse. The chain link fence was gone, and the yard was dirty now, which was understandable since it was being used as a parking lot. The paint was gone, leaving just grayed and weathered wood in its place. Two large young black men were hunched under the hood of a Crown Victoria, their shirts stained with engine grease.

"Kyle lived here," she told Talia. "It wasn't a great house, even then, but we had fun. Wrote a bunch of songs there."

The men with the car noticed her idling in the street and started to stare.

"I think you're making them nervous," Talia said, pointing it out.

"Yeah, we better move on." She waved to the dudes in the yard and rolled on. Another dead end on a trip that was feeling like a waste of time. "This isn't working out how I planned. I got one more place I want to go."

Finding the recording studio where she and her band had recorded *Southern Hospitality* with Kyle producing wasn't hard. It also wasn't worth it. The first thing she noticed was the For Lease sign. She pulled into a parking lot overgrown with weeds. The front doors were padlocked, and every visible window was broken. "Well, shit. So much for that." Danielle slammed her palms against the steering wheel. "He's gone. Every little snippet of our time here is either gone or changed beyond recognition. I'm sorry to waste your time."

"It's not a waste to me," Talia said. "I've had fun, seen new places. Snuck into a bar."

"I'm glad for that, at least." She backed out of the parking lot and headed back to the hotel. "I guess we'll rest up tonight, and in the morning, we'll head back home." She glanced over at Talia. "Or to Austin. I know Ms. Luster will be expecting you."

"I guess she will," Talia said softly. "I think she had a foster home picked out for me already."

They fell silent for several miles until Danielle finally spoke again. "We don't have to wait until the morning. We could start now. It's a two day drive, no matter how you slice it. We could at least get down the road a bit."

"Whatever you want to do. It's your call."

Danielle sighed. "Yeah, we'll do that. No need to keep you out here any longer than necessary. Besides, I'm sure my therapist would love to have a few words with me, and I haven't checked on Randy and Terri in a while."

"I guess it's on to Austin," Talia said.

"I guess so."

There was little talking on the drive. Talia spent most of the drive staring out the window. Danielle tried to start some small talk, but found her unresponsive and gave up. She refused to go to dinner when they stopped for the night in Memphis, so they ate room service in silence. The next morning they left early for Austin.

Another day of driving and more silence. Nine hours to do nothing but wrestle with her thoughts was a recipe for disaster. By the time they reached Austin that night, Danielle's guilt was turning to anger. She couldn't understand what was going on with Talia. All she wanted from her sister was some sort of sign that she wanted to stay, but in these moments, she had gone cold.

They checked into a Holiday Inn on the outskirts of town and bedded down for the night. It was a long night for Danielle.

She tossed and turned, her emotions a knot in her stomach. It was crazy to her to think that when Talia had first come into her life, all she wanted to do was get her out. Now she was hours away from getting her wish, and it was making her sick.

In the morning, they dressed hurriedly, still not talking. Their appointment with Luster was less than an hour away.

CHAPTER TWENTY-ONE

Danielle sat on the edge of the bed with her keys held loosely in her hand. Her hair was in a ponytail, and she wore faded blue jeans, dirty tennis shoes, and a plain gray T-shirt. Feet away, Talia stood in front of the sink, studying herself in the mirror. She wore one of the outfits Danielle had bought for her that first day, a gray blouse over a ruffled yellow skirt and a black belt with black flats. Her face was freshly washed, her skin fresh and flawless, and her blonde hair pulled away from her face and held in place by a faux-antique clip. She was making last minute adjustments, looking more like a girl readying to go on her first date, not to a foster home.

With a deep, shaky sigh, Talia finally turned around, killed the bathroom light, and strode past Danielle without a look. She plucked her suitcase off the bed. Danielle had already watched her meticulously pack it earlier that morning.

"Well, let's go. Ms. Luster is waiting."

"All right," Danielle said. It was the only thing she could force out of her mouth.

She held the door open, and Talia strutted right past her and into the hallway. Danielle trailed her to the elevator, and they stood on opposite sides on the ride down. They stepped out into the muggy heat of a morning that promised to be an absolutely unbearable day. Again Talia walked ahead of Danielle to the car and waited impatiently for Danielle to catch up. When she did, she popped the trunk for Talia's suitcase, but she refused.

"I'd rather put it in the back so I can get it easier. You don't need to get out that way."

"Whatever you want, kid."

Danielle slammed the trunk lid down, and they got in the car. Danielle's every motion was violent as she started the car and jerked it into gear. She took the long way, seeking out traffic, delaying their arrival, praying for one flicker of regret from Talia.

"Why are you taking this way? You're going to make me late."

"Right," Danielle said. "Gotta get you to the church on time." She said it thinking of Talia's story of the first time she'd been assaulted. She sped up and began to weave through traffic. If she was in such a hurry, then Danielle would surely get her there.

The message hit, and Talia smirked. "Like you care."

"I don't care? We're here because of you, kid. I was ready to go back to Brett's, maybe take the long way and do some sightseeing. You're the one who wanted to come down here."

"Yes, you're right. I did. Can't imagine why."

Danielle, who had been driving in the inside line, threw on her brakes and jerked the wheel to the right, making an almost ninety degree turn into the neglected parking lot of a boarded up Long John Silvers. She slammed the car into gear.

"No, I can't imagine why, so do me a favor and enlighten me. I thought we were having a good time and connecting."

Talia's façade broke. She turned toward Danielle, her face contorting with anger. It was a look Danielle had seen on her mother's face more than once. And on her own.

"You mentioned Austin. Not me."

"I had told you that if you wanted me to bring you back after Nashville, I would. I was just throwing it out there. You didn't have to jump on it so fast."

"Because I'm tired of people pretending to care about me. It's been happening all my life, and I'm sick of it. At least Ms. Luster cares a little. So I'll go to her because there is literally nowhere else in the world I can go."

"Oh, that's bullshit," Danielle said. "We wouldn't be here if I didn't care."

Talia pushed open the passenger side door. "If you cared,

you wouldn't have left me with a stranger for four days. No one has ever cared. My father just wanted me for a toy. Mother was always hung up on her own guilt. You were all she ever talked about. I was just the price she paid for her terrible decisions. Well, I'm tired of being an afterthought." She hopped out, slamming the door behind her, and started walking west.

Danielle jumped out the other side. "Where are you going?"

"I can find it on my own. I'm not stupid."

Danielle stood beside the idling car, struggling to find the right words. The easiest thing in the world would have been to let her keep walking. Let her walk right out of her life. She started thinking about Brett. Did she have anything of value at his place? Anything she couldn't live without? If not, she could just drive away. She was already convinced that leaving her exile had been a mistake. Now, if she left, no one would care.

Talia kept storming down the street, never pausing, never looking back. Then Danielle's own anger boiled to the surface. She'd be damned if some fifteen-year-old was going to get the last word on her. Danielle dropped back into the car and raced forward, cutting Talia off just before she crossed a side street, the ass end of the Camaro jutting out into traffic.

"You know, I told you at first that I didn't know what I was doing, and that I was selfish and that I disappointed everyone. So I don't know why you're so surprised. You knew exactly what type of person I was. I thought I was getting better. Slowly. You were helping me to be better. But I guess that was just a lie. No shock from one of Dorothy Regan's daughters."

"I'm not a Regan. Maybe that lying streak comes from the other side."

Danielle slammed her door and ran around the front of the car quickly, so quickly that Talia stumbled backwards in shock. Danielle shoved her backwards further. "Don't you dare." She jabbed her finger in Talia's face. "Don't kid yourself. You're every bit as much her kid as I am, regardless of the name. You sit here and try to blow her up to be some saint. It's all such bullshit.

You're just as manipulative."

"Maybe I learned it from watching you," Talia said, but her confidence was waning in the face of Danielle's force.

"You didn't learn shit. It comes naturally." Danielle stopped her advance, letting Talia retreat. "You wanna go back? Go then." She pointed south. "It's that way. Go until you cross the next major intersection, then two blocks to the west. But you know what's going to happen to you in foster care. Pretty thing like you."

Talia stopped backing up and stood straight. "It's happened before. I can handle it."

"You're in such a hurry to get back. I think you like it. Just a perv, like your dad."

Talia screamed and ran at her, flailing at Danielle with limp fists that could never do any damage. "Screw you," she screamed. Talia punched herself out, briefly leaned against Danielle for support, then pushed away. "All I wanted you to do was fight for me."

"What?"

"You'll run off to another state and make an ass out of yourself fighting for your career. You'll risk going to prison to fight for your twisted ideas about independence. But when it comes to me, you can't even be bothered to try and talk me out of it?"

"That's why we're even here. Why we went on this trip. When I went back to the station, that was me fighting for you. I don't do that. I'm the one who always walks away before I get hurt. I took a chance on you, and now see where we are."

"That's all I'm worth? One moment? This trip had nothing to do with me. You just didn't want to be alone—that's why you came here and whined about your dead boyfriend. It's all just an act for you anyway. You didn't care about him any more than anybody else in your life."

Danielle slammed her fist on the hood of the car. A car narrowly missed slamming into hers, and the driver shouted an insult as she drove by. "Don't you dare fucking say I didn't care about Kyle. He was the only person I ever loved, and the only one who ever loved me."

"I'm sure he did love you," Talia said softly, but with a rising edge of nastiness. "But don't tell me that you loved him. In all this time you've talked about him, never once have you cried, or even gotten teary eyed. He was just another piece of your puzzle."

"It was seven years ago. I'm out of tears."

Talia sized her up across the roof of the car, looked Danielle dead in the eyes, and called her bluff. "Are you really? Because I don't think you are. I don't think you have the heart to cry over him, or anybody else. You're just an empty, pathetic shell of a person who can't see past her own selfish desires. You toy with Mr. Walls. You toy with your friends, and you toy with me. Well, if I'm going to be somebody's plaything, I can do that anywhere."

Danielle's rage melted into the steaming pavement. With one well-placed verbal assault, Talia had laid bare everything Danielle had always known about herself but been reluctant to admit. She had no comeback. Her mind went blank.

Talia walked around the front of the car and squared up to the shaken Danielle. "The truth hurts. But maybe in the long run, you'll be better for it. Have a nice life, Danielle. Underneath it all, I believe you are a good person, and I hope you find that in yourself." Danielle collapsed into the driver's seat, and suddenly Talia was kneeling in front of her. "I want you to know that I forgive you for everything. You weren't ready for this, and it was unfair to throw you into it. You need to go fix yourself. Don't worry about me. I'll be fine."

Talia stood, straightened her skirt, and started walking south. She left her suitcase in the backseat. When Danielle had first seen her, she had nothing, and now as she walked out of Danielle's life, that was still all she had. Danielle couldn't bring herself to watch, and by the time she finally looked up, Talia was nowhere to be seen.

She sat even longer until the squawk of a police siren caught her attention. An Austin PD cruiser with lights flashing pulled in behind her. Danielle stood on shaky legs and ran a nervous finger through her hair. The cruiser door popped open, and a youthful officer stood. "Ma'am, are you all right? Are you having car trouble?"

She glanced back in the direction Talia had been walking, hoping to see her. "I'm having trouble," she managed to say. The dam she had spent so many years building was cracking, and she felt all the emotions she hadn't let herself experience pushing on her crumbling walls.

The officer came to her. "What kind of trouble?" The car was still idling, so he looked at the tires. "Did you have a blowout?" He looked at her with kind eyes, saw her fighting a losing battle, and put a hand on her shoulder. "Ma'am?"

Danielle gave up the fight and collapsed into the officer's arms, blubbering like a fool, talking gibberish she knew he couldn't understand. She let it all out to a complete stranger: her parents, Kel, Adam, Kyle, Brett, Shannon, and Talia. She cried for them all. For the pain they had inflicted and the hurt she had paid forward. He held her close and let her cry, not saying a word.

She finally pulled away. It felt like she'd been in his arms for days, but she knew it was only minutes. "I'm sorry," she managed to say. "I'll move the car. I have something I have to go do."

She started to get in the car, but the officer grabbed her arm. "Ma'am, I'm not sure you're in a condition to drive. Maybe you should talk to someone."

"I do need to talk to someone," she answered. "But you can't help me with that. I'll be fine. But I need to go. I promise you, I'm not going to hurt myself."

He loosened his grip, and Danielle slithered out and down into the driver's seat. She had, for the first time in years, a clear vision of who she was and what she needed to do.

"Are you sure I can't help you?"

Danielle started to close the door but stopped and looked back up at the officer. "Well, maybe you can do one thing for me."

***

Danielle pulled into the parking lot of the Health and Human Services building cautiously. She had been looking for Talia the entire time, hoping she would catch up. Either she walked fast, or she got a ride, but Talia was gone. After she parked, Danielle took a moment to straighten up, wishing that she could disguise that her eyes were red from crying. No. Talia needed to see that. The time for hiding was over.

With all the composure she could muster, Danielle walked in and right up to the counter. The tired woman on the other side of the glass knew who she was instantly, and the metal door to her right buzzed. "Go on in. Luster is expecting you."

She weaved her way through the hallways and soon found Luster standing alone, waiting for her. She hurried up to Danielle. "Ms. Regan. I have to tell you, I have reservations about this. Talitha has been telling me about everything."

Danielle stopped walking and stared at the woman. "Her name is Talia now. And I don't blame you for doubting me, but I'm going to make this work, and I need someone to believe in me. I need you to be that person."

They exchanged stares, and then Luster sighed. "Well, let's see how this works." She retreated to the office door, cracked it open, and stuck her head inside. "Talitha dear," she said, ignoring Danielle's assertion of her new name, "there's someone here to see you now."

Luster stepped aside and held the door open wider. Danielle walked through, head held high, and felt better when Talia's eyes got wide. She pulled up a chair and sat facing her sister. "Hey, kid."

"Danielle."

Danielle leaned forward, resting her elbows on her knees and clasping her fingers together. "You got me. You nailed me in a way no one ever has. You're one hundred percent right, and I needed to hear it." She reached for Talia's hand. "I need you. I need you to show me how to be a better person. And to teach me this weird forgiveness thing you do. I'm asking for one more second chance here. This time it's all about you. I'm through chasing rainbows."

Talia started to smile, but caught herself. "I'm not sure I believe you."

"That's fair. I know I'm going to have to earn your trust. I'm just asking for a start."

Talia looked over Danielle's shoulder to Ms. Luster. "It's your call, honey. I have a family ready to take you if you want. They're a decent family."

"I won't be mad if you go," Danielle said softly. "I'm starting over one way or another. You do what you've gotta do. But I couldn't let you go without letting you know that you got through."

"Your eyes are red."

Danielle smirked. "Yeah. I just spent ten minutes crying like a dolt on the shoulder of some poor rookie police officer who had no idea what the hell to do with me. It was kind of embarrassing."

"You finally cried for Kyle? That's good. You needed to do that," Talia said.

"I cried for you," Danielle answered. "And me. And every goddamn thing in the world." She laughed uneasily. "It was a lot of tears."

"I thought you were out."

"I did, too," Danielle said. "Turns out I've got more than enough. Now that I've tapped them, I'm not sure I can stop. I figure I'm gonna spend a lot of nights crying myself to sleep."

Talia laid her hand on Danielle's cheek. "It's not a bad thing." Danielle put her hand over Talia's, reveling in the touch. Finally, Talia spoke again. "Could we live somewhere near Mr. Walls? I like it up there."

Danielle opened her eyes, which were trying to fill with tears again. "Really?" Talia nodded. "We'll live anywhere you want. I promise I'll be better this time. A whole new Danielle."

"You don't have to be new," Talia said. "Just be my sister. For real this time."

"You got it."

***

Two days later, Danielle and Talia stood shoulder to shoulder on the banks of the Colorado River. They both wore lightweight floral print dresses to combat the heat. In her hands, Danielle held a simple pewter urn.

Talia laid her hand on the urn. "Mother," she said softly. "Thank you for bringing me to Danielle and for the sacrifices you made for me. I know you weren't perfect, and you were burdened with guilt and regret, but you did the best you could, and I forgive the rest. Rest easy." She looked to the sky, a brilliant blue dotted with the occasional puffy white cloud. "Lord, please take Dorothy James Regan McLain into your arms and shelter her in your eternal love. Forgive her sins as I have, and cleanse her soul of her guilt. Prepare for her a house of gold, and reunite her with those she loved. Amen."

Talia pulled her hand away and nodded at Danielle. Danielle popped the lid and stepped forward.

"Wait," Talia said. "Don't you want to say something?"

Danielle looked back at Talia. She didn't want to say anything, but she knew Talia wanted her to. She put the lid back on. "Mom," she said, her voice quivering. "Um, this is weird," she said to Talia, but Talia nudged her on. "So, Mom, I know it was a crazy trip. I wasn't always the best kid, and you didn't get any breaks. I want you to know it wasn't all bad, even if that's what I always focused on. I guess you did the best you could." She glanced back again, and Talia nudged her still. Danielle knew what she needed to say. "So I guess what I'm saying is...I forgive you." The words stung coming out of her mouth, but a second later, her soul seemed lighter, if even by just a fraction. She took away one more step forward and popped the lid. "Say hi to Dad if you see him."

She held the urn upside down, and the last earthly remnants of Dorothy Regan cascaded down to the gently rolling waters of the Colorado and were whisked away. Danielle held the empty urn loosely in one hand, and Talia stepped forward to claim the other. They watched in silence for several minutes before Danielle broke the silence.

"Well, come on. We've got moving to do."

CHAPTER TWENTY-TWO

The ride out was beautiful. Tasty blues licks slowly melting into cascading piano chords, the drums rising from the mix to meet them, and then it all slowly faded. Danielle edged up to the microphone, tossed her hair, licked her lips, and hit the button. "That was 'Time Waits For No One' by the Rolling Stones, wrapping up another fantastic morning here on Amarillo's home for real rock. I'll be back tomorrow morning to see all you fine folks back to work. Don't fret, because Melody is next to take you to quitting time. Make sure you get your requests in now for today's Rock Garden, Amarillo's number one request show. Stay cool out there, and thank you for listening to the KATT. Here's some White snake for ya." She killed the mike as the keyboards for "Here I Go Again" filled the air.

Danielle muted the booth monitor and turned to the aforementioned Melody, an attractive blonde who was a legend in the Amarillo radio community. Melody grinned as she switched places with Danielle. "You know, I'll never get tired of hearing that," she said in a whiskey rich voice.

"You mean, number one call-in request show?"

"Yep." Melody hopped onto the bar stool that sat behind the board and adjusted the mic. "And to think, when you walked in here three years ago pitching this idea, I thought you were full of shit. Shows what I know."

Danielle scooped up a legal pad and manilla folder and tucked them under her arm. "It wasn't a big deal. You couldn't find anything in this damn town but holy rollers, Top 40, country, and Tejano. Sometimes all you gotta do is offer something different. Lots of people out there still like to rock."

"But this," Melody said, referring to the top of the line equipment that surrounded them in the tiny booth. "And the format. If you had told me that you could follow Stone Temple Pilots with Paul Revere and the Raiders and people would dig it...."

Danielle moved to the door. "I guess I just believe that good music will find an audience. Call me an optimist." She pushed the door open. "Have a good shift, Champ."

She ducked out of the studio as Melody prepared to go on and strolled down the hallway. The studios of K-A-T-T may have gotten a new face, but they still resided in a building that didn't know the seventies were over. She padded down a hallway covered with faded grayish blue carpet to a lobby that still had wood paneling on the walls.

Jyme, the receptionist, sat at a workstation that consisted of a thrift store desk and a folding table set at a ninety-degree angle to each other. She was banging away on her computer, her normally kind face twisted in intense concentration. Jyme had been the first person Danielle had spoken to when she had walked in two years earlier with time on her hands, money to burn, and no direction. She had gotten Danielle an audience with the station's owner, and the rest was history still in the making.

Danielle sidled up to the desk. "What the heck are you working on that's got you so tense? Are you making up a will or something?"

Jyme slid her eyes over and failed to disguise her reaction. "Just fell behind and trying to catch up."

"Oh." Jyme was the kind that never frowned, never had a bad day or a bad word to say, so Danielle knew she was hiding something. She leaned over the desk, and Jyme shifted to block her view. "Okay." She stood and backed away. "Has Sammy called about the new signage yet?"

"Um, yeah. He dropped off a proof sheet for you to look at. I've got it...."

Jyme swiveled in her chair, which Danielle knew she would do because she had seen the proof sheet lying on the desk.

When Jyme slid away, Danielle moved quickly to spy her screen. "What is this?"

Jyme froze. "Um, well...." She swallowed hard, looking for words she didn't have.

"This is commercial copy. You aren't supposed to be working on commercial copy."

"Yes. But, it was an emergency. You see—"

Danielle cut her off by picking up the phone and smashing buttons she had well memorized. After three rings, a female voice that had smoked several packs too many came on the line. "This better be important. I'm about to go into an important meeting." Behind her, Danielle distinctly heard pool balls colliding, a jukebox pumping out Toby Keith, ice clinking in glasses, and some dude bitching about the Cowboys.

"Christine, this is Danielle. I want you in this office in ten minutes typing up your copy, and I swear to fucking God, the next time you pawn your work off on somebody else, I'm going to kick your ass. Pound back that last Captain Morgan and move."

"I wouldn't dare drink during business hours," Christine said, puffing herself up with zero shame at getting busted. Everyone knew that shame was one thing she didn't have. "I'm insulted you would even think that."

"Spare me. If I cut you, you'd bleed Crown Royal. Get down here and do your goddamn job." Danielle slammed the phone down and turned her attention to Jyme. "Quit letting her take advantage of you."

"Yes, ma'am," she said.

Danielle pointed at her screen. "Delete all of this. I want her to start from scratch."

"Some of this was hers," Jyme protested. "She came in with some ideas. She just asked me to help proofread and organize, and then before I knew it...."

"Yeah, her kids probably wrote the rest. If the Big Guy would let me, I'd run her out of here so fast. I swear she's got some blackmail shit on him."

"It's not that," Jyme said as she rolled back to her natural position. "They've been friends forever. He keeps her out of loyalty. Oh, speaking of friends. You have one waiting in your office. I knew your shift was almost over, so I didn't think it would hurt."

"Oh, yeah, no problem." She snatched the proof sheet off Jyme's desk. "I'll go over these real quick." Danielle moved on, heading to her office just off the lobby. "If Christine gives you shit—"

"Tell her to go fuck herself. I know."

"And use those exact words," Danielle called out. "Don't go all Suzy Homemaker on me and be nice. Cuss, for God's sake."

She opened the door and stepped into her office to find the raven-haired Ashley Brooks reclining in one of the metal and cloth visitor's chairs, her black boots propped up on one corner of her desk. She broke into an easy smile as she swung her feet down. "There she is." Ashley was up in a heartbeat, sweeping Danielle in a big hug. Time had changed her little. She looked a bit more mature now, but her youth was still upon her face, and her eyes still glittered. "Man, it seems like forever."

"A whole lifetime," Danielle said as she broke the hug and retreated behind her desk. "I gotta say, I'm surprised to see you here. I figured you were out on the road somewhere."

"I have been," Ashley said as she sat gingerly on the corner of the desk. "Nice digs," she said, gesturing to the spacious office that contained only one personal memento—a framed certificate of completion from Franklin Ridgeway's grief program. "Seems wrong, though."

"What's wrong with it? I think it's very professional."

"That's what's wrong with it. You're professional. Look at you, wearing a business suit," Ashley sneered. "Sad to see a sister cash in her chips for a normal life."

"I guess we all gotta grow up sometime," Danielle said. It had taken her several months to get over feeling the same way. "What can I do for you, Ash?"

"Right," Ashley said, skittering off the table like a schoolgirl. Hell, she was only twenty-three.

Ashley produced something from an inside pocket of her motorcycle jacket and tossed it on the desk. Danielle picked it up. It was a CD with Ahsley on the cover. She was made up like an eighties glam rock queen, clutching a Flying V guitar close to her chest. Above her head were the words *Six String Goddess* in eighties style lettering. Danielle glanced up and smiled warmly.

"You made it? Good for you." She flipped the CD over. "Sabre Records. Can't say I've heard of them before."

Ashley rounded the desk and knelt next to Danielle. "You haven't yet. It's a start up label. I'm their first signee to have a release. But it's going to be great. The owner has money, and he's going big to support me."

"And you want me to slip it into the rotation? I'll certainly give it a listen and see what I can do."

"I would appreciate it, but that's not why I'm here. I was hoping you could do something else for me." She slipped into a puppy dog face.

"What do you want?"

Ashley scooted closer, putting her hands on Danielle's arm. "Well...the first single is 'Club 17,' and we rented this old theater outside of town to shoot a video. And since you're on the song, I was hoping you might come out and be in the video with me."

"Oh God," Danielle muttered. She rubbed at her eyes, wishing that the thought didn't send tingles shooting up her spine. "I couldn't, Ashley. But thanks for asking."

"Why not?" She nudged Danielle in the ribs. "Come on, it would be fun. And it might help the song. I'd really appreciate it."

Danielle leaned back in her chair and studied the woman, who was a younger copy of herself. "What's the video about?"

"Not much," Ashley said seriously, but they both knew that if Danielle was asking, then she was tempted. "We're making the place up to look like a top notch club. We'll perform on the stage while the crowd parties it up. The director will pick people out at random and just ask them to adlib some stuff. It's fairly cheap. Most of the cast are kids from the local colleges. You could bring some people if you wanted to. The more, the merrier."

"That's easy. Shouldn't take more than a couple of hours to shoot enough footage, as long as your director isn't a doofus."

"So you'll do it?"

"I don't know," Danielle said. She sat back up and started shuffling the papers on her desk. "I'm pretty busy, and I'm retired, you know."

"Uh huh," Ashley said. "Retired. Right. It's just a video shoot. Besides, if you're really retired, then this will be your last song. It would be a shame not to do something to acknowledge it." Danielle stared hard at Ashley, who met it with a smile. "Tell you what. Why don't I leave you directions, and if you want to come, then come on. We're at the old Adobe Showplace out on east Highway 60. Shooting starts tomorrow night at about seven and goes until we get what we need. We have the place all night."

"I know where it is," Danielle said. "So, how does a girl from Missouri know about the Adobe? How did you come to pick there to shoot?"

Ashley tucked both hands in the pockets of her jacket. "Because it was close to you, and I thought it would be harder for you to say no that way."

"You're a tricky little minx, aren't you?"

"You might say that," Ashley said, beaming from ear to ear. "Seriously, please come. I really want you there."

"We'll see," Danielle said as noncommittally as possible. Inside she felt the old familiar stirrings beginning. There was no doubt what her heart wanted. "I make no promises."

"Good enough."

Ashley turned down an invitation to lunch and left, saying that she had business to attend to elsewhere. Danielle instructed Jyme to hold all calls, and she shut herself up in the office, threw Ashley's CD in her computer's CD drive, and put it on repeat as she worked, trying to keep herself busy. The album was solid enough, much more straight ahead classic rock than Danielle's sound. She could hear the familiar influences: Zeppelin,

Aerosmith, Bad Company, etc. Ashley's voice was passable, but her playing was razor sharp, and her authenticity sold it all. Still, Danielle doubted that she had the star power to really make it.

At three, Danielle headed out. It was a gorgeous May afternoon with a pleasant southwesterly breeze and plenty of white puffy clouds dotting the high blue sky. She hopped into her new ride, a professionally restored Jeep Wrangler, black with silver and red trim and oversized tires for off-roading fun, the top fully removed for the summer. She tied her hair back, slipped on some Ray Bans, and took off, Ashley's offer still bouncing around her head.

She stopped at a Sonic on the way out for two large cherry limeades, hit I-40, and headed west to Vega, noisily pulling into a parking spot on the street across from the high school with ten minutes to spare. She killed the engine, but turned the key so the stereo would keep spitting out tunes at a volume that the soccer moms in the area had complained about often. She sipped at her drink and drummed on the steering wheel as ZZ Top sang about "Legs," while behind closed doors, the other moms sat in silent judgment. Danielle didn't care.

The boys had moved on to "Viva Las Vegas" by the time the bell rang, and the school grounds began to fill with teenagers. Danielle was keenly aware that the boys in the school made a point of walking by just to spy a look at her. It made Danielle feel a little better about herself to know she was the hottest mom there, and refused to let Talia tell her what MILF meant because she knew it would ruin the vibe. The modern kids and their silly acronyms.

Talia emerged eventually, surrounded by a ring of friends. The timid girl of three years earlier was gone, replaced by a confident and competent young woman. A summer of intense tutoring had gotten her close enough to level, that the school district was comfortable letting her in, and from there, Talia's natural intellect did the rest.

Talia had embraced life and threw herself into it eagerly. She was in the choir and the drama club, student president of the Fellowship of Christian Athletes, and started her own club, Students For A Bright Future, a group of kids of all ages who volunteered in the community and encouraged kindness and acceptance on campus. She was unshakable, tireless, and annoyingly upbeat.

She was also three weeks from graduating and three days from her senior prom.

She smiled and laughed and bounced along the grounds with her friends, a sight to behold in white Keds, a frilly black skirt with pink and white flowers she had bought off the discount rack at Target, a cream colored blouse she had sewed herself as a Home Ec project, and a black leather vest rescued from a vintage clothing store on Sixth Street. Her gold hair was long and thick with natural waves. She caught sight of Danielle and excused herself from the group, jogging the rest of the way to the Jeep.

Talia jumped into the shotgun seat. "Ooh, Sonic. Yummy." She plucked hers up and took a hearty tug. "Is it ready yet?"

Danielle shook her head as the Jeep's engine roared to life. "Got the call this morning. I thought about grabbing it on the way out, but I know you want to be there."

"Can we go?"

"Already on the way," Danielle said as she navigated back to the interstate. As she raced back toward Amarillo, neither tried to talk over the road noise and wind. On the western outskirts of town, Danielle turned into a shopping center that contained, among other things, a dress shop.

Talia clapped her hands. "I'm so excited."

"I couldn't tell," Danielle smirked. As she whipped into a parking spot, Danielle got serious. "I'm glad you let yourself enjoy this stuff. So many kids think it's beneath them. I used to be one."

"Yes, but you were born a forty-five-year-old woman," Talia joked.

"That's true," Danielle said. "Come on, let's get this over with. Girlie places like this give me the creeps."

They were there to pick up Talia's prom dress, a stunning

crimson off-the-shoulder piece that had required a few minor alterations. Talia held it to her chest. "Will I be the belle of the ball in this?"

"You'd be the belle of the ball in a garbage bag," Danielle countered. "You got all the accessories you need? Handbag small enough to conceal a .380 Colt?"

"Stop it," Talia chided. "Yes. I have everything else I need."

"Let's get out of here then." Danielle's phone buzzed, and she took it out of her pocket, read her text, and made a face.

"Problem?"

"Nah," Danielle said as she put the phone away. "Just Brett. Said he won't be able to make dinner tonight. Somebody got sick, so he's got to cover one of the school's athletic banquets tonight. Can't believe this town is small enough that athletic banquets make the news."

Talia carefully put her dress back in the long white cardboard box and hustled to Danielle's side as she started for the door. "That's too bad about Brett," she said. "It's steak night. He always comes on steak night."

"Hey, at least we already got the steaks, or we'd be eating toaster crumbles tonight."

"Hey, whatever," Talia said. Her demeanor changed as they hit the parking lot. "Are you all right? You seem a little on edge today."

"It's nothing," Danielle said. "Had to get on to somebody at work today, that's all."

"No, this isn't one of your Christine moods," Talia said. "This is something else. You're not so good at hiding your emotions anymore. Come on, what is it?"

"Don't worry about it. I'm just tired, that's all. Worried about sweeps coming up. Rumor is that we might be dropping a couple of spots."

"Bull," Talia said. Danielle wasn't sure what she was calling bull on and didn't press. Talia was right about her losing her ability to hide her feelings. Had to do some work on that.

Home for the two of them was a modest one-story red brick

house in a new housing development in the northwest corner of Amarillo. It offered quick access to the interstate to get Talia to school in the morning before turning around and turning around hauling back into downtown for work. Talia had a driver's license and her own car, but she preferred Danielle to take her to school so they could bond during the drive. With college around the corner, they both knew those moments were fleeting.

Danielle grilled up two petite sirloins for dinner. Talia cut hers into small pieces and threw them in a salad, while Danielle took hers straight. On most Wednesdays, Brett would have joined them and hung out until it was time to go to the station, and she found herself missing him. Talia ignored it and kept her abreast of all the school news that was fit to print.

It had been Brett's suggestion to enroll her in tiny Vega High instead of one of the much bigger city schools, feeling that Talia would be more comfortable in the cozier setting. It had been a good call, though the commute was a killer.

Later that night, Danielle laid in bed thinking about her meeting with Ashley and the temptation it presented. It was impossible to keep her mind from racing at the possibilities. After an hour, Danielle forced herself out of bed and crept into the hallway. There was no light coming from under Tali's door, so she thought it safe.

She retrieved her laptop from her closet and snuck into the kitchen, where she poured a tall glass of milk and grabbed a bag of Oreos, booted up the computer, slipped a thumb drive into the USB port, and put earbuds in as the music started up.

As a way to say goodbye to the life, Danielle had put all of her unrecorded music on the drive, making her own little album out of it. She had also used the practice to teach Talia, and discovered that on top of everything else, her sister was a natural musician. Together they played all the instruments, made what would have amounted to a solid demo, and then moved on. They both still played, but only for fun, and they never talked about it.

After only two cookies, Danielle pushed the snack away, finding it unsatisfactory. She sensed more than heard Talia coming up behind her and quickly killed the music and minimized the media player on her screen.

Talia leaned over and rested her chin on Danielle's shoulder. "Whatcha doin?"

Danielle tried to play it cool. "Nothing. Couldn't sleep, so I figured I'd catch up on some work. Brainstorm some ideas for Sweeps."

Talia reached out, unplugged the earbuds, and hit the k button on the keyboard, and the music started back up. "Catching up on work, huh? It's okay to miss it."

"That's the thing. I had gotten to where I didn't miss it. Until yesterday."

Talia moved around behind Danielle and sat at her left, drug the package of Oreos over to her, and dug one out. "I knew something happened yesterday. So tell me about it."

Danielle again paused the music and pushed the laptop away, and Talia again restarted it, and this time kept it close to her so Danielle wouldn't keep messing with it. So Danielle relayed the story of Ashley's visit. When she was done, Talia sat quietly, chewing on her cookie and her thoughts. She looked up with a starry grin on her face. "So what time are we going?"

Danielle was taken aback. Even as she was teaching Talia to play and they were working on her catalog of songs, Talia had been skeptical, fearing for good reason that Danielle would fall off the wagon. So her eagerness now was a true 180.

"You want to do it?"

"Of course. I think it would be fun. And my friends would love it. I mean, how often do you get to be in a music video?"

Danielle rubbed her hands together and looked away. "I don't know. Maybe it's not such a good idea."

"Why not?"

"Because I made a commitment to you for one thing. And besides…." She paused, reluctant to even speak the words. Talia waited expectantly. "You don't give a junkie another taste. You do, and he winds up face down in a gutter somewhere. Especially since he's not so young and strong anymore, and he can't take it like he used to."

"You're not a junkie. You're a musician." Talia leaned forward and cupped Danielle's face in her hands. "It's who you are. It's in your soul. I am so thankful for what you have done for me and what you gave up, but now it's time to take it back. I'm eighteen now. I'm going to college in the fall. You saved me. You deserve a chance to rediscover yourself."

Danielle tried to slough it off. "It's just a music video. Let's not make it bigger than it really is."

"If it's just a music video, then why are you so worked up about it?" Danielle didn't answer, so Talia turned off the music and pulled out the drive. "It's a start," she said, answering her own question. She held the drive out to Danielle. "Give it to her tomorrow. See if she'll pass it along for you. Then see what happens."

Danielle took the drive. "I'll think about it. Now you get to bed. You've still got school in the morning."

***

The Adobe Showroom had been built by some aspiring and misplaced Bohemians in the late nineties, who thought they could launch an independent music scene in the Panhandle. Beyond wildly miscalculating the support their idea would garner, they made some key mistakes. The first was building it too far from the city, northeast of town and a couple of miles down a back road. The place was too damn hard to find, and too distant for most people to bother with. It was a shame, because the building itself had been beautiful, with neo-Art Deco designs and carefully constructed acoustics that, she had been told, made it a fabulous place to catch a band.

That was then. The Bohemians took a bath on the project, gave up, and moved on. From there, it found new life as a porn store for a while but had sat empty for many years. Chain link fencing was put around it after the county cops got tired of busting teen keggers, and that seemed to be the end of The Adobe's life.

After Danielle had set down roots and started pumping money into the station, some true believers in the community had pitched her the idea of renovating the building, giving her the history and taking her to the building, but Danielle passed. There was no way the Adobe would ever thrive, not given its location and not in this town.

Now, as she and a gaggle of girls bounced over the broken parking lot in Danielle's green Ford Explorer, a sadly necessary purchase made expressly for carting around gaggles of teenage girls, the Adobe had been given at least a temporary stay of execution. The fencing had been peeled back to allow workers access, and they had cleared away the weeds in the immediate vicinity of the building, fixed broken windows, and given the whole thing a quick black paint job. A temporary marquee was perched over the double glass front doors with Club 17 in neon lighting and One Night Only: Ashley Brooks featuring Danielle Regan underneath it.

Danielle and Talia exchanged glances. "A bit presumptuous, don't you think?" Danielle asked.

"No," Talia said. "She had faith."

An officer from a local security company stopped them long enough to check them out, saw Danielle's name on a list, and passed them through. There was a swirl of activity outside of the club, workers setting up lights and camera crews catching B roll that might be of use later. To the right, a series of RVs sat, and Danielle parked near them. "All right girls, sit tight and let me find out what's going on."

She got out and stood, eyeing the RVs and wondering which one Ashley would be in if she wasn't already inside. She didn't want to interrupt the busy workers and began to feel a swell of panic rising inside her. This was no longer her element. Had it not been for the girls, she would have bolted, but Danielle swallowed hard and did her best to find her courage.

The door of the RV at the far end of the line banged open, and Ashley appeared in the doorway. "Dani!" She rushed down the steps and ran over, swallowing Danielle up in a hug. "I had hoped you would come." She chuckled and pointed at the marquee. "I guess you knew that, though." She stepped back but wore a mile wide smile on her face. "Man, this is going to be great. Thank you so much for coming. What do we have here?" She looked past Danielle at the SVU. "Friends?"

Danielle looked back and waved, and Talia hopped out of the passenger seat. "This is my sister Talia. Talia, this is Ashley Brooks."

"From the Black Heart Chokers," Talia answered. "I've heard your work."

Ashley smiled bigger. "Ya heard of me? That's cute. I'm assuming those are your friends in the car?" Talia acknowledged that they were. Ashley surveyed the scene for a minute and then called out, "Hey, Paulie! Come here!"

A harried young man in a headset with a clipboard in his hands rushed over. "Yes?"

Ashley pointed at Talia. "Would you please take Talia and her friends here and get them a prime spot? Let Jesse know that I want them to get plenty of camera time, would ya?" As Talia got her friends from the truck, Paulie acknowledged the order and led them all away. "Come back to the trailer, and we'll get you in make-up and wardrobe. God, I can't believe it." As they walked, Ashley grabbed her arm. "I really think this song is going to be huge, and I was thinking it might be huge for you too."

"Oh yeah," Danielle said. She could feel the USB drive in her jeans pocket. "How do you figure?"

They reached the last RV in the line, and Ashley went up the steps and opened the door. "Come on in." Danielle went ahead. The RV had been modified to make it a mobile makeup studio, and several technicians were inside scurrying about. The other members of her band were sitting in chairs, getting ready for the shoot. "Hey, Clara."

One of the technicians answered and hustled over. "Clara, this is Danielle, our surprise VIP. Would you get her all fixed up?" She turned to Danielle. "I'm gonna let Clara do her thing, and I'll catch up to you when it's showtime, all right?"

A half hour later, Danielle emerged into the night air decked out in skin tight gray jeans, high heeled boots, and a thin salmon blouse under a blue leather jacket that she decided was going to go missing when the shoot was over. Clara had put extensions in her hair to make her look more like people expected her to look. An assistant then walked her into the building to the backstage area, where the band and crew were readying for the shoot.

Ashley saw her and strode over, a gold top Les Paul slung around her waist. She wore a thin red kami — which left little to the imagination — over black jeans, and her black heart choker around her neck. She stuck her finger under it and pulled it out a bit. "I thought this would be a cool little Easter egg for the fans we had. Whattaya think?"

"It's cool," Danielle answered. "I wish I had something like that to pay tribute to my band. I don't have anything left from that time."

"I thought of that. Paulie!" Paulie materialized so fast that Danielle was beginning to think the kid was magic. "Where's Danielle's surprise?"

"Oh yeah, right over here." Pauline skittered off and back again, carrying a boxy leather guitar case. He sat it down carefully and made a production of opening the case. Out of the case, he produced a shimmering, candy apple red Stratocaster, the Danielle Regan signature model she had first seen in an AxeMasters in Kansas City four years earlier. He held it out to Danielle like Moses handing over the stone tablets.

"I want you to use this tonight," Ashley said. "We're really going to plug in and play, no lip synching. It'll make things more authentic." She watched Danielle slip the guitar over her head and fiddle with the strings. "That's my baby, so be careful with her. I can't believe I spent that much on a guitar, but it's The Danielle. You pay for quality."

She put an arm around Danielle and led her to the lip of the stage. The dance floor was full of people, mostly younger people milling around talking, some getting some last minute direction from the que. She pointed at a single mic at the very front of the stage. On the floor around the mic was a half circle marked off with black duct tape.

"You and I will spend most of our time there, inside the circle. The version we're releasing is the duet, so you'll have a verse all to yourself. When you're not at the mic, just do whatever feels natural to you. Have fun. We're gonna shoot several takes straight through, so don't worry if you screw up or something. Just keep on keeping on."

The shoot went on just as she said it would, and they played and replayed "Club 17" while the kids danced and partied. After the first two takes, Danielle began to loosen up, and she started to interact with Ashley's band, which brought a huge smile to the younger girl's face.

For the last take of the night, Ashley had Talia summoned to the stage, and she joined them. By now, she had heard the song enough to be able to sing the chorus, and the three of them stood at the mic belting it out. When the director yelled "Cut" for the last time, Paulie appeared out of thin air to take the guitar from her, and she was swallowed by the crew wanting to thank her for her participation. She noticed Ashley and Talia drifting off to the side of the stage together but couldn't get to them. Whatever they talked about didn't last long, and soon Ashley was sweeping in to the rescue.

"Thank you again for coming. I think it went great. I'll email you when it's done so you can see the finished product. I got the info from your secretary."

"Thank you for asking," Danielle said. Sadness crept over her as she saw the kids file out of the room and the crew begin tearing down equipment. It was over too soon. "I had a blast," she said. "I'll just go change clothes, and then we need to be headed out."

Ashley waved her arm. "Don't worry about it. I had Clara take your stuff to your car. Keep the outfit. It looks good on you. So much better than that stupid business suit." She fiddled with the lapels on the jacket. "Especially this jacket. You fuckin' own this jacket."

Danielle blushed. "Thanks. Well, be careful out there.

Rock'n'roll is a vicious game, you know. I'll be watching the charts for you." They hugged again, holding it this time. Danielle wasn't sure if it was Ashley she didn't want to let go of or the moment. She finally did let go. "I'll be adding the song to our rotation," she said softly. "If it's okay, I'd like to premiere it tomorrow morning on my show."

"That would be freaking awesome," Ashley said. "Thank you."

CHAPTER TWENTY-THREE

True to her word, Danielle premiered "Club 17" as the last song on her shift. Next to her in the booth, Melody danced like a schoolgirl. "What a great song," she gushed. "Makes me feel like I'm in college again. This could've come straight out of 1977. How did you discover this again?"

Danielle slid from behind the board to trade places. "Ah, I'm always getting records from independent labels looking for exposure. Most of it is trash, but every so often, you find something cool."

Melody hopped on the stool and prepared to take the reins. "Is that why you're on here?"

Danielle had anticipated that she might pick up on her involvement and had practiced swatting away the suggestion. "That's not me. It's a sister act. I don't know if I should be honored or upset that you think that's me."

"Oh, don't give me that load of hogwash," Melody said. "Honey, I've been in this business since you were in diapers. I've heard all the greats. I know your voice, and I know your style. Don't try to play dumb with me. And since we're on the subject, may I just say again that it's stupid that you won't let us put your songs in the rotation."

Danielle gathered her papers and moved to the door. "What difference does it make? You get 'requests' for my songs all the time."

"I have to do something. Here we are, we have this awesome station playing all these great artists, but there's this one huge, gaping hole you won't fill."

"I already let you talk me into adding the goddamn

Beatles. What more do you want?"

"You know what I want. I want the Queen of Blues/Rock. The High Priestess of Guitar. I want you to quit pretending you don't exist."

Danielle popped open the studio door. "Well, maybe one of these days I'll pass this beast over to you, and then you can add all the songs you like. Until then...." She ducked out the door, leaving Melody to her shift.

It was a quiet Friday at the station. The sales staff dispersed early in the morning, supposedly to get an early start, but she knew they were all kicking off early. It didn't matter. Fewer salespeople hanging around meant less drama. The traffic girl finished her work by noon, and Danielle let her off early too. Talia had voluntarily driven herself to school, so Danielle had the afternoon free and clear, and she spent it working, staying busy to avoid thinking too much about the previous night. Everything had happened so fast she hadn't even attempted to give Ashley her demo, which was for the best in the long run.

After work, she rattled around town, enjoying another beautiful day. The temperatures were rising, and the heat would soon get oppressive, but for now, it was tolerable. She cruised and blared her stereo, the day's CD of choice being The Stone's *Voodoo Lounge,* and generally enjoyed life and wondered how things might have turned out if she'd had the presence of mind in her younger days to just take her foot off the pedal sometimes.

The first thing she noticed as she ambled down the street toward home was Brett's truck parked in front of the house. He had traded his red and gold one for a new blue and silver Ford, and it still had the dealer's tags on it. Talia's car was in the driveway, a white 2010 Camry. When Talia had gotten her license, Danielle had offered her any car she wanted, from just off the assembly line high performance to fully restored classic American muscle. She opted for fuel efficiency and practicality, and Danielle knew she had failed her in some fundamental way. Behind Talia's car in the two-car driveway was a strange car, a rented black Chrysler 300 with the Enterprise stick visible in the back window.

She pulled the Jeep in next to Talia's Camry and noticed the unmistakable smell of ribs cooking on an outdoor grill. As she walked up the driveway, Danielle was prepared for some kind of surprise to be sprung.

She walked in and found a group of people lounging around in the living room. Talia and Brett were on the couch. Brett looked like he had just stepped off the golf course in khaki shorts and a powder blue polo shirt, wrap-around shades up on top of his head, and a Shiner Bock held loosely in one hand. Ashley sat on their loveseat next to a skinny man with thin blond hair and a high forehead. She also had a Shiner in hand, and in a folding chair at the head of the group was another man. He looked to be in his thirties, with short brown hair and a slightly crooked nose. He had been loudly entertaining the others with a story, a bottle of Shiner held in both hands as he spoke. The story ended as she walked in.

"Sis," Talia called, sounding imminently guilty. She popped off the couch and came to Danielle, taking her briefcase out of her hand. "I was beginning to think you got lost."

"I was cruising," she said, studying the strangers in her living room.

Brett stood, took a swig, and adjusted his beltline. "I'm gonna go check on dinner." He gave Danielle a nod and disappeared into the kitchen.

"Come," Talia said. "Sit."

"Can I? In my own house?" She was still eyeing the strangers carefully and felt more than a bit annoyed that Talia had conspired to bring these people into their home.

Ashley set her beer on the coffee table in front of her. "I heard you play the song this morning," she said. "Sounded amazing. Did you get any feedback?"

"The afternoon DJ loved it. Said it could have come straight out of 1977."

"Good enough for me," Ashley answered, and she playfully slapped the thigh of the man next to her. "Now, let me introduce you to the man responsible for it all." She gestured to the dark haired man in the folding chair. "Danielle Regan, this is Ben LaFontaine, founder and president of Sabre Records."

He tipped his bottle toward her. "Ms. Regan."

The name immediately hit home. "Ben LaFontaine? Like, the fifth richest guy in the world? That Ben LaFontaine?"

"In the flesh," he said. "Actually, I'm the fourth richest in the world. My dad is always telling me that I'd be number one if I'd quit blowing money on foolish things like vanity record labels, but what good is money if you don't use it? Besides, he's only nineteen on the list, so he hardly has room to talk." He chuckled, and Ashley and the blond guy followed suit.

Danielle, who could count a former president as a personal friend, was not impressed. "So why are you in my living room, Mr. LaFontaine? And who is this guy?" she asked, referring to the blond on Ashley's left.

"This is Alan, one of my most trusted advisors. We'll get to his role in a bit. First, however, I believe your friend was about to serve us some honest to goodness real life Texas bar-b-que, and I'm dying to try it."

"Oh yeah," Talia said. "Dining room is this way. Everybody, come on. Sis, would you help me put everything out?"

"Sure." Danielle sidled up next to Talia. "What are you doing?"

"Brett and I decided to do this last night after I talked to Ashley. We're giving you a shove because we know you won't do it on your own. Now play nice and put on your businesswoman face."

Talia and Danielle put bowls of potato salad and baked beans, and a plate of corn on the cob on the table, while Brett came in from the patio with a platter piled high with ribs and sausage. "Bon appetit," he said. "Anybody need another beer while I'm up?"

"Hook me up, Cowboy," LaFontaine said as he stabbed at a rib with his fork. Danielle settled into her seat at his side. "I love trying new foods, especially local foods. Gotta say I've never spent much time in Texas, though. Toured NASA once, but that's about it."

The dinner conversation was light and dominated by LaFontaine, who regaled the group with the typical rich guy stories about exotic vacations and daring deeds. He talked a little about some of the software he had created, which was how he made his first fortune during the dotcom boom of the late nineties.

That presented Danielle with the opening she waited for. "So how did you go from computer programming and Wall Street speculator to starting a record label?"

"Ah, good question." He set aside the stripped bone of a rib, wiped his face and hands, and swiveled to face Danielle. "I'm a music lover, Ms. Regan. A true believer in the power of rock and roll. I started looking at the popular music landscape, and I didn't like what I heard. Rap and hip hop, EDM, and what goes for pop music today is just suburban white kids ripping off rap, hip hop, and EDM. There's no rock anymore. When I grew up, I had a poster of Eddie Van Halen on my wall. Now kids want to be Skrillex. It's sad."

"So you started this label to bring rock back?"

"Exactly. Rock is still out there, but it's smaller. It's a niche. The big labels don't want to sign rock acts or promote them. And the labels are in league with the radio stations. You work in radio. You know how corporatized it has become."

Danielle nodded. That she knew well. KATT was the only station in town that was independently owned, but she was aware that the owner had been weighing offers.

"They have a monopoly," LaFontaine continued. "They collude. These kids these days, they don't know there's anything else out there. They are force fed this electropop silliness and told it's cool. I want to change that, and I can. My money can open doors other independent labels simply can't."

He turned his attention to Ashley. "When I first heard of Ms. Brooks here, I knew I had found what I was looking for, which is the face of a generation. She's gorgeous and talented, and charismatic. The kids will go crazy for her."

Danielle breathed out slowly. "That's all very interesting, but I doubt you needed to come all this way to tell me this. So why are you here?"

LaFontaine looked around the table. "She doesn't beat around the bush, does she?" On that, everyone agreed. "I'm here because Ashley called me last night and said she had something I needed to hear. She sent me a file, I listened to it, and I hopped on a plane."

Danielle's head snapped around to Talia, sitting on her other side. "I may have slipped Ashley my copy of your demo last night," she said. "I knew you wouldn't."

"I'm glad she did," LaFontaine continued. "Because it was excellent, or at least the song I heard was. It was enough to convince me to drop what I was doing and come here. This afternoon, your sister played us the rest." He reached across the table for Danielle's hand. "The world needs to hear this, Ms. Regan. You've been in exile long enough."

Danielle pulled her hand away. "That's very nice of you to say, but those songs are just...whispers. That's not a demo. It's an epitaph. A goodbye."

"Maybe that's what you intended," Ashley said. "But it can also be one hell of a reintroduction. Listened to that last night, and I cried. Do you know why?"

Danielle stared across the table at her. "Why?"

"Because your music showed me just how far I still have to go. I can mimic your playing. I can cop your style. But I don't have your depth. I haven't lived the blues—you have, and it shines through in your playing. Let us help you."

LaFontaine retook Danielle's hand. "This is what I'm offering. A one album deal, no advance, but I'll give you a 45% royalty rate, which is far above what any major label does. I'll fund the studio time." He waved a hand at Alan, sitting next to Ashley on the other side of the table.

"I'll help you put a band together," Alan said. "I've already made some calls. We'll work together to find you some people, the right people."

Danielle pointed to him, but spoke to LaFontaine. "This dude is going to help me? No offense, but honestly, he looks like a pharmacist."

"Don't let his looks fool you. This is a cool, cool cat right here. He's got a great ear for talent and is a good judge of character. He'll steer you right."

"And I'll help when and where I can," Ashley volunteered. "I'd love to be a part of it. And I've got tons of friends, and you have friends. We put out the call, total All Points Bulletin."

LaFontaine picked up the thread. "You've already got the start of a great album, and I know you have a reputation for working fast. You go in the studio, cut me an album, and then we'll stage your grand comeback. Obviously, you'll have to tour, but I want to relaunch you with one big show. Really put it all out on the line right out of the gate. I'll pay for everything. We'll make it the grandest comeback ever."

"What if it's not good enough? What if it's too late and nobody cares anymore?"

LaFontaine shrugged. "I'm betting on you, Danielle. I heard what you and your sister did in a home studio—I have no doubt that you can still do it. And we will make them care. If you didn't know this already, drawing attention is one of my many skills." He sighed. "I know you're anxious, but everybody in this room believes in you. What matters is if you believe in yourself. If you don't think you can handle this, then I move on with no hard feelings. One thing to keep in mind, though." He leaned forward as if to bestow some secret on her. "I know for a fact that Cumulus is in serious negotiations to buy your station. You've been kicking the shit out of their stations, and since they can't beat you, they're going to buy you. I know you think you've got an ally in Dan Edwards, but a man of modest means can only say no to big money for so long. When he's sitting on a beach in Cancun, he won't have many regrets about throwing you under a bus."

"That's bullshit," Danielle said, but even as she said it, she remembered the station owner cryptically mentioning a "big deal" he was working on in their last conversation.

"Believe it or not. It's up to you." LaFontaine wiped his hands one more time, checked the gold Rolex on his wrist, and stood up. "I have to be in Seattle in the morning, so I need to run. I just need one thing from you, Ms. Regan. Yes or no? Are we in business?"

Danielle stood and looked him in the eye. Her mind raced back, thinking of the great time she'd left behind, as well as the horror show of her attempted comeback. She thought of Steve and wondered where he was and what he was doing. She thought of Talia. Finally, she made a decision she thought she could live with.

"Yes."

CHAPTER TWENTY-FOUR

A pink stretch Hummer idled noisily outside Brett's ranch. In the living room, four awkward teen boys in tuxedos waited while four teen girls finished getting ready in the bedroom. Brett and Danielle sat in twin recliners, watching the boys fidget on the couch. They knew they were under the watchful eyes of adult supervision, and therefore tried hard to subdue their nature.

One by one, they came out, strutting into the room like they were on a runaway in Paris. Each girl stopped in the doorway to do a little twirl and paused for her date to pin a corsage on her. Talia came last, and after her date pinned her, Brett steered her away. "My beautiful girl," he said softly. "Who would've thought, huh? Keep your head on straight, don't let any of the boys get handsy."

Talia simply laughed. "I've got it under control." She turned to Danielle. "So? Am I the belle of the ball?" She twirled, showing off her crimson gown with the silver accents. Her hair was piled high atop her head.

"No doubt," Danielle said. She held Talia's chin in her hand. "Have fun tonight, but be careful. If you feel uncomfortable in any way, you call, and I'll come get you."

"It's just a dinky high school dance," Talia said. "You act like I'm going to war or something."

"Boys get ideas on nights like tonight," Danielle answered. "You are going to war, whether you realize it or not. All I'm saying is, use your best judgment." She called Talia's date, whose name was Carter. "Anything happens to her, and you're the first domino that falls, got it, bud?"

He rolled his eyes and acknowledged her comment,

and the whole flock moved from the living room and out into the brilliant sunshine of a dying day. Brett and Danielle stood shoulder to shoulder like proud parents sending their child out into the world but watching until the limo was fully out of sight.

When they were gone, Brett slapped her playfully on the arm. "Let's go sit on the patio."

Danielle glanced at Talia's Camry, now alone in the driveway. "I don't think I can do it," she muttered.

"Do what? Let her go?"

"Drive that stupid car home," Danielle said with a grin. "I'm gonna lose what's left of my cool cred if anybody sees me in that thing."

"Oh, good lord, Danielle. Come inside." Brett grabbed a Shiner and a Coke from the fridge and led them to the back patio. He popped the lids off both, and they clinked the necks of their bottles together. "We did good," he said. "And you thought she was doomed."

"I was wrong. I admit it. But I tell you, that girl did more to save me than I ever did to save her. She really does have a special light, doesn't she?"

"That she does."

"How strange," Danielle said, her eyes focused on the wide prairie beyond the chain link fence that surrounded the property. "Dorothy Regan, fucked up as she was, gave birth to an angel and a devil, and somehow they made a life together."

"You're hardly a devil," Brett said. "It's so weird how you always look at yourself like that. On the list of Hollywood bad girls, you're pretty far down on the line."

Danielle smirked at him. "I beat the shit out of a widow. On video."

"Angelina Jolie wore a vial of blood around her neck."

"Yeah, well...." Danielle shrugged. "She was fucking bizarre. The point is, I always felt like there was a devil on my shoulder, a darkness I just couldn't get away from. And it took her light to drive it away."

"At least it did," Brett said. He sat his beer down, stood,

took Danielle's Coke, and pulled her to her feet. "Remember when I threw you a prom out here? And we danced barefoot?"

He started to sway, and Danielle let him pull her in. "I remember." She wrapped her arms around his waist, and they swayed to music only they could hear. They danced for a while, neither keeping track of the time, but darkness was creeping around by the time Danielle broke free. "Guess I ought to hit the road."

"Guess so."

They closed up the patio, and Brett drained the last of his beer.

"Well, I know things didn't work out quite the way we planned, but I guess it all worked out. I got another shot, anyway. That's all I ever really wanted was a chance."

"You'll knock 'em dead. I have no doubt. Tally plays me your stuff every time she comes over. It's great. Maybe your best stuff. I like that you've softened up a little bit."

"Softer? You think I'm softer?" Danielle felt herself go hard inside. He didn't know it, but Brett had thrown down a gauntlet. "You think I've wussed out, don't you?"

Brett stammered for a response. "No, no. I didn't say that. I just mean that this new stuff you're writing is more introspective and mature. It's not about wild, screaming solos anymore. I like it."

"Uh huh," Danielle said. "You think I've wussed out. God." She turned a slow circle. "Everybody is going to talk about how I've gotten old and calmed down."

Brett came up behind her and stopped her circling by wrapping his arms around her. He whispered in her ear. "Calm down. The music is still great. Keep in mind that your audience is more mature now."

Brett's hot breath on her neck magically banished her sudden bout of anxiety. She wanted to feel his lips on her skin, and she rolled her head to give him the opportunity. He took it, lightly kissing her as his hands moved slowly up and down her arms. Danielle moaned softly, enjoying the touch. Every time his lips touched her, she felt parts of herself awakening. She was rapidly approaching a point where she would either have to leave or let this wave take her wherever it wanted. She quickly spun around.

"That night, the prom night? You do know that I almost —"

"I know," he whispered. His lips hovered tantalizingly close to hers. "I stayed up all night waiting for you to come to my room. I fell asleep sitting up, staring at the door."

Danielle chuckled. "I was waiting on you. But then the cop came, and...our window passed."

"Did it?" He kissed her softly, and for a fleeting moment, she almost went with it. It took everything she had to pull away.

"Don't start thinking we're alone tonight. It'll just get you into trouble." She stepped back out of his hands and took a moment to collect herself. "I'm going home now. See ya Wednesday."

"Steak night," he said.

"Not many of them left. Best not miss anymore."

She made her way to the door, car keys in her hand as lame discussions about steak night bounced around in her mind. She stopped at the front door and paused, debating, and then realized she couldn't leave it like this. She put the keys down on an entryway table and turned to Brett, who was still standing in the living room. She walked up to him. "Here's the thing," she started, a half dozen reasonable justifications in mind. Their eyes locked, and whatever it was Danielle had intended to say flitted away. "Oh, screw it."

She pulled Brett into her, kissing him with passion left untapped for too many years. He met her and kissed back, and they twirled some more, neither wanting to break first.

Finally, Brett pulled back and smiled down at her. "You really don't want to drive that Camry home, do you?"

Danielle laughed out loud and laid one hand against his stubbled chin. "I'm making up for lost time." Danielle looked into his face, waiting for Kyle to step in, to invade her memory as he always seemed to do. But this time, there were no ghosts at her side. It was just the two of them, neither one with a reason in the world to say no. "Come on." She took his hand and started for the bedroom. Brett started to go, then stopped.

"Are you sure about this?"

"I'm trying to live in the moment, which I've never been particularly good at, and you're kind of killing it." She let go of Brett's hand. "Maybe I should just go home."

"No, don't do that," Brett said, closing the distance between them and stealing another kiss. "We've wasted too many moments to let this one go."

Danielle slithered up close to him. "Then quit yapping and take me to bed."

***

Much later that night, gentle fingers brushing on her bare arm woke Danielle. She had been sleeping with her head resting on Brett's chest and wasn't sure if she'd ever slept as peacefully. She craned her head, trying to see who had touched her, but all she could make out was a silhouette in the dark. The silhouette leaned down.

"I brought your car," Talia whispered. "I left the keys here on the nightstand."

Danielle, only partially awake, groaned. "Did you have fun?"

"Not as much as you did," Talia said. A finger of regret started to form in Danielle's heart. She started to roll over, but Talia stopped her and gave her a gentle peck on the cheek. "Go back to sleep. You deserve this. You both do. I'll see you in the morning."

Danielle didn't fight and easily slipped back into her slumber. The next time her eyes opened, daylight was peeking around the drapes. Brett was staring at her and playing with her hair.

"Well, that happened."

"Yes, it did," Danielle purred. She stretched and propped herself up on one elbow. "And I don't regret it one bit."

"You weren't sure about that, were you?"

"No," Danielle admitted. "I almost bolted last night, but I made myself stay. Gotta quit being afraid. My God, I'm almost forty, and I've been loving a ghost for a decade. I'm tired of just existing."

Brett started running one hand up and down her arm. "So, where are we now?" Danielle didn't understand his question. "I mean, where do we go? Was this just a one time thing, or...?"

She playfully slapped him on the chest. "You've known me for three years. Have I ever struck you as the Wham Bam Thank You Ma'am type?"

"That's not what I meant," Brett whispered. He was being serious, and it was bringing Danielle down. "Do we go back to platonic friends, or are we friends with benefits? Are we together?"

Danielle laughed. "I don't think we could be much more together."

"Danielle," he sighed. "Be serious for a second. I don't know where your head is at. You're about to go back to your career. You're going to go on tour. Once that happens, once you're gone for a while...."

Danielle answered his concerns with a kiss. "My heart is here, and here is where it will remain. This thing about going on tour and all, there's no guarantee that will even happen. I could bomb out night one. I just need you to do one thing for me."

"What's that?"

"Keep a light on in the window for me, and I'll find my way back to you. I promise." She smiled sweetly and ran one finger across his lips. "My house is just a house—I've got nothing invested in it. Most of our memories are here. It wouldn't be a big deal at all to move in, if that's what you wanted."

"Seriously? Wow."

"Is that commitment enough for you, or do I need to go buy a ring and propose?"

Brett answered by closing his fingers around a handful of her hair and pulling her down for a long kiss that promised to turn into more. "I don't need any of that. You're enough," he whispered.

   "I damn well better be," she said. Then the time for talking was through.

CHAPTER TWENTY-FIVE

Alan proved to be just as good as advertised, somehow convincing a wide assortment of musicians to make their way down just to jam with Danielle and see how things meshed. Danielle took advantage, conning the more well known members to come into the station to record some custom promos. The station was her lifeline, the Plan B, in case everything crashed and burned again.

After a week of serious rehearsals, they had a short list of musicians who were available, willing to tour, and comfortable being contract players, at least for the time being. Once word began to filter into the grapevine that Danielle was working again, old friends began reaching out to offer support. Yet Danielle still wasn't happy.

That evening at dinner, surrounded by boxes, Danielle picked at her food, her thoughts a thousand miles away. "What's wrong?" Talia asked as she watched Danielle push uneaten food around her plate.

"It just doesn't feel right. I think maybe I've made a mistake. I was thinking about calling LaFontaine and ending this whole thing."

"Don't do that," Talia said. "You're just nervous. I get it. The last time you tried to perform, things went really bad. That was then. Times are different—you're different."

"Yeah." Danielle stood and gathered her dishes, pushing her uneaten food into the trash. "It's just, I've always had a band. Now, I'm putting together a team. They're all good musicians, but there's no comradery. For these guys, it's just a job. Used to be, me and the band, we were family. I didn't do a good enough job of showing them that. I pushed them all away, but they were my family, and I miss 'em."

"Reach out to them. Maybe enough time has passed that everything will be forgiven."

"It's too late," she said as she leaned against the counter. "Those guys went on with their lives, and I can't blame them. Who would be fool enough to trust Danielle Regan?"

"Me," Talia answered. "Wait here." She pushed away from the table and hustled to her room, and came back dragging her backpack along. "Give me a sec." She sat and started rifling through the backpack, found a purple folder and pulled it out, and went through several papers until she found the one she needed. "I've been doing some digging," she said, looking up at Danielle. "DeShon, your bassist, right? He lives in a little town in Connecticut and works in New York as a session musician and producer. The other three still live in the Austin area. Garrett's club closed about a year ago, and now he's working for an ad company doing their artwork. Trish is still teaching, Ty still runs the store. Go to them. Melody can handle the station. I can take care of myself."

Danielle came to the table and took the paper from Talia's hands. "How long have you been working on this?"

"Since they all came to dinner, and you agreed to try a comeback. I was going to reach out to them directly and try to surprise you, but maybe this way is better."

Danielle squatted in front of her. "You have two weeks of school left, finals coming up, college admissions to deal with, and you've spent your time doing this?"

"I can multitask," Talia said. "Go to them. Even if they say no, you at least need to face them."

"I faced three in Austin, and it wasn't pretty."

"That was four years ago. Wounds have had time to heel. Go. I'll even reserve the plane tickets and the hotels for you." Danielle started to balk at the word planes. "You don't have time to drive. You'll be fine. You have to do this."

***

In a coffee shop on 42nd Street, DeShon Welch sat at a window table, waiting, when Danielle walked in. The years had been kind to DeShon. A bulky man when he was the bassist in her band, DeShon still looked fit but leaner. His head was clean shaven, and he had a fuzzy soul patch beneath his bottom lip. He looked stylish yet casual in black slacks and black shirt open at the collar under a white jacket, which contrasted sharply against his black skin. When he saw her, he stood, approaching her like you would approach a rival businessman at a negotiation, respectful but wary.

"Danielle Regan," he said in his still booming voice. "Long time, girl."

She stopped and held out her hand. "Yes, it has been."

DeShon took the hand, and they shook, then he broke out in a grin. "Get in here," he said, pulling her in for a hug. "Sit. Have a drink." She took the chair opposite him as he waved a waitress over. She ordered a French vanilla cappuccino, which caught his attention.

"Drinking coffee now? My my."

"Somebody got me started on them. They're not too bad."

DeShon nodded as he sipped at whatever frothy concoction he had ordered. "Still putting down three Cokes a day?"

"I've scaled back a little bit. I've actually changed quite a bit. Not always of my own volition, but still."

"Yeah," DeShon agreed. "I've always kept tabs. Kept rooting for you to pull yourself up off the canvas. I used to look for you everywhere I went, figuring that eventually you'd track me down and ask me to come back."

The waitress brought her drink, and she sipped at it. "I was going to. I talked to Garrett, and he told me not to bother."

He laughed. "You listened to that shithead? Man, he don't know." He moved his drink to the side. "Dani, listen. I was pissed at you for that shit with the flag and all that. Royally pissed, and I still think it was a shit thing you did, but I got over it. I saw that interview you did where you were talking about your hillbilly, and I got where you were coming from. I couldn't have played with you right then, but...I would've come back if you'd asked."

"I know I put you in a tight spot," she said with a sigh. "I know I was extremely selfish back then. If I could do it over—"

"You'd have done the same thing. You had to. You were in love, and that was the only way you could say it. I get it now. I think, maybe, we were all a little worn out, you know? Man, you ran us hard. Working all the time. We just needed a break."

"Is twelve years enough of a break?" DeShon's eyes got big with surprise. "No promises, but I got a record deal. One album, one shot. I need a band. I promise, no Confederate flags this time. Just rock and roll."

"I don't know, man." DeShon leaned back in his chair and gazed out the window at the throng of people shuffling down the street in the bright summer sun. "I don't really perform anymore. Strictly studio stuff now. I got projects lined up."

"Okay," Danielle said. "How about this? Just help me with the album, and I'll put together a touring band. You can co-produce."

"Oh really," DeShon said. "Co-produce? What about songwriting?"

"Most of the songs are already written," Danielle said. DeShon reacted the way she expected him to. "But I don't mind sharing the credit across the board. I don't get caught up in all of that like I used to. That was my ego that always wanted all the credit. That bitch is dead."

DeShon stared at her silently for a long minute. "I think you might be right. I see a different light in you now. So, I'm co-producer, and I get songwriting credit on every song?" Danielle confirmed the offer. "One more thing."

"What's that?"

DeShon licked his lips, perhaps working up the courage to ask. "You record it up here, not down in Texas. Doesn't have to be in the city. There's actually a nice facility outside of Hartford. Perfect for the guys who don't need the temptation of being in the city. It's kind of a dealbreaker. I can't leave my life to go down to Texas for a month."

Danielle thought it over. "I need to start ASAP. Can you squeeze me in next month?"

"Guaranteed. We got a deal?"

"We got a deal," she said. "Now, if I can just convince the others."

"All right," DeShon said, satisfied with the results. He should have been. Not many people won negotiations with Danielle Regan. "You want me to call them for you? Maybe if they hear I'm back in the fold, they will be more receptive."

"No, I'll talk to them first. But I may give them your number in case they need independent verification."

"Works for me," he said. "I'll tell ya, though. Garrett will come if he knows I'm in. Besides, last I heard, he was punching a time clock, so he'll probably jump at the chance. The other two are all on you."

"That's the trick. Last time I saw them, it didn't go so well. Trish was seriously pissed. Not sure how that one's going to play out.

"Best of luck to you. I'm in, even if they aren't. So, you sticking around or hopping back on the plane?"

"I got tonight," she said.

***

They spent the day together, DeShon dragging her to his office and his studio in the city and his apartment. DeShon was an eternal bachelor, and his place screamed it. They had dinner in a fancy restaurant that made Danielle's skin crawl, and then they said their goodbyes. The next morning, she hopped on a flight for Dallas, where she caught a connector to Austin.

She rented a car and drove to her hotel. There she checked in with Talia and Brett and rested up. She knew the next day could go two ways, and one of them was incredibly bad.

She caught Ty Woods at the store the next morning. Ty, her former rhythm guitarist, ran Austion SoundSource, a music supply store struggling to survive against competition from the big box stores like AxeMasters.

The store looked much like it had when she had last been

in it four years earlier, though maybe a bit more rundown. The competition didn't seem to be going his way. Ty was behind the counter when she walked in while a young woman was busy straightening up the sheet music section.

"Here comes trouble," Ty said upon seeing her. His hair had grown out a little, and he'd put on a few more pounds, but otherwise, Ty hadn't changed much.

"Always," Danielle said. "So, I was wondering if we could pop back into your office for a couple of minutes."

Ty looked around the deserted store. "I don't think we can get any more private than we already are."

Danielle eyed the girl, who glanced back at her. She shrugged. "Well, I just wanted you to know that I'm keeping the baby, and I expect you to do the right thing."

The girl gasped and dropped a book on the floor.

"Danielle!" Ty cried out, but he said it with a smile.

"You asked for it. Anyway, the real reason I'm here is to ask a tiny little favor. Hardly a thing at all."

"What would that be?"

Danielle bit down on her lip, suddenly finding it hard to speak the words. "Well, I'm trying to put the band back together."

"Oh, Jesus."

"No, listen. I'm different now. Things will be different. I've already talked to DeShon, and he's on board. He's already blocked out two weeks of studio time in Hartford the middle of next month. School will be out by then."

"Dani…." Ty ran his hands through his hair. "Geez. You know we don't play much anymore, and we've got the kid."

"Family vacation," Danielle said. "I won't work y'all like I used to. Plenty of downtime for y'all to go sightseeing. I'll pay for your airfare and hotel and even throw in some per diem money if you need it." Ty's eyebrows went up. "I got a quadzillionaire footing the bill for this thing. Spend his money before he spends it on something stupid, like trying to fly to space."

"You've only got two weeks."

"I've got solid demos. If we were starting from scratch, it

would be one thing, but I just need y'all to help build them up. And I want my old band back. I don't expect you to go on tour with me. We never got to say goodbye, you know? I think maybe we all need this a little bit."

Ty debated it, then relented. "Come by the house tonight for dinner, and we'll work on Trish. If you can convince her, then I'll come." He leaned forward. "You really got DeShon?"

"I sure did," Danielle said. "I've still got a little badass in me after all."

"I guess you do. What about Garrett?"

"He's next on the list," Danielle said. "Though DeShon says he'll be an easy sell. Heard his club went under. That's too bad."

Ty shrugged. "Not much future in being a club owner. Especially in this town. Things are changing around here. It's not the place you remember. Sixth is going to shit." He waved his hands at the store. "Honestly, this place is on life support. We've been thinking about packing up and heading somewhere else. I feel like I'm trying to fight back the ocean."

"That's a feeling I know very well."

***

Garrett Hardesty had a forty-five minute lunch and was halfway through a Reuben at a downtown Schlotzskys when Danielle caught up to him. He looked funny in an ill-fitting suit. His hair was closely shorn, and his earrings were gone, though the holes were still visible. He was skinnier and more pale, and looked stressed.

"I already know why you're here," he said as Danielle approached his table. "DeShon called me this morning. Fucker woke me up because he doesn't pay attention to time zones." It sounded like a bitch, but Danielle had the feeling he was happy to hear from his old friend.

"He was supposed to leave it to me."

"Take it up with him. As you can see, my fortunes have taken a turn for the bizarre. My club went out. Fucking millennials with their goddamn White Claw and Coldplay and shit. All the good bars are shuttering up."

"Sorry to hear it. Seemed like a pretty cool place."

"It was," he said. "But, I'm making a shitload more money doing what I'm doing now. And it's still art, even if it is commercialized. About as satisfying as a five second circle jerk, but it pays the bills."

"You got any vacation time coming? I could use a man with your specific set of skills. Don't know how well it's going to pay, but I can handle your expenses."

Garrett pushed his sandwich aside. "You going on tour after this?"

"Yep. Trying to put together a touring band as we speak. But I want you guys with me in the studio."

"I'll go with you. All the way, man." He loosened his tie. "I hate this shit. Suit and tie and button down bullshit. Can't stand it. You need a drummer. I'm your guy. Just don't throw me under the bus again."

"I been under that bus too," Danielle said. "Sucks. Nobody's getting thrown under the wheels again, I promise."

***

They all agreed that Trish would be the toughest nut to crack, which was why Garrett insisted on coming to dinner. Danielle called Ty, and the three of them worked it out. That evening, Danielle picked up Garrett at his North Austin home, and they made the drive to the suburb of Buda to the south, taking the long way to avoid I-35 gridlock.

Trish Woods met them at the front door of their modest suburban home, her red hair worn loose and curly over her thin shoulders. She was not surprised in the least by Danielle's appearance on her doorstep.

"Come on in," she said. "Table is already set. Hope you like beef stroganoff."

"Yummy," Garrett said. He gave Trish a quick peck on the cheek. "Been too long, Chica. You look great. Still, you look like a kid."

"You're a liar, but thank you for the effort," Trish said. She turned her attention to Danielle. "Danielle."

"Trish," she answered. Neither made any show of affection.

She followed Trish to the dining room and took a seat beside Garrett. Ty sat at the head of the table, Trish on his right, and their little girl, now school age, sat on his left, eyeing the two strangers with a mix of fear and curiosity.

Everyone filled their plate and made small talk. Danielle was thinking it would be best to wait until after dinner to broach the subject of her visit. Trish beat her to it.

"So, I'm not such a fool that I can't see what's going on here," Trish said as she delicately folded her napkin and dropped it in her lap. "You still can't let go of the past, can you?"

"It's not that. I want to end things better. And maybe try to make up for how I left things. I'm asking for two weeks. Two weeks so we can all close this up and quit living with regret."

"That regret is yours. I have nothing to regret. None of us do. You were the one that messed everything up."

"I know that," Danielle said calmly. The old Danielle would have already had her back up, but she kept herself steady. "I'm trying to make it up to you, all of you. I know that you and Ty have your own life, and I'm not trying to screw that up. But don't tell me that some part of you doesn't miss it. This is an opportunity for us to finish things right."

"What amazes me," Trish said, still calm but with a searing edge to her voice, "Is that you convinced these two to go along with this. You don't fool me. This is typical Danielle nonsense. You still think we're going to be there to pull you out of the pit. Well, not me."

"I'm out of the pit," Danielle said. "And things are different now. I've got no illusions anymore. There's no guarantee that any of this amounts to anything. But it doesn't matter. This is my chance to walk away on my own terms, and it's yours as well."

"Until the first bad break, and then you'll freak out like you always do."

"I won't. I'm not that girl anymore. I've let go of all that." Trish didn't respond, but her eyes still held plenty of skepticism.

"Look at it this way—y'all get a two-week, all expenses paid vacation to lovely Hartford, Connecticut, and all you have to do is play a little piano and sing some harmony. I fuck up, and you jump on a plane and head home. If it works, you get one last taste of the limelight and some tasty songwriting royalties. It bombs, and you still have the vacation."

"I want at least one weekend completely off so we can go into the city and enjoy ourselves."

Danielle didn't bat an eye. "Tell me what you want, and I'll make it happen. Tickets for a Broadway show? Five star hotel? Car service? You name it."

"Are you trying to bribe us?"

"Absolutely," Danielle said, feeling the tide turn. She finally broke into a smile. "But I'm using someone else's money, so it's all good."

***

In a crowded gymnasium with temperatures hovering somewhere just north of hellfire, Talia James graduated high school three years after being left alone in a motel room in Austin. She graduated without honors, in the middle of her class, but she held her head high as she strode in with her black cap and gown. She smiled her million watt smile when she saw Danielle and Brett sitting in the front row, beaming like proud parents. Her journey was just beginning.

Two weeks later, the two of them packed their bags, said goodbye to Brett, and boarded a plane to New York, and from there on to Hartford. She had provided the band copies of her demos, and bright and early on a Monday morning, the five members of Reckless Passions stood together for the first time in twelve years. The first day they just ran through the songs. For Ty and Trish, they hadn't played more than casually since Danielle first left Austin, and they needed to shake off the rust.

The second day, they started recording. It did not feel like the old days. The togetherness wasn't there. But there were moments when it almost felt right, like the first time she stood at a microphone next to Trish singing harmony or when she and Ty traded licks during the ride out of a song.

Other times it felt cold and professional. The music was good, but the fire was missing. Talia slotted in where needed, singing harmonies and playing any instrument needed. Old boyfriend Colin Nix heard of the proceedings and stopped by to add some guitar to two songs.

True to her word, Danielle had run a loose ship, leaving everyone plenty of time to their own devices. Recording nine-to-five was strange for a woman who would gladly spend twenty hours in a day in the studio, but she forced herself to do it.

On the last day, with time to kill, Danielle introduced one last song, a new lyric she'd been working on for weeks. It was titled "Reckless Passions," and it was nothing else but a love letter, apology, and goodbye to her bandmates. She played it for them once, and the mood in the studio turned.

On that last day, on that last song, Reckless Passions finally did return. When the song was complete, they all gathered around to listen to the playback. DeShon opened with a soulful bassline. Ty joined with some understated chord work, slowly building with Talia on percussion. Then the drums came alive, with Danielle joining the fray and Trish adding organ. The song shuffled along, a loose and infectious groove that dropped out three quarters of the way through. Danielle delivered the final heartfelt lines of the bridge before the song kicked back up for a final run through the chorus. The entire band added call-and-response lyrics as Danielle let loose, soloing them through to the finale. The song ended, with the last sound being Trish's organ fading out.

They looked around at each other, and each had tears running down their face, and no one of them tried to hide it.

***

The Cinderella ending that Danielle wanted didn't materialize. Returning home to Amarillo, Danielle listened to the master tapes and knew that, with the exception of "Reckless Passions," the songs weren't there. With more time, maybe they could get it, but time was not an ally. Instead, Danielle and Garrett packed up again and headed west.

Alan met her in Los Angeles with the roster of hired hands they had agreed on to finish the album. Talia did not make the trip, choosing to stay behind with Brett. The new band consisted of Bernie Patterson on rhythm guitar. Bernie had been pounding away since the early eighties after finding himself in name bands, replacing original parts when the band was on their way down. Despite an impressive resume, he had never tasted mainstream success.

Carmen Esperanza took over on bass. Considered an up-and-comer by Alan, she had experienced success in a pop band in her home country of Venezuela before fleeing declining fortunes for a shot at the good life in L.A. She brought a sense of Latin rhythm, and her voice would be a sassy counterpoint to Danielle. Joey Arnold took pianos and keyboards. Originally a tech for Billy Joel in his younger days, he's spent years as a contract player for bands such as Aerosmith and Whitesnake, among others, toiling in the shadows and grasping for whatever shards of reflected glory he could get.

They took a week to rehearse before heading into the studio and meshed well enough. They were all professionals, and it was a job for the others. Danielle had every confidence that they could hold their own, but she had to hope they would gel into a real band, and soon. Ben LaFontaine wanted her on the road by mid-August. The clock was ticking, and Danielle's confidence was waning.

***

Danielle sat on her bed in her room at a seaside hotel, watching the waves roll in. Her mind was racing. She worried that, in spite of all her work, the album wasn't going to come together. She could see Ben LaFontaine giving one listen and pulling the plug, sending her back to her little radio station to live out the rest of her life as a has-been.

At other times, being this close to the beach, she wondered about her former flame Adam and where he was, what he was doing. She hadn't seen or heard from him since she rebuffed his last pass at her four years earlier. She knew he was still in L.A. and still acting, but she hoped that he was happy and that he had found someone to tame his wild streak.

Her eyes were starting to get heavy when someone knocked on the door. The sound jarred her into awareness. As a second knock came, Danielle shook the sleep out of her head and walked to the door. On the other side, Ashley Brooks radiated confidence in a tank top under a flannel overshirt and stonewashed denim skirt over black boots. "Hey there, pal," she said. "Thought you might could use a little company."

"Sure," Danielle said, surprised to find Ashley on her doorstep. "Come on in."

Ashley smiled bigger. "Mind if my friend comes in too?"

Ashley stepped aside and Shannon peeked around the doorjamb. "Hey there, beautiful. Remember me?"

"Shannon? What the hell?" Danielle felt the weight on her shoulders lift ever so slightly. "Y'all get in here." Ashley stepped in first, followed by Shannon, who was decked out as always, this time in a lavender dress, her blonde hair freshly curled. Danielle snapped her up in a warm embrace. "Where have you been? You just dropped off the face of the earth."

Shannon's eyes hit the floor, but she locked her fingers with Danielle's. "I messed things up for you, Danielle. I ruined everything. I just couldn't face you after that. I know how you are with people who fail you."

Danielle pulled Shannon closer, lifted her chin, and gave her a gentle kiss. "Someone came into my life that taught me about forgiveness, and somehow, someway, it took root. I've missed my friend."

Shannon visibly relaxed, and instantly her familiar cockiness returned. "You know, if you want to try that kiss again but make it a little longer, I wouldn't be upset."

Danielle pushed her away. "Get outta here." Turning to Ashley, she said, "What are you doing here? You're supposed to be on tour."

"I am," Ashley said as she plopped on the end of Danielle's

bed. "We're on a West Coast swing, so I was in the neighborhood. Besides, Big Al called and said you were struggling, thought you might need a friend. I knew Shannon was living out here, so I called her up. I told you I'd bring the cavalry."

"That you did. But how much can you help if you have shows to do?"

"We'll have to work in the morning, so I can catch a plane to my shows at night. Then I'll fly back overnight and be back at the studio in the morning."

"Jesus, Ashley, you'll kill yourself running that hard. Talk about burning your candle at both ends."

"I'm young. I've got a big candle. How often do you get to record an album with your hero? It's totally worth it."

Shannon put her arm around Danielle's shoulder. "This time, there's no sneaking around. Your friends are at your side, and together we're going to knock down the door. Nobody's keeping us out. Keeping you out."

Ashley jumped up and took Danielle's other side. "She's right. The girls are storming the castle walls."

Danielle smirked, but she couldn't deny the warmth she felt in the moment. "Well then. I guess let's go shake the pillars of heaven."

***

Ben LaFontaine sat behind his expansive mahogany desk on the top floor of an office building that carried his family name. Under his right hand was a yellow legal pad where he had been furiously jotting down notes. Danielle sat on the other side of the desk, and neither said a word as the music flowed freely from surround sound speakers discreetly tucked into the walls.

LaFontaine sat so still, eyes closed tight, that Danielle wondered if he had fallen asleep. She had done everything she could. Following the sessions in California, she had returned to Austin, where she oversaw the final mixing and mastering at a studio she knew well. She had culled the best performances from both sessions, sometimes mixing and matching between the two bands. What they listened to now was her best shot. Her last shot.

Only as the final notes of the final song died did he finally budge. "Well," he said. He rubbed at his chin and looked around the room, anywhere but at Danielle. His reaction confirmed her worst fears that the album wasn't up to par, but she would not back away from it. She was proud of it, even if it never saw the light of day.

"I, uh...you know, this was always going to be a risk," he said, finally managing to look at her. "That's why I didn't want to give you any guarantees. I believe in doing business the right way across the board. I didn't want there to be any false pretenses."

"A bunch of people worked their asses off on that record," Danielle said.

"I know that. I paid for them." He smiled, but Danielle was in no mood for joking around. He recognized it and let it go. "I know you put your all into this, and I appreciate it. Ashley and Alan both told me how hard you worked. I couldn't have asked for anything more from you."

"But you don't want it." Danielle collapsed back into her seat, her breath escaping her lungs in a jagged burst. "Son of a bitch."

LaFontaine rested his elbows on his desk. "It's not that I don't want it, Danielle. I just don't know what we're going to do."

"About what?"

"About the rest of the musical world after we get through stomping a mudhole in their ass." Danielle made no effort to hide her confusion. "This album, this is *The White Album* and *Exile on Main Street* rolled into one, and then injected with super soldier serum and genetically engineered to kick maximum ass. To sit on this would be tantamount to a crime against humanity. I can't wait to drop this thing."

"You're kidding."

"No, I'm not. One thing. Two songs, 'Laid Bare' and 'Down On You.' I like the demo versions you did with your sister better. Swap those out, and we're in business. We can put these versions on the B side of a couple of singles. What do you say?"

Danielle looked at the ceiling. She was torn somewhere between laughing like an idiot or crying like a sap. She knew she was grinning from ear to ear. "I say we've got a deal. What next?"

"Hang around town for a few days," Lafontaine said as he started thumbing through an old-fashioned Rolodex on the corner of her desk. "I'll make some calls, and we'll shoot some videos real quick. You should get your sister to come out here with you. I've got some ideas for her. Besides, it will give you something to do while I finalize your big comeback show."

Danielle stood and hugged herself. "About that. I was thinking it might be better to play some club shows first. Maybe do a small tour. Just to get my feet wet and get everybody used to playing together."

LaFontaine wasn't looking at her when he said, "September 24."

"September 24. What's September 24?"

LaFontaine leaned back with a satisfied grin on his mug and laced his fingers together behind his head. "That's the date of your big comeback show. I've had the date reserved, but I was waiting for the album before I finalized it. Now I know that you've got the goods. It's a go."

"That's a month away. There's no way I will be ready. That we will be ready. I need more time. Don't you think you should be consulting me about this stuff?"

"Why? I'm footing the bill. Besides, if you're involved, you'll stall and let your insecurities get the better of you."

She knew he was right on that. "So, where is it?"

"That's the best part." LaFontaine sounded almost giddy. "The show that never was. Austin. Erwin Center. Back to the scene of the crime."

"Jesus Christ," Danielle shouted. "Are you intentionally trying to sabotage me? You want me to fail? That's way too big a venue. And the pressure. My God. People are going to be coming out of the woodwork to watch me fall on my face."

LaFontaine finally popped up out of his chair and tucked his hands in his pants pockets. "Nonsense. Danielle, you're a lion, and you've been locked up in a zoo for too long. I'm dropping you back into your natural habitat, back in the lion's den. All you've got to do is be a lion." He approached her but stopped just short of arm's length. "Be the fucking lion, Danielle."

***

Danielle and the band hunkered down in Los Angeles and waited. They rehearsed daily, sometimes for hours at a time, jamming on every song Danielle had ever recorded and then moving on to important covers as well. They were getting tighter by the day, and everyone was a professional, but how they would hold up when the lights went on was something different.

The unexpected extra time in L.A. forced Danielle to miss seeing Talia off to college, but LaFontaine made it up by flying her to L. A. from San Marcos, Texas, for a weekend so they could star in a music video together.

Shot on the set of a soon-to-premiere sitcom, the video for the song "Down on You" featured Danielle and Talia reenacting the recording of the song in their living room. Danielle wore a thin, untucked blouse, ripped jeans, and walked around in bare feet, her hair stylishly unkempt, preening around the set, while Talia had a blast mimicking her time on drums and acoustic guitar. The song, an upbeat rocker with a slight pop tinge, wound down with a wailing solo. Danielle pulled out all the stops, hamming it up with all the cliché guitar god moves: playing behind the head, behind the back, on her knees, fretboard tapping. She hammed it up, and the more she did, the more the director encouraged her. Just before the song faded out, she took off the guitar and held it out for Talia, who slipped it on and pretended to play the final lines of the song as it faded. The director loved the symbolic passing of the torch. LaFontaine loved it so much that he decided the song would be the first single.

The second video was more difficult to film. For the song "Kill the Lights." Danielle faced the missteps of her past, sitting in a dark room, lip synching the song as a montage of Danielle's darkest moments played on a screen behind and sometimes on her. The director told her it was cathartic, a way to take ownership of her past. Literally, wearing her sins on her sleeve was not something that sat well with her, but she agreed to try it.

Her redemption came in the third and final planned video, "Chase the Highway." The video portrayed Danielle leaving those failures behind and heading out on the road. As the song says, she was chasing the highway that would lead her home. She spent an entire day on a closed road in the desert, driving fast and showing off in a pristine '63 Corvette convertible and loving the horsepower in her hands again. Plans were to shoot the final scenes for the video back in Austin before the big show, with the final shot being of her pulling up in front of the Erwin Center. Despite her best begging, the producers would not allow her to drive the Vette all the way to Austin.

Then she was out of time. September 24 drew ever closer, and it was time to make final preparations. The band would have two afternoons to soundcheck in the building affectionately known as The Drum before the big day.

LaFontaine was putting on a full court press in the buildup. He took out ads during prime time to promote the upcoming album titled *Kill the Lights*. He dropped the video for "Down On You" during halftime of the Steelers-Bengals game on Monday Night Football eight days before the show. He planted stories of Danielle's redemption with favored reporters, trading insider access to his future endeavors for carefully orchestrated puff pieces. He even went so far as to publicly offer Nicole Moore the opportunity to open the comeback concert by introducing Danielle, doing so on *The Tonight Show*, because outgoing host Jay Leno had always been a supporter of Danielle's. Moore, whose reality show had crashed and burned, was nowhere to be found.

At his behest, a cadre of entertainment reporters flocked to Austin to cover the show. Critics and comedians had a field day predicting disaster. Danielle removed herself from it all, staying at a bed and breakfast in San Marcos near the Texas State University campus to be near Talia. When she went out, she fell back on her Renae Tucker persona and drove around in a rented Chevy Impala so as not to draw attention.

With each passing day, the pressure intensified. On Monday, September 23, 2013, Danielle refused to leave her room, insisting that she needed the quiet to get her mind right. Talia checked in, and they ate dinner together in her room. Neither mentioned the upcoming show. She went to bed early that night, knowing that regardless of how things turned out, her life would never be the same again.

In twenty-four hours, she would either be Danielle Regan once more or would never be her again.

CHAPTER TWENTY-SIX

The first thing Danielle heard that morning was Huey Lewis's unmistakable voice crackling to life from the cheap alarm clock, singing "If This Is It." She laughed. If this is it, indeed. She shuffled to the bathroom and splashed cold water on her face, and looked at herself hard in the mirror. She was somewhere between that ballsy eighteen-year-old who came to Austin with nothing but a guitar and an attitude and the broken shell of a person she had been on that cold Kansas morning when fate started dragging her back home. She could see both in her eyes, fighting for control. Young Danielle dying to kick ass again. Broken Danielle ready to run at the first sign of trouble. She knew her future rested with whichever one won out.

She took a long, hot shower and ate a light breakfast. Against her better judgment, Danielle turned on the TV and flipped through the channels, and caught several stories on news stations about the upcoming show. She got a chuckle when polls conducted by both CNN and Fox News determined that there was a 71% chance the night would end in disaster. The two news giants never agreed on anything, but on this, there was a consensus.

Just after ten that morning, she checked out of the B&B and started back toward Austin. Her plan was to slip quietly into the Erwin Center before the crowds started to form and hide out there until showtime. Unlike four years earlier, there were no meet-and-greets. No one other than the band, crew, and a handpicked list of friends would be allowed anywhere Danielle before the show. She was taking no chances.

Optimism bubbled deep under the surface as she made

the trek back up I-35. Danielle refused to embrace it or even acknowledge it, but she knew it was there. That was Talia's doing, and she knew that none of this would have been possible without her little sister. When she was around, Talia had a way of making Danielle better.

That optimism vanished when she pulled up to the venue. A huge banner announced "Danielle Regan Live In Concert, TAKE TWO," and featured two publicity photos of her, a recent one leftover from shots taken for the new album and one that had been taken for her doomed performance with Shannon in this same theater four and a half years earlier. Seeing herself in that shot, wearing the same outfit she was wearing when the big fight broke out, squashed that trickle of hope, and she slipped past security with a growing darkness gnawing at her soul.

Most of the crew was already at the arena, making preparations. Some said hello as she strode past, but most ignored her, either because they were too busy or they were afraid. Danielle walked on. She made a quick stop on the coliseum floor and worked her way backstage, just checking things out. Standing just off the stage, Danielle had a flash of Shannon's assistant Tara tackling her as chaos erupted all around. On suddenly shaky legs, Danielle skittered away and found her dressing room.

Brett surprised her with lunch, and they enjoyed finally spending some time together, however fleeting it was. Officially they were dating and living together, but they had scarcely seen each other all summer, and neither had said the Three Magic Words to the other. It was an odd relationship, but it was working. Neither saw the need to borrow anymore trouble.

In the afternoon, the band arrived. They did a brief soundcheck and went over the set list a final time. They had decided at the last minute to include a brief acoustic set in the middle of the show, but Bernie, the second guitar player, felt it was wiser to move the set up. They also agreed to scrap the set altogether if the show wasn't working or the crowd wasn't into it.

Ben LaFontaine was backstage with his crew ninety minutes before showtime, strutting like a peacock. Shannon arrived shortly thereafter. Then Ashley, her often mentioned but seldom seen younger sister in tow. Various musician friends dropped in for quick hellos. Danielle visited with everyone but kept an emotional distance. With each minute that passed, the air got heavier. Even from her dressing room, she could hear the crowd gathering. In her mind, it was a split crowd, some eager to see her perform again, while others were there for the train wreck. She prepared herself for a lukewarm reaction.

Franklin Ridgeway worked his way backstage and took Danielle aside. Perhaps seeing the worry on her face, he wanted to pump her up and assure her that she could handle anything that came her away as long as she didn't let her anger get in the way, and then he moved on.

Half an hour before showtime, Talia finally arrived as Danielle finished changing into her show clothes. Talia's presence brought Danielle some much needed peace. They went over the big surprise of the night, when Danielle would call Talia onstage to perform "Down on You" together. Talia had been open to it previously, but now Danielle saw the nerves creeping up on her even while she tried to project confidence.

At ten minutes to showtime, LaFontaine gathered the band together and banished everyone else from the dressing room. The six of them formed a tight circle, arms on shoulders, and looked each other dead in the eye.

"All right, people," LaFontaine crowed. "This is what we've all been working for right here. It's been a lot of hard work and sacrifice, but tonight it's all about the glory."

Danielle cringed and saw in the faces of her new band that the words hadn't hit the way he intended. She stepped into the breach. "Fuck glory," she shouted. "Nobody cares about glory." She looked every member of the band in the eye. She knew she was shaking, but she hoped the others couldn't see it. She smiled big and wide. "Let's just go have some fun."

Once they made it to the lip of the stage, the house lights dropped. Danielle peeked out. There wasn't an empty seat to be had, and flashbulbs popped all over the hushed crowd. Again she flashed on her night at Shannon's concert and how everything had fallen apart at once. Now there was no hiding her shudder, and her breath came out in short spurts.

"You okay, Boss?" Bernie asked.

She looked back at him, but any attempt to display confidence was gone. "I'm fine," she whispered, her voice lilting. "I got this."

"Oh shit," Carmen, the bassist, muttered. "Here we go."

"Shut the fuck up," Garrett snapped. "Got get in your positions and be ready to rock." He came to Danielle, sneering, angry. He snapped at her until she looked into his eyes. "You are not going to fuck this up," he said sternly. "This is your world. This is where you belong, and you are the fucking queen. You're the best goddamn guitar player on planet Earth." His face softened. "And it's been a blast playing behind you again. This ain't shit. This is a tune up. Just go out there and let 'er rip, man, because I got your back. Okay?"

Danielle giggled. "We're a long way from Colin's tour bus, aren't we?"

Garrett gestured toward the stage. "Go take your crown like the bad bitch you know you are."

***

The PA system had been keeping the crowd entertained with a steady stream of classic rock, setting the mood. When the music suddenly stopped, the crowd surged forward. Stray whoops and hollers originated from points throughout the crowd. The air filled with the electric hum of instruments. Yet the music did not start. There was a pause, and a ripple of worry audibly made its way through the crowd. From somewhere at the back, a young woman's voice began to chant, "Dani! Dani!". It gained steam and moved forward until the entire crowd was shouting at the top of their lungs.

And then she appeared, materializing out of the darkness in gray jeans, black boots, a white shirt, and black vest. The lights glinted off the pearlized purple guitar slung around her waist. She stood in a single spotlight, and the crowd roared at her. Danielle felt her molecule vibrating—her legs were jelly, and her hands didn't want to move. She let her eyes sweep over the throng of humanity splayed out in front of her, she heard their chant, and she felt what she thought she would never feel again. She felt the love of the crowd washing over her. She stood perfectly still, and the longer she stood, the louder they chanted. Then she raised the guitar, pulled her right hand back, pick in hand, and stopped, holding the position. The fingers of her left hand found her chord and held it. Still, Danielle did not play, and the crowd screamed even louder.

There was, in those moments, nothing else in the universe. No past to run from or future to fear. There was only the moment. Then Danielle brought her right hand down in a vicious arch, a wicked power chord exploded, and an instant later, the band joined in. Fireworks went off, and confetti cannons spewed brightly colored paper over the crowd as the band launched into "Tremble," a hard rocking song from Danielle's *Stripclub* album. They were off and running.

They played three songs in rapid succession before they finally took a break. Danielle approached the mic while the others took advantage to grab some water. "So, uh, the last time I was here, things didn't go so well." There was applause and a little bit of laughter mixed in. She thought she heard a little bit of jeering as well, but it didn't matter. "But I want to tell you, I'm happy as hell to be here with you fine folks tonight. I know it's kind of rote, and every band says it at every show, but I am really and truly thankful that each of you could be here with me tonight. It has been a long, long road to get to the moment. So thank you for coming. Let's get on with it!"

They launched into the first slow song of the night, her 1997 hit "Alone in the Night," which segued directly into the brand new "Laid Bare" before she approached the mic again. Only five songs in, and Danielle was drenched with sweat, but they were playing better than she had expected, and she knew this would be a night when she could play forever. Behind her, the band took advantage of the little break.

"This next song we're going to play is one you might especially like, or at least I hope you will," she chuckled nervously. "Once upon a time, I was going to get married...." The was an empathic wave from the crowd. "It's okay. But we had a few spectacular months together, and this song is about that. For a long time, all I could ever think about was how I missed him, and it poisoned me. All that heartbreak and the pain and the anger corrupted my soul, and it almost ruined my life. Luckily, with a lot of help from a lot of fantastic people, I'm here. This song is the first time I've allowed myself to look back on those moments and feel joy. Maybe this song will help you feel the way I do every time you catch one of those awesome Austin sunsets. Let's go!"

Breaking out the acoustic guitars, they premiered the new ballad that Danielle felt was the best song on the new album. She had written some ballads over the years that she felt were pretty good, but this tribute to Kyle was her very best. "Austin Sunset" was supposed to be the start of the acoustic set they had planned on doing, but as the song ended, the lights went dark. Danielle was hit with the spotlight. Confused, she looked around for support, but could see nothing. She let out a long hissing breath, trying to calm herself down as panic threatened to overtake her. Things had been going so well. Maybe too well.

"Ladies and gentlemen," a female voice boomed over the PA system. Ashley maybe? "You are in for a real treat tonight. Performing together onstage for the first time in fourteen years. Give it up for Austin's own...Reckless Passions!"

Danielle whirled as the lights came up, and there they were, DeShon, Trish, and Ty, grinning like fools, instruments at the ready. Danielle's knees buckled at the sight of them behind her. She went to a knee. "Get up, girl," DeShon called out. "We didn't come all this way for you to take a knee."

Trish let her fingers walk across the keys. "So what's the deal? Are we playing or not? The crowd is getting restless."

"What do you want to do?"

Ty sidled up next to her. "We'll follow your lead, Captain. You just pick the song, and we've got your back."

Danielle smiled and wrapped her arm around his shoulder. "You got it. Let's try this one for size." She surged into the opening riff of the song "Wrecked," a Zeppelinesque song that had easily been the hardest song the band had recorded. She wasn't going to let them off easy, and they responded, keeping up with her as they churned through the song.

She led them through "Wrecked" and "No Regrets," and then Ashley emerged on the stage, dragging Talia with her, guitar in hand. Ashley shouted out to her, "I couldn't miss this." Danielle nodded. The planned setlist was out the window now, anyway. The show was devolving into a party, and she loved it. Someone had brought beach balls, and the crowd was knocking them around, which brought a laugh out of Danielle.

"Y'all don't mind if I bring some friends along, do you?"

Two more songs, and then Reckless Passions took their leave of the stage, and the new band came back on, this time with Shannon in tow. She strutted up to Danielle. "We never did get a chance to play any of our songs live."

"No time like the present." With that, they started into "Already Fallen" and "Tamarind" off their collective album. On record, their voices had sounded fantastic together—Shannon's operatic range offered an interesting counterpoint to Danielle's sultry, roadhouse vocals. Onstage, it was even better. Shannon had an onstage flair Danielle couldn't compete with, but vocally they pushed each other to be better.

When Shannon was done, Talia returned for their duet on "Down on You," and then they brought the show to a rocking close with a charged up version of her signature song, "Blessed Poison." The final song built to a crescendo as the band jammed. Bright strobes began going off, and confetti rained down as they wrapped up the song, Garrett's thunderous drums and Danielle's wailing solo reaching a fever pitch before crashing down with one last boom of sound. Garrett stood behind his set and tossed his sticks into the crowd while Danielle hugged the other members of the band and turned to the crowd. She punched her fist into the air while the audience chanted her name once more.

She beat a quick retreat to the side of the stage, where Brett and Talia were the first to greet her, but she was instantly swallowed by the arms of her friends. There were tears and laughter all around.

"That was a heck of a show."

Danielle turned and found Steve standing just beyond the crowd with his girlfriend Aja at his side. "I'm proud of you, kid."

Danielle pushed her way to him, and they hugged. "I can't—"

"You don't have to say a thing," Steve said. "What is understood need not be discussed."

Instead, he hugged her again. "I'm not alone," he said again. Danielle looked up and saw Randy and Terri had snuck in as well. Randy was even standing with the assistance of crutches. She went to them too.

"Hey, stranger, can I get some of that?" Danielle turned and found Adam Quisenberry, her long-time on-again but mostly off-again lover, looking suave and casually dangerous.

"Get over here," Danielle said, pulling him in for a hug as well. "Where?"

"Your new Sugar Daddy thought it would be a pleasant surprise, but he was afraid if you knew everybody was here beforehand, you would freak. Steve-O and myself have been trying to lay low for days."

There was a tug at Danielle's sleeve, and she turned to find Carmen, the bassist, at her elbow. "Boss? They're calling for encores. Are we going to give 'em one?"

"Fuck yeah, we are. Let's go." Turning to her friends, she said, "Everybody hang loose. If you play an instrument, grab one and get your ass on the stage. Show's not over."

The crowd of eighteen-thousand people, who were sure to have the world's worst cases of laryngitis in the morning, somehow found the way to scream even louder as both bands, Ashley, Talia, and Shannon, all took the stage together. "Y'all want more," Danielle teased. They responded. "All right then."

They played three more songs, each loose jams, every

member being given ample time to solo and show their stuff. The last song, a cover of Stevie Ray Vaughan's "Texas Flood," featured each of the five guitar players taking a solo, then taking a second round of solos. Finally, with the entire band bordering on exhaustion, Danielle screamed more than sang the final verse of the song, and they brought it down for good.

As the crowd chanted again, Danielle called the band to her side. They stood arm-in-arm and bowed before the audience. Yet it felt incomplete. She glanced to the side of the stage where her non-musician friends stood applauding. "Everybody stay here," she commanded her band as she hustled to the side of the stage. "Come on. All of ya. Out on the stage with me. Come on."

When they resisted, she took them one by one by the hand and pulled them onstage: Adam, Steve, Aja, Ben LaFontaine, Terri and Randy, and Brett. They fell in line with others, arms around one another, and took another round of bows as the audience showered them with love.

Danielle looked right and left at the string of people she had gathered around her. Old friends that she had abandoned and new friends she had picked up, her first love, her new love, and the girl who had brought her back from the brink. They stood together now, all as one in the burning glare of the stage lights. Danielle knew it didn't matter what happened after tonight, good or bad. She had everything she needed.

For the first time in her life, Danielle Regan was at peace.

In Loving Memory of Danny Neal Hunt (1951-2021)
A true man among men

Donny Hunt is a lifelong Texan with a passion for music and writing and an amateur sports historian. Reckless Passions is his fifth novel.